Jared didn't want to see her as a woman . . . to think of her as one. She was the enemy. A traitor. But the smell of her was intoxicating. The feel of her soft body stimulating. His jaw relaxed and his breathing quickened and he knew . . . knew she felt it too.

It was like when they were on the cliff, when his body had covered hers. This same something had drawn them then. He had fought it then and failed. He didn't even want to fight it now. Besides, there was more than one way to persuade.

Intimidation.

Seduction.

He leaned into her, a devilish gleam in his green eyes.

"You wouldn't dare," Merry began, and knew by the slight lifting of his brow that he dared this . . . and more. "Let me go!"

"I think not."

"I don't want you to—"

Merry never had a chance to finish. His mouth crushed down on hers, hot, hard, and hungry. She tried to fight him. Tried to twist her face away. But fire raced from him to her and muddled her resolve.

And it sparked an explosive reaction in her. One that shocked her nearly as much as the feel of his lips on hers.

"Blazing passion, non-stop adventure and a be-still-my-beating-heart-hero are just a few of the highlights in this captivating second novel in Ms. Dorsey's delectable Charleston Trilogy. SEA OF DESIRE is not to be missed!"

ROMANTIC TIMES

CHRISTINE DORSEY

SEA OF DESIRE

ZEBRA BOOKS
KENSINGTON PUBLISHING CORP.

To my second son,
Chris,
for all you've accomplished
and because I love you.

And as always to Chip.

"I cannot but lament . . . the impending Calamities Britain and her Colonies are about to suffer . . . Passion governs, and she never governs wisely . . ."

Benjamin Franklin
February 5, 1775

ridiculous. There was no [...] of said. She shouldn't

Prologue

Land's End, England
Late Summer, 1777

A storm was coming.

Merideth Banistar shivered beneath her scarlet cape. Taking a deep breath of sea-scented air, she wrapped the folds more tightly about her body. She stood on a granite ledge overlooking the inlet. When the midday sun burned off the mist she could see for miles across the channel below, but tonight, with even the moon obscured by rain-heavy clouds, darkness enshrouded her. Only the incessant pounding of the surf told of the beach below.

But she hadn't come here for the view. She'd come to escape. Her father's anger. The uncomfortable naggings of her own conscience.

Could her father be right? Was she dooming them both because of her stubborn refusal to accept Lord Chadwell's proposal? Merideth swallowed, remembering the rheumy eyes and warted nose of the elderly earl. His skin was parchment thin, and when he spoke to her his breath smelled of soured wine.

Yet, as her father was quick to point out, he seemed kind. He had that to recommend him . . . that and his fortune.

Merideth sighed, the sound caught by a gust of moisture-laden air and carried toward the looming house behind her.

Banistar Hall. It had been in her family for generations, ever since Charles II awarded the wind-swept land at the ends of the earth to Richard Banistar in 1665. And they, she and her father, were going to lose it.

Because she couldn't . . . or wouldn't . . . make a suitable match.

Lord Chadwell was their last chance, according to her father. So yesterday when Merideth stated her refusal to accept him, Alfred Banistar declared all hope gone. And through most of the day and evening placed the fault for their near-impoverishment squarely on Merideth's shoulders.

The wind whipped about her, tugging at her velvet hem and freeing strands of wildly curling golden hair from beneath her hood. But she refused to accept the blame for their problems. "I won't," she yelled into the face of the storm.

As if in response, the sky crackled, flaring the darkness with a sizzle of white lightning.

And in that instant Merideth's heart leaped to her throat.

For the split second of brilliance revealed a man on

10

the beach below. The flash of light caught him bounding from a small boat into the ebb tide, his movements registering raw power. Like herself he was wrapped in a cloak, though his was black as sin and enfolded a form both tall and large of frame.

Merideth stood frozen, like the imprint of the man on her mind, as night again enveloped her. Shaking her head, she tried to convince herself that imagination was playing her for a fool. There was no logical reason for anyone to risk coming ashore mid the rocks below— not in the dark of night. At least no licit reason.

The hair at Merideth's nape bristled as another streak of lightning seared the sky. The man was gone. The boat, now pulled onto the shore, was not. This was no apparition. His presence was as real as the pistol he held.

Her heart pounding, Merideth grabbed up her skirts and ran toward the twinkling lights behind her. By the time she reached the garden, huge raindrops pelted her cloak, soaking through to her gown, wetting her hair and face.

The storm was upon her.

Chapter One

Nothing was as he'd expected.

Jared Blackstone paced across the threadbare Aubusson rug, past the empty bookshelves, then turned back to face the traitor. No, not traitor. Informant. Jared had to remember not to let his prejudice be obvious. The Americans, his countrymen, needed the information this man could give.

Forcing the scowl from his dark features, Jared settled into the leather chair opposite Alfred Banistar and watched as the older man squirmed.

Alfred cleared his throat nervously and brushed his hand over his ruffled cuff. "You have the money with you?"

"Aye."

Nodding once, Alfred rose and moved toward his ornately carved desk—one of the few pieces of furniture in the room. After jerking the top from a crystal decanter, he splashed amber liquid into a glass. "Madeira?" he asked, and downed the contents quickly when Jared declined.

Feeling a bit more himself, Alfred poured another portion, his hand a little steadier, and resumed his seat. "I didn't expect you this night, not with the storm."

Wind-lashed rain pelted the tall casement windows and Jared wondered himself why he had chanced coming ashore tonight. The only reason he could come up with was that he wanted to put this task behind him. Meeting with a British spy did not sit well. Jared was much happier commanding the privateer *Carolina* then delving into the world of intrigue. If not for the plea from his cousin Daniel Wallis, Jared would be harassing British shipping on the high seas, not sitting in the run-down library of an English lord.

"I hope your surprise in seeing me doesn't mean you don't have the information," Jared began. "Because if it does—"

"No! No. Never fear." Alfred licked his thin lips. "I've the name you wish."

"And proof of his betrayal?"

"Yes." He pulled a lace handkerchief from his waistcoat pocket and dabbed at his brow. "I've all the proof you'll need."

"Then, may I suggest we get on with this? I don't wish to—"

"Papa! Oh, thank God!" Merideth Banistar rushed into the library, heading straight for her father. She stopped short when she spied Jared Blackstone. Instinctively she turned on the stranger, who now stood looming over her. "What are you doing here? What do you want?"

"Daughter." Alfred's voice was tight." That's no way

14

to speak to a guest. Apologize straight away."

Merideth ignored his reproach. She'd run through the storm, breathlessly racing into the house, only to have to search through rooms until finding her father. Her heart pounded and she fought back fear. "He came ashore," Merideth said, keeping her eyes on the stranger. She was certain it was the same man, though he seemed even larger and more formidable at close range. "He beached a small boat below the cliffs." Merideth steeled herself. "And he has a pistol."

Jared stared down at the woman. He hadn't followed his first impulse and pulled the gun when she'd rushed into the room. He couldn't be sure this prearranged meeting with Banistar wasn't a trap. But the pistol, though it was primed, was still hidden beneath his waistcoat, nestled in a pocket next to the gold.

"Nonsense, Merry. Mr. Blackstone is a friend of mine from London. He's from my club." Alfred draped an arm around his daughter's damp shoulders. An arm that she immediately shrugged off.

"So you owe him money, then," Merideth stated, not that she necessarily believed her father. She knew some of his gambling and drinking friends, and Mr. Blackstone didn't seem the type at all. He looked hard and dangerous, dressed in clothes as black as his raven-wing hair.

"Daughter, you forget yourself." Alfred spoke loudly, yet his voice lacked conviction.

But Merideth's didn't as she turned on him. "Perhaps *you* forget that I know of our circumstances." Whirling back toward Jared, the hem of her wet cloak swirling out, Merideth faced the stranger. "We have no money. As you can see, we have almost nothing of value either." Her hand arced out to indicate the barrenness of the room. "It will do you no good to threaten my father."

She angled her chin higher and Jared felt the corner of his mouth twitch. The chit acted as if she could protect her traitor of a father from him, and her looking as if she weighed less than eight stone, soaking wet. Which she was. Water dripped from the tip of her impudent nose and trailed down through the tangled ringlets.

He had half a mind to tell her exactly why he *was* here, and that it most likely was none of her concern, but Lord Alfred was babbling on about his being a friend, chatter that his daughter was totally ignoring. Jared shrugged. "I am here neither to collect money from your father nor to threaten him."

Lightning flashed, amplifying the brightness from the branch of candles on the desk, moments before thunder shook the panes. Alfred cut short his explanation and Merideth only stared. The stranger's voice was low and firm, oddly believable coming from a man such as he.

"Then why are you here?" Merideth didn't know why she bothered to ask, except that for some reason she thought if he lied she would know. He didn't give her the opportunity to test her theory.

"My business is with your father, but rest assured it has naught to do with collecting money."

"There, you see," Alfred said, pulling Merideth's gaze slowly away from the stranger. "You blustered about for nothing. Mr. Blackstone is a friend of mine."

"Friends don't come sneaking ashore in the dead of night brandishing a pistol," Merideth pointed out. She was far from convinced that the stranger was harmless. One had only to look at him to know different.

"That will do, Merry. Mr. Blackstone is our guest, and, as such, he deserves our courtesy. Something I've ignored too long." Alfred moved to the door and gave the frayed bell cord a yank. "I'll have Thurston show you to your room."

"That's not necessary. If we could simply conclude our business, I can leave."

"Nonsense. The weather is frightful, and, besides, now is not the time to discuss our concerns." Alfred's eyes rolled ever so slightly toward his daughter, who still studied Jared as if by staring she could detect what he was doing in her house.

Jared came close to demanding they proceed with the exchange—coin for information—as planned. Send the chit from the room if necessary. But he hesitated. Something about Lord Alfred touched a chord of sympathy within him. Jared was prepared to despise the man for his traitorous ways, but found he couldn't quite summon that emotion. And Lord Alfred seemingly wanted his daughter to know nothing of Jared's real reason for being here.

In the end Jared shrugged and followed the aged servant when he appeared.

"Give Thurston your waistcoat and he'll dry it by the fire. It doesn't do to be wet when there's a chill in the air," Alfred said.

Jared paused beneath the corniced doorway. His eyes slipped over the woman, from the tip of her dripping head to the small puddle beneath her square-toed shoes. "Perhaps you should see to your daughter's needs before her frolic in the rain leads to illness."

"I was not frolicking," Merideth shot back, but the stranger was already behind the heavy mahogany door and thus insulated from her words.

Merideth stood still, staring at the spot where she'd last seen the infuriating man and fighting to control her shivering. It was only now, after he had left, that she realized how chilly the room, with its meager fire, was. During his last survey of her, Merideth had actually forgotten how wet and cold she was.

Casting that foolishness aside as quickly as she shed her cloak, Merideth moved to the fireplace and spread her hands toward the flickering flames. With a sigh she glanced over her shoulders. "Now are you going to tell me the truth?"

"Mer-ry." Her father drew her name out in the beseeching way he'd used for years, the way she used to find so comical as a child. Tonight she only found it annoying.

"I know this has something to do with money. It always does. You said the sale of Mother's jewelry paid off the most pressing of your debts." Merideth fingered the gold locket at her throat—the piece was one of the few saved from the factor's sale—and wondered why she'd been naive enough to believe him.

"For the last time, Mr. Blackstone is not here to collect money." Alfred's demeanor changed quickly from cajoling to vexed. "Besides, we both know lack of coin wouldn't be a problem if you'd accept Lord Chadwell's proposal."

18

Anger coursed through her veins. She turned in time to see her father gulp down his glass of wine and reach to replenish it. There were so many things she could say, starting with an admonishment to stay sober. But that never did much good. It was as futile as pleading with him to curb his gambling. He would promise, and in his heart, Merideth believed, he was sincere. But her father could keep his addictions at bay for just so long.

Now they were in such dire financial straits that their only salvation was for Merideth to marry a man older than her father.

Slowly, trying to contain her anger and suppress words that would do neither of them any good, Merideth gathered up her cloak and headed for the doorway.

"Merrryyy . . ."

Her father's voice drifted after her, but Merideth ignored it as she crossed the cavernous great hall and headed for the servants' dining room.

Thurston and his niece, a woman as rotund as the old servant was spare, were huddled close to the peat-fed fire, their gray heads bent in gossip. Neither bothered to rise when Merideth entered, though they both jerked around in their seats when she spoke.

"Where did you put our guest, Thurston?" Merideth saw no reason to add to their speculation about Mr. Blackstone by referring to him in any other way. As servants, Thurston and Belinda were lacking, but they were two of only a handful of retainers who remained at Banistar Hall.

"In the king's room, your Ladyship," Thurston replied, wrapping his gnarled fingers about the stem of his clay pipe.

"It weren't cleaned," Belinda added, settling her wide bottom more comfortably in her chair. "I didn't get no warning that we'd be having a guest."

"That's fine, Belinda." Merideth turned to leave, but stopped to drape her cloak over the back of a chair. She noticed Mr. Blackstone's was across another, presumably to dry by the fire.

As Merideth climbed the broad staircase, she considered going to her own room first. Chances of there being a fire in the grate were slight, but she could at least change into a fresh gown before facing the stranger. And perhaps towel-dry her hair. While one hand trailed along the ornately carved banister, Merideth used the other to brush damp curls from her face.

It would be a relief to be dry and warm. But then it would be even more of a relief to know the truth of Mr. Blackstone's visit. With a sigh of determination she turned down the long, dark hallway leading to the king's room.

She paused before rapping on the heavy, paneled door, wondering whether their guest was impressed when informed he would stay in a room once frequented by James II. Merideth had no doubts that Thurston had related the story to Mr. Blackstone as he'd led him toward the room. If there was one thing Thurston could be counted on to do, it was act as the Hall's historian.

What a shock it must have been to hear of the room's grand past and then see it like it was today, stripped nearly bare of anything that could command a price.

Perhaps Mr. Blackstone wasn't surprised. After all, he had seen the library.

Merideth knocked on the door, deciding she didn't care in the least about Mr. Blackstone's observations. He was an unneeded annoyance at the very least, and more likely a dangerous threat.

In answer to his summons, Merideth entered the room. He stood by the tall window, silhouetted by a dazzling burst of lightning. The clap of thunder drowned out the sound of Merideth shutting the door behind her.

The stranger stood still, watching her for a moment before a sardonic smile curved his full lips. "Ah, Merry is it? Have you come to see to my comforts?"

"Hardly." Merideth's chin notched higher. "I've come to discuss something with you. And to make you an offer." Despite herself Merideth was drawn to the hearth, where someone, she assumed Mr. Blackstone, had built a roaring fire.

"An offer?" Jared left his post at the window and moved toward the two chairs grouped in front of the hearth. His gaze roamed over the damp gown that clung to Merideth Banistar's slender frame. His voice was smooth and suggestive. "What might that be, I wonder?"

He was arrogant as well as vile, and Merideth had no trouble believing he was sent by some of her father's dandified acquaintances to extract money from him. Doing her best to ignore his stare, Merideth seated herself in one of the tapestry-covered chairs. With a shrug the stranger sat in the other.

He'd removed his waistcoat, draping it over the back

of the chair. Though his shirt was white, a contrast to the stark black of his waistcoat and breeches, it was just as severely cut, with no lace or ruffle to break the harsh lines of his broad chest.

He frightened her.

Swallowing back the fear, she crossed her hands and began. "First, I need to know what you want."

He turned his head to the side, a slightly bemused expression on his face. "Are we still discussing your offer?"

Merideth felt heat flood her cheeks, but she refused to look away. "No. We are not. You are about to tell me why you came here."

"I am?" Jared fought the grin tugging at his mouth. The woman had brass. He had to give her that. Another time, and most certainly another place, he might enjoy a game of verbal sparring with her. Partly because, by the looks of her, he had a notion it might lead to quite an enjoyable tussle among the sheets. Not that he believed she came to offer him her body. He only alluded to that possibility to see the angry color rise in her face.

Merideth stiffened her spine. "Unless you tell me what it is you want, I can't see to your payment. And please don't repeat your story that you wish nothing from my father, because I don't believe you."

"I didn't say I wanted nothing," Jared pointed out. "I simply said it wasn't money."

"Then what?"

She certainly wasn't coy. "Perhaps you should ask your father that question."

"I'm asking you."

"And I, Lady Merideth, am not telling you." Jared met her stare and wondered if she would take his statement as final. She didn't blink, but only continued to look at him through eyes the color of a Carolina summer sky.

Merideth tried to decide what to do next. She would offer him money; that seemed the most expedient way to be rid of him. But she had no money, and, if she were to believe him, that wasn't what he was after anyway. Then what?

She took a deep breath. "You're a colonial, aren't you? From one of the southern colonies, by your accent."

"Very astute." Her ears were as sharp as her tongue. Jared might have been born in Charles Town in the South Carolina colony, but he had spent most of his life on the high seas. And he didn't think his speech was characterized by the lazy drawl of slow summer afternoons spent beneath moss-draped oaks.

"One might wonder what a colonial is doing in England in the midst of your revolt."

"One might," Jared agreed. "But then one's birthplace doesn't necessarily decide one's politics." Jared wasn't a fervent patriot because he happened to be born in America. At least he hoped his loyalties were born of a higher ideal than that.

However, the way she was studying him—as if he had mistakenly spoken his last thoughts aloud—made him pause. If he was going to act the spy, no matter how much he disliked the role, he'd be well rid of her suspicions. It wouldn't do for the army garrison nearby to be summoned by Lady Merideth before he could get

23

his information and leave.

Another lie was in order.

"You make too much of this, Lady Merideth." Jared smiled the smile that had captured more than one female's attention. "I merely came to Banistar Hall to pay your father a short visit."

"By boat? At night? During a storm? Or have you forgotten I saw you arrive?"

Leaning forward, elbows resting on his spread knees, Jared resumed the bald-faced lies, amazed at how easily they slipped from his lips. "I came by coach." He seriously doubted she'd brave the storm to check the coach house tonight. And by tomorrow he'd be gone.

"I saw you from the cliffs not more than an hour ago. You leaped from a boat, then pulled it ashore."

"Dear Lady Merideth, a man would have to be insane to attempt a landing such as that." Or desperate. "Besides, unless I'm mistaken, it was quite dark an hour ago. Too dark to see what you obviously imagined." Jared could have sworn no one had seen him come ashore.

She wasn't going to argue with him. Merideth was certain it would be a waste of time. But she knew what she saw, and she knew, too, that she didn't trust Mr. Blackstone. Never mind that his smile transformed him, making her wonder why she ever thought he looked dangerous.

With a dimple flirting with his cheek, and the show of fine white teeth softening the harsh contours of his face, he was handsome. Sinfully so.

But that was of little consequence. There was no point remaining, since he refused to tell her the truth about his reason for coming to Banistar Hall. Whatever he wanted from her father, she would find out soon enough. Papa was never able to hide his indiscretions for long.

She stood, obviously considering their discussion closed. Jared hoped he'd alleviated some of her suspicions, though by the look she shot him as she brushed a strand of hair from her cheek, he doubted it. Her hair was light, a soft honey gold that went well with her blue eyes and pale skin. Now that the heat from the fire had dried it, her hair curled widly about her face. She looked like his perception of an angel.

But he couldn't allow her appearance to fool him. She was going to cause trouble if he stayed here much longer. Following her to the door, Jared decided to return to Lord Alfred as soon as she left. There was no need to delay further. And afterwards, as soon as the storm passed, he'd return to his ship and put this behind him.

Merideth's hand rested on the brass doorknob, and she turned. Mr. Blackstone, following her closely, now loomed over her. He smelled of sea and storm. She swallowed, forcing herself not to be intimidated by his size and obvious strength. "How long did you say you planned to stay with us?"

"I didn't," Jared said with an arch of his brow. "But I imagine I shall be gone in a few days."

"Back to London?"

"Back to London," Jared confirmed with a smile that didn't quite reach his eyes. She might be lovely, but she wasn't the soft, pliant female he was used to. Jared expected her to call him a liar. From her expression it was apparent that was what she thought. Instead she simply opened the door and walked down the hall, her carriage—despite her damp, rumpled gown and tangled hair—regal.

Merideth slammed into her room, the simultaneous crash of thunder drowning out the noise. The fire in her hearth was lit, but dying, and with a sigh Merideth moved toward it. There didn't seem to be anything she could do about the stranger tonight, but in the morning she intended to send word for the village constable to pay a visit to Banistar Hall.

For now, she would change from her damp clothes, then return to the library. If she knew her father, he had drunk himself senseless by now and would need help finding his bed.

Shadows shrouded the stairs as Jared made his way back to the library. The few sconces that were still lit burned low, their flames sputtering in pools of melted wax. Jared glanced about when he reached the huge entrance hall. There wasn't a soul about. Actually, he hadn't seen anyone since entering Banistar Hall except Lord Alfred, the servant Thurston, and, of course, Lady Merideth. It seemed odd for a house this large to have so few people around.

But then that was hardly the only unusual thing about the place. The Banistar family had obviously fallen on hard times. He knew the gold hidden in his waistcoat wasn't near enough to restore the family to prosperity, but it provided a motive for Alfred's treasonous venture.

Not that Jared considered lack of funds justification for becoming a traitor. But it did provide a motive where until tonight Jared couldn't fathom one. After all, for a British lord to contact an emissary of Dr. Franklin's in Paris and offer to reveal the name of a well-respected American who was in truth working for the British intelligence was at least suspicious. And that suspicion was part of the reason Jared had come ashore at night. *And* wanted to be done with this quickly.

As Jared knocked on the library door, he wondered briefly if Merideth Banistar knew of this intrigue. She hinted broadly that she took charge of her father's affairs. Did those affairs include spying? It wouldn't be the first time a beautiful woman had used her wiles to discover secrets. But though Lady Merideth was undeniably beautiful, Jared couldn't see her steeped in subterfuge.

It appeared that if Merideth Banistar wanted to know something, she asked—or, more accurately, demanded.

Shaking his head, Jared entered the library. He had neither the time nor the inclination to ponder the daughter's personality. It was Lord Alfred and his secrets for sale that should be occupying his thoughts. Getting the secrets and getting the hell back to his ship.

Jared shut the library door with a soft click, then turned, a scowl darkening his features.

"Now, I know what you're thinking, my boy, and believe me, i' 'tisn't true. I'm not too drunk to transact our business." Alfred Banistar lifted his glass toward Jared in a wavering salute.

"As you say." Jared's voice was tight. "Then may I

27

suggest we conclude our transaction as quickly as possible?"

"Ah, yes. You would be the one who chafes at delays." The final word was cut short as Alfred took another gulp of wine. "The interruption because of Merideth was unavoidable. We can't have her here when we are discussing the fact that her father is a . . . a . . . What would you call me, Mr. Blackstone?"

"I don't think my label for you is important."

"Ho." Alfred's laugh was short and not very jolly. "But I already know what you consider me, as do you. For a spy, you aren't very adept at hiding your feelings of contempt."

"Distaste for your duplicity is closer to the truth," Jared said as he shook his head at Alfred's silent offering of wine. "And I am not a spy, simply a courier." And an unwilling one at that, Jared added to himself.

Alfred brushed the difference aside with a wave of his hand, spilling amber liquid on his already stained waistcoat in the process. He didn't seem to notice the mishap, and Jared sighed in frustration. His Lordship was obviously skunked.

Jared moved closer to the chair where Alfred sprawled. "If you will give me the information, or tell me where I can find it, I'll give you the money and take my leave." Waiting out the storm in the cave off the beach seemed preferable to this. Then he could leave at first light to reboard his ship. The longer the *Carolina* stood anchored off shore, the greater the chance of being spotted by a British cruiser. For tonight, with the rain still lashing and the thunder booming, his ship was safe enough, but come tomorrow . . .

"I've always admired you colonials. Did you know that?" Alfred's words were slurred, and he completely ignored Jared's suggestion that they move forward with the transfer. "I even spoke in Parliament once about giving in to some of your demands. Not too vehemently, you understand. It wasn't a popular sentiment. But I for one was distressed with the onset of this war." He paused long enough to upend his glass. "Nasty business, war. Of course, you have no chance of winning this one, but still I hate to—"

"The name, Lord Alfred! I need the name."

His eyes owlish, Alfred stared up at Jared. The younger man was losing patience, and it didn't help when Alfred began laughing uncontrollably.

"Don't have it. I—"

"Damn your bloody hide." Jared grabbed Alfred by the front of his waistcoat and hauled him up. "You said—"

"Not me. Merideth," Alfred sputtered. "Too dangerous for me to keep, but no one would suspect Merry. She has the name."

Jared's fingers loosened and Alfred sank bonelessly into the chair. Hell, he should have discussed this with the daughter from the beginning. So much for his assumption of her innocence. Blue eyes and an angel face did not a pure heart make.

"Wh . . . where are you going?" Alfred leaned forward, reaching for Jared, who'd retreated toward the door. "I want my money."

Jared paused and turned, his expression dark. "You won't see a single penny until I have the information I

29

came for. If I have to get it from Lady Merideth, I shall."

"But the money is mine. You must give it to me. She doesn't even—" Alfred sucked in his breath. His heavy-lidded eyes, focused on a spot behind Jared, widened in shock.

"What the—" Jared jerked around, but only caught a glimpse of scarlet before blinding pain exploded in his head.

Good Lord, he hurt! Jared moaned and the sound amplified the drums pounding in his head. He tried to move his hands, to cradle his aching temple, but he couldn't move them. What the hell? He tried again, this time forcing his eyes open.

He'd obviously died, for there staring down at him was the most beautiful angel. His eyes narrowed. Hell, that was no angel. It was Lady Merideth Banister, and he was . . .

Memory crashed down on him and he fought against the pain to sit up. Rough hands grabbed at him, knocking him back to the floor.

"Ye aren't going nowhere," came a voice from behind him. Jared twisted but could only catch a glimpse of thick-soled boots.

At the same time, he realized his hands were tied. "What's going on here?"

"I'll tell ye what's going on. Yer going to hang."

"Hang?" This time Jared struggled to sit up, but the boot slammed into his shoulder, flattening him. His head landed on the worn carpet with a thud. "What the hell for?" Jared managed after the bolt of pain subsided a bit. Had they discovered why he was on British soil?

Jared's gaze sought Merideth's. She still stood over him, and she took a deep breath, her bottom lip trembling before responding. "Why did you do it? I would have gotten you the money . . . somehow."

"Do what?" Jared tried to keep the panic from his voice. But he was in so much pain he could barely think straight, he was trussed up like a Christmas goose, and it felt like an ox was standing on his shoulder.

"Murder him," Merideth sniffed. "Why did you murder my father?"

Chapter Two

"What the hell are you talking about?"

"That'll be enough outa ye." The boot ground harder into Jared's shoulder as he strained to sit up. He tried to see past the black dots that swam before his face. "Her Ladyship done sent for the constable, she did. He'll take care a the likes a ye."

Jared's eyes met Merideth's and followed the slight shift in her gaze to the motionless form on the floor, not ten feet away. Even though it was covered with a sheet, one didn't need much imagination to know it was a body. And it didn't take her accusing words to know it was her father. Tears shimmered in her eyes, and she seemed barely able to keep them from pouring down her cheeks. While he watched she took a deep, quivering breath.

"You can leave now, Mort. I can handle Mr. Blackstone," Merideth said to Belinda's son. She'd sent the maid running to the stables to find him.

"But yer Ladyship, what if he tries to get away?"

"You've tied him securely, and I do have a pistol." Her glance strayed back to where Jared lay on the floor. "And I won't be shy about using it."

"But Lady Merideth . . ."

"That's enough, Mort. Tell Thurston to watch for Mr. Samuals, and inform your mother that I'd like some tea." Merideth strained to control her voice and emotions. She couldn't break down now. Later, when she learned the truth, and when the diabolical Mr. Blackstone was bound for his hangman's noose, then she could give her grief free rein.

"Ye wants I should take his Lordship . . ." Mort paused, as if not knowing exactly where to suggest he take him. "Up to his bed?"

"No." Merideth wondered if Mort's question was prompted by his long history of helping her get her father up the staircase to his room when the earl was too far in his cups for Merideth to handle alone. "I don't want him moved."

"But it ain't fittin', him just lyin' there."

"We'll take care of him directly." Merideth tried not to look at where her father lay. But the sight of him as she had found him earlier, crimson blossoming from a hole in his chest, his face bloodless, was etched on her mind. She stiffened her spine. "I want everything to be as it was when the constable arrives."

"As ye wish, your Ladyship." Mort moved then, giving one last heel dig to Jared's arm before heading toward the door.

Jared twisted and got his first look at the burly redhead as Mort left the library. When he was gone, Jared slowly hiked himself to sitting. Merideth didn't seem to mind that he sat. She simply watched his labored efforts, the pistol she held never wavering.

Something warm trickled down his ear, and Jared imagined his efforts had caused the wound on his head to bleed. But it was better than lying on his back beneath the yeoman's boot.

"I want to know why." Merideth had allowed him to struggle to sitting, but now she aimed the gun toward his chest. Even though he was tied, his size and obvious strength frightened her.

"Do you mean, why was your father killed?" Jared watched as she sucked her lower lip into her mouth before nodding. He took a deep breath, wincing slightly at the pain in his head. "I haven't a clue. Because I didn't kill him."

Why was he blessed with a voice that inspired belief? Merideth knew better, yet she was still tempted to accept his words. She cocked the pistol. "When I found you, there was a spent gun clutched in your hand. And there was . . ." Merideth felt tears threatening and paused. When she gained control of her emotions, she continued. "You shot him. Of that I've no doubt. I just thought you might be . . ." She almost said, ". . . good enough to tell me why," a completely ridiculous thought. "I thought you might tell me why you did it."

"Dammit, I didn't shoot anyone!" God, he wished he'd never agreed to this plan of Daniel's. "It would have been a neat trick, since I was unconscious. Or didn't you notice that detail when you discovered your father?"

Merideth bristled under his sarcastic tone. "My father obviously tried to defend himself. It's just too bad he didn't kill you rather than graze your head. Apparently you were still able to fire your pistol. Or perhaps you fired first and his shot wasn't true."

"Or perhaps," Jared mimicked, "someone knocked me over the head and used my pistol to kill your father." Her noise of disbelief and disgust infuriated Jared. "The hell with what you think. That's what happened. I was in here discussing business with your father, and someone came up behind me. The next thing I knew there was a ten-ton giant standing on my shoulder."

"That's a preposterous story. I'm surprised even *you* have the nerve to suggest it."

"I'll suggest something even more preposterous. The person who hit me was wearing scarlet." Jared cocked his brow. "You were wearing a scarlet cape earlier, weren't you, Lady Merideth?"

"You can't be suggesting that I . . . You obviously have more nerve than sense, Mr. Blackstone." Merideth took a moment to rein in her anger. When she spoke again, her voice was tight with control. "I shouldn't have even wasted my time talking with you." Merideth moved toward the door, determined to watch her prisoner, yet keeping as much distance between them as possible. "I shall leave it to the constable to discover why you were at Banistar Hall."

There was a pounding on the door, but it wasn't so loud that Merideth missed the cold deliverance of Mr. Blackstone's next words.

"For your father's sake, and yours, I don't believe you want the constable to know why I came here."

Merideth's eyes locked with the stranger's. "What do

you mean by that?" she asked. But there was no time for him to answer, even if he planned to; for Thurston, usually notoriously slow in answering the door, had already opened it. The constable, followed by two of his deputies, entered the library.

"Your Ladyship." Constable Samuals bowed toward Merideth. His stoic expression wavered only slightly as he took in the sheet-shrouded form sprawled on the floor, the pistol Merideth still held. "What happened here? Your man came pounding on my door, squealing something about an emergency. And this not a fit night for man nor beast."

"I can hardly control the weather." Merideth didn't much care for the constable's attitude. She didn't believe that the retainer she'd sent to fetch him hadn't explained what the problem was. But then Amos Samuals hadn't held the Banistars in very high regard since Lord Alfred had run up a large tab at the Three Gate Tavern, the establishment owned by Amos's brother. Neither of the brothers was happy when Alfred was unable to pay. But that shouldn't keep the constable from discharging his duty, Merideth thought. She nodded toward Jared. "This man murdered my father."

"I see." Samuals pursed his lips as he glanced toward Jared and then knelt beside the body. "Looks as if he was shot."

"Of course he was shot!" Merideth felt her patience slipping as sure as the weight of the gun pulled her hand down.

"No need to get yourself all uppity." The constable flipped the sheet back over Lord Alfred's lifeless form.

"You say this fellow done it?"

"He did." Merideth glanced toward her prisoner, wondering why he wasn't saying anything in his own defense. He simply stared back.

"Who is he? Don't think I've ever seen him in these parts."

"I'm Jared Blackstone." Jared kept his tone even. "And if you wouldn't mind, I'd like a moment alone with Lady Merideth."

Her jaw dropped. Merideth couldn't help it. Of all the gall! The stranger made the request as easily as if he were asking for an introduction.

"Well, it so happens I do mind. You ain't getting no special privileges here. A moment alone, indeed. I imagine you'd be likin' untied and a sound horse too."

"I'd like to speak to him."

"What?" The constable turned on Merideth, his eyes bulging. "This ain't no tea party here, your Ladyship."

"Do you think I don't know that? This man killed my father . . . my *father*, Mr. Samuals. And I want to speak with him alone."

Hands on his knees, Samuals pushed to his feet. He mumbled something about the gentry—a remark that Merideth neither caught nor truly cared about—before he headed for the door. With a nod he motioned for his two deputies to follow.

"We'll be right outside, so don't think of trying anything," he said to Jared before closing the door behind him.

"Well?" Merideth leveled the pistol with both hands.

Jared's eyes met hers. He didn't completely trust her. Hell, he didn't trust her at all. But even pointing a gun

38

at his chest, she seemed a better choice than the constable. Besides, she might have a stake in this deception too.

"I didn't come here to take money from your father. I came to give him some."

Her snort of disbelief was anything but ladylike.

"It's true. He was selling me something for a generous amount of gold."

"I didn't send the constable out of the room so I could listen to lies. My father didn't have *anything* worth a great deal of gold . . . except Banistar Hall. And he never would have sold that."

"He had information."

Jared spoke the words softly, but he saw them spark interest in Lady Merideth's face. She was either a superb actress or she knew nothing of her father's activities. But from what Lord Alfred had said about his daughter knowing the name of the traitor, that was impossible.

"What kind of information?"

"It's not important now." No sense chancing her turning him in as a spy as well as a murderer. "What is, is that I had no motive to kill your father."

"I still don't believe you came to give him money." Merideth started toward the door.

"I can prove it." Jared twisted to his side, groaning at the pain that caused. "It's in my waistcoat pocket. I never had the chance to give it to him." Or to receive the name of the American traitor, Jared thought. But Lady Merideth knew who it was. He'd bet on that.

Merideth let her eyes drift along his broad chest to where his black waistcoat draped open. This was ridiculous. There was no packet of gold. She shouldn't even be tempted. But she was. Something about the way he spoke or the look in his sea-green eyes made her move toward him.

"Even if you have gold, it doesn't prove anything." Merideth bit her bottom lip and took another step. Closer.

"It proves I came here to give money rather than take it," Jared said, though he knew she was right. It didn't prove anything. But desperation spurred him on. "It shows I had no motive to kill Lord Alfred."

She could smell his scent now, dark and mysterious, like the sea during a storm. His green eyes were rimmed by a darker hue. They drew her.

The silk of her skirt brushed his bent knee. She was standing above him now. Looking down. The pistol still aimed at his chest. If she fired it, there was no chance she would miss. But if he somehow managed to get hold of the gun, he would kill her.

Merideth's gaze flashed to where his hands were tied behind his back. He couldn't grab the gun. But she stepped back and placed it on the desk just the same. Then, before she could change her mind, Merideth knelt beside the stranger.

The heat from his body seemed to scorch her fingers as she reached inside his waistcoat. Merideth's knuckles brushed his shirt and she could feel the hard muscles through the fine cotton, smell the sticky sweetness of his blood. She tried to ignore his nearness as she hurriedly rifled the pocket he indicated with a thrust of his jaw.

"It's empty," she said, leaning back on her heels and

giving him a look that clearly meant she should have expected nothing else.

"It can't be." Jared twisted around as best as he could, his shoulder knocking into her arm. She skittered back as if his touch were poisonous. Tucking his chin, Jared tried to see. "Check again."

"I will not. There's nothing there, I tell you, and you know it." Merideth tried to stand but something caught her, and when she glanced down she saw her lavender overskirt trapped beneath the stranger's knee. "Let me up."

"Why should I?" Jared hadn't purposely snared her gown, but now that he had he shifted his weight to hold her captive. His expression was hard. "Look again."

Grabbing the flap of his waistcoat, Merideth rummaged her hand in the pocket. Nothing. "As I said before, it's empty. Now, if you don't let me up," Merideth began, her words grinding out between clenched teeth, "I shall scream."

Jared paid no heed to her threat. "Someone must have stolen it," he mumbled more to himself than her. "I had it when I entered the library. Whoever killed your father must have taken the money too." His eyes met hers. "Don't you see?"

"Don't be absurd. I don't believe in fairies or pixies of old legends. There was no one here but the servants and me . . ." Merideth stopped. What was she doing even discussing this with him? Of course, he had already implied that *she* might be the killer. He was grasping at anything. With a determined yank she freed her gown, falling back on the floor in the process. She scrambled to her feet.

"No, wait—" But Jared could say no more as the constable slammed open the library door.

"Ain't waitin' no longer to take the prisoner into the village. Looks like there's a break in the storm." He motioned for his deputies to haul Jared up, and they did with obvious delight for the pain they inflicted.

Merideth straightened her gown and kept her eyes averted. She didn't want to notice what they were doing to the stranger . . . and she didn't want to see the way she knew he was looking at her.

"What you want me to do about . . . him?" Amos Samuals twisted his grizzly head toward the covered body on the floor.

"If you would get word to the vicar, I would appreciate it."

Samuals nodded his agreement, then led the way out of the room. Merideth glanced up in time to see the deputies yank Jared Blackstone through the door. His head was bleeding, and crimson dripped onto his waistcoat. Merideth wished she'd thought to suggest they bandage him before he rode the three miles to the village. But then her gaze swung around to her father's body and her heart hardened. What did she care what happened to the man who had murdered her father?

By the time the door clicked shut she was down on her knees beside the linen shroud, tears streaming down her face, her breathing punctuated by heart-rending sobs.

Merideth stared down at the array of papers spread

across the mahogany desk. She had spent the sennight since her father's funeral trying to make sense of them . . . trying to figure out a way to save Banistar Hall. Not just for herself. One conclusion she came to during the long night she grieved beside her father's body was that she cared little about the ancestral home. It was her father who had prized it, though he'd spent little of his time here until age and finances forced him to curtail his travels.

Yet she couldn't help wondering where she would go . . . what she would do . . . without Banistar Hall.

Sighing, Merideth let a parchment note fall from her fingers. Perhaps she could find a solution to her dilemma if her concentration would stay focused. But like the parchment, it slipped . . . often. And then she was looking into Jared Blackstone's sea-green eyes. *For your father's sake, and yours, I don't believe you want the constable to know why I came here.* What did he mean?

"Don't be a fool. It was nothing more than a ploy to save his murderous neck," Merideth said to herself. "And it won't work."

Because tomorrow he was to hang. For the murder of Lord Alfred Banistar.

"'Tis only just," Merideth assured herself as she started to read the document she picked up from the desk. If there was a good reason for him to be here that night, Mr. Blackstone would have mentioned it during the trial.

Oh, he had repeated his preposterous lie about delivering gold to her father and someone stealing it. But no one believed him. Especially when he could give

43

no logical reason why he would have money for Lord Alfred.

Merideth snorted. "Because there was no gold."

Jared's entire defense was based on half-truths and maybes. Dr. Foster couldn't say for sure that the wound on Mr. Blackstone's head was from a pistol ball. But he couldn't say he was knocked over the head either.

"No, I couldn't swear the cut wasn't caused by the defendant being hit with a sharp object," Dr. Mason had said. "But there *was* the spent pistol clutched in Lord Alfred's lifeless fingers. I'd say it likely his Lordship shot wildly, grazing the defendant's head," the white-haired doctor pronounced.

Jared Blackstone's only response was to vehemently insist he was hit from behind.

"Ridiculous lies," Merideth mumbled, pushing herself away from the desk. "Mr. Blackstone might as well have confessed and saved everyone the aggravation." Merideth walked to the window and looked out over the heath to the cove. "At least he didn't mention his contention that someone wearing scarlet hit him."

During the trial Merideth had expected Jared Blackstone to cast suspicion on her with his story of a scarlet-clad assailant. But he hadn't.

"He probably forgot he even made that up," Merideth said, then shook her head. "Now I'm talking to myself. Not just talking but holding an entire conversation."

In frustration she marched back to the desk and sank into the chair. She reached for the locket hanging from the ribbon around her neck. Her fingers closed over the smooth gold.

"I have to find out," she finally whispered. "Oh, Papa, I have to find out what he meant."

Her shoulders squared, Merideth stood. After asking Mort to saddle her horse—one of the few her father hadn't sold off—Merideth went to her room to change into a riding habit.

"I ain't sure I should be doin' this." Lester Hawson scratched his grizzled head and looked around the anteroom to the jail as if the answer might lie in the stone walls.

"I shall take full responsibility," Merideth assured him. She was glad to find Lester, one of Samuals's deputies, on duty, rather than the constable himself.

"Still ain't rightly sure. 'Course, I can't ask the constable, since he went to Foxworth to visit his lady friend. Usually makes the trip on Saturday, but weren't 'bout to do it on the morrow. Not with the hangin' set for then."

"And by then it will be too late for me to say what I must to your prisoner."

"Now that's for sure," Les answered, with enough enthusiasm in his voice for Merideth to know he looked forward to tomorrow's "festivities."

"So, may I see Mr. Blackstone now?" Merideth tried not to fidget, but Les still leaned against the door leading to the cell, his bulky shoulders blocking the way.

"Well, I guess it won't harm nothin'. You ain't

plannin' on shootin' him or nothin', are you? Wouldn't want to cheat the hangman?"

"No. I simply want to talk to him about something."

"Good luck to you." Les shifted his weight. "He ain't the talkin' kind. Hardly said two words since we locked him up. Real unfriendly."

Merideth paid no attention to Les's harangue as he fiddled with a large brass key. The heavy door swung open and Les lead the way inside.

"I best stay here with you."

"No!" Merideth paused. "I mean, that won't be necessary." She couldn't possibly find out what she wanted to know with Les hovering about.

"But this man's a killer. I can't let you—"

"I said I shall take responsibility. Besides, he has no weapon and you do. If there's a problem, I shall simply call out."

"I don't like it."

"Nothing will happen."

Jared lay on the cot, staring at the cobwebbed ceiling, his head cradled on his crossed arms. He was listening to Lady Merideth plead her case with the jailer. At this point he didn't much care which of them won. He probably should, but hell, he was going to hang tomorrow.

"Do I have your word you won't do nothing to her Ladyship?"

Jared twisted his attention away from the spider crawling across the beam when he realized the deputy was talking to him. "But of course," he responded in his most sarcastic tone. What the hell did the man think, that a killer would keep his word?

But apparently the subtlety was lost on the jailer, for he grunted his approval and backed out of the cell.

Lady Merideth seemed less assured. She remained by the door. But she stood her ground. Jared watched her, his lids partially lowered, and had to admire her courage. That is, he would have if he thought she believed him a murderer. He doubted she did, because he wasn't so sure she didn't know who the real killer was.

Merideth cleared her throat. "I . . . I came to ask you a question."

"And here I thought this a social call." Jared stretched and crossed his booted ankles.

"You needn't be so . . . so . . ."

"So *rude?*" Jared cocked a raven brow. "Is that the word your *Ladyship* is searching for?"

"Actually, I was thinking more along the lines of 'barbaric.' But then that's all one can expect from colonials, isn't it?"

For someone with the face of an angel, she could look pretty haughty when she raised her chin a certain way. Jared came close to smiling at the picture she made. Then he remembered his circumstances, and all traces of mirth left his face.

"What is it you want? I'm somewhat busy, and time *is* running out."

"You don't look occupied to me." Merideth took a step forward, away from the security of the door. Though it was midmorning, the light inside the cell was dim, filtered through the narrow bar-covered window. She brushed her hands down the deep-blue skirt of her riding habit.

"Perhaps I'm contemplating my life," Jared said, his tone bored, his gaze once again focused on the process of the busy spider.

"I thought maybe you were begging God's forgiveness."

That got his attention. Merideth nearly flinched at the look he shot her. His green eyes were dark and intense, bright with barely controlled violence. Merideth swallowed, wondering anew about the prudence of coming here.

Damn the woman. When he first saw her in the cell doorway, he felt . . . what? Relief? Hardly. But a fissure of comfort. At least he wasn't going to go to his death without talking to anyone but the surly constable and his dim-witted deputy and the foul-smelling cleric. A beautiful woman was certainly preferable to either of them. And Merideth Banistar was undeniably beautiful.

But hell, he didn't need this. He was going to hang tomorrow. For a murder he didn't commit. And he was busy. Trying to decide how he'd let this happen to himself.

Jared shifted, then settled more comfortably on the hard cot. The spider had made some progress since he'd looked away. Industrious little thing.

He was ignoring her, hoping she'd go away. Merideth knew it. But she hadn't come here to leave without an answer. She moved closer to the cot. It was too short for him, and Merideth noticed his boots stuck out over the end. "Why did you come to Banistar Hall? What was your business with my father? And don't tell me to ask him, because thanks to you he's dead."

"You can drop the pretense of ignorance. I know you're privy to the information. Lord Alfred told me before he was shot."

"What information?"

Lady Merideth stood over him now, forcing him to look at her, blocking his view of the spider. A shaft of sunlight hit her golden hair and for a moment Jared forgot everything but the desire to pull her down on top of him. That would certainly be a nice treat for the condemned man. But he didn't think anyone else would agree . . . especially Lady Merideth. Her mouth was pressed into a straight line.

Jared shrugged his shoulders. "You needn't worry. I've decided to take the Banistar secret with me to the grave." Actually, he'd decided it would do him no good to confess Lord Alfred's treason or his daughter's involvement. Most likely no one would believe him. And even if they did, he'd still hang as a spy. Was it better to die as a spy rather than a murderer? He hadn't been able to come to any conclusion on that, so he'd decided to say nothing.

Lady Merideth still had the information the Americans wanted. This way she could contact someone else and make the trade. So in a sense it was damn heroic of him to keep quiet. Now, if she'd just go away and let him dwell on that for a while . . .

"What are you talking about? What secret? I want to—"

Merideth sucked in her breath, stifling the scream. She had never seen anyone move so fast. One minute he was prone, seemingly ignoring her presence, the next he was on his feet, looming over her, backing her

49

against the damp cell wall. His hard thighs pressed against her; his chest was only a deep breath away.

"Don't play games with me." Jared's words were gritted through clenched teeth. "Your father told me you had the name. You're involved in this treason just as much as he was."

"Treason?" Her voice was hardly more than a whisper.

Jared's brow arched. "You really should consider the stage. You certainly have the looks for it." His gaze dropped insolently from her face to the rise and fall of her jacket-covered breasts. "And you *can* act."

"Get away from me." She gave his chest a shove with the heel of her hand, surprised when he moved. "I don't know what you're talking about. And I don't believe for one minute my father was involved in treason." As she watched he merely shrugged, as if he didn't care whether she doubted him or not. He moved to the small window, the violence seemingly drained from his big body.

She felt dismissed.

"You're simply saying that to save yourself." Merideth marched over toward him. "But it won't work. No one will believe such a ridiculous lie." Certainly her father's reputation hadn't sunk that low. "I imagine the constable laughed in your face when you—"

"I haven't told anyone. And I just assured you I wouldn't."

His eyes held hers, and for a moment—one irrational moment—Merideth found herself lulled by his voice into believing him. Her breathing stopped, and she could feel the pounding of her heart.

Noise from outside the cell broke the spell.

Merideth tore her gaze away, and she remembered that Jared Blackstone had accused not only her father of treason but her as well. As disloyal as it may be, Merideth found herself wondering if her father, out of financial desperation, could have entertained traitorous thoughts. She quickly pushed that from her mind. Besides, this man was accusing her of the same deed.

"What the hell was in your mind, Les? I should kick your ass to Penzance for this!"

"She done said it was all right," came an answering whine as the cell door banged open.

Merideth turned, an explanation on her lips. But she never had a chance to use it. A steel-hard arm snaked around her waist, forcing the breath from her body and dragging her back against Jared Blackstone. From the corner of her eye she caught the glimmer of a knife blade.

"Either of you move and I'll kill her," the man behind her said. His arm tightened. The knife point traced along her ribs. And this time she had no trouble believing him.

Chapter Three

"This ain't a good idea at all, Blackstone."

"Oh, I think it has its merits." Jared gripped the carved knife handle and kept his gaze on the constable and the flustered deputy. He didn't bother to glance down at his captive. He knew she was scared. Jared could feel her heart thumping against his arm. Well, hell, he was scared too.

"What we gonna do, Mr. Samuals?" Les was sweating profusely, the perspiration running down the sides of his fat face.

"What you're going to do is move away from the door." Jared kept a firm grip on Merideth.

"I can't let you just walk out of here." The constable was trying to keep some control over the situation, but Jared could tell he was nervous. "You've already murdered one Banistar."

"So then it makes no difference to me if I get rid of another." The pinch he gave Lady Merideth made her cry out. Some of the ruddy color left the constable's face.

53

"There's no call to hurt her none."

"Whether or not I hurt her is entirely up to you. Do as I say, Lady Merideth lives to see her grandchildren. Cause me any more trouble . . ." With a slight shrug Jared let the two men fill in the rest for themselves. Apparently they'd decided to take him at his word, something for which Jared was extremely grateful. He didn't know what he would do if they called his bluff.

But the constable took a step away from the doorway, bumped into his cowering deputy, and gave him a shove toward the cot. "Get a move on with you, Les."

"You aren't going to let him get away with this, are you? He killed my father!"

Jared had momentarily let his grip loosen on his captive—a move he regretted. He didn't need her arguing against him. Foolish woman. Didn't she understand what he could do to her?

With a jerk Jared yanked her up against him. She sucked in breath and hung onto his arm as he backed up, dragging her toward the door.

"Do something!" Merideth couldn't believe the constable and his deputy were simply standing there, watching this happen. She tried to dig in her heels as he inched them across the straw-covered floor, but her toes were barely touching the ground. All manner of things she could do to stop his escape ran through her head, but nothing seemed like it would work—not with the knife pressing against her every time she took a deep breath.

Suddenly it was too late. He lunged backward, out of the cell, pulling her off her feet. Her skirt swished around them and Merideth wondered if she was taking her last breath. But then just as abruptly she was let go. Her momentum sent her spinning against the stone wall of the anteroom as her captor slammed the cell door shut. He turned the brass key, pulling it out and tossing it onto the heel-scarred desk top.

They both noticed the pistol lying on the desk. But Jared Blackstone had it in his hand before Merideth could push away from the wall.

He checked the pan, seemingly satisfied that it was ready to fire, and aimed it casually at her.

"Come along, now, Lady Merideth. We mustn't tarry."

"I'm not going anywhere with you." Merideth tried to keep her voice calm. She raised her chin in determination.

"Oh, but you are." He wasted no time slipping the knife inside his boot.

"I can't believe the constable didn't search you before putting you in the cell."

Jared glanced up. The dimple in his cheek flirted in and out as he grinned. "Neither could I."

As quickly as the smile had transformed the hard contours of his face, it was gone. His scowl made Merideth shiver.

"You lead the way, your Ladyship."

"I said I'm not going."

"You have information I want and I'm not leaving you here."

Merideth's only response was to lift her chin higher.

Jared clenched his jaw. "It would be a shame to shoot you."

"Go ahead. You'll no doubt do it anyway, and I'd rather die here than—umph!"

"Hell!" Jared tossed her over his shoulder, ignoring her struggles to get free. Just his luck to pick a defiant hostage. She kicked, her boot coming dangerously close to his groin, and Jared hoisted her higher and tightened his grip on her legs. He stuck the pistol in his pants and brought his hand down hard over her bottom. "Do that again and you'll be sorry. Now hush up."

Merideth could hear Amos Samuals and Les yelling from inside the cell. But her captor didn't seem to notice. He simply strode to the door. Merideth prayed the yard in front of the jail was packed with people. But apparently it wasn't—though she couldn't see from her upside-down vantage—because after a quick glance around he proceeded outside.

Jared Blackstone sat her on her horse, but before Merideth could brush her hair back enough to see, he grabbed the reins and walked her mare over to another horse, one presumably belonging to Constable Samuals. In a quick, fluid motion he was in the saddle, leading her horse down the crooked, narrow path away from the small hamlet.

He may have anticipated Merideth's plan to jump from the saddle, for before she could, he urged both horses into a gallop. It was all Merideth could do to hold on to her sidesaddle.

There was no sound save the horses' hooves and the incessant whistling of the wind as they rode along the hills and moors. They passed a stone house, small and low, sheltered by a slight rise, and Merideth hoped to see the farmer or his wife. But they were nowhere in sight. And as they galloped alongside the stone hedge covered with bracken and furze, Merideth realized it was for the best. No simple yeoman or his mate was a match for Jared Blackstone.

"Where are you taking me?" Merideth called out as they headed off across a field following the footpath.

He didn't answer.

"You'd make better progress without me. I'm just slowing you up." Merideth waited a moment. "I won't tell them which way you went."

"Be quiet," was his only response. He didn't even look around, but simply kept them moving.

Late-afternoon sunlight shone off the white feathers of a gull circling overhead. Merideth was tired. Her muscles ached from the long hours on horseback. Riding had never been something she enjoyed, perhaps because for as long as she could remember, Banistar Hall had not had much of a stable. She'd ridden, of course, but never for this long, and certainly never under such trying circumstances.

But the agony in her arms and back was nothing compared to the distress she felt in her mind. What *was* he going to do with her? Merideth felt she could withstand almost anything if only she knew what to expect.

It had been the same with her father. Once she'd discovered their alarming financial predicament, she'd been better able to cope. It was the unexpected—the surprise—that frightened her the most.

And she had no idea what to expect from Jared Blackstone. She asked him repeatedly. She asked when they slowed to ride around a stand of wind-tormented hawthorn, its limbs bent inland, nearly touching the ground. When they paused to allow the horses to drink from a small swift-moving stream. When she refused to remount after the horses had drunk their fill.

But he never answered her. He never even acknowledged that she spoke by so much as a nod of his head. When she crossed her arms, refusing to take his proffered help into the saddle, he simply picked her up and set her there, ignoring her flinch of discomfort as her tender backside met the hard leather.

Now they were riding through another rock-strewn stream. Rather than crossing it, they followed the current as it made its way to the river. Merideth shifted, her physical and mental agony heightened by every step.

"I want to know where you're taking me."

Jared snorted and turned in his saddle, the leather creaking. "So you've said . . . numerous times."

Startled that he had bothered to respond, Merideth straightened her shoulders. "Then perhaps you will answer me."

"To Banistar Hall," was all he said before clicking her horse to a faster pace.

"Banistar Hall? But that's the first place they'll look for you."

"Don't tell me you're concerned for my welfare?"

That wicked grin was back again. Merideth ignored it. "Not in the least." She couldn't imagine why she had said that. "I certainly hope the constable apprehends you as quickly as possible."

"I'm sure you do," Jared said, throwing the words over his shoulder as he led her along.

"Of course I do. You murdered my father."

His horse—rather, the constable's horse—stopped so suddenly Merideth's mare nudged into him before jolting to a stop. Jared Blackstone's expression was fierce when he stared around at her.

"I shall tell you one last time: I did not kill your father."

"Do you expect me to believe that?"

Jared took a deep breath, then shrugged. "I suppose it matters naught what you believe." After that he started their little procession moving again.

The sun was setting before Merideth caught sight of anything that looked familiar. They must have taken a very roundabout route to Banistar Hall. As a matter of fact, Merideth was almost certain they'd been traveling in circles most of the afternoon, though she wasn't certain if it was by design or not. She did imagine it would be difficult for anyone to follow their tracks.

But then it didn't really matter if they were followed. Amos Samuals was certain to go straight to Banistar Hall and find them. And even if the constable didn't come, Merideth knew her way around the manor well enough to get away from her captor. She would even force herself to go into one of the secret passageways if necessary.

Except they weren't heading along the path toward the house. They were traveling along the narrow ridge that separated the granite cliffs from the waters of the channel. When they reached the beach he guided them down toward the surf. Droplets sent spraying by the horses' hooves sparkled in the last rays of sunlight.

"We can't reach the house from here. At least not on horseback."

"We're not headed for the house."

The caves.

Merideth knew before he turned the horses that that was where he was taking her.

The dark, enclosed . . . mysterious caves.

The shudder that ran through her was involuntary. As was the image her mind drew from the past. Of a child . . . a little girl . . . defying her nanny and climbing down the stairs chiseled in the rocks. To explore the caves.

It was nap time, but it always seemed to be nap time as far as Miss Alice was concerned . . . or so Merideth thought. She wasn't tired. Not in the least. She flopped back on the bed in the nursery in disgust. If anything, she had too much energy. Tomorrow was her birthday. She was going to be eight. And her father had promised to return from London for the occasion.

Merideth rolled to her side, propping her cheek in her palm. Father said she was growing up, becoming a young lady. But grown-up ladies didn't nap the day away. At least she didn't think they should. Of course, she wasn't around many ladies, young or old, but she just knew she'd outgrown the need to sleep all afternoon.

After sliding over the edge of the bed, Merideth climbed down the steps and walked to the window. Sitting down on the window seat, she smiled. She loved to look out over the cliffs to the channel. She imagined if the sky were really clear she could see the whole way to France. Papa went there often, to a place called

Paris. And he promised to take her there too . . . when she became a young lady.

"But he'll never think me grown enough if I'm treated like a baby." Merideth tossed back her pale ringlets and glanced around the small room. It was a baby's room. It was dark and dreary. Not like the rest of the house, which glimmered and shone. And certainly not like the view from the window of sparkling sky and glittering water. The view that beckoned.

With a quick glance toward the door to the adjoining room where Miss Alice snored peacefully—she was one grown-up who needed her sleep—Merideth slipped from the nursery. Most of the servants were accustomed to her little forays while her nanny slept, so no one stopped her. And no one noticed when she slipped out of the massive front door.

As she ran along the cliffs, the sea-scented air blowing in her face, Merideth grew more and more excited about the morrow. A visit from Papa. He was always such fun. He brought presents, but more important, he sometimes took her with him when he visited neighbors, or allowed her to sit with him in the big dining room. Wonderful adventures.

She found the steps by accident. Crude stairs, hacked in the rocks. Leading down to the beach. To the water.

Hesitantly at first, she climbed down. She'd never gone beyond the cliffs by herself, and wouldn't even be this far if Miss Alice knew about it. The steps were weathered, some of them worn away almost entirely by the salt-water-charged wind. And they were overgrown with bracken and tangles of ivy. But the farther down she went, the more anxious to reach the bottom she became.

"Ouch!" A thorn pierced her skin, but Merideth stuck her finger in her mouth and kept going. The beach was wide and sandy, and the waves broke with sparkling white foam . . . a silent invitation. With a squeal Merideth stuck both hands into the surf and swirled them around. When her sleeves got wet she pulled them out, fanning her arms in the spring air. It wouldn't do for Miss Alice to find out she'd come down here.

Racing across the sand was fun. Merideth did it several times, chasing the seabirds, the black-headed gulls and puffin, who pranced along the shore. Out of breath, she bent forward, hands on knees. And that's when she saw them.

The caves.

Dark and mysterious. Compelling.

Merideth took a deep breath and walked toward the gaping mouth, drawn as she never was before to explore something beyond her narrow world.

At first it was fun. Light from the outside flirted with the darkness, sending shivers down her spine and raising gooseflesh on her arms. But as she moved deeper into the cave something happened. The thrill turned to disquiet, then panic. The air smelled rank, and the ground beneath her slippers seemed slick. She slipped, a scream erupting from her slight body. The sound echoed off the walls and was followed by another sound. An eerie, scary sound like a thousand fans swishing the air. Then came the squeaks, louder and louder.

Merideth crouched on the floor, covering her head. "No!"

"No! No!"

Jared twisted around when she screamed. What the hell . . . ? Before he knew what she was doing, Lady Merideth grabbed hold of her mare's mane and dug her heels into the animal's ribs. Wild-eyed, the frightened horse whinnied, throwing its front legs into the air. The reins were yanked from his hand, and he nearly lost his seat grabbing for them.

How she stayed in the saddle he didn't know, for the horse bucked again, then took off down the beach, sending sand flying from beneath its hooves.

With a flick of the reins Jared was in pursuit. The mare acted crazed . . . or was it the rider. "You're going to kill yourself!" Jared yelled, a touch of panic in his voice. She was heading toward the rocks at the end of the crescent-shaped beach.

Digging his heels into his horse's side, Jared leaned forward, coaxing every bit of speed from the animal. Oh, to have one of his family's thoroughbreds beneath him! But this was the constable's horse, and though he appeared to have heart, the speed wasn't there. Still, Jared was gaining on her. Given another ten rods, he'd overtake her.

But he didn't have another ten rods. The rocks loomed, grotesque and shadowed by the gathering twilight.

His bay's nose inched alongside the mare. "A little more," Jared urged, his body low and straining. "Just a little more and we've got her." But time had run out. With a lurch Jared threw himself forward and to the side. His arms outstretched, he grabbed hold of Merideth, knocking her from her horse. For one frantic moment they flew through the air, clutching each other, then with a thud they landed on surf-packed sand.

The jolt knocked the air from Jared's lungs and sent his ears ringing. He landed on his back, Lady Merideth on top of him, her hair covering his face. He lay still a moment, trying to decide if he was in one piece. His body ached, but he didn't think anything was broken.

Lady Merideth was alive. He could hear her breathing, feel the beat of her heart next to his.

"Are you all right?" Jared ran his hands down her arms and back. She sucked in breath and raised her head. Her response was weak, but certain: "Yes . . . yes, I'm fine."

She was fine. She was fine? Anger flowed through Jared at her words. Anger stimulated by a crisis just ended. When he'd leaped from his horse, he wouldn't have bet on either of them surviving. He had only done it because he'd thought the odds were better than smashing against the rocks. And now all she could say was she was fine?

"What in the hell got into you? Are you crazy? You could have gotten yourself killed!" His hands cupped her shoulders and he gave them a shake. "You could have gotten us both killed."

She was trembling. Jared let out his breath on a frustrated sigh and studied her face. Her hair formed a curtain about them, blocking most of the light, but he could see her eyes. They were wide and crystal blue . . . and frightened.

Jared had seen her reaction to her father's death and to being abducted at knife point. Both had scared her, but there was never this uncontrolled fear in her eyes. The harsh edges of his anger blurred. "What is it? What's the matter with you?"

Merideth shook her head. Emotions rolled through her in undulating waves. She struggled to contain them. "I . . . I can't go in there."

"Where? What the hell are you talking about?" Jared shifted to lift her off him.

"No! No." Her voice held a hint of its earlier panic. "I can't. Please don't make me." Rolling over on her back, Merideth raised her arms to cover her head.

"What the . . . ?" He grabbed her wrists, pulling them away from her face, and positioned himself over her body. His voice softened. "What is it? Where don't you want to go?"

"The caves," she whispered on a sob as tears rolled down the side of her face.

Her reaction didn't make sense, but then neither did his. She was his hostage, and his life depended upon getting out of England as quickly as possible. She was also a traitor, and he wasn't completely convinced she didn't have something to do with her own father's death.

But he couldn't stop himself from comforting her.

Jared touched her cheek, surprised when she turned her face into his palm. "Don't cry." He repeated the words tenderly as his fingers brushed sand-strewn hair from her forehead.

Her weeping slowed and her eyes closed. Jared thought her asleep and started to pull away, but her voice stayed him. "Don't let them get me."

"I won't," Jared promised, wondering what he was vowing to protect her from. But his arm curled around her shoulder as he added, "You're safe with me."

She seemed to take him at his word, for Jared noticed a slight smile tilt the corners of her mouth, and she snuggled deeper into his embrace. He lay for long minutes holding her. Breathing in her flowery scent and feeling her soft body mold to his.

Night was truly upon them when he stood, gathering her up in his arms, and headed for the caves. She was sound asleep, doing nothing more than sighing as he carried her.

Jared's mind raced with the things he had to do. Build a fire . . . a signal fire. And hope against hope that the *Carolina* was still around to see it. That she hadn't been captured by the British frigates that cruised these waters. Or that the crew hadn't given up on him and sailed back to France.

Chances were good that one or the other had happened. He'd missed the rendezvous day by nearly a week, but he was going to try. Jared started into the cave with his sleeping bundle, but paused. Placing her out of sight was the logical thing to do while he gathered wood for a fire and tried to find out what had happened to their horses.

But, good Lord, she was frightened of the caves. In the end, Jared laid her in the sand near the entrance. Chiding himself for his foolishness, Jared wandered off toward the bramble-covered rocks.

Merideth opened her eyes slowly. It was dark and she was outside . . . near the sea. Memory drifted over her, making her jerk to sitting.

"Oh." She covered her mouth to muffle the groan of pain. She felt battered and bruised all over. But there was no time to worry about that. Rustling noises to her right sounded and Merideth turned her head, searching through the darkness. He'd built a small fire. She could make out Jared Blackstone's shadowy form standing over it.

As stealthily as she could, Merideth pushed to her feet. Skirting the caves, she made her way to the steps carved into the cliff. She could still hear him, and he seemed to be closer than before.

Merideth's heart pounded, and she couldn't believe her captor couldn't hear it as she started up the steps. At first she moved slowly, conscious of every rustled leaf, of every broken twig. But when she heard his hearty curse, and realized he'd discovered her gone, she grabbed up her skirts and climbed as fast as she could.

If she could only make it to the house and get inside before he caught her, she might have a chance. Thurston would be there, and though he could do little against Mr. Blackstone, there *was* her father's pistol. In the library. If she could only get to it. If she could only . . .

The worn-away step. She wasn't concentrating and she'd forgotten about the worn-away step. The small cry that escaped her as she fell seemed to echo in Merideth's ears, and she knew it was heard by the man pursuing her. Jagged rock cut into her knee and her breath caught on the pain. Hair fell across her face, and her hands clutched at the coarse marram grass woven into the side of the cliff.

Sobbing, Merideth pulled herself up, yanking her sleeve free from a prickly blackthorn bush. Fabric tore as she scrambled to the next step . . . then the next.

She could hear him behind her now, growing closer with each pounding footfall of his boots against the carved-rock stairs. Her raspy breathing sounded in her ears, her head pounded, as she fought her way up over the top.

The terrain was flat now, easier to traverse, and with her last reserve of strength Merideth bounded toward Banistar Hall.

But her pursuer was faster, and before she'd traveled five rods he was so close his mumbled curses singed her ears. Something grabbed her legs, and the next thing Merideth knew she was sprawled on the soft grass, a hard male body on top of her.

"Let go of me!" Merideth tried to flail at his restricting weight, but he easily caught her wrists, pinioning them above her head.

"Stop it! Just be still." Jared tightened his grip when she tried to squirm free. "I've had enough of your lying and deceit."

"Lying and deceit?" Merideth spit hair from her mouth. His broad chest loomed above her, and her every breath skimmed her breasts against him.

"Don't put me in the caves," he said, mimicking her earlier plea, his voice thick with disdain. "I should have remembered whom I was dealing with."

Merideth stopped struggling. The moon was out, casting an eerie glow on the bodies entwined on the top of the cliff. "What do you mean, whom you're dealing with?"

"Traitors are rarely to be trusted."

"Traitors! I'm no traitor!" Merideth jerked her knee upward with considerable force. His groan was satisfying; the added weight of his unsupported body was not. Merideth couldn't move, could hardly breathe. He was going to kill her, squash her, and there was nothing she could do about it.

"What . . . what are you going to do with me?" Her question was a breathy whisper.

Jared shifted some of his weight to his elbows, but was careful to keep her hands and legs restrained. "Do? Well, unless you wish to tell me who the spy is, I plan to take you with me."

"You can't do that."

"Oh, I think I can." Jared certainly hoped he could . . . hoped he could get *himself* away at least. "But then the decision is yours. Tell me what I want to know and I'll leave you here when I go. If not . . ." Jared left the rest to her imagination.

"But I don't know any spy." Merideth squirmed. He no longer was cutting off her air, but she found the feel of him on her . . . unsettling.

"Then I'm afraid you're going with me."

"That's kidnapping."

"Aye. But then for someone who would have hanged today for a murder he didn't commit, that doesn't seem such a dastardly crime. Besides, my great-grandfather was a pirate. He kidnapped beautiful women all the time."

"I'm sure your great-grandmother loved that."

"Actually she did. She was one of them."

Merideth could see the flash of his white teeth in the

moonlight. She could only imagine the dimple. She lay very still, thinking of it and wondering why everything seemed different. She was still pinned to the ground. Her wrists were still held captive in one of his hands. But she could feel his eyes on her, and it made her skin tingle.

His face moved nearer. Merideth could feel the whisper of his breath on her cheek. And then, before she knew what he was about, his lips pressed to hers.

Resisting was her first reaction. She yanked at her hands and her body arched, trying to push him away. But it only made the contact more intimate.

His mouth was firm, like the rest of him, hinting at something dark and erotically forbidden. She gasped and her lips parted. The touch of his tongue made Merideth jerk, but she couldn't contain the moan that drifted off across the mist-shrouded cliff.

She'd been kissed before. Lord Chadwell had maneuvered her alone into the gardens. His hands had fumbled with her hair, and his mouth had slobbered down her neck. And she'd been revolted.

So why wasn't she repulsed by Jared Blackstone? It wasn't a civilized kiss. It was hard and forceful and wild.

Like him.

And he was the man who had killed her father.

Reality slammed into her, blocking the sensual feel of his body against hers. He let loose her hands, and now she used them to shove at him. Unlike before, he rolled away when she pushed. But he did take hold of her arm.

What had gotten into him? Jared stared down at the

woman lying in the grass, only able to make out her shadowy form, and shook his head. She was a traitor, and certainly someone he couldn't trust. He had absolutely no business kissing her. But it was almost as if he couldn't resist.

Damn, he was going to turn her over to Daniel as soon as he reached France. If he ever got to France. Jared shook his head again. And when he did, his gaze wandered out over the channel. What he saw made him jump to his feet, grabbing Lady Merideth up beside him.

"Oh, I couldn't. Cap'n would have me killt sure."

looked like she was twisting the boy's arm.

Chapter Four

"What is it? Where are we going?"

Ignoring Lady Merideth's questions, Jared searched the darkness, a grin spreading across his face when he saw it again. "They're still here."

"Who's still where?" Merideth resisted, trying to yank away when he pulled her toward the steep steps. "I demand to—" Air whooshed out of Merideth as she was forced against his hard body.

"Your demanding days are over . . . at least for a while. Now come along."

"I won't. I—ah! Put me down!" Again Merideth found herself thrown over one of his broad shoulders. Her fists pummeled his back and she twisted about, trying to pull loose.

"Be still unless you want to go tumbling down the cliff."

Merideth froze. "You wouldn't throw me down." Her voice, breathless because of her awkward position, quivered. "Would you?"

"I won't have to. If you aren't careful, you'll simply fall."

"Then put me down and let me walk—" Merideth grabbed his broad back, clutching the linen shirt as he moved down the carved stairs, ignoring her request.

By the time they reached the beach, Merideth's head pounded. She was plopped unceremoniously in the sand—thankfully not in the cave. The fire near the rocks still burned.

After Merideth swiped curls from her face, she watched him run to the blaze. He was pulling his shirt over his head as he went.

"What are you doing?"

No response.

Merideth was getting tired of being ignored, but she had no choice but to endure it. She could see him clearly now, silhouetted against the orange flames. His upper body was bare, the muscles bronzed by the fire. His dark hair, loosened from the queue, hung nearly to his shoulders, giving him a primitive, untamed appearance.

Merideth sucked in her breath, remembering how close she'd come to weaving her fingers through that thick mane of hair. Thinking of how her fingers itched to do it even still.

He was moving his shirt in front of the fire, then away. Signaling.

Merideth pulled her gaze from him and searched out across the channel. At first she could see nothing but endless miles of blackness. Then, just as she was ready to turn away, she caught a glimpse of something.

A faint light, flashing in the distance. It blinked three times, then there was nothing but the infinite darkness, the rolling splash of surf on the sand. If she hadn't seen Jared Blackstone's reaction, Merideth would be convinced the sighting was a hallucination.

Her captor stood, staring out to sea, while Merideth sat huddled on the sand. Waiting. For what, she didn't know.

Merideth considered running again. Jared's attention was focused away from her; he seemed to have forgotten she was there. But the memory of what happened the last time she ran stayed her.

She listened, but could hear nothing but the crashing waves, the crackle of the fire, and her own heart pounding in her ears. Then the colonial was wading into the surf, waving his white shirt. Her eyes narrowed, Merideth made out the dark shape of a small boat riding the waves toward shore.

Again Merideth thought to run. She could hide in the caves. They were a twisting maze of tunnels. No one could find her in there. She would hide and he would leave. She'd be safe.

But though she wanted to escape him with all her being, Merideth couldn't . . . she just couldn't make herself inch toward the caves.

"There ye be, Cap'n." The booming voice startled Merideth. She clutched her hands together to stop them from trembling. "We'd 'bout given ye up fer sure."

"I came close to giving up on myself," Jared admitted, reaching for the boat's prow.

Three men leaped from the longboat, wrestling it onto shore.

"What happened to ye? We was supposed to meet a sennight ago. And where's the other boat?"

"Gone. No doubt the new property of a fisherman." Finding it missing when he reached the desolate beach had given him a moment of panic. "As for what happened to me, 'tis a long story, and one best told after we've distanced ourselves from Land's End. Marcus, douse the fire. We won't be needing that anymore."

As one of the men moved off to follow Captain Blackstone's order, hope flickered in Merideth's breast. Perhaps her captor had forgotten her. He hadn't even glanced her way since dumping her on the beach. She tried to make herself as small as possible. Now that the fire was out, the only light came from a sliver of moon, newly risen in the sky. She was fairly certain none of the other men had noticed her.

She could barely see Captain Blackstone and his friends, though she could hear them. They were discussing the light that now glowed from the ship in the channel. The beacon appeared as the fire on shore went out.

"We best be hurryin', Cap'n. Caught sight of a ship a the line before sunset. Wouldn't do for them to get a bead on us."

"You've got the right of it there, Mr. Simpson. Let's be shoving off, then."

They were leaving. He *had* forgotten her. Merideth shut her eyes and held her breath, a silent prayer floating round in her head. But when she heard footfalls in the sand, and felt his presence, Merideth realized it had been a foolish hope.

"Come along, your Ladyship." His words were mocking.

"What ye got there, Cap'n?"

"The sum total of my accomplishments here. A very lovely traitor." His hand closed around Merideth's arm.

"I am *not* a traitor." The yank she gave her arm had no more effect than her denial. He simply hauled her to her feet.

"But she be a woman."

This remark from one of his men made Jared chuckle. "Aye, she is." His head bent toward her till Merideth could feel the whisper of his breath on her cheek. "But then some of the best spies are." His voice was silky smooth and meant only for her ears.

"I don't know anything. Please, don't take me away from here." She was reduced to begging, but she didn't care.

Neither did he. Without another word he pulled her toward the longboat. When they neared the shore, he lifted her high against his chest and walked into the water, depositing her on a hard wooden seat near the back of the boat.

Merideth clutched the seat as the men pushed off from the shore, taking the longboat into the dark waters of the channel. Taking Merideth into the unknown.

Little was said on the way to the ship. It was too dark

to see more than vague shadows of anyone, but Merideth felt as if three sets of eyes studied her, and she had to force herself not to tremble. When they reached the ship, the captain's large hands guided her to a rope ladder, and she could sense his heat behind her as she climbed.

It was dark on deck—apparently the captain was serious about not letting his presence known to the British ships that patrolled the channel. He led the way below, where tallow candles sputtering on iron holders protruding from the bulwarks offered some light. Merideth swiped tangled hair from her eyes and followed.

At the bottom of the ladder the captain threw a hasty order over his shoulder before striding down the companionway. "Take her to my cabin."

She had no time to protest before a beefy hand clamped around her arm. "This way, wench," the man said, hauling her toward the ship's aft. He didn't seem to care when she tripped on her torn skirt; he simply yanked her along. If she ever thought to solicit help from any of the crew on this ship, it certainly wouldn't be this tattooed giant.

Merideth feared what he might do when they reached the cabin, but he only shoved her inside and slammed the door . . . him on the outside. She heard the turn of a key and sank to the deck, her skirts billowing out around her.

The cabin was dark and confining, with only a feeble glow from the moon to cast eerie shadows on the furnishings. Merideth reached for her locket, rubbing the smooth surface with her thumb, trying to calm her panic. The wall seemed to press in upon her, and she tried to think of something else to help her fight the feeling.

Once her eyes adjusted to the lack of light, Merideth could make out a cot, a desk covered with piles of ledgers, and two trunks. Windows lined one wall of the cramped room, but unless she planned to swim to shore—a feat she knew was beyond her—they offered no escape.

Her head lolled back against the bulwark, and tears burned her eyes. No one—not even she—knew where she was bound. She had no one to turn to for help. Merideth sniffed and impatiently scrubbed at the moisture on her cheeks. She would not become a sniveling whine. She could overcome this problem. She could!

But the cabin walls pressed closer. And then she thought about what Captain Blackstone wanted from her. The name of a traitor. A name she didn't know.

And he would likely kill her if she didn't give him what he wanted . . . perhaps even if she did. After all, he had killed her father.

Merideth clenched her fists and tried to come up with a plan. But all she could think of was the gleam in Jared Blackstone's eyes as she and he lay entwined on the cliff.

"So you were to have your neck stretched," Padriac Delany said with a chuckle.

"I'm glad you find it so amusing." Jared backhanded rum from his mouth and grinned at his friend. He'd met Padriac in France the year before, after the Irishman had escaped from a British prison. Since then the lighthearted Delany had served on the *Carolina* as first officer.

"Well, now, I think every man needs such a brush with death," Padriac offered. "It makes one appreciate life all the more."

"I appreciate life just fine. And *your* brush with death, unlike mine, was caused by something you actually did."

"Smuggling," Padriac said with a snort. "Hardly something to lose your life for."

"The British Admiralty seems to think it is."

"They find privateering and spying equally offensive."

"True enough," Jared admitted. "But I was to be hanged for murder. A murder I didn't commit," he added after noticing the widening of Padriac's eyes.

Delany leaned back against the bulwark, mirroring Jared's pose. "Any idea who did do it?"

Jared's pause was brief as he recalled the blur of crimson before pain had exploded through his head. "Nay." She was a traitor, but Jared couldn't bring himself to believe Merideth Banistar had killed her father.

Padriac took another swig from the pewter mug. "I thought perhaps that pretty baggage you brought aboard had something to do with it. Or is she just here to warm your bed till we reach France?"

"Hardly." Jared straightened. "She's Lady Merideth Banistar. Lord Alfred's daughter. And apparently his fellow traitor."

"I caught but a glimpse of her, and admittedly the light was poor, but she seems a comely wench."

Delany's blue eyes shone with a sparkle Jared knew well. He shook his head and grinned. "She's a beauty all right, but not for the likes of you, Paddy."

"'Tis no need to pull rank on me. You did see her first."

"'Tisn't rank but friendship I'm offering. She's not to be trusted." Jared's green eyes narrowed. "She's but someone else willing to sell out their country for gold."

"They make our job easier."

"They're despicable." Jared jumped to his feet and paced the small wardroom. The cabin, often crowded with officers, was empty now except for Padriac and himself. They'd outstayed the others, who had either sought their hammocks or taken up their watch.

Delany leaned back in his chair and let Jared stride the length of the room several times before he spoke. "This has nothing to do with John, you know."

Jared turned abruptly. His hands fisted and he speared his friend with an icy stare. But a moment later his broad shoulders slumped and he swiped relaxed fingers down over his face. "I just can't help thinking if John hadn't gotten mixed up with this whole intrigue business . . ."

"He'd be alive today," Padriac finished. "But it was an accident. He was thrown from his horse. Besides, your brother knew what he was about. 'Twas his choice

81

to become a spy."

"Well, it isn't mine." Jared leaned toward Padriac, his palms planted firmly on the scarred table separating them. "I've no taste for secrets and subterfuge. I've a wish to wash my hands of it once and for all."

"Aren't you forgetting one small thing?" Paddy's dark brow arched questioningly.

"I'm not forgetting her, if Lady Merideth is whom you're alluding to. Nor am I forgetting that someone knocked me out and killed Lord Alfred. And,"—Jared raised his hand for emphasis—"stole the gold I planned to use as payment."

"Lady Merideth?"

"'Tis possible. She was certainly there." Jared gave an exaggerated sigh. "Unfortunately there seems to be naught I can do about it now." He paused. "Not unless I can convince the lovely Lady Merideth to talk."

"If she's an informer, that shouldn't be difficult."

"She insists she knows nothing."

"But then perhaps she's telling the truth." Paddy lifted his palms in question.

"Before he was killed, her father told me a different tale. I think perhaps the lady is trying to control who she tells her information to *and* for how much."

"And you . . . ?"

"Want her to tell me what she knows . . . and for payment most likely already received."

Padriac held up his mug in salute, then downed the contents in one gulp. "Good luck to you, then."

Jared shrugged. "If she doesn't answer to me, I'll turn her over to Daniel when we get to France." But he didn't want to. *He* was the one who had been sent to get the name of the traitor. *He* was the one who had been lied to and robbed and very nearly hanged. And, by God, *he* should be the one to discover the truth. Jared splashed rum into his mug.

Delany held up his hand when Jared reached to fill his. "I've had enough, and think it past time I seek me bed. Good night, good friend." Paddy pushed himself to his feet, only a bit unsteadily. "I'm glad you're back among us, safe and sound."

"And I'm glad you decided to stay around Land's End. Even though it was against my orders."

"Now as I recall, your orders only said something about not getting the *Carolina* captured by some damn English cruiser. To that I followed them precisely."

Jared's deep laughter filled the cabin. "Remind me to write my orders down in the future, for that's not at all as I remember them. Still"—Jared clasped his friend's shoulder—"I'm grateful that you hung around."

"'Twas nothing you wouldn't do for me." With those words Padriac left the wardroom, and Jared sat down to finish his rum.

A half-dozen mugs later, he was still in the wardroom, more sprawled than sitting on the wooden chair. Memories wouldn't let him seek the oblivion of sleep.

John.

His twin brother, older than Jared by mere minutes.

On the surface they'd been as different as two people could be, but underneath, where it counted, they were close.

They seemed as different as two sides of the same coin. John was fair and slight, where Jared was tall and dark. John was the thinker, the reader of books, where Jared was the doer, the impetuous one who rushed into things without thinking them through.

"Except for that one time," Jared whispered, closing his eyes. "Why did you have to pick then to rashly follow the cause?"

Because John was also passionate and good. Jared was the cynic, John the believer. A man committed to the ideals of Adams and Jefferson. A man who knew his effectiveness wouldn't be at the helm of a ship or in the heat of battle.

"I can do this, Jared," he'd said that last time they were together. "We Americans need information, and I can see that we receive it."

"Don't be foolish," argued Jared, the selfish brother. The brother who wanted to keep his twin safe. "You're needed here at Royal Oak now more than ever."

"So you can go off on one of your ships? I'm sorry, Jared. I didn't mean that. I know what you do is important. You cause havoc with the British navy as few can. But I must do this." His face had split into a grin. "I can't have you being the only Blackstone to gain all the glory, now can I? Besides, Daniel is going to France with the delegation from Congress, and he wants me to go also. It's something I can do to help us win our freedom."

In the end nothing Jared had said persuaded John to stay at home. John sailed for France. The next thing Jared heard, his brother was dead. His cousin, Daniel, gave him the full account. How John had gone to England to meet with an informant. How he had fallen from a horse and died.

It should have been me.

Jared leaned his forehead on his balled fists as that thought echoed in his mind. *He* was the daredevil, the wild one who took chances. The less-than-perfect brother. If one of them had had to die, it should have been he.

Jared slammed the mug down, spilling rum that pooled, then quickly became a rivulet, dripping off the scarred tabletop with the next pitch of the ship. This was doing no good. Thoughts of John only filled him with impotent anger. That's why he tried to fill his mind with other things.

That's why he shouldn't have listened to Daniel's plea that he act as courier for a traitor.

She couldn't sleep.

Merideth clutched her locket and paced to the other end of the cabin. It was a mess, and prudence dictated she try and restore it to some order before her captor returned. Mr. Blackstone—no, apparently it was Captain Blackstone—wouldn't like it that she had ransacked his quarters. But she couldn't make herself straighten up his things.

If only she knew what was happening. Why her father had been killed. What she was supposed to know about a traitor. And where they were taking her.

The cabin's contents gave no clue. After lighting the

lantern hanging over the desk, she searched carefully. Though she could decipher some of the writing, the charts were no help. The captain's papers dealt more with cargo, captured and otherwise, than with anything resembling espionage.

And the only weapon to be found was an ancient sword. Though it shone from careful preservation, and seemed sharp enough, Merideth didn't think she could use it effectively. But she intended to try.

Kicking aside a pair of breeches—pulled from one of the trunks—Merideth walked to the windows. Her hand closed over her mother's locket in an unconscious gesture. The worn gold felt warm and familiar . . . soothing. But in the next instant Merideth lifted the ribbon from around her neck and buried the locket deep in her pocket. It was the only thing of value she had. She hated the thought of parting with it, but if the need arose, she would. But she didn't want it stolen by some murdering colonial.

Merideth was so deep in thought she failed to hear the key turning in the lock. She whirled around, her hand spread beneath her throat, as the door flew open.

"Good Lord, what have you done?" Charts and papers were scattered everywhere, as was every article of clothing from his sea chests.

Merideth raised her chin, refusing to show how intimidated she was by his tall broad-shouldered form. He nearly took up the entire doorway, and she was certain his booming voice could be heard all over the ship.

Captain Blackstone stepped into the cabin, kicking aside a tangled shirt, and slammed the door. "Answer my question, woman. What were you about?"

"I should think that obvious. I was searching your cabin."

Jared looked around in amazement. "And what, pray tell, did you hope to find? I'm not in possession of any state secrets."

"So I noted." Merideth stood her ground, though his green gaze seemed to slice through her.

"If this is your usual method of spying, I should think you aren't too successful."

"I was looking for a weapon." As one, their eyes slid to the sword lying on the window seat beside her.

"I would think a pistol more your style," Jared said.

"I have no *style* where weapons are concerned."

"My mistake." He bowed, his gaze never leaving her. "Now, may I suggest you repair the damage you've done?" His voice was low, like smooth silk encasing solid steel. But it did nothing to disguise his intensity.

Merideth swallowed. Helplessness was not a feeling she enjoyed. She'd felt it too much during the last year not to recognize it. With all her being she wished to toss back her hair and send him a look filled with disdain. To tell him he was free to do with this mess what he chose, but she would do naught.

In the end she bent and in an angry motion swept up a rumpled shirt. A slightly musky scent she recognized as Captain Blackstone's drifted from the linen. To salvage her pride, she balled the shirt and tossed it toward the open chest. It caught on the lid.

Jared could barely keep from laughing. At that moment she reminded him of his younger sister, Betsy. She was a stubborn child, woman now, and used to getting her way. Then Lady Merideth spoke and her words erased that image from his mind, reminding him that their business together was serious—deadly serious.

"I want to know where you're taking me . . . and why."

Her chin was set at a defiant angle, and though she swept up a chart rolling near her feet, Jared didn't think she planned to do much more toward cleaning his cabin, regardless of his implied threats.

"I thought I made myself clear as to the why." Jared crossed his arms and studied her face. She still had the look of an angel about her. But a fallen angel to be sure.

"And I think I've made myself clear that I don't know the information you seek."

"Your father indicated differently."

"Before you killed him." Merideth watched a dull-red stain his bronzed face. "Is that why you did it, because you thought me easier to coerce?"

"If I thought that, I most certainly was wrong. Your father was willing to traitor himself for mere coin—"

"That's a lie!"

"You, on the other hand," Jared continued as if she hadn't spoken, "have yet to name your price."

"There is no price because there is no information." She didn't know why she took the effort to dispute him. His smirk made it obvious he didn't believe her. But she didn't care what he thought. She knew. Knew her father wouldn't be a party to treason, no matter what the rewards. He wouldn't.

Perhaps he had let their finances get out of hand. And he did have a weakness for gaming tables and drink, but he was a loyal Englishman. He was!

"I've had enough of this." Before she could back away, the captain's grip, iron hard, shackled her arm. Merideth yanked but it did no good. He held her still. His eyes burned into her, and his hot breath wafted across her cheek as he spoke.

"If you think to demand more money in France, think again."

"That's where you're taking me, France?" Merideth tried to mask the panic from her voice. But he seemed to notice neither her tone nor her words.

"I've a notion you've already been paid. And I wish to know the name."

"I've been paid nothing, and for the last time there is no—"

"I carried gold when I came ashore. I still had it when I met with your father."

"You mean when you killed my father!" Merideth swung her fist, but never knew the satisfying feel of flesh against hated flesh. He caught her wrist as easily as if she'd told him what she intended to do. Her fury—and fear—mounted as he yanked her up against him. She could see the prisms of fiery green radiating from the center of his eyes.

"I did not kill your father."

There it was again. The temptation to believe him. But what he said was a lie. It had to be. He'd lied about

89

everything else. Her father. The money. If there had been gold, they would have found it.

Besides, there had been a trial. The magistrate had found him guilty. He *was* guilty. He had to be. There was no one else.

"Now, if we could get on with this." He scowled down at her, and Merideth wondered if he could hear her heart pounding. "Just tell me what you know and I shall be done with you. I might even manage to put you ashore on this side of the channel."

She raised her chin. Her eyes met his. And she wished—oh, how she wished—that she could tell him something. At that moment, with him scowling down at her, his hair dark as a raven's wing, his expression hostile and untamed, she could readily believe his earlier claim that the blood of pirates ran through his veins. But she knew nothing. In the end that's all she could say.

Damn her to hell.

She was afraid. It was obvious she tried to hide it, but the trembling of her full bottom lip gave her away. She was afraid, yet she still defied him.

He should be in control. He knew he wasn't. Not only did she refuse to tell him what he wanted to know, he could feel the tiny fissures of desire cracking away at his anger. Nay, more like fueling it.

Jared didn't want to see her as a woman . . . to think of her as one. She was the enemy. A traitor. But the smell of her was intoxicating. The feel of her soft body stimulating. His jaw relaxed and his breathing quickened and he knew . . . knew she felt it too.

It was like when they were on the cliff, when his body had covered hers. This same something had drawn them then. He had fought it then and failed. He didn't even want to fight it now.

Besides, there was more than one way to persuade.

Intimidation.

Seduction.

Jared ruthlessly shoved aside the sting of guilt as his lips moved toward hers. She was a spy after all. A traitor. And wasn't all fair in love and war?

A gasp, a puff of air, escaped Merideth as he bent toward her. She had feared his touch on the cliff, and ever since. She jerked, trying to put space between them, and managed only to press them closer.

Wriggling only rubbed her breasts against his broad chest. Fighting only made him lean into her, a devilish gleam in his green eyes.

"You wouldn't dare," she began, and knew by the slight lifting of his brow that he dared this and more. "Let me go."

"I think not."

"I don't want you to—"

"You make such a practice of lying, 'tis no wonder you're so good at it."

"I'm not ly—"

But she never had the chance to finish the word. His mouth crushed down on hers, hot, hard, and hungry. She tried to fight him. Tried to twist her face away. But fire raced from him to her and muddled her resolve.

And it sparked an explosive reaction in her. One that

shocked her nearly as much as the feel of his lips on hers.

With a growl he deepened the kiss, forcing her mouth open. Merideth's mind went blank. Tingles of anticipation raced across her skin and she sagged against him. Too shaken for rational thought.

Letting loose of her arm and wrist, Jared let his hands roam over her. His fingers tangled in the depths of her golden hair, tugging for better purchase. Passion burned in him like a white-hot fever, fast and furious. Steeling his determination, Jared strove to control it before he gave in and drowned in the sensation.

His seduction had a purpose. He must remember that.

But oh, when she opened to him so easily, so completely, it was hard to remember. She was sweet and womanly, wanton and alluring. Everything a man could want.

With a yank Jared opened the front of her riding habit and shirt, sending buttons flying. Neither of them seemed to notice. Still covered by the sheer linen of her shift, her breasts teased and tantalized, soft, pink-tipped, and puckered in anticipation. Her head fell back when his callused hand covered her.

He squeezed and she moaned, the vibrations humming across his lips as he followed the curve of her exposed neck with his mouth. He had never tasted skin so erotically flavored. He had never wanted a woman so desperately. Jared's mouth clamped over the straining tip of her breast and her legs spread, welcoming his hard body. He rubbed his aching

92

tumescence across her and she trembled.

Her desire matched his. Her surrender was complete. She responded to him without reservation, without hesitation. Quickly. So quickly.

Too quickly.

The words echoed through Jared's passion-drugged mind, taking hold and forcing him to think. She professed to hate him, to believe he murdered her father. Yet she writhed, moaned . . . seduced.

Tearing his mouth from her soft skin, disgusted at his reluctance, Jared held her at arm's length. Her eyes blinked open, those blue angel eyes. It took a moment for them to focus, longer still for her breathing to slow.

He had meant to seduce her, to use sex if he must to learn her secret. But he'd underestimated her. And he'd very nearly been seduced himself.

"Don't think I don't know what you are," he said. "Or what you were doing." With that he turned on his heel and stormed from the cabin, leaving Merideth to wonder what in heaven's name she *was* doing.

Chapter Five

The door wasn't locked.

Merideth had noticed last night, not long after Captain Blackstone stormed out of his cabin. But she hadn't done anything about it . . . until now.

At first, she was too stunned. Whatever had happened between them had shocked her completely. Not *his* behavior. She expected no better from him. He was obviously an uncouth colonial unfamiliar with gentlemanly behavior.

But what of herself? Merideth was honest enough to admit that beyond the initial contact, she hadn't been forced to do anything. Not kiss him back. Or clutch his shoulders. Or writhe against him wantonly. She also knew in her heart that he was the one who had stopped. Stopped, leaving her bewildered and feeling like an abandoned toy.

"That's just plain foolish," Merideth mumbled to herself as she lifted the latch and heard the door squeak open. "The entire thing is foolish." And she wasn't about to let it bog her down. She would simply put it behind her.

Whatever she'd felt when Captain Blackstone had held her would be forgotten, thrust from her mind. For she had far more important things to think about.

Like the cannon fire that still echoed in her head.

The booming sound had woken her this morn with a suddenness that slashed away any grogginess caused by a near-sleepless night. She'd scrambled from the window seat, where she'd perched when her legs had grown too heavy to continue her pacing. A quick search out the transom windows had told her nothing except that whatever they were firing at wasn't in their wake.

There had been few shots. The battle, if that's what it had been, was over almost before it began.

And now Merideth was going to see what was happening. She peeked into the companionway, found it empty, and walked toward the hatch. Slowing her pace, she listened to the noises overhead. Was it too much to hope that an English cruiser had captured the *Carolina*? Merideth hoped not, for she wished it with all her heart.

But it was not to be. As she came above deck for the first time in daylight, Merideth realized it was the *Carolina* who had been victorious. Her crew, not a one of which appeared wounded, was busy securing an English merchantman to its side with grappling hooks.

At the sound of the only voice on board she recognized, Merideth turned, brushing back her hair when it was caught by the stiff breeze. She found Captain Blackstone on the quarterdeck yelling orders to some of his men as they scrambled over the deck railing onto the captured ship.

Tall and imposing, with his dark-blue jacket flung open by the wind, her captor stood with his legs spread, his arms clutched behind him. He appeared very much in charge and even more intimidating with the sun banishing the shadows from his handsome face.

He'd yet to notice her, and for one cowardly moment Merideth considered backing down through the hatch and slipping back into his cabin. But she didn't. Her chin held high, her resolve but a tad shaky, Merideth moved through the sailors who seemed to pay her little heed.

It wasn't the captain who saw her first, but the man standing by his side. He was nearly as tall as Jared Blackstone, with deep-auburn hair, and a pleasant expression. His blue eyes sparkled and an engaging grin split his face when he spotted Merideth.

She watched as he nudged the captain, an elbow in the lean ribs beneath the billowing white shirt. Jared stopped his study of a chart to follow the other man's gaze.

Captain Blackstone seemed to find her presence less than amusing.

A scowl blackened his countenance as he took a menacing step toward her. "What in the hell are you doing up here?"

She would not be intimidated. She wouldn't. Merideth stood her ground on the gently rolling ship. "I came up to see what was happening."

"What does or does not go on upon this ship is no concern of yours. Besides," Jared added, annoyed that

97

this had been his first concern when he saw her, "'tisn't safe. We've just captured a British vessel."

"I'd rather hoped it might be the other way round. And I seriously doubt I've good loyal Englishmen to fear."

The other man chuckled at her remarks, which earned him a frown from his captain. "Don't encourage her, Paddy. She's difficult enough as it is. As for you . . ." He faced Merideth again, those green eyes that reminded her of the sea near sunset boring into her. "You are to get below and stay below. Lord only knows how you managed to escape through a locked door," he finished, turning back to his chart.

"Easily enough, since you failed to lock it when you left last evening."

At that the man he called Paddy let out a loud guffaw, and Merideth realized the captain hadn't truly been angry before, merely annoyed. Now, however, he was furious. But before he could reach her, the other man stepped forward.

"We've yet to be introduced. I'm Padriac Delany, at your service. And you must be the lovely Lady Banistar of whom I've heard so much," he said, his words embossed with a Gaelic lilt.

He took her hand, and he smiled so charmingly as he brought it to his lips that Merideth couldn't help but respond. Perhaps here was someone she could turn to. Ignoring the captain, she moved with him to the rail when he suggested she might have a better view of the proceedings.

"Don't bother yourself, Jared," he said. "I'll see Lady Merideth back to the cabin when she's had a look."

98

Expecting a verbal rebuke at the very least, Merideth slanted a glance under her lashes. But the captain's only response was a brief shrug of his broad shoulders before he went back to work.

And though Padriac Delany seemed very courteous, he soon had her below deck. And as soon as the door closed behind her, Merideth heard the unmistakable click of the lock.

"What in the hell was that about?" Jared met Padriac at the top of the ladder. He'd already sent a prize crew aboard the merchant ship, which had been bound for Waterford from London with a cargo of iron and dry goods. With any luck both vessels would reach Morlaix in three days.

"What was what about?" Padriac began, but thought better of playing coy after gauging his friend's mood. "I simply thought it better if you didn't throttle the wench in view of the entire crew."

"Have you gone daft?"

"More to the point, have you? From the look of you when she mentioned your failure to lock the cabin door, I thought you would strangle the poor girl."

"That 'poor girl,' as you call her, can take care of herself. She's a liar and, unless I miss my guess, an accomplished spy."

"You've let your imagination run amuck."

"Have I?" Jared's brow arched. "Or have you simply let her beauty cloud your common sense. I told you her history."

"Aye, you did." Padriac shrugged. "But she does

99

have the look of an angel about her."

"Deceiving as hell."

"I gather she didn't give you the information you sought."

"Nay, and you needn't look so amused. I doubt she reveals anything until the gold is sufficient."

"So you're giving up?"

"Hardly. Since we spotted this prize off our bow this morn"—Jared gestured toward the captured British schooner, now trailing behind them—"I've had scant time to think of Lady Merideth."

"Really?" Padriac arched a bronzed brow. "I should imagine her hard to forget. But since she's taken a shine to me, I shall be only too glad to get what I can from her—information, of course."

"She's my problem, and I shall handle her," Jared said before clambering down from the quarterdeck. He failed to see any of the humor Padriac found in the situation.

The knock, a faint brushing of knuckles against wood, stopped Merideth in mid stride. Kicking aside a waistcoat, her attention flew to the sword. With a sigh she dismissed the idea of fighting off whoever stood in the companionway.

"Who's there?" she queried, and realized how ridiculous her precaution was. *She* was the one locked in.

"'Tis Tim, yer Ladyship. Cap'n Blackstone sent me."
He sounded like a child. "Come in, then."
There was a fumbling with the lock and the door

veed open. A narrow, boyish face peered around the edge. He shyly studied Merideth a moment with big brown eyes, then glanced around the cabin.

His eyes grew round as saucers. "Gawd, what happened? Cap'n said his cabin needed straightening, but I never thought . . . Did ye do this?"

The inquiry was so sincere that a wave of guilt rushed over her. "I did," she answered, then hastened to explain. "I was searching for a weapon."

"Cap'n keeps his pistols under the bed," Tim began. "But they ain't loaded," he continued when Merideth instantly doubled over to see that under the mattress there was a box large enough to hold a brace of pistols.

Sighing, Merideth plopped onto the bed. It was probably just as well she hadn't found them earlier. As she watched, the boy, whom she imagined to be no older than ten, began picking up the captain's clothing and folding it. Or, rather, attempting to fold it. He mostly wrapped things around his thin arms till there was no material left. Then he transferred them to the open chest.

"Why are you on this ship?" Merideth leaned forward, resting her elbows on her knees.

"Me? Why, I'm the *Carolina*'s cabin boy, I am. Cap'n Blackstone picked me out special for the job."

"He did, did he? Don't you think you're a little young for such a job?"

"No sir . . . I mean yer Ladyship. I be nearly twelve." Tim picked up a boot and, after polishing the toe on his sleeve, laid it on top of a clean but wrinkled shirt.

She hated gambling, but in this case she'd make a hefty wager that the boy was lying about his age. Years of living with her father had given her clues to the telltale signs. And Tim was showing all of them. His eyes darted around the room, refusing to meet hers. His hands, judging from the way he rubbed them down his sagging breeches, were sweating, and his voice was too firm.

But there was something else there, fear possibly, and Merideth decided not to pursue it. Perhaps he was afraid that Captain Blackstone would throw him off the ship if he knew the boy's true age.

Of course, he might be thrown off when the captain saw his wardrobe stuffed into the sea chest.

Picking up a shirt that lay strewn across the foot of the bed, Merideth folded the shoulders together. When she had Tim's attention, she proceeded to fold it neatly. "There," she said, placing the garment in the other chest she'd dumped earlier. "That should keep the wrinkles at bay."

Tim picked up another shirt and tried to copy her actions.

"Arms together," she said. "Like this." She proceeded to fold another. The captain's scent drifted up to her, and Merideth tried to ignore the memories it evoked.

"Ye think I should refold them others?" Tim asked after they had cleaned up most of the shirts and breeches strewn around the cabin.

"It probably would be best." Merideth sat back on her heels. She was straightening into a neat pile the charts she'd scattered. She watched Tim fumbling with the deerskin hunting shirt. "How can you know so little about folding clothes if you take care of the captain's?"

"Don't usually have to do none of this. He takes care of hisself for the most part. 'Course Mr. Padriac, he done told me that the captain has a blackamoor to care for his needs when he's at home. But he don't bring him on the ship."

"How very democratic."

"Huh?"

"'Twas nothing."

"Ye make messes like this often?"

"Actually, this is my first." She was far more used to cleaning up messes her father made.

"Was it fun?" Tim asked, his pinched little face so intent Merideth laughed.

"Well, yes," Merideth began, surprised at her admission. "It actually was." She was searching for something, true enough, but she was also mad at Captain Blackstone for bringing her aboard and telling her nothing. More angry than fearful, which under the circumstances was foolish.

But it *had* been fun to throw his things around the room. It reminded her of all the times she'd wanted to grab the decanter from her father's unsteady hands and slam it against the paneled wall of the library. To show Tim, Merideth retrieved one of the ill-folded shirts from the trunk and gave it a toss.

Tim looked at her as if he thought her ready for Bedlam.

She threw another.

"Here, you try it." When the lad shook his head vehemently at the breeches she offered, Merideth flung it over her shoulder. "We have to refold these anyway," she said, pushing a blue silk waistcoat into his hands.

"Oh, I couldn't. Cap'n would have me hide sure."

"He won't know. Goodness knows I shan't tell him. Besides," Merideth said with a conspiratorial smile, "I'll help you put everything away again. I promise."

"Nay," Tim said, but Merideth could tell he wavered. "'Twouldn't be fittin'."

"Like this," Merideth coaxed. She sent a shirt flying across the cabin.

It was followed by the waistcoat.

When Merideth turned, Tim had a big grin on his face. With no more than a nod of her head as prompting, he grabbed up another shirt and tossed it high. It caught in the rafter and hung like canvas in the doldrums.

"That's the way of it." Merideth scooped up another garment, laughing as she threw. Tim's giggle joined hers, and before they knew it they were competing to see who could throw the fastest. And having a grand time doing it.

"What in the hell is going on?"

Merideth and Tim turned in unison toward the doorway when they heard the captain's booming voice. Apparently their laughter had hidden the sound of his entry. But he now stood, feet apart, arms crossed, surveying the disarray of his cabin.

His dark features looked even darker than usual. His expression, harder.

Merideth caught only a glimpse of Tim's beet-red face before she grabbed his thin shoulders and thrust him behind her. "It was my fault, Captain Blackstone. I made him do it."

"I've no doubt of that," Jared said, though it hadn't

looked like she was twisting the boy's arm.

"'Tain't true, Cap'n." Tim squirmed around Merideth, though she tried to keep him out of harm's way. "I done it, and I'm ready to take the consequences."

Jared rubbed his chin to hide a grin. The boy showed courage, but then Jared had thought so from the time he'd found Tim alone and hungry down by the wharf in Charles Town.

"Just exactly what do you think these consequences should be?" Jared asked, his expression serious.

"You won't flog the boy. I won't allow it!"

Jared went from amusement to annoyance at the sound of her voice. His brow arched. "*You* won't allow it? I didn't think you were in a position to allow or disallow anything."

Merideth felt heat flood her face. How could she have done this? Poor Tim. She'd only wanted him to have a good time because he'd seemed so serious. But if anything happened to him it *would* be all her fault. And the captain was right. There was absolutely nothing she could do about it.

"I'm ready to take me punishment, Cap'n sir." Tim's shoulders straightened.

Jared's attention focused back on Tim. There was no sense frightening the boy just to scare the woman. "Cook's making bread pudding tonight. I think you should forego yours."

"Aye, sir."

"And to bed with you early tonight. I should think by two bells in the second dogwatch."

"Aye, sir."

"And Tim?"

"Aye, sir?"

"You'll have to clean this mess up later."

"Oh, aye, sir. Is there anything else, sir?"

Jared smiled at the boy, his dimple deepened, and then he tousled Tim's blond hair. "Nay. Now run along while I have a word with Lady Merideth."

"Aye, sir." Tim bolted for the door, but paused, his hand on the latch. "Cap'n Blackstone, sir? We didn't mean no harm, neither of us. We was just havin' a bit of fun."

Jared nodded and Tim escaped through the door.

When the captain's stare focused on her, Merideth realized her mouth was agape and closed it with a click of her teeth. She had expected . . . Merideth wasn't certain what she had expected the captain to do to Tim.

Whip him? Yes, hadn't the boy said the captain would have his hide if he caught them? But he hadn't so much as raised his voice . . . to Tim, anyway. And the punishment, if you could call it that, was more one an indulgent father would pass on to his son.

It surprised her, this different side of the captain.

But though his attitude toward Tim seemed friendly enough, Merideth doubted she'd receive similar treatment.

"Now would you mind telling me what all that was about?"

His tone was calm, but Merideth didn't miss the agitation behind it. She swallowed, wondering how she ever convinced herself the captain didn't frighten her. "We were straightening your cabin," she said, her voice as firm as she could make it.

106

Jared said nothing.

"Well, we would have gotten around to it eventually. We were simply . . . Oh, for goodness' sakes, you know what we were doing. We were throwing your clothes about."

"Might I inquire as to why? Or is this simply a penchant of yours?"

Merideth shot him a look that clearly showed her regard for his wit. "I thought Tim might enjoy it." Merideth decided the truth couldn't get her any deeper into trouble than she already was.

Tim obviously had. Jared had rarely seen the boy so animated as during the ruckus. Not that he hadn't tried to get Tim to enjoy himself. He had. The boy loved sailing on the *Carolina*, and would do anything for Jared and the crew. But Jared had never seen that childish glee in Tim's eyes until minutes ago.

He supposed he had Lady Merideth to thank for that.

But there were still many reasons to distrust her. Jared pulled his thoughts to the problem at hand. "I imagine my shirts are in need of a good scrubbing after all they've been through."

"Most of them are clean."

"That was before they were used for your amusement." Jared hesitated a moment. "I want them washed . . . by you."

"I'm not your servant."

"No," Jared agreed. "My servants are in Charles Town. I think, though, you shall do in a pinch." Jared held up his palm when she started to protest. "They need to be cleaned before they can be put away. And I need

107

the cabin straightened before Tim's punishment ends."

He was using the boy as leverage. Merideth saw through his scheme straight away. She also felt fairly sure that the captain wouldn't do anything to harm Tim. But she wasn't absolutely sure, so in the end she narrowed her eyes and agreed to do his wash.

His grin of satisfaction was harder to swallow than the thought of washing his shirts.

"Sorry, I can't do nothin', but the cap'n, he made me promise not to help ye none."

"That's all right. I'm nearly finished." Merideth sunk her hands into the murky rinse water. Wringing out a white linen shirt, she took considerable pleasure in pretending it was the captain's neck. She brushed hair from her cheek with her shoulder and plopped the shirt over the makeshift clothesline that crisscrossed the cabin. She'd strung it earlier, when rope, along with two buckets of seawater and a bar of soap, was delivered to the cabin by a smirking sailor.

She imagined the entire crew knew of her escapade with Tim, as well as their punishments. When Tim arrived shortly thereafter to watch her wash the captain's shirts, he confirmed her speculation.

Not that she cared one way or the other. Getting off this vessel and returning to Land's End were all that concerned her.

And punishing her father's killer.

"Guess ye ain't used to this, ye bein' a lady and all," Tim mumbled as he bit into an apple.

"Actually, sometimes ladies have to do more than

you might think." Merideth dragged another shirt through the wash bucket.

"Ye mean ye washed clothes before?" Tim stopped munching and looked at her wide-eyed.

"Not exactly," Merideth admitted. "But I have helped Belinda. She's one of the servants." One of the few servants left. If indeed there were any at Banistar Hall now.

"Hmmm." Tim seemed to ponder this as he took another bite of his apple.

"What about you? Was your punishment so bad?"

"Nay. Cap'n had a talk with me about how important it was to follow orders on a ship. Me bein' sent down to clean up and not doin' it was goin' against orders, he said. 'Tweren't so bad this time, but durin' a battle it could be real dangerous."

He quoted the captain as if it were the Gospel. Merideth reminded him of the rest of his punishment.

"Aye, well, Cook didn't give me any puddin'—which I felt was right and just. But when I was cleanin' up the dishes cap'n said he didn't have much of a sweet tooth tonight, and that I could eat his if I'd a mind."

Merideth straightened, drying her hands on the skirt of her riding habit. "He gave you *his* bread pudding?"

"Aye." Tim started straightening the charts on the desk. Merideth just stood, her mouth open in disbelief.

"But you said he'd skin you good. You were so afraid to cross him. And he gave you his dessert?" *She* didn't receive *any* bread pudding with her simple fare of pork and potatoes last night.

"He did. And the cap'n's one who likes his desserts," Tom proclaimed in all sincerity. "But the cap'n ain't like old Luke was. The cap'n, he ain't the kind to go hurtin' ye."

Such a shadow of dread came over the young face at the mention of Luke that Merideth moved toward the desk and touched Tim's arm. "Who's this Luke?"

"Ain't nobody important." He shrugged off her hand, and Merideth imagined it was more to keep her from seeing how afraid he was than because he didn't want her touching him.

From the open doorway Jared watched them, Lady Merideth and the boy. He hadn't heard what they were discussing, but he knew he didn't want the woman getting too close to Tim. She may have made him laugh yesterday, but she wasn't to be trusted. Not with her country's secrets. And not with Tim.

"Mr. Padriac's looking for you, Tim." They both turned, and Jared thought he saw a flicker of guilt flash across Lady Merideth's face.

"Time for me lessons?" Tim asked, his face contorted into a scowl.

"'Past time' would be more like it."

"Sorry, Cap'n. I was just gettin' a start on yer cabin. But I weren't helpin' her with the laundry none," he added quickly.

"Didn't think you were." Jared jerked his chin in the direction of the companionway. "Better get along with you now."

Merideth hoped the captain would follow his young charge, but he only leaned against the doorjamb, his arms folded across his powerful chest, acting as if he had all the time in the world.

Well, she wouldn't be intimidated. There was naught

110

wrong with honest work. If he wished to watch her launder his shirts, so be it. She grabbed the last garment. This one he'd worn recently. His scent clung to the soft linen. Annoyed that she'd noticed, Merideth plunged it into the water, doing her best to ignore her captor looming so close.

She'd removed her jacket. Her shirt was cut in a man's style, though made of a softer, finer fabric. It became her. Even with the sleeves turned up and her arms near elbow-deep in sudsy water.

Jared considered leaving. He didn't like noticing the way she looked. His interest in her was simple; discover the name of the spy. He thought now that she felt defeated was a good time to try again. He was prepared to offer her a quick return to England. Certainly she wished to return to where servants did the laundry.

"Did you want something, Captain Blackstone?"

She didn't sound defeated. "Nay. I just wondered how you were enjoying your captivity. Thinking perhaps you might wish to barter for your freedom."

Merideth's head shot up and she swiped damp curls from her forehead with her arm. "My captivity is barbarous, sir. But as for bartering, I have nothing to trade." Merideth grabbed up the shirt and slung it into the rinse bucket. Water splashed out in a crystalline arc, sloshing over the captain's boots.

Merideth heard his sharp intake of breath and tried unsuccessfully to keep from smiling. With an enthusiasm she hadn't felt before, Merideth proceeded to slosh the shirt around in the bucket. Then, before he could comment on his wet boots, she seized the sodden shirt, gave it a perfunctory squeeze, and flung it over the rope.

Water splattered everywhere, but nowhere so much as on the captain.

Merideth glanced up in time to see anger flash behind his green eyes. All thoughts of mischief fled as he lunged toward her.

Overturning the wash bucket with its load of soapy water was an accident. But as he jumped from its path, Merideth knew she'd never convince the captain of that. He rounded on her and she darted, thrilled that for the moment she had escaped him.

But the deck was slick, and as she headed for the open door her half boots skidded. She threw out her hands as she fell, catching onto the captain's sleeve at the last minute.

Instead of breaking her fall as she hoped, clutching the captain threw him off balance just enough to slip on a sliver of soap that had sloshed from the bucket into the puddle of water. They fell together, amid petticoats and curses, onto the wet deck.

"Hell Almighty!"

Water sopped through Jared's shirt as he landed on his back, Merideth atop him. Her hair cascaded about them, curtaining their faces. And her expression, instead of penitent, revealed an irreverent smile.

Why he grabbed fistfuls of her golden curls he wasn't sure, but the next thing he knew, he was tugging her closer and her amusement had vanished.

Kissing her was everything he remembered. Hot and wild, and so impossibly erotic Jared didn't know what

112

kept him from rolling her over and taking her on the water-covered deck. She opened to him immediately, welcoming his tongue and moaning when he swept it through the honeyed interior of her mouth.

His hands slid down her back, molding her body to his. Her legs spread, and she seemed to wrap herself around him. A promise of the ecstasy to come.

Years of sea duty, years of war, caused the loud rattle to penetrate his passion-drugged mind. He heard it, and his hands stilled.

"What is that?"

She raised her head and looked at him, her angel eyes heavy-lidded, her mouth rosy and wet.

"The call to battle stations," Jared answered, already pushing to his feet and pulling her up with him. There was no time to say anything more, and that suited Jared fine.

For he had no idea how in the hell to explain away what had just happened . . . again.

Chapter Six

"Don't ask!" Jared said as he strode across the quarterdeck. His shirt and breeches were soaked and he didn't want to explain to Padriac how they got that way. And from the expression on his friend's face, Jared assumed that question was on the tip of his tongue.

Scooping up his spyglass, Jared focused on the armada of sails dotting the horizon. "My God," he breathed, slowly lowering the brass tube.

"Rather impressive, wouldn't you say?"

"'Disastrous' is more the word I'd use. Pile on the topsails."

Padriac relayed the order, then leaned forearms on the rail. "What's your guess? Have they spotted us?"

"Spotted? Aye. Whether or not they choose pursuit is another question. Perhaps they'll think us of too little consequence to bother with. But regardless, I'd wager we're dealing with the British Grand Fleet here."

Padriac only nodded as the *Carolina*'s crew set about

skimming the vessel across the water with all haste.

By the beginning of the next watch the question was answered. The British were in pursuit. Not the entire fleet. However, two cruisers had peeled off and were gaining on the American schooner.

"Damn." Jared pounded his fist on the railing. "I was hoping they'd consider us unimportant."

"I think they recognize the *Carolina*. Your reputation comes back to haunt."

"Very amusing," Jared said as he studied the sky. "'Twill be twilight soon. If we can hold them off till then, we might have a chance to lose them in the dark."

But two hours later, as the shadows lengthened and the ocean lost its sun glow, the British vessels drew closer. The two cruisers each sported more guns than the *Carolina*, and as Jared watched from the quarterdeck the British tars were busy opening the gunwales.

"They mean to make a battle of it," Padriac said, coming up behind where Jared paced from the wheel to the rail.

The *Carolina* was a whirlwind of activity. Cannons were rolled into place, and sand strewn on the deck. But the American ship sported only sixteen guns, all four-pounders, and thirty swivels. No match at all for the heavily armed British duo.

"We have maneuverability," Jared said, a worried frown creasing his forehead, "but they certainly have us beat in firepower and speed."

It had been hours since the captain left his cabin.

116

Merideth had sopped up the soapy water, and waited. If there was to be a battle, it was certainly taking its time in coming. Earlier, from the transom windows, she'd noticed two ships. But now she couldn't even see them.

She was tired and hungry and bored. And more than a little curious to find out what was going on. No one had brought an evening meal, and Tim hadn't come back to see her. After testing the door and finding it unlocked, she decided to go above deck.

Merideth stepped through the hatch just as the first broadside hit the *Carolina*. The evening twilight was brightened by an explosion of orange-gold light as the thunderous roar split the silence. Men screamed, and as Merideth watched, stunned, a sailor threw down his comrade and rolled him on the sand-strewn deck, extinguishing the flames that licked up his back.

Horrified, her hand clasped to her mouth, Merideth retreated till her spine straightened against the mainmast. Men sweated and swore, sponging the great guns and lighting the fuses. There wasn't a moment of quiet . . . a moment of peace. Smoke filled the air, making her eyes smart, and Merideth scrubbed at the tears that flowed down her cheek. This wasn't what she'd expected.

This was horrible. and she couldn't imagine how these men endured it.

More screams and curses drowned out Merideth's sobs as another explosion filled the air with splintered wood. Fires erupted on the deck, and tars scrambled to dump sand and water on the burning wood.

This was war and death. And Merideth could do naught but cringe against the mast.

She heard a voice, loud and commanding above the din, a voice somehow reassuring in the midst of chaos. "Prepare to repel boarders! Prepare to repel boarders!"

Merideth twisted her head to follow the sound of his voice. He stood on the quarterdeck, surrounded by smoke, his once white shirt grimy and torn, his dark hair loose from its queue. Surprisingly, she knew a moment of relief when she realized he wasn't bleeding like so many of the others around her. But any such emotion was short-lived as he grabbed up a cutlass and ran toward the ladder leading from the quarterdeck.

Another explosion was followed by a sound like a score of trees cracking in the wind. Merideth looked back toward Jared Blackstone. He was glancing up, into the sails, and then his eyes dropped and locked with hers. She saw shock, then anger and fear, and before she knew what he was about to do, the captain leaped from the quarterdeck.

He landed on the run, grabbing her and throwing them both toward the far rail. They landed with a thud against a giant coil of rope just as a section of shrouds and sheared-off mast crashed onto the deck.

Pain radiated from her shoulder and Merideth could barely catch her breath. She needed a moment to think about what had just happened, but the captain gave her none. With no compassion for her bruised arm, he clutched her to him.

"You could have been killed," he yelled above the tumult, his face close to hers. She concentrated on the

118

flashing prisms of green in his eyes as the meaning of his words sank into her befuddled brain. "Do you never listen to orders?" With that he pulled her none too gently toward the hatch, climbing over large fragments of oaken mast that cluttered the deck where Merideth had stood just moments before.

"Get below and stay there," were the captain's final words as he left her by the hatch and rushed toward the rail. Merideth swallowed and obeyed, but not before her gaze registered the carnage on the deck.

Those sailors not manning guns were running about barefooted, grabbing pikes and firing muskets. The British ship was close, so close Merideth could plainly see her crew as they swung giant grappling hooks toward the *Carolina*'s deck.

These were Englishmen, countrymen, and they were obviously winning the day. But Merideth couldn't help wondering what would happen to the Americans who fought them so ardently.

"Yer Ladyship. Why ain't ye below?"

Merideth turned as Tim came barreling toward her. He grabbed her arm, much as the captain had earlier, and pushed her down through the hatch.

"Cap'n said I was to watch out for ye. But he said ye were down in his cabin." The boy spoke as he scrambled down the ladder, forcing Merideth to bunch up her skirts and hurry to keep ahead of him.

"Ain't no place for ye up there," he said, pulling her along the companionway.

"It's no place for anyone." Merideth leaned against the bulkhead after she was shoved into the captain's

119

cabin. Here the sounds of fighting were only a little less vivid than on deck. "I wanted to see what was happening," Merideth explained as she tried to catch her breath.

"We've got ourselves in a tight one," Tim said. He yanked something from his breeches. It was dark in the cabin, with no candle, but Merideth could make out a pistol.

"Wh . . . what are you going to do with that?" Hard-faced and smeared with sweat and grime, he didn't seem the same boy who had tossed his captain's clothes about the cabin.

"Protectin' ye, like the cap'n said," he answered simply.

"I see." Merideth didn't think it wise to point out that she probably needed more protection from the captain than from the English attackers. But she couldn't help the feeling of sympathy that swept over her when she thought of the American crew.

Except for Captain Blackstone. He deserved whatever befell him for killing her father. Who cared that he swore he hadn't done it? Who cared that he'd saved her from being buried beneath the falling mast? None of that mattered . . . or so Merideth tried to tell herself.

She became so used to the musketry and clamor of battle that the return to quiet was jolting. Merideth sprang up from the bunk where she was sitting. "What is it? What's happened?"

"I ain't rightly sure." Tim sat in the captain's chair, the pistol pointed toward the door to the passageway.

Night smothered the cabin under a blanket of uneasy darkness.

"Let me light the flint so we can—"

"Nay! We'll keep it dark."

"But we can't see," she said, hoping Tim didn't hear the panic in her voice.

"Nor can we be seen." Merideth heard the creak of the chair as Tim rose. He moved toward the door, cracking it open and allowing a sliver of light from the companionway to slice into the darkness.

"Do you think the British have won?" The light was sufficient to read the look of disgust Tim sent her way.

"Hush, someone's comin'."

Merideth peeked over Tim's shoulder in time to see Captain Blackstone striding toward them. He looked tired and dirty . . . but not defeated.

Tim stuffed the pistol back into his breeches and swung the door wider in welcome. All his seriousness seemed to evaporate, leaving in its place the curious lad. "What 'appened, Cap'n? Did you blast them back to Lan's End?"

"Not quite." Jared let out his breath, quickly assuring himself that Lady Merideth and Tim were all right. "We did keep them from boarding us. But I've got to tell you, it doesn't look good." Jared addressed his comments to Tim, though he watched his English captive from the corner of his eye.

"But if ye repelled them, then—"

"The onset of night had as much to do with that as our crew. The British are a cocky lot." Now his gaze did shift to Merideth. She met his stare square on. "They're thinking we're doomed and have pulled back to wait for first light to finish us off," Jared continued.

"Finish us off?" Tim seemed unable to comprehend the meaning.

"The mainmast is down, and we've a leak on the lee side."

"So we're just . . ." Tears clogged Tim's throat. "Givin' up?"

"Nay." Jared's voice was firm, but Merideth could see in his eyes that he wasn't certain. "We're hoping we can patch up the hull. But we won't surrender without a fight. 'Twas why I came below." That, and to check on their safety. "There's work to be done."

"Ye can count on me."

"I knew I could." Jared clasped the boy's shoulder. "Get above, and be quick about it."

Tim scampered out of the cabin, leaving the captain framed in the wedge of light. He seemed so large and formidable that Merideth couldn't help a small step back. "I hope you aren't giving him anything dangerous to do."

"Everything on a privateer is dangerous. But Tim can handle more than you think. He's a good sailor."

"He's a boy," Merideth countered.

"True enough. But he's a sensible lad who listens to orders and knows what he's about."

His earlier chastisement about her failing to obey and nearly getting herself killed in the process echoed back to her ears. Merideth straightened her shoulders. "I suppose I owe you my gratitude for—"

"I'm not interested in your thanks." Jared stepped

122

further into the cabin when he noticed her chin jerk up. "I've come to give you a choice."

"I'm listening."

"Stay here, locked in the cabin alone . . . with no light." He saw the color leave her face, and wished he didn't have to insist on the darkness. Her eyes held a shadow of the same expression as when he planned to put her in the cave. "Or assist in the surgery."

"I don't know anything about taking care of wounds."

Jard shrugged and moved into the companionway. Her hand on his arm, where his sleeve was torn, stayed him from shutting the door.

"I would help if I could." A subtle lift of his brow had her adding the word "really." She couldn't stop thinking of those poor men she'd seen during the battle. Burned. Bleeding.

"Wait!" Merideth called out before he could latch the door. "I'll do it. I'll help in the surgery."

Jared swung back into the room. "If I let you out of here, I must have your word that you won't cause trouble."

"You'd take my word?" Now it was Merideth's turn to arch her brow.

"Aye. At the moment I have little choice. My men are suffering, and there's much to do this night."

He did care about the wounded she'd seen on deck. Merideth saw the concern in his eyes. And she couldn't fault him for it. No matter what else there might be between them. "You have my word, then." Merideth hesitated. "For this night."

123

He seemed to think on that a moment, then nodded. Taking her hand, he shut the cabin door behind them and led the way toward the makeshift surgery.

As they approached the afterhold the pitiful cries of the wounded grew louder, and Merideth came close to changing her mind. Surely she could stand a night in the closed-up cabin, especially knowing the morn would bring release from her captivity. She owed these Americans, especially their captain, nothing of herself.

But before she could make known her change of heart, the captain's hand tightened around hers. Not in punishment, but in empathy for his suffering crew. Merideth couldn't help squeezing his fingers in response. He paused before the ladder that led down to the surgery, and looked at her. The only light came from a sputtering candle stuck into the bulkhead.

Merideth held her breath, waiting for him to say something . . . to do somthing. But he only stared, his expression unreadable, before leading the way down the ladder. He did little more than point out the surgeon before climbing back up to the companion-way, leaving Merideth alone with the blood-splattered doctor and the wounded men.

This area contained no windows and was ablaze with light from many candles. Large planks had been set on barrels to make a platform. On that flooring were tables and pallets where wounded men lay. Merideth watched as the surgeon, a large man with grizzled hair that stuck out in every direction, tightened a tourniquet around a sailor's arm.

Below the metal sleeve with its grisly-looking screw,

nothing remained but a bloody stub. Merideth stared at it and her knees grew weak. Smells of blood and camphor filled the air, turning her stomach into a quivering knot. She must have made a sound, for the doctor shifted his attention from his patient to where she stood, back against the ladder rungs.

"Don't just stand there looking like death warmed over, girl. There's work to be done. Fetch me that bottle." He jutted his chin toward a corked container, and Merideth jumped to comply. She brought it toward him, careful to keep her eyes away from the man spread out on the table.

"Now," he ordered, "give me a swallow." While the doctor's hands stayed on his patient, Merideth tipped the bottle to his lips. He drank of the rum greedily, but shook his head when she offered him another drink. "They be needing it more than me," he said, motioning toward the men lying on pallets.

After that, Merideth had no choice but to move among the wounded, offering a drink here, a comforting word there. She packed cuts with lint and smeared grease over burns. And though she thought she'd be sick, she held down a man while the doctor pulled large splinters of wood from his leg.

Merideth had no idea how long she'd been in the makeshift surgery when she straightened, rubbing the small of her back as she did. Work was not new to her. She did her share and more at Banistar Hall. Work that wouldn't get done if she sat in the drawing room stitching all day. But she'd never been as tired as she was now.

"Give yourself a break," the doctor whose name she'd learned was Abner Pochet said. She'd also learned that his qualifications for the job of ship's doctor included a deft hand with the saw, a strong stomach, and a smattering of apothecary knowledge. During quieter times aboard ship, he was a carpenter.

"You've been at it longer than I," Merideth countered, though she dearly wished to return to the captain's cabin, bury her head neath the down pillow, and forget all that had happened in the past fortnight. But she was realistic enough to know that could never be.

"Aye." Abner scrubbed his hands down the leather apron covering his breeches, smearing it with more blood, then reached for the bottle of rum. He swallowed loudly . . . appreciatively. "But I be a burly man, and you but a slip of a lass."

Merideth couldn't help the laughter that escaped. Abner had first told her that when she'd offered to hold down a tar whose leg was broken. She'd but looked at him, grabbed the sailor's shoulders as gently and firmly as she could, and held on while Abner set the bone.

The good "doctor" had repeated his comparison several times during the ensuing hours . . . each time Merideth helped with some task he deemed unsuitable for her. And each time his black eyes sparkled a bit more.

"I've an idea," he said now. "What if we both rest ourselves a spell?"

"Do you think we should?" Merideth quickly scanned the hold with its cargo of wounded and dying.

126

Abner's gaze followed hers. "Won't do any of them a speck of good if ye drop over, now will it?"

"No." Merideth tucked a loose curl behind her ear. "But I'm a far cry from dropping over."

"Maybe so. But I ain't. Besides, that appears to be Tim with some victual."

Merideth turned to see the boy coming down the ladder balancing a tray on his hip. Rushing forward, she grabbed up the bucket he carried.

"'Tis some fresh water for ye," he said. "And some gruel. Ain't hot," he added with a grimace. "Cap'n said no fires till we're outa this mess."

"Out of it?" Merideth's surprise was obvious. "I thought we were simply holding on until morning." Keeping afloat until the British came aboard. That was certainly what *she* thought they were about.

"Phew," Tim snorted, and Abner rolled his eyes. "She doesn't know the cap'n very well, does she?"

"Actually I barely know him at all . . . and that's fine with me, but I fail to see what that has to do with anything. From what I understand, we are sinking and have no mast to hold sail. It seems obvious our only choice is to surrender." She was counting on it. She'd been working this long night away, knowing in her heart that the morrow would see her safe and sound upon an English vessel bound for home.

Now Tim's and Abner's expressions—as if the two were privy to a wonderful secret—deflated her feelings of anticipation. "What is it? Why do you find the notion of surrendering so humorous?"

The boy looked at the man, who merely shrugged.

127

With a mim movement of his shoulders, Tim spoke. "Cap'n, he patched up the leak. Used a stretch of canvas and tied it on hisself."

"So what if we aren't sinking. We've no way to move."

"We're moving right now," Tim countered. "Them Limeys gonna wake up at dawn and find us nowhere at all. Maybe they'll think we just sunk under their noses."

"I . . . I don't understand." All of a sudden the hold seemed very warm.

"We used our sweeps to get away," Tim chuckled.

"Sweeps?"

"Oars, yer Ladyship. Cap'n had us muffle 'em with bits of sail to keep the noise down, then we stuck 'em through the oar ports and rowed away in the dark. And all the while crews were up in the shrouds jury-rigging' the sails."

He seemed proud enough to bust about his captain's achievements—sneaking away from the cocky enemy. And Merideth . . . Merideth felt sick. They weren't going to be captured by the British. She was going to remain a captive of the horrible Captain Blackstone. Gray dots swam before her eyes, and her stomach recoiled. She glanced about for a place to sit, but her two companions were faster.

"Me God, she's a gonna swoon clear away."

"Here, yer Ladyship, sit yerself here."

"Sittin' ain't enough."

"No, really." Merideth held up her hand in protest, but her head was forced down between her spread knees anyway.

"What's going on in here?" As if on cue, Jared stepped into the hold in time to see Abner and Tim kneeling beside Merideth Banistar.

"Her Ladyship took sick," Tim explained, giving Jared no more than a glance.

"She did, did she? 'Twas my impression she was to be helping with the wounded rather than adding to the sick list."

"I'm fine, really." Merideth bobbed her head up and Abner caught it with his wide-palmed hand, shoving it back down.

"She ain't well, Cap'n. But it ain't her fault. She done a powerful lot . . . especially for a little slip of a—"

"I said I'm fine and I am." Merideth bounced out of the chair before Abner and Tim could stop her. She wasn't going to let the despicable captain think she was some whiny female who fainted at the first sight of blood. Unfortunately, her abrupt movements didn't allow time for her head to adjust to the idea of standing.

She'd barely taken three steps toward the captain when everything went black.

"What the . . ." Catching her before she hit the deck was a reflex action.

The first thing Merideth saw when her eyes drifted open was the captain's broad, bare back. He was standing beside his sea chest, unfolding a clean shirt—a shirt she had washed. Blinking, she tried to remember

129

what had happened. Why was she lying on the cot in Captain Blackstone's cabin, watching him . . . change his clothes?

His breeches were wet, clinging to the taut muscles of his buttocks and thighs. He reached down to unfasten the flap and Merideth gasped in her breath.

The captain turned quickly, spearing her with his green gaze, and suddenly all that had happened—the battle, her fainting—came flooding back.

"Well, I see you've come around," he said with a lift of his raven brow. Apparently he had decided against stripping from his breeches, for he was rebuttoning his pants. But the dampness made them just as snug in front. Merideth swallowed and forced her gaze away from the muscled thighs and the obvious bulge at their apex.

Pushing to her elbows, Merideth ignored him as he moved to the cot; she looked instead out the transom windows to where the first blush of dawn had tinged the sea a pearly pink. They were moving all right, and, by the look of their wake, at a goodly speed. And there was no sign of the British vessel. "You've escaped again, I see."

"It's something I seem to do passably well." His grin flashed; the dimple appeared, but it just as quickly disappeared as a cynical expression darkened his face. "Almost as well as you swoon. Is that something you practiced back in England?"

"I never fainted before you happened into my life. And I hardly think one time qualifies me as accomplished at it." Merideth held his stare and tried to swing

130

her legs over the cot's side. There wasn't any room to get up without brushing against him. "Would you mind moving?"

"Abner thinks you should stay abed for awhile. And this wasn't the first time. On the beach at Land's End you very prettily swooned away. Of course, that's when you were trying to gain my sympathy."

"How foolish of me not to realize the emotion was foreign to you." Merideth shoved against his leg, but he didn't budge. He just stood there, arms crossed over his hair-covered chest.

"I told you Abner thinks you should rest."

"Why should you care what he thinks? I'm quite sure my *pretend* swoon has afforded me enough time to lie about."

The hint of a smile tilted the corner of his mouth and lit the depths of his eyes. "I rely on Abner when it comes to the health of those on my ship. Besides, he mentioned that you worked very hard last night. He thought 'twas only natural the blood finally got to you."

"But then *he* apparently thinks my faint was genuine?"

"Aye."

"Unlike his captain."

"Genuine or no, it doesn't change the fact that you tended the wounded last night." He stepped away to retrieve the clean shirt and Merideth bounded from the bed.

"Well, for your information, caring for the men did not cause me to swoon." He turned, looking at her in surprise. Obviously he had thought she'd be happy with the chance to stay in bed. "It was discovering that you weren't to be captured . . . this time . . . that made me ill."

Merideth advanced on him till she had to tilt her head to look him in the eye. "Knowing I had to remain in your loathsome presence."

Jared's eyes narrowed. "Being rid of me is easy enough. Just tell me what I want to know."

"For the last time, I don't *know* anything."

"Then there's nothing more to discuss." Turning on his heel, Jared slammed out of his cabin, realizing too late that he still wore wet breeches from working on the hull. But he refused to turn back, especially when he passed Tim in the passageway, heading toward his cabin.

"Abner wanted me checkin' on her Ladyship," the boy began before Jared cut him off.

"She's just fine!"

Scratching his head and wondering at his captain's brusque manner, Tim watched him stalk off, his breeches wet, his chest and feet bare. He was still pondering it when he entered the captain's cabin.

"I'd a thought the cap'n would be feelin' tip-top, seein' how we done snookered them British."

"Maybe he fears you'll be attacked again. The ship must be in pretty bad shape." Merideth hoped she didn't sound too pleased by the prospect. But Tim dashed her hopes with his next words.

"Not much chance of that happenin'. We'll be salutin' the fort at the head of Morlaix Roads within the watch. Then there's nothing more to do but sail up the river."

"That's where we're headed? Morlaix?"

Tim nodded. "That's where we take our prizes."

Including her. Merideth sighed. Perhaps it was better they were here. Someone in France had to believe she knew nothing about a traitor. Someone had to listen.

But even as she tried to believe the best, a creeping doubt made a chill run down her spine. What if they didn't believe her? What if her father *had* been involved in treason and had somehow pulled her into it?

He wouldn't do that, Merideth thought. But her conviction wasn't as strong as it had been. Whatever Jared Blackstone was, a killer or not, he believed she was involved. He truly believed it.

Shutting her eyes, Merideth leaned her forehead against the glass panes. For better or worse, they would soon be in France.

Chapter Seven

"What do you mean he's not here?"

Jared stood on the steps in front of the half-timbered house and stared at the wizened, tight-lipped woman. She simply screwed her face into more of a grimace and started to close the door.

"No, wait, please. *Pardon.* I did not mean to be so abrupt." It wasn't this woman's fault that Daniel Wallis wasn't here. And even Jared's manners usually weren't this lacking. He'd never been as polished and courtly as his brother. But his mother had taught him better than to yell at elderly ladies.

Smiling, Jared tried again. *"Pardon,"* he repeated. He never had picked up more than a few words of French. "I am a friend of Monsieur Wallis . . . his cousin. Do you know where he is?"

"Non." This time she did shut the door of the boardinghouse where Daniel had stayed, and Jared let her.

Damn.

What was he to do with her now?

Jared strode down the rue du Mur, toward the docks, wondering just where in the hell Daniel could be. Jared's instructions had been explicit. *Procure the name of the traitor from Lord Alfred and return to me here in Morlaix.*

It had seemed so simple at the time . . . though Jared hadn't liked the idea of it. "I'm a privateer . . . a sea captain," he'd said. "Spies and intrigue are not for me."

But Daniel had countered smoothly . . . knowing just the words to say to get Jared to agree to his scheme. "You and John were more alike than you realize. Believe me, I grew up with both of you. If he were here, he'd do this without hesitation."

"Aye, but John is dead."

"And so I'm asking you. It's important, Jared."

"So where are you now, Cousin Daniel?" Jared mumbled to himself as he crossed the narrow street and walked along the wharf. The warm air vibrated with the sound of mallets striking hawsing irons, and it smelled of tar and salt water.

Morlaix was a favorite with Yankee privateers, and the packed shipyard bore that out. Vessels in various stages of repair and refitting lined the shore, their masts pointing skyward like skeletal spires.

Jared spotted the *Carolina*, her ocher-and-red hull, which made her resemble an innocent merchantman, shining in the sun. It wasn't till one noticed the sharp, sleek lines of the hull that her true beauty came to light. But that beauty was marred now, and Jared shook his head as he realized again how much.

The crew had cleaned up the debris of shattered

railings and splintered spars, but the shorn mast left a void. That and the hole in the hull made Jared recall how lucky they'd been to escape the British cruisers. But their luck didn't seem to be holding out.

The *Carolina* would be land-bound for a time . . . longer than Jared wished to be. And he didn't know where to find Daniel.

"Appears the lady's had a rough time of it." Padriac came up beside Jared and stood for a moment. Like his friend, he studied the schooner.

"Aye, she has."

"But she'll be good as new in no time."

Not exactly how Jared would have described it, but he nodded all the same. Together they walked toward the gangplank.

"So, did you find your cousin ready to question our little spy?"

"I didn't find my cousin at all." Jared stepped aside as a tar carrying a bucket of treenails passed by. "It seems he's off to points unknown. At least his landlady couldn't tell me where he is."

"What's to be done with Lady Merideth?" Padriac called as Jared strode across the deck toward the hatch.

"A good question. A good question indeed," Jared called over his shoulder before climbing down the ladder. And one he couldn't honestly answer. Except to know he wished to be rid of her. She wasn't going to tell *him* a thing . . . she'd made herself clear on that point. And if she was to do the Americans any good at all, he needed to get her to someone she would talk to.

Daniel Wallis wasn't available. That left one man.

*　　*　　*

"Come in." Merideth stopped pacing the small cabin when the knock sounded. She was almost pleased to see Captain Blackstone, which was ridiculous considering their distrust of each other. But perhaps he would tell her what was going to happen to her.

They'd been in port . . . a French port . . . for several hours, and no one had told her a thing.

"He's not in Morlaix." Jared shrugged. "Possibly not in France at all."

"Who?" Merideth's eyes narrowed when he scowled at her.

"Your contact."

Would he never cease this silly notion that she was a traitor? Weary of even trying to explain, Merideth sighed. "Pity." Her tone was sarcastic, but in truth she was sorry to hear the news. Perhaps a face-to-face meeting with this man who'd told the captain she and her father were traitors was needed before she could return to England. Unless, of course, Captain Blackstone planned to release her because her so-called contact was gone.

But Merideth didn't think there was much likelihood of that. Jared was leaning against the bulwark, his arms crossed. He was staring at her. Despite all she'd been through at his hands, Merideth had a foolish desire to smooth out her skirt and straighten her hair. Not that either would do much to improve her appearance. There were neither clean clothes nor pins to dress her hair since her abduction from British soil. Add to that the trials she'd been through, and Merideth imagined she was a sight indeed.

She didn't care, Merideth reminded herself as she returned his stare. What the captain thought of her mattered naught.

"I suppose we'll be off to Paris, then," he said, taking a deep breath and letting it out slowly.

Paris. For a moment Merideth was a small girl again, wanting more than anything for her father to take her with him to the French capital. But she wasn't eight, and the man before her had most likely killed her father. Turning, Merideth settled onto the window seat, almost afraid to ask, yet fearing the unknown more. "What's in Paris?"

"Not what . . . *who*. And the answer is Dr. Franklin."

Benjamin Franklin. Merideth had heard of that colonial from her father. He'd been fascinated by Dr. Franklin's work with electricity, though Lord Alfred hadn't completely understood the concept. "What have I to do with Dr. Franklin? Surely you don't think that I—"

"I don't know what to think anymore. Daniel told me he was Franklin's emissary. Daniel isn't here." Jared shrugged as if he'd explained the situation . . . or as if it were unexplainable. In either case he seemed tired of the subject and their discussion, not bothering to answer her inquiry as to who Daniel was. He only paused before taking his leave to order over his shoulder, "Gather your things together. We'll leave for Paris on the morning post."

Her laugh made him stop. "My things?" Merideth mimicked. "Just what 'things' am I to gather?"

A scowl spread over Jared's face as he looked at

139

her . . . really looked at her. He'd studied her on this voyage more than he liked to admit, her face, the blue of her eyes, the curve of her cheek. And her hair. God, how he loved to see the sun shining in her hair.

But as his gaze drifted down over her form, he noticed the torn, bloodstained gown instead of the womanly curves beneath. What in the hell was he thinking? He couldn't take her to Paris like this. "Hmmm." Jared cleared his throat to hide his embarrassment. "I'll send Tim out to fetch you something."

"Tim?" Merideth questioned, but the captain was already out the door. Leaning her head back, she decided it didn't matter. She doubted Tim was very accomplished at selecting ladies' apparel. But anything would suit so long as it was clean.

Oh, how wrong she'd been.

Merideth tugged on the gown's bodice. It did no good. Her breasts still seemed ready to spill over the narrow row of lace. The deep breath she took only made matters worse. "Good heavens," she whispered to herself on a moan.

Tim obviously had a penchant for bright colors. The gown was a vivid red, with bright-blue swans embroidered on the quilted underskirt. A dress to catch the eye if ever there was one.

"Ain't it a beauty?" Tim asked, obviously pleased with his purchase. He'd come into the cabin after she'd dressed, but so far Merideth didn't have the nerve to let him see the front.

140

"Yes, oh, yes it is." Closing her eyes, Merideth turned from the small looking glass the captain used for shaving. Maybe it wasn't as bad as she thought. When Tim said nothing, her lashes drifted open. She couldn't help smiling at the way the boy's eyes bulged.

"I . . . I didn't know it were so . . . so red," he mumbled, as his face turned nearly as bright as the gown.

When the knock sounded at the door, Tim reached back and opened it without shifting his gaze from the dress.

"Are you read—" Jared stepped into the cabin, his mouth clamping shut when he saw her. What in the hell was she doing dressed like a strumpet? A quick glance from Merideth to Tim almost made him groan. What in the hell was he thinking, sending a lad to buy her a gown?

Without a word, he strode to his sea chest. A moment of rummaging and he pulled out a cloak. It was long and black, obviously not made for a woman, but he heard Lady Merideth's sigh of relief when he swept it around her shoulders.

"We shall miss the coach if we don't hurry," was all he said.

Merideth followed him off the gangplank, doing her best not to trip over the hem of the too long cloak. With an unexpected feeling of regret she stepped onto the wharf. To be off Captain Blackstone's ship should be a relief beyond words, but as she glanced back to see Tim waving from the deck, she longed to turn about and race back.

"Don't be silly," she admonished herself just before

stumbling over the long, fluttering hem. As she caught herself before falling, Merideth decided it was fear of the unkown that caused her foolish longing to return to the vessel. But unlike her recent experience, this foray into the shadowy future would hopefully be better. At least she wouldn't have the pigheaded captain to contend with. He'd made it perfectly clear he couldn't wait to be rid of her.

Jared paused to look around when he heard her mumbling . . . grinning in spite of his ill humor. Lady Merideth—who often, despite her angel face, managed to appear haughty—looked comedic. Beautiful, Jared had to admit, but comedic all the same. Again he chastised himself for not personally seeing to her attire. He hadn't much experience with buying ladies' clothing, but he could have done better than the trollop apparel she wore under his cloak.

Slowing his pace, Jared offered his arm, which she took after a moment's hesitation.

The air was warm and humid, smelling of salt water and the press of humanity. The cobblestones were uneven and difficult to traverse while holding up the heavy cloak. Merideth was tired and hot by the time they reached the courtyard of the inn where they were to catch the coach to Paris. She welcomed the chance to enter the cool, ivy-covered taproom and rest.

The barely perceptible hush of voices that accompanied their entrance lasted only a moment. The captain seated Merideth on a bench near the door and went to purchase their passage. He returned with a short, rotund man who introduced himself as Monsieur Gerald, the innkeeper. A smile creased his fleshy face and his chins quivered as he asked how he might serve her.

"Some tea, please."

"Ah, tea for the lovely lady, and for the gentleman, rum," he said in his thickly accented English before turning and yelling something in French to a serving girl. She scurried to do his bidding so quickly that Merideth wondered if Monsieur Gerald was as amiable as he seemed.

In any case, he appeared determined to stay about, hovering over the captain and herself.

"Captain Blackstone tells me you are off to see Dr. Franklin."

"Yes, we are."

"He is a wonderful man, Dr. Franklin. So beloved by the French."

"Yes, I suppose he is," Merideth agreed.

"But then all Americans are. Especially men like Captain Blackstone, the famous privateer."

Merideth raised her brow at the innkeeper's description of her companion and saw the captain flush beneath his sun-darkened skin.

Monsieur Gerald seemed not to notice. He went on wringing his fat hands and grinning his insincere grin. "Captain Blackstone has told me of Charles Town, his home in America. Are you from the Carolinas also?"

"Actually, no. I live in England, Banistar Hall. Captain Blackstone kidnapped me after killing my father."

Merideth thought she could feel the air grow still. Jared Blackstone, sitting across the small round table from her, scowled, his jaw clenched so tight she could

143

see a muscle jump in his cheek. The little innkeeper glanced from one of them to the other, seemingly at a loss as to how he should react. Then suddenly he laughed, tentatively at first, then with more gusto.

"It is a joke," he chortled. "You are making light with me."

Since Captain Blackstone was already chuckling along with the innkeeper as if he saw humor in her words, Merideth smiled. Obviously the innkeeper was so enamored of Captain Blackstone he would not believe anything she said. Besides, she doubted he could be much help against the captain. But that didn't mean she wouldn't find someone later who could.

At least Monsieur Gerald turned his attention toward the captain after her "joke." Merideth drank her tea and surveyed the room while the innkeeper questioned his guest about the prizes he'd brought to port.

Most of the patrons spoke French, and spoke it much too quickly for Merideth to follow their conversations. Years ago, she had tried to teach herself the language in anticipation of going with her father to Paris. But learning without the aid of someone who spoke the language had been difficult. Miss Alice, her governess, had not known French, and her father had seen no need for a tutor.

Even when she'd proudly displayed her hard-earned knowledge during one of his visits home, and he'd laughed at her accent, he'd refused to hire a tutor.

"Someday I shall take you with me to France. Then you can learn to speak the language," he'd said before riding off.

144

But, of course, they had never gone anywhere together.

By the time the coach for Paris arrived, Merideth concluded it was not a great deal cooler in the inn than out in the sun. Still, she refused to slip the cloak from her shoulders and display herself in the gaudy gown.

The coach was cramped, so much so that the captain decided to rent a mount to ride alongside. And, Merideth suspected, to allow himself a more comfortable trip. At any rate, she was happy not to be subjected to his presence.

But after a day of traveling she had to admit to feeling a little different. No one else packed into the coach spoke more than a word or two of English. Though, to Merideth's disgust, every time they stopped to change horses and rest, her traveling companions all seemed to flock around Captain Blackstone.

"How do you know all these people?" she finally asked as they were sharing an evening meal. Though he seemed pleasant enough . . . for the captain . . . around the French, he certainly wasn't the gregarious type.

"I don't know them."

Merideth paused, a spoonful of beef soup suspended in midair. "Well, they certainly seem to know you." One young lady, whose dress Merideth thought more revealing than her own, had nearly swooned when she'd talked with the captain.

"Of me, perhaps."

"*Of* you?" Merideth returned the spoon to her bowl, untouched.

Jared shrugged, then leaned back against the paneled wall. "I'm a privateer. We're a popular lot in

France for now."

Merideth sat very still for a moment. When she met the captain's gaze, her eyes were thoughtful. "I suppose France will join the war on the colonists' side."

"I don't think it's been decided, though my guess is yes. However"—Jared tossed his napkin aside and stood—"if it's secret information you're after, I can't help you. I'm only a sea captain."

"Information?" Merideth jerked her arm away when he touched her elbow to help her rise. "I'm not trying to get information from you. Of all the—"

"Perhaps we should continue this conversation outside." This time when Jared took her arm, he held her fast. Already several patrons were watching them, and Jared didn't wish to make any explanations. He was able to laugh off her insistence to the innkeeper in Morlaix that she'd been kidnapped, but Jared didn't want another such incident. The French might be fond of American privateers, but they didn't approve of abductions.

"What are you doing? Let go of me."

"When you keep your voice down and cease making a spectacle of yourself, I shall." Jared steered them into the rear courtyard. Ivy-covered walls enclosed them, throwing shadows across the cobblestones. The area was secluded, the noise from the inn a distant murmur.

"I am not making a spectable of myself, unless it's by wearing this, this . . . gown." Merideth flipped the cloak off her shoulders, baring a good deal of her breasts to Jared's view in the process.

"Put the damn thing back on." Jared scooped up the garment, clenching his teeth and trying to ignore the ache in his groin that hadn't completely disappeared since she'd walked into his cell.

"I shall not. I'm hot and weary and sick and tired of wearing it." Merideth couldn't recall ever throwing a tantrum before, but she was on the verge of one now. Her life, while difficult when her father had been alive, was now bordering on the impossible. Merideth tried to comfort herself with the idea that when she got to Paris a change for the better was almost certain. But it no longer helped.

Jared was in no better spirits as he flung the cape around her, closing it with fists gripping the fabric. "You will wear this, *and* do as I say."

"Or what?" Eyes flashing in moonlight filtered through the oak trees, Merideth faced him. "Will you kill me as you did my father? Is that what is to happen to me?"

"If murder were to my liking, I would be sorely tempted." Jared tightened his fingers, pulling her closer to him. "As it is, I shall have to console myself with seeing that you follow my orders."

"I will n—" Merideth's words were cut off as his hold on her tightened.

"Aye, Lady Merideth, you will. For if you don't keep yourself covered, I shall not feel obliged to rescue you when one of your 'admirers' becomes too amorous. And I don't suppose even a woman such as *you* would welcome some of the men you would no doubt attract."

"Let go of me, you disgusting . . . Whatever do you mean, a woman such as I?" Merideth could feel his knuckles against her breasts with each breath she took. It had such an unsettling effect she needed to con-

147

centrate on his answer.

"Come now, Lady Merideth, you don't think I believe you limit your espionage technique to smiles and sweeps of your big blue eyes?"

Those eyes widened. "You're not suggesting that I . . . ?" Merideth clamped her mouth shut. "Never mind. You seem to be convinced that I'm a . . . a . . ."

"A traitor? Someone willing to sell out their countrymen for coin?" Jared loosened his grip, letting her shift slightly away. But he could still smell her fragrance. And the memory of her flesh against his fingers heated his blood.

"Whatever you think I've done, it can't be as bad as murder."

"Ah, the murder of your fellow conspirator."

"You mean my father."

Jared's fingers splayed, pressing into the creases of his cloak. At that moment he came close to apologizing to her for his words. Whatever she might be, she loved her father. In the frail dusting of light from the moon, he could see the sorrow etched on her lovely face. His voice grew low. "I think we both know I didn't do that."

"You're forgetting I found you with his body, a spent pistol in your hand."

Hard proof indeed, she thought. Enough to condemn. But as Merideth stood close to the man she accused of murder, she found herself doubting the obvious. He said nothing more, no heated denials, but she found the wall of her conviction cracking.

They stood in the courtyard, surrounded by a smattering of night sounds. The chirp of distant crickets, the lonely hooting of an owl. It struck

148

Merideth that if someone were to happen upon them, they'd be looked on as lovers sharing an embrace in the moonlight. Not as the adversaries, the captor and captive, that they were, exchanging oft repeated accusations and denials.

His gaze held hers, drew her like a lodestone. Closer. Till the whisper of his breath brushed across her face. His lips touched hers, softly at first as he and she stood in the cocoon of night, then with a dark, demanding hunger that Merideth could do naught but match.

His hands clutched the cloak, pulled her toward him. Through the layers of silk and doeskin Merideth could feel steely hardness, and she melted around him like hot wax.

Tongues met, mated, and mimicked the dance of love as Merideth worked to free her hands from the confines of billowy wool. To touch became her desire, and when she did, when her fingers finally burrowed beneath his waistcoat, his pleasure-drugged moan was her reward.

Hers followed as his mouth tore away, forcing an erotic path under her jaw. He nibbled and caressed, his whiskers scraping her soft skin, causing shivers of anticipation to course through her body.

The cloak was torn open before his mouth met the restraints of fabric. Now he was free to feast upon her flesh, the warm, tingling skin of her breasts. He skimmed, he suckled. When the lazy sweep of his tongue dipped between her breasts Merideth thought she might swoon, so intense was her pleasure.

And all the while he nudged, his chin, then his teeth, forcing the lace-trimmed edge of her decolletage lower.

The anticipation was exquisite torture, and Merideth, squirming in the clasp of his large hands, nearly tore the offending fabric away herself. Then it was gone, pulled below her nipples, offering the torrid tips to his greedy mouth.

Her knees grew weak, and Merideth's head fell back, spilling moon-silvered curls down across the black cloak still skimming her shoulders. This was intense pleasure, more darkly satisfying than any fantasy. Merideth became swept up in it, writhing and moaning as he feasted on first one and then the other taut nipple.

Behind the brick wall the tavern door opened, filling the night with raucous laughter. Merideth, her mind passion-drenched, didn't care until the moist heat of his mouth was removed. She made a low sound of protest, startled when he grabbed the cloak.

As suddenly as he had earlier yanked the cape's folds aside, the captain now forced the garment shut. He removed from sight her pearl-toned breasts, their nipples rose-tipped and wet, glistening from the touch of his tongue.

As he glanced toward the noise, a scowl darkened the captain's handsome features. He remained close, so close Merideth could feel the heat radiating from his body. But a gulf of embarrassment and shame slowly seeped between them. And it grew wider with each vivid memory that flashed through her head.

Merideth couldn't believe it. Was it possible that moments ago, nay, not even that long, she slid against him, pressing her breasts into his mouth? Wanting. Aching.

Careful to avoid looking him in the eye, Merideth

tried to pull away, to get away. Anywhere that she wouldn't have to face the captain's icy green stare. But he would have none of it. He held on tight, wrapping her in the voluminous depths of the cloak. The satin lining skimmed across her sensitive nipples, a poor substitute for the sweet roughness of his mouth, and Merideth longed to readjust her bodice.

But he allowed her no time as he hustled her toward the inn. Once inside he guided her toward the steep stairs, following so close behind as she climbed that she had no choice.

They were headed toward the rooms he'd taken earlier. One for him and one for her. Merideth remembered how relieved she'd been when he'd requested them from the innkeeper. The thoughts of sharing a room with him had seemed abhorrent then.

What were they now?

Even the comparative glare of candlelight hadn't penetrated the hazy glow of arousal that clung to her. She ached in places that instinct alone told her he could assuage. But that would mean . . . Merideth could scarcely conceptualize what it would mean, let alone attach words to it. Yet she knew she was torn. Knowing what she should do, and knowing how opposite that was from what she wanted.

At the top of the stairs, he took her arm from behind, the hallway being too narrow to walk by her side. The key was out of his pocket and into the door before Merideth could catch her breath from the rapid climb. The door creaked open. Merideth was propelled inside and less than gently placed in the one chair gracing the room.

A pair of brass sconces on either side of the tiny window splashed light across the bare wood floor. Merideth kept her eyes trained on the knothole blemishing one of the wide planks. She could just see the toe of the captain's boot, and she could sense him looming over her. Merideth fought the urge to look up until he spoke. Then she couldn't help herself.

He appeared angry and as confused as she felt, but his voice was firm. "I'll see you in the morning," was all he said before turning on his heel and leaving her alone in the room.

Merideth let out a breath she didn't realize she was holding as the lock clicked behind him. Then she sat in stunned silence. Making sense of what had happened was her first priority. She could accept her feelings if only she understood them. But she couldn't, and finally, exhausted from the day's journey and the evening's encounter, Merideth prepared for bed.

She lay awake long into the night, disgusted with her inability to sleep. The crowd below in the tavern had long since departed when she finally drifted off. But even then her rest was not peaceful. Her slumber was full of dark, dank caves and men of the night, who taunted and teased, offering but a glimpse of a dimpled grin.

Then there was but one man, coming toward her through the darkness. She could hear him, his breathing, the stealthy way he moved, all one with the shadows.

She didn't want him. Merideth had decided she was glad the captain had turned away from her. But he was here in the room with her. His presence making her tense.

Slowly Merideth opened her eyes, focusing into the darkness. Relief washed over her. Captain Blackstone wasn't in the room. She realized, with a sigh, it was only a dream.

It wasn't till her lashes started to drift shut that she caught a glint of moonlight off the knife blade.

Chapter Eight

The scream woke him, loud and shrill and full of fear.

Leaping from bed, Jared grabbed the pistol from the small table and flung open the door. The candle at the end of the hall sputtered, offering more smoke than light, but Jared found his way to Merideth's door. It was locked . . . just as he'd left it. But he could swear the scream had come from her room.

"Merideth!" His pounding caused Monsieur Flaubert, one of the coach's passengers, to crack open his door. He mumbled a few questions in French while scratching at his nearly bald pate. Jared ignored him.

From the far side of the panels he thought he heard sobbing. "Dammit, Merideth, answer me." His hand reached instinctively for the key. He'd stuck it in the pocket of his breeches. But, of course, he wasn't wearing his breeches. He wasn't wearing anything but thin cotton underdrawers, and those rode low on his hips.

Hell.

Two more doors opened, and he thought he heard a gasp coming from one of them. But he paid little heed because he *knew* he heard a keening sound from behind Merideth's door.

The thud as his bare shoulder slammed into the wood shook the jamb. The second thrust splintered it and he fell into the room.

It struck him first how normal everything looked. He didn't know exactly what he'd expected after waking to that scream, but certainly one or more rough intruders. But though he brandished the pistol, seeking out the shadows for the person bent on harming Merideth, she was the only one in the small room.

She was backed up as far as she could get against the headboard on the bed, her eyes wide as saucers, the blanket clutched in her white-knuckled fists. Golden hair tumbled over her bare shoulders. Jared took a moment to prop the broken door against the opening, blocking out the curious faces that peered into her room.

"What is it? What's wrong?" Jared rested his hip against the bed. He reached out to touch her, thought better of it, and busied himself with lighting the candle on the commode.

"There was a man . . . with a knife." Merideth hated that her voice quivered. She took a deep breath, forcing her fingers to relax. The captain was looking at her the same way he did whenever she denied knowing the name of the traitor.

"A man with a knife," he repeated, saying the words without inflection.

"Yes!" Merideth tossed down the blanket she was clutching, then remembered she wore only her shift and pulled it up again. Her jaw tightened, but she lowered her voice. "Yes, there was a man. And he had a knife. If I hadn't screamed—"

"The door was locked," Jared pointed out.

"He must have used the window. I don't know. But he *was* here."

With a casualness that raised her ire, the captain moved to the open window. He glanced out into the darkness, then back at her. "'Tis a fair drop. Not to mention climb."

"What is that supposed to mean?"

"Not a thing." Jared turned back toward her. "Merely an observation."

"Well, I don't like the way you're acting . . . as if I'm making it up. There *was* a man, and he *did* have a knife." When the captain did nothing but stare at her, Merideth continued. "Perhaps he used the door." Merideth held up her palm when he started to respond. "And don't tell me the door was locked. I'm aware of that. I also know that *you* have the key."

"Then I sure don't know why he didn't use it," the innkeeper said in his halting English as he pushed aside the door to face Jared and Merideth. "What's all the commotion up here? And what happened to my door?"

"There was an intruder," Captain Blackstone replied before Merideth could answer. "Now, as you can see, the lady is not dressed for visitors." After turning the grumbling innkeeper out into the hallway, and promising to compensate him for the damages, Jared repropped the door shut. When he looked back at

Merideth his arms were folded across his chest. He did nothing but stare.

Merideth felt like a rabbit caught in a snare.

She wet her lips. "I thought it was you . . . at first." She ignored his arched brow and continued. "But then I knew it wasn't."

"This man, what did he look like?"

"I don't know. It was dark."

"But you are sure it wasn't I?" His tone was cynical.

Merideth ignored the question. "He was dressed in black, and he stood over my bed. Then . . . then I saw the knife."

"Was he big? Little?"

"I don't know, I tell you. It happened so quickly." Merideth searched her memory. "I awoke from a dream and sensed someone was here. Then my eyes focused and I saw him."

"But not clearly enough to tell if he was large or small?"

Merideth returned Jared's stare for a moment, then threw off the blankets and scrambled from the bed. While he watched, annoyed that he noticed the way the fine linen of her shift clung to her body, she grabbed up her gown. "I saw the knife clearly enough," she insisted as she poked her arms into the sleeves.

Jared regretted it when she yanked the bodice up to cover herself. "What are you doing?"

"Obviously, I'm getting dressed. It's apparent you don't believe me, and frankly I don't care. But I have no intentions of lying abed and waiting for whomever it was to return."

"Just what do you intend to do?"

His unconcerned tone infuriated her. The trembling fear was only now leaving her limbs, and he acted as if nothing had happened. *"I* intend to stay awake and keep watch."

"'Tis hours till dawn."

"I don't care." Merideth strained against the window, shutting it with a bang, fighting to ignore the feeling that the room was closing in on her. Suddenly the air seemed suffocating. But she sat on the only chair in the room and crossed her arms.

"What will you do if he returns? You barely have a door."

"Apparently a locked door didn't help last time. In any case, I shall scream."

"For me?" Jared's brow arched, and his lips lifted in a mocking grin.

"For anyone who will help me."

"I see." Jared leaned against the wall, one ankle crossed over the other. He let out a deep breath before continuing. "First of all, I never said I don't believe you."

Merideth's snort sounded unladylike. "You didn't have to. I think I know when someone thinks I'm lying."

"In this case you're wrong. It happens I do think you saw someone."

"With a knife," Merideth reminded.

"Aye, with a knife. But I imagine it was simply a local ruffian infatuated with your comeliness."

"So he decided to kill me?"

"Nay, chances are he had nothing more in mind than to partake of your charms."

"Partake of my . . ." Merideth leaped from the chair, crossing the room to stand before him in four angry strides. "I am Lady Merideth Banistar. People do not break into my room to . . . to . . ." At a loss for what to say, Merideth lifted her chin. "You may leave now," she finally said, her voice and countenance regal . . . haughty. To Jared's way of thinking, amusing.

But he didn't have the time or inclination to be amused. He was tired, and sleepy, and wishing he could be done with this business soon. Though he doubted the intruder would return after all the commotion, he wasn't taking any chances with Lady Merideth Banistar while he was responsible for her. And thanks to his cousin, Daniel, that would be until they reached Paris.

"Come along."

"Where? What are you doing? Let go of me." Merideth batted at the hand clasping her arm.

"*I've* no intention of sleeping in here with the door broken, and you obviously need someone to watch out for you."

Regardless of her reluctance to accompany him, Jared pulled Merideth into the hall. Several faces reappeared at the doors, but no one seemed willing to offer her assistance against the captain. When he ushered her inside his room and shut the door, Merideth could have sworn she heard a collective sigh of relief from the other passengers.

This room was similar to hers, with a chair, broken-fronted chest of drawers, and a ratty-looking bed that took most of the space. It was there that Merideth focused.

160

"If you think I shall be so grateful for your questionable concern for my welfare that I'll . . . I'll . . ."

"Listen, Lady Merideth. Despite what happened in the courtyard, I've no interest in you other than the information you have about a certain traitor."

"But I have no—"

Jared held his hand up to stop her protest. "Therefore, if you would simply climb into that bed and get to sleep, I'd be most grateful."

Merideth pursed her lips. "Where do you intend to sleep?"

"In the chair." Jared's jaw jutted toward the rickety piece of furniture. "I assure you it will be fine. I've done it before on board the *Carolina*." Without further discussion Jared settled onto the rush-bottomed chair and leaned it back on two legs.

Merideth slowly climbed into the bed. The mattress was lumpy and smelled of unwashed bodies, but Merideth imagined it considerably more comfortable than the captain's chair. She was about to make some comment about it when she heard his muffled snore.

He was asleep. Some protection he would be if the intruder returned. Even so, Merideth found she felt safe. Before she knew it, dawn had paled the eastern sky and it was time for their journey to continue.

For nearly a sennight they followed the same routine. Merideth would ride in the cramped coach by day surrounded by French-speaking strangers and roasting in the captain's heavy cloak. At night they would share a room.

He kept his distance.

After that first night the captain made arrangements at every inn to have an extra cot or pallet moved into the room. He stayed downstairs until Merideth had slipped out of the gown and covered herself, then he entered, removed his shirt, and settled in for the night.

He fell asleep quickly, always before Merideth. But he was also quick to wake. When the dream recurred, the suffocating feeling that walls were closing in on her, it only took a strangled sob from Merideth for him to be at her side.

One night she woke with his knuckles tracing a gentle path down her tear-streaked cheek. "What is it? What's wrong?" His voice was so low and soothing, Merideth hesitated before turning away. But she knew better than to share her fears. Her father had simply found them amusing. He'd teased her often. And in the light of day, inside a large-enough room, Merideth could laugh too. But the terror was still there.

Miss Alice's reaction had been different. The governess had felt the only way to conquer fear was to face it. And if you couldn't do that on your own, you could always be forced. Memories of the times she was locked in the huge wardrobe in her bedroom made Merideth tremble. Her breath caught and she leaped from the bed, knocking Captain Blackstone aside.

"What the hell are you doing?" Jared stood and watched her frantic movements, his hands resting loosely on his hips.

"Opening"—Merideth paused to shove—"the window." A rush of air escaped her when the sash gave.

"For God's sake, it's raining. You'll get . . . wet." His

last word was only murmured as she stuck her head outside.

Two steps brought him to her side. Cupping her shoulders, Jared pulled her inside. Her hair was soaked, the water drooping her curls and spiking her long lashes. "Are you daft?" Jared looked down into eyes as bright and prismed as the droplets on her skin. "What's gotten into you?"

"I don't like to sleep with the window closed," she said before trying to twist away.

His hands tightened. His laugh held no mirth. "Drenching yourself is not the answer." As he spoke, Jared's gaze roamed over her. He almost groaned at what he saw. Her shift was nearly transparent, made so by the wetness that also caused it to cling to her body. Pink nipples, tight from the chill, beckoned. His own body responded, hardened.

God, he wanted her.

Tomorrow they'd reach Paris. And he'd hand her over to Dr. Franklin, or Daniel, if he was there. He'd never have to see her again. He never *wanted* to see her again.

Their eyes met, and though she tried to make her expression defiant, Jared saw burning in those blue depths the same hunger that he felt. In the past, whenever he'd touched her, she'd opened to him, responded in a way that no other woman ever had. She would this time too. The moisture on her body nearly sizzled.

She swallowed and Jared watched the sweet curve of her neck. Then, as if trying to fight the inevitable, she twisted away.

Jared jerked her back. Closer. Contact with her dampened his skin. The feel of her warm, wet breasts against his bare chest turning his blood to boil. His arousal pressed her stomach and her eyes drifted shut.

Surrender.

Jared could taste it. Anticipated tasting her.

But though his lips hovered near hers, he hesitated. At one point he'd thought to seduce her; now he greatly feared he was the one being seduced. By a traitor.

Jared closed his eyes, trying to steady his ragged breathing. Slowly he pushed her away, separating them, denying himself the erotic sensation of her body against his. "You'd best get out of those wet clothes," he said, his voice gruff.

"What . . . ?" Merideth's eyes snapped open. "Oh . . . oh, yes." Moments ago, she thought, he had planned to kiss her . . . and heaven help her, she'd wanted him to. But his expression had hardened. Hands that had caressed now turned her toward the bed.

"Hang your shift on the chair. It should dry by morning."

"Where are you going?" Merideth watched as he grabbed up his shirt, pulling it over his head with jerky motions. He strode to the door, removed the key from his breeches, and opened the lock.

"I'm going out. You get some sleep."

Before Merideth could remind him that it was raining, the captain closed the door behind him. Instinctively she followed his instructions, removing her wet shift and climbing into bed. But she couldn't go to sleep.

The chafing of the bed linens against her skin made her long for the feel of his hands. Try as she might to ignore the sensation. Try as she might to call herself a fool. It did no good.

And when slumber finally did come it wasn't the nightmare of confinement that filled her mind. 'Twas the far more frequent dream of Captain Blackstone.

The coach entered Paris in midafternoon, rattling along the narrow cobblestone streets. Merideth had her usual seat by the window, which by this time the other passengers gave her without argument. When the coach stopped, Merideth stepped out, her head turning with the splendor of all she saw. Before she could take in a fraction if it, Merideth was hustled into a rented chaise and she and the captain were driven to the Hôtel du Hambourg.

"Damn," Jared mumbled after speaking with a man in powdered wig and silk waistcoat.

"What is it?"

"Neither Dr. Franklin nor Daniel are here."

"Who is this Daniel?" Merideth inquired, but received no answer. The captain was busy asking questions of his own.

"Is Samuel Dayton here?" Jared remembered Daniel telling him Samuel Dayton had also been sent to France by the American Congress.

"*Oui,* Monsieur Dayton is registered and, I believe, in his rooms."

After receiving the room number, Jared led the way up the stairs. The door was answered by a small, swarthy man who spoke little English. His head bobbed as Jared explained who he was and why he wished an audience with Monsieur Dayton. The man motioned them into an ornately decorated drawing room and backed into the hallway.

Jared offered Merideth a seat, which she refused. She was much too concerned about her welfare to do aught but pace. She measured the length of the Aubusson rug twice before turning on the captain.

"Who is this Daniel, and what does he have to do with me?"

Jared crossed his arms and looked at his captive from heavy-lidded eyes. "He's the person who arranged this fiasco."

"Exactly what fiasco are we discussing?" Merideth tilted her head, but her eyes remained locked with his.

"The one where I went to England acting as a courier to receive information about a spy."

"Ah . . . so you admit now that the entire incident was a mistake. My father would no more sell out his—"

"Oh, he would sell out, all right. He was more than willing to do that, as I'm sure you will once sufficient payment is offered." Jared ignored the angry jut of her chin. "It was other circumstances that made the trip ill fated."

"Such as my father's untimely death at your hands."

"His death was unfortunate. I believe we both know it wasn't at my hands."

Merideth turned away. In truth she had no ready answer for that, because against all evidence to the contrary she almost believed him. But if the captain hadn't killed her father, who had? That unanswerable question always formed a stone wall in Merideth's reasoning. She walked to the window and looked out on the street below.

She didn't think she had ever seen so many people in one place. The narrow roadway was packed with ladies and gentlemen from all walks of life. Peasants in their ragged brown wool mingled with the gentry in their bright-colored silks. And now and then a chair would pass below, the bearers dressed in the livery of some noble family. Merideth was so absorbed watching the events, she didn't hear anyone enter the room until he spoke.

"Ah, Captain Blackstone, it is a pleasure to finally meet you. I've heard so much of your exploits. All Paris is abuzz with them."

"Thank you." Jared stood and returned Samuel Dayton's bow. "I've come to see you on an unrelated matter that involves Daniel Wallis."

"He's not here. Off to London, I believe. Oh, perhaps I shouldn't have let that slip." Samuel's gaze slid toward Merideth, who watched the exchange from the alcove surrounding the window. "'Tis a secret, I fear."

"Lady Merideth understands all about secrets," Jared said before introducing the two.

"A most charming and lovely young lady," Samuel said with such intensity Jared was surprised he didn't drool.

For her part Merideth was polite, but cool. She seemed not to notice Dayton's popping eyes or lewd smile.

"When do you expect him to return?"

"Who?" Samuel turned his attention back to Jared reluctantly.

"Daniel Wallis."

"Ah, yes. I haven't a clue. Would you care for some wine?" Dayton took Merideth's arm and drew her toward a marble-topped side table with an array of decanters glistening in the light streaming through the windows.

"Nay, she doesn't want wine." Jared grasped Merideth's arm, effectively halting her progress across the room. "Nor do I. We do wish, however, to see Wallis."

Though obviously taken back by the captain's manners, Samuel tried to remain composed. Only the dabbing of his upper lip with a lace handkerchief indicated he'd failed. "I told you at the onset that I have no idea when he shall return, or even where he is for certain."

Jared dropped Merideth's arm and stood still for a moment, trying to calm his impatience. "Listen," he said at last, startling Dayton, who was now nervously twisting the fine linen in his hand. "Daniel Wallis asked me to act as courier for him . . . a matter of national security. Don't concern yourself with her knowing," Jared added when he saw Samuel's small eyes dart toward Merideth. "She's part of the entire scheme." Jared forged ahead before Merideth could repeat her denial. "I was to go to Land's End, meet with Lord Alfred Banistar, and retrieve certain *information*. Daniel impressed upon me how important this *information* was to the success of the revolution." If Daniel hadn't been so persuasive, Jared thought, there

168

never would have been an agreement. "I was to meet him in Morlaix, but he wasn't there. I'd hoped he might be in Paris."

"Which, obviously, he isn't."

"Obviously." Jared clasped his hands behind his back to keep from grabbing the front of Samuel's dandified waistcoat. "So my question is, since I am a sea captain and need to return to my ship, what am I to do with her now?" Jared didn't intend his smile to indicate good humor.

"Very well, then." Dayton went to the delicately carved writing desk and with a sigh settled into the chair. "Where is the information? I suppose I can see that Daniel receives it."

"Lady Merideth *is* the information."

"Pardon?"

Jared decided Dayton had been in France too long if he was speaking the language when flustered. But as long as he was ridding himself of this obligation so he could return to the *Carolina*, he didn't care. He couldn't keep himself from meeting Merideth's eyes, however.

"Lady Merideth is in possession of the information Daniel wanted."

"I most certainly am not." Deciding she'd had enough of sitting quietly and listening to these two men decide her fate, Merideth sprang to her feet. She was by Captain Blackstone before he could stop her. Leaning over the desk, she grabbed Dayton's hand. "I don't know anything that will be of use to your country. And as a loyal Englishwoman, I wouldn't tell you if I did."

169

"She simply needs the right monetary compensation," Jared injected. When Merideth bent forward, the cape still covering her gown slipped open. Jared resisted the urge to yank it shut as he watched Samuel Dayton follow the rise of her chest, from the gold of her locket to the shadowed valley between her breasts.

"Don't believe him," Merideth said, clutching Dayton's fat hand in both of hers. "This man broke into my home, killed my father, and kidnapped me—"

"Damn!" Jared thundered. "She knows that isn't true. I simply—"

"He did! He was to be hanged when he escaped from the jail and—"

"She's a traitor, pure and simple." Jared joined Merideth in leaning over the desk. Palms flat on the glossy surface, he scowled at Dayton. "You can't trust a word she says—"

"I do not lie. And I most assuredly am not a—"

"Enough!" Dayton clasped his hands over his ears, knocking his wig awry in the process. "I've heard enough!"

Jared and Merideth straightened as one. Their expressions were accusatory as they glared at each other.

"I won't listen to another word," Samuel continued. "You will have to take your argument elsewhere."

"This isn't an argument," Jared said, holding up his hand when Merideth started to disagree. "I simply need for you to take charge of Lady Merideth until Daniel returns."

"And I simply need for you to see that I'm returned safely to my home in England," Merideth said.

"After she tells us what she knows."

"I don't know anything to tell you." Merideth turned toward Jared.

"'Tis not what your father said." Facing her, Jared bent till they were nose to nose.

"Before you killed him."

"I did not—"

"Out! Out, out, out." Samuel Dayton rose and shooed at them as if they were troublesome children. "You must both leave. I can do nothing for you."

"Well, what in the hell am I to do with her?" Jared stood his ground; Samuel took a step back, but the expression on his doughy face was determined.

"I don't know. Perhaps Dr. Franklin will. Yes," Samuel said, a smile creasing his face. "Dr. Franklin is who you must see." As he spoke he walked forward, backing his guests toward the door. To his relief they seemed to be going.

"But I was told Dr. Franklin isn't in Paris." Jared stopped his backward progress.

"True. But he is in charge of the American delegation in France. He is the only one who can help you."

Letting out a frustrated breath, Jared reached for the doorknob. "Where can I find Dr. Franklin?"

"In Passy, I believe," Samuel said, continuing to inch them through the doorway. "He is using part of the Hôtel de Valentinois." With that he shut the door.

Merideth stared at the closed portal a moment. "What a rude man."

Jared looked down at her, arching his brow, but said nothing. After a moment he straightened his waistcoat, then offered his arm. "I suppose we shall have to go to Passy."

Merideth hesitated only a short time before placing her hand on his sleeve. "I suppose we shall. From what I've heard, Dr. Franklin is an enlightened man. I'm sure he will listen to me."

"I'm not taking you there to engage in another discussion like we just had. And for God's sake keep yourself covered." Jared reached down and yanked the cloak together. "I thought Dayton's eyes were going to pop from his head when you leaned over his desk."

Merideth clutched the woolen material. "*You* paid for this gown."

"Tim chose it, as I recall, *I* supplied the cloak."

Merideth merely shrugged as they stepped out into the sunshine. She felt more confident than she had in some while. Surely the Dr. Franklin she'd heard so much of, who was respected even in England, would see that she was returned home safely.

Chapter Nine

The short ride to the village of Passy was pleasant enough. Captain Blackstone had rented a chaise, and Merideth appreciated the openness after the cramped, closed-in coach. Once they passed the Quai Conti, the area was rural. A gentle breeze held the fragrance of summer flowers, and Merideth couldn't help taking a deep breath and leaning back against the cushions.

"Why so pleased?" Jared inquired.

Turning her head, Merideth studied the captain's dark profile as he returned his gaze to the road ahead. Rays of sun slipped beneath the chaise bonnet and highlighted the strong angles of his face. A handsome face, Merideth admitted to herself, with its high forehead, straight nose, and curved, sensual lips. She was certain most women found him irresistible.

But that was most women, not her, Merideth reminded herself forcefully when he twisted to stare at her, his green eyes questioning. "Have you decided to refuse to speak? If so, I'd have thought back at the

Hôtel du Hambourg a much more advantageous time."

"I'm sure that would have suited *you*. However, I've no intention of remaining quiet while you spout lies about me. And"—Merideth tilted her head—"I think your countrymen should be aware that you were tried and convicted of murder."

"Tried and convicted? That sounds a tad less damning than your usual assertion that I killed your father. Are you having doubts? Perhaps my repeated denials are having some effect after all."

"If repeated denials were effective, I should be safe and snug in my own home rather than traipsing across the French countryside as your . . . your prisoner."

Jared's smile was fleeting, but the trace of his dimple remained. "You forget, I've your own father's assertion that you are in possession of the spy's name."

"And you forget, I found you holding the gun that killed my father. Besides, if you didn't do it, who did? There was no one else at Banistar Hall."

"The servants?"

"They had no reason to hurt Papa. They are worse off with him dead than they were before. And not a one of them has the cunning to kill him and make it appear as if you did it."

"That is something, isn't it," Jared conceded. "I can think of only one person capable of that."

"Who?"

"You." Jared watched as a shadow crossed her face. She lifted her chin and turned away, but not before he noticed the glisten of tears filling her eyes. He had the strongest urge to reach out and cover her folded hands with one of his. Instead he snapped the reins, forcing the horse to pick up his pace.

Not another word passed between them until they reached Passy. They found the Hôtel de Valentinois at the corner of the rue Basse and the rue des Vignes. A large stone mansion, it had wings projecting from the center, each of which ended in a raised turret supported by Tuscan columns.

Jared drove the chaise to the left wing. At the door, which was answered by a wigged servant in livery, Jared was directed to a small building in the garden. As they approached along a brick path that wove among fruit trees and boxwoods, Merideth heard the sound of children's laughter.

They rounded a giant yew and Merideth got her first glimpse of Benjamin Franklin. He leaned against the side of a stone building; a plain brown coat covered his slightly stoop-shouldered frame. His long hair was frizzled, and he looked like a prosperous merchant. As he read from a parchment he held, he occasionally glanced up, laughing at the antics of two boys playing tag in a grassy area.

"Dr. Franklin." Jared called out the name as they approached. "A moment of your time, please. I'm Captain Jared Blackstone."

The older man glanced up and examined Jared and Merideth through bespectacled eyes. A welcoming smile brightened his face. "Ah, Captain Blackstone, the privateer. I've heard of your exploits."

"And I of yours," Jared said, and the older man chuckled.

"Oh, but that I could brag of daring adventures at sea, I'm sure I'd have all the young ladies' hearts a-flutter." His sparkling eyes shifted slightly toward Merideth.

The captain's introduction of her was less than glowing, but that didn't stop Ben Franklin from being gracious. His manners were charming, and Merideth decided she liked him despite his being a colonial.

"What can I do for you, Captain?" Ben said when they were seated on wooden benches beneath the shade of a cluster of trees. Franklin had dispatched his grandsons, William Temple and Ben Bache, off to the house in search of refreshments.

"'Tis a matter of some delicacy," Jared began.

"Nonsense, we are among friends here," Franklin insisted.

"Lady Merideth is English, of course."

"Of course she is." Ben leaned forward to pat her hand. "Would you care to remove your cloak? The day is quite warm."

"No. No, thank you. I'm very comfortable."

"As you wish," Franklin straightened, turning his attention back to Jared. "Now I think we should conclude our business so that we can enjoy ourselves when Will and Ben Bache return."

Jared cleared his throat. "Let me begin by saying, I would not be bothering you if I could only determine the whereabouts of Daniel Wallis."

"Ah, Daniel." Franklin waved his hand. "He's about, I'm sure. Though, like you, I don't know exactly where."

Jared shrugged, wishing Franklin knew where his cousin was, but deciding in his absence he had no choice but to proceed. "Little more than a fortnight ago

Daniel approached me while I was in port at Morlaix. He is my cousin and . . . friend." Jared hesitated using the term "friend" to describe his relationship with Daniel. But they *were* cousins, reared in the same house.

"At any rate, Daniel confided in me . . ." At this point Jared hesitated, his gaze straying toward Merideth, who sat, her expression guileless, on the bench beside him.

"Do go on, Captain Blackstone. What did Daniel confide?"

"He spoke of your negotiations with the Comte de Vergennes, the minister of foreign affairs, and of the attempts to form a French alliance for America."

"Yes, yes, that is my ultimate goal. But 'tis hardly a secret."

"He also mentioned a plan underway in England to offer Congress some concessions and bring an end to the war . . . an end that would not include independence." Since Franklin said nothing, only smiled at him, his eyes winsome, Jared continued. "According to Daniel there was someone, someone powerful in the American government, who was selling information about your negotiations with the French to England."

"My heavens," Franklin chuckled. "That certainly sounds like some intriguing espionage."

Though slightly baffled by the older man's reaction—Jared would have thought he would take this information more seriously—Jared continued. "The identity of this traitor was known by an Englishman willing to give us the information . . . for a price."

"That's a lie!" Merideth sprang to her feet and faced

177

both men. With her hands fisted and planted on her hips, the cloak opened, revealing the gaudy gown beneath.

"Sit down," Jared said, resisting the urge to grab the cloak and wrap it around her tightly.

"I will not. You are telling lies about my father and I won't have it."

"You will have it, for 'tis not lies I speak." By this time Jared was on his feet, nose to nose with his captive.

"Lies, lies," she taunted. "You don't know the meaning of the truth."

Jared's jaw clinched. "I'm not the one who—"

"Children, children." Franklin's voice was like a gentle balm. "Contain yourselves. I assume the Englishman of whom you speak, Captain Blackstone, is Lady Merideth's father?"

"It was."

"He wasn't a traitor." Merideth turned her attention to Dr. Franklin, jerking away when the captain reached out to close the cloak.

"Of course not, dear," Franklin soothed. "But let's allow the good captain to finish his story, then we shall hear what you have to say. I'm certain we can untangle this unpleasantness."

Jared wasn't confident of that, but he saw no alternative to resuming his seat and his narrative. He noticed that Merideth also took her seat *and* pulled the edges of the cloak together, hiding the swell of her breasts.

"Before my last cruise Daniel asked me to go ashore at Land's End to meet with this gentleman. I was given

178

a goodly amount of gold to ply his tongue, and set sail."

"And did you speak with this man?"

"Aye. Lord Alfred and I met and he was very agreeable to the exchange."

Merideth opened her mouth, but Franklin's hand on hers kept her quiet. "You shall have your turn."

"Anyway, Lord Alfred and I were about to conclude our deal when he began insisting that his daughter was in possession of the name of the traitor."

"And then what happened?"

"My father was shot and killed," Merideth said before Jared could respond. "By him." She pointed her finger straight at Jared's chest.

Trying to remain calm, Jared looked away from the accusing eyes. "I did not kill Lord Alfred. Someone knocked me out from behind. When I awoke, Lord Alfred was dead and I was holding the pistol that shot him."

"A British court found the evidence sufficient to sentence Captain Blackstone to hang."

Franklin wrinkled his brow in surprise. "A fate you somehow eluded."

"He broke out of jail and took me hostage," Merideth informed her host.

"Goodness."

"She knows the name of the traitor," Jared pointed out.

"I haven't a clue what he's talking about."

"Her father said—"

"Now, now." Franklin motioned for both of them to resume their seats. "We do seem to have a dilemma here." He rubbed his hand down over his sagging jowl.

"First of all, let me say, I think you're both telling the truth—"

"But—" Their protests were voiced at the same instant.

"The truth as far as you know," Franklin said. "This entire incident is most unfortunate, not only because of the death of your father, Lady Merideth, but because it was all so avoidable."

"Avoidable? How?"

"Ah, Captain Blackstone." Franklin stood and paced across the grassy knoll and back, walking slowly. "Spies and traitors are part of every war. It seems to be a requirement. However, in this instance it matters not that the British know what I'm about. I actually welcome spies. The more the British and French know of each other's plans, the better for me."

"But Daniel said—"

"I'm sure he did. But I'm afraid he was taking his job as my aide too seriously. His orders to you did not originate with me."

"And the gold?"

Franklin shrugged his stooped shoulders. "I'm barely allowed enough to keep body and soul together. There is no extra coin for buying information."

"Then Daniel must have lied to me." Jared stood and gripped the back of the bench, wishing he were more surprised by the news.

"He most likely thought he was doing what was best. There no doubt is a traitor. And Daniel wanted the information."

"But you don't want it?"

"No, Captain, I don't. Now, it looks as though my

grandsons have found us something to eat." Franklin motioned toward the boys racing across the garden, a servant in their wake. "Perhaps we can sit down and enjoy some of this marvelous French food. I normally prefer my sustenance coming from the good earth." He leaned forward and confided to Merideth, "but Ray du Chaumont, who graciously allows me the use of part of his home, keeps excellent chefs. I admit to being tempted beyond my ability to resist."

While the servant spread the food on a nearby table, Jared stood, hands clasped behind his back, staring out over the garden. His expression was dark, far too bleak for him to be contemplating the flowers and trees. As if an invisible clock dictated his actions, his fingers opened and closed, slapping against each other with dogged regularity.

"Please, Captain, you'll ruin my digestion. We shall discuss this further after our repast. Do sit down."

Seeming to have no choice in the matter, Jared took his seat. The wine was good, though he drank little. Beside him Merideth was talking freely, answering some question put to her by Franklin. He should pay heed to their conversation—politeness, which his mother had tried to drill into him, demanded it—yet he couldn't. Franklin's words kept drumming through his head.

He cared little about spies or counterspies. He cared less about the information Lady Merideth possessed. Yet a man had died because of this . . . this useless information. A man had died and Jared was blamed.

Obviously, not everyone held Franklin's view on the matter.

181

"Blackstone," Dr. Franklin said, breaking into Jared's thoughts. "I know of Blackstones, from Carolina. Thomas and John Blackstone. They are fellow members of the Royal Society. If I recall, John is doing some interesting studies on plant fertilization. I've read several of his articles."

"John was my brother. Thomas my father." In all the concern over spies and traitors, Jared had almost forgotten his link with the philosopher from Philadelphia. Most of his family were very interested in the natural sciences. His father and brother were fellows of the prestigious Royal Society, as was Franklin. The members studied the sciences and exchanged information. "My father and brother spoke of you often. They admire you."

"And I them. When I read your brother's paper on carbon dioxide supporting plant growth, I wrote him expressing my agreement." Franklin took a bite of cheese. "Do you share your family's love of natural sciences?"

"Nay, I fear the study of philosophies is not something at which I excel."

"Ah, but 'tis not for everyone. From what I hear of your conquests at sea, you obviously excel there."

"You are too kind, sir."

"Nonsense, you do our country an immeasurable service. What we would do against the world's greatest navy without privateers such as yourself, I do not know."

From there Franklin launched into a discussion on the merits of privateering. In spite of herself, Merideth found the topic of interest. Apparently Dr. Franklin made a study of maritime escapades; at least he seemed to know all about Captain Blackstone. The captain, contrary to the arrogant impression she had of him, appeared embarrassed by Franklin's praise. Merideth found the emotion endearing till she reminded herself they were discussing victories over her own countrymen.

Besides, with his dark sardonic looks, the captain was not someone who would be described as endearing.

"Does your brother share your passion for the sea?" The question seemed innocent enough, simply part of the conversation, but Merideth noticed the stiffening of the captain's broad shoulders. His hand, holding a fork balanced in his long fingers, stilled.

"My brother is dead, Dr. Franklin," he answered, and Merideth thought his voice unusually husky. She had the odd desire to reach out and cover his hand resting on the lace covered table. But, of course, she didn't. Why did she constantly have to remind herself they were enemies? Especially when he shed his arrogant veneer and appeared vulnerable. Like now. She had a hard time remembering she was his captive. It was almost as if they were friends.

Pushing aside those foolish thoughts, Merideth decided it was time she took matters into her own hands—at least as much as she could. Franklin's two grandsons had finished their tea and wandered into the small building, to work on today's edition of the single-sheeted newspaper Franklin published.

"Dr. Franklin," Merideth began, setting aside her napkin. "I do appreciate your hospitality, but I believe we have some important matters to discuss." She saw the captain's head jerk around, but she ignored him. "By his own admission, I was kidnapped by your countryman. A man, I might add, who, I repeat, was to be hanged for killing my father. Now, I realize you feel some loyalty to Captain Blackstone; however, as a humanitarian you must feel some compassion for my plight."

"I do, sweet child. My sympathies are with you."

"There is more to this situation than that," Jared interrupted.

"Now Captain." Franklin held up his hand, palm out. "Let us give Lady Merideth a chance to speak her piece."

The captain didn't like it—Merideth noticed the stubborn jut of his jaw—but he sat back, arms crossed, and held his tongue. If Franklin noted Captain Blackstone's reaction, he made no comment before again facing Merideth. "What do you propose be done at this point?" he asked, as the breeze caught a lock of his long frizzled hair.

"It's quite simple. I should be returned to my home at Land's End. As for Captain Blackstone . . . before he began this . . . this wild adventure, he was sitting in a cell awaiting the hangman."

"Now wait just a minute!" Jared leaned forward, hands on knees. Only Franklin's placating hand kept him from leaping up.

"Are you suggesting Captain Blackstone should be returned to that cell?"

"Well . . ." Merideth swallowed. "He was convicted of the crime."

184

"The hell you say!"

"Now Captain."

"With due respect, Dr. Franklin, I cannot sit by and listen to her advocate I voluntarily hang for a crime I did not commit."

"I am simply trying to ascertain what Lady Merideth thinks is fair. She has been through an ordeal."

Both Merideth and Dr. Franklin pretended not to hear Jared's derisive snort.

"Lady Merideth." Franklin took a sip of wine and leaned back into the cushions of his chair. "Do you feel Captain Blackstone killed your father?"

The question was succinct and to the point, surprising coming from a man who appeared to be completely relaxed. "Well, I . . ." What did she think? At the time, Merideth had been convinced of his guilt. Now . . . ? "The constable and court thought so."

"But the question is, do you?"

She couldn't help it; her eyes strayed to the captain's, drawn in a way she couldn't explain. He stared at her with those green eyes as if he could see clear to her soul and was privy to her thoughts. But that was ridiculous.

She cleared her throat, forcing her attention back to Franklin. "What I think is immaterial. Captain Blackstone did come to my home at night, uninvited. I did find him in the library with my father. He held a pistol, a discharged pistol. He was wounded, and my father was . . . was dead."

Merideth lifted her chin and took a deep breath. When she recounted the circumstances, it certainly appeared that the court was correct in their verdict.

"I didn't kill your father."

How could one softly spoken denial counter all she knew? But it did. Had she lost her mind?

"So, Captain, you deny Lady Merideth's claim."

"Aye. To begin with, I was invited to Banistar Hall. At least Lord Alfred expected someone. Whether you wish to know of a spy in your midst or not, Lord Alfred had the name of one. And he was very willing to exchange that information for gold."

"He didn't!" Now it was Merideth's turn to object to what was being said.

"You're right there. He was killed—and not by me—before he could give me the name."

"Aren't you going to repeat your preposterous notion that he said I knew the name?"

Jared said nothing. He merely crossed his arms and leveled his ice-green stare on her till she swung her head around, spilling golden curls over her shoulder.

"It appears we have ourselves a quandary." Franklin templed his finger tips and peered through his spectacles at both young people. "I tend to believe Captain Blackstone—now, wait till you hear me out, Lady Merideth. I tend to believe that he didn't kill your father. You yourself appear to doubt his guilt there, unless I'm mistaken."

Merideth wanted to but could not deny his assumption. She said nothing, and moments later Franklin continued. "As for the question of a spy, I really have no thoughts. Since I have no funds to purchase a name, even if I wished to do so, it seems to be a moot point. Lady Merideth"—Franklin smiled sadly—"I'm very sorry for your loss, but I will not attempt to return Captain Blackstone to a fate I doubt he deserves. You, however, must be returned to your home, with all haste."

"I shall see her returned safely," Jared said. Damn, when he got his hands on Daniel, he'd throttle him soundly.

"Nonsense, you are a persona non grata in Lady Merideth's neighborhood. I shall see our guest safely returned through diplomatic channels. In the meanwhile"—Franklin stood and brushed crumbs from his lap—"she can stay here with my grandsons and me."

"I couldn't impose."

"Don't be silly, dear child. Look at his place." His arm swept toward the mansion. "The du Chaumonts afford me too much room for just the three of us. Besides, it shan't be for long."

It was decided.

Jared had his wish of having Lady Merideth taken off his hands. He could return to his ship, which hopefully was near to being refitted, and head for the open seas. It wasn't as if everything was the same. A man had been killed. And though Franklin might believe him, and Lady Merideth might begrudgingly admit his guilt was in question, the fact remained that he was wanted for murder in England. But, then, he was also wanted for piracy, a hazard of being an American privateer.

All things considered, he supposed he was getting out of this debacle pretty well—certainly a lot better than his brother had when he had dabbled in espionage. Then why couldn't he shake the mantle of despair that hung over him?

Lady Merideth.

The part of him that couldn't wait to be rid of her warred with the part that was fiercely attracted to her. It had been this way since the moment he first saw her, and try as he might, it hadn't abated.

Leaving was by far the best thing he could do. What self-discipline had failed to do, distance would surely accomplish. So as soon as the decision was made that he would return to his ship and Merideth would stay, Jared took his leave.

Franklin arranged for the loan of a horse from the du Chaumont's stable. Jared's good-byes to Lady Merideth were brief, and done in the presence of Dr. Franklin. She seemed satisfied with the arrangement, and so, Jared reminded himself, did he.

Merideth watched Captain Blackstone ride down the lane, his broad shoulders straight, and wondered why she felt so dejected. She was rid of him at last. Safe with Dr. Franklin, who promised her speedy return to England. Considering the circumstances, everything had worked out as well as possible. Her father was dead. Nothing would ever change that. But at least she could now mourn him in peace.

At the foot of the lane, with the sun dappling through the arched leaves overhead, the captain reined in his horse and turned in the saddle. His wave was meant for Dr. Franklin, she was sure, but it made her stomach flutter. With that he turned the corner and disappeared from sight. And Merideth sighed. She didn't mean to, and 'twas not a loud noise, but she was certain Dr. Franklin heard it, for he chuckled softly.

Drawing herself up to her full height, Merideth faced him, hoping her cheeks were not red. "I thank you, sir, for your hospitality, but I should very much like to return to my home as soon as possible."

"Of course you would. I shall write a correspondence this very afternoon to my good friend Lord Tinsly. Together we should be able to arrange something."

"I thank you, sir."

"No need to thank me." Franklin offered his arm, and together they walked back through the garden. "It shall be pleasant having a young lady about, even for a short while. My grandsons miss the gentle ways of a woman, as do I."

"Well, I shall be most pleased to offer what assistance I can."

Ben smiled and patted the hand resting on his sleeve as they strolled along the brick path. "How very kind of you. And now I think I shall send word to Madame Geaudaux. She is a dear lady who lives very close. Do not breathe a word of this, but I think she is enamored of me." Ben laughed and Merideth joined him. "At any rate, she is a wonderful friend and just the one to help us."

"Help us?"

"That is your only gown, is it not?"

Merideth glanced down to where the captain's cloak covered her dress. "Yes," she admitted.

"And I gather, the way you keep it covered, it is not to your liking."

This brought another peal of laughter from Merideth. "Hardly. The gown I wore when kidnapped was soiled, so the captain had one of his crew purchase this for me."

"Well, we must see that you get another. You are far

too pleasing to the eyes to keep yourself covered so."

As much as Merideth longed for something else to wear, honesty forced her to speak. "I haven't any coin."

"'Tis naught to worry about."

"You don't understand. I can't even pay you back when I reach Land's End. I'm afraid . . . there are debts." She couldn't even imagine how those debts had multiplied since her abduction from Banistar Hall.

Dr. Franklin seemed to ponder this a minute; then he looked up, his eyes shining. "Have you ever considered becoming a governess, Lady Merideth? No, no, of course you haven't. But I think you'd make an excellent one . . . if only temporarily. And I know two boys who could use one."

"But I—"

Franklin paused as they neared the small garden building. From inside came the sound of young voices. "You'd be doing me a favor and paying for your gown at the same time." As he spoke, the voices became louder, raised in argument.

"I shall tell Grandfather if you don't."

"I don't care what you say. You think you are so smart, just because you're older."

"Give me that or I'll show you just how much older and *larger* I am."

"Grandfather! Grandfather!"

As Merideth watched, the boys exploded from the building and rushed toward Dr. Franklin. He looked at her, a wry expression on his face. "I think perhaps two gowns," was all he said before his grandsons surrounded him.

Chapter Ten

He had been summoned back to Passy.

The post, nestled snugly in the pocket of his waistcoat, crinkled as Jared dismounted in front of the Hôtel de Valentinois, the large estate where Franklin was staying. It had been nearly a month since he'd ridden away. And, Lord help him, he couldn't suppress the thrill being here again created.

Was Merideth Banistar still here?

Benjamin Franklin hadn't mentioned her in his letter, the letter that had awaited Jared in Morlaix when he'd returned from his latest foray into the channel. Franklin had simply stated that he needed to see Jared about a matter of great importance, and could the captain possibly call on him at his earliest convenience.

The request suggested a jaunt to the country rather than the long trip it was, but Jared hadn't taken the time to eat a hot meal before he was galloping across the French countryside. En route he repressed thoughts about why he'd rushed off to Passy. But now, with his bootheels clicking a staccato on the stone walk leading to the door, he knew.

He wanted to see Merideth Banistar again. Or, if she was gone, at least have some word of her. She'd never been far from his thoughts since he'd left. The sky reminded him of her eyes; his cabin held her scent, so hauntingly strong on his pillow that it kept him awake nights. He ached for her in a way he'd never experienced before.

And he wanted it to stop.

If absence didn't work, then he welcomed this opportunity to see her again. Certainly she wasn't as beautiful as he remembered. Surely she had some flaw he'd yet to notice. Besides, of course, the fact that she was a traitor to her country. But Jared found that even knowing that didn't quell his obsession with her.

Pushing away those thoughts, Jared knocked on the door. Evening had fallen, and the hallway was aglow with candlelight when the servant answered. Jared was ushered into a large room where murals of pastoral scenes in muted colors adorned the walls. He had always considered his own home at Royal Oak grand, but it didn't compare to this.

"Ah, Captain Blackstone, you've come."

Jared turned from his examination of one of the paintings at the sound of Dr. Franklin's voice. The older man stood stooped over a gnarled walking stick. He carried a simple felt hat in his other hand.

"I was just on my way to Madame d'Abbeville's soiree. Won't you join me?"

Jared had not known what to expect from the request that he come to Passy, but he hadn't thought it an invitation to a soiree. "I . . . I'm hardly dressed for socializing. I rode from Morlaix as soon as I received your message."

"Nonsense, Captain." Franklin let his gaze travel over Jared's black waistcoat. Snug breeches were stuffed into high black riding boots. "You look splendid. Besides, the ladies expect us colonials to garb ourselves simply, and they love it." This last he said in a loud whisper, punctuated by a wink.

Jared had to admit, Franklin's own clothes were almost Puritanical in cut and cloth. With a shrug he followed the older man, who obviously thought the matter closed, into the hallway.

"Madame du Chaumont offered me the use of her coach, so we needn't walk. It isn't far, perhaps three miles, but my gout seems to be reminding me of its existence tonight."

Jared helped Franklin into the coach, then climbed in himself. When they were settled, he gave the signal to the coachman to begin.

"Testy problem, old age," Franklin began. "The spirit is still so willing. 'Tis the body that rebels."

"You seem quite active."

"Not nearly so much as I'd like." After that admission Franklin steered the conversation to a series of inconsequential topics. The merits of Monsieur du Chaumont's chef. The unseasonably cool weather. The sexual exploits of his friend, Madame de Beaumarchais.

The dialogue was interesting, but not once did Franklin touch upon the two subjects of most interest to Jared. Why had he been summoned to Passy? And what had become of Merideth Banistar?

Finally, he could stand it no more. During a lull brought on by Dr. Franklin searching his mind for a name, Jared said, "I assume Lady Merideth has returned safely to Land's End by now."

If Franklin was surprised by the abrupt change of subject, he didn't show it. Instead he smiled, that smile that made Jared think he knew more than he pretended. "It would seem such things take longer than I thought."

"Do you mean she's still in Passy?" Damn, he hated that his heart was racing.

"Oh, of course. Didn't I tell you? She's already at Madame d'Abbeville's estate. She spent the day there."

"I thought she'd be home to England by now."

"Did you really?"

Jared couldn't make out Franklin's expression in the dim light of the coach, but his tone was distinctly skeptical. Jared had the uncomfortable feeling that the older man knew exactly what he was thinking.

"She's been quite a blessing, you know."

"Has she?"

"Yes. She is wonderful with the boys. Don't tell her I said this, but I think both of them fancy themselves in love with her."

Jared remained quiet.

"Will especially. He rushes to fulfill her every wish."

"How nice for her."

"Now Captain, don't sound so cynical. Lady Merideth is very careful not to take advantage. She gives much more than she receives."

By the way Franklin spoke of her, Jared would wager Franklin's grandsons weren't the only ones who fancied themselves in love. It was time to bring him back to reality. "Has she mentioned the name of the American traitor yet?"

"What?" Franklin reached for his cane as the coach slowed, brushing the inquiry aside. "Oh, no. I truly don't believe she knows anything about a traitor."

"But her father said—"

"Yes, yes, I know what he told you. Let's speak of it no more tonight." Franklin opened the coach door himself and alighted before Jared could even reach out to assist him.

They'd stopped before a lavish stone mansion. Each one of its myriad windows sparkled with light, casting a pale-yellow wash over a circular drive clogged with coaches. As soon as the front door was opened, Jared could hear the melodic sound of women's laughter mingled with the strains of violins.

A spiral staircase led to the second-floor ballroom. No sooner were they announced than two ladies with rouged cheeks and nearly exposed bosoms approached Dr. Franklin. Each of them grabbed an arm and pulled him into the room. Where the butler's voice had barely carried over the din of noise, the one woman's loud chatter did.

She announced for all to hear that the beloved Dr. Franklin had finally arrived. Standing where he was left when the women dragged away the ambassador, Jared watched the proceedings with amusement. Though a fairly tall man, Franklin's entourage dwarfed him by virtue of their preponderance of powdered hair and billowy gowns. They seemed to adore the old man, and, judging by the liveliness of Franklin's step, the feeling was mutual.

More people were moving toward Franklin, and Jared scanned the group, a smile etching his face. He realized he was looking for Merideth, and he felt a stab of regret when he didn't see her. His focus broadened. Though the room was large, the crush of wide silk gowns and humanity made it appear crowded. His gaze skimmed across the dancers near the raised stage at the far end of the room and froze.

She was dancing. Jared stopped himself from moving toward her. Instead he watched, losing sight of her occasionally as other dancers stepped between them.

She was more beautiful than he'd remembered, and he was transfixed.

Her head tilted and she smiled at her partner. Jared felt the air tingle as if a storm were approaching. He swallowed and forced himself to look at her partner.

A dandy. No doubt about it. And a rather conceited one, if Jared could tell from the way the gentleman arched his bewigged head and looked down his large nose. He was older than Merideth by at least three decades, but that didn't curb his lustful expression. Again Jared found himself fighting the urge to move forward. He relaxed, crossing his ankles and leaning against the silk-covered wall. What did he care how people looked at her? *She* certainly didn't seem to mind.

Jared let his attention stray back to Lady Merideth.

She was radiant. Her gown, an icy blue confection of silk and lace, shimmered when she moved. She bowed, dipping forward, and the candlelight pearled the soft skin of her shoulders and neck. Her hair, undimmed by powder, shone golden, the curls piled fashionably atop her head inviting exploration by a man's hands.

His hands.

Jared tightened his fingers into fists when that thought struck him. The idea was ludicrous. Besides, if anyone was apt to sample the delights of Lady Merideth's locks, it was more likely the partner graced by her sweet smile.

"She's lovely, isn't she?"

Jared jerked around at the sound of Franklin's voice. When had he escaped the bevy of ladies paying him homage? And why in the hell had Jared allowed himself to simply stand there, staring at Lady Merideth? Denying it was impossible, so Jared merely shrugged. "Aye. She appears to be enjoying herself."

"What?" Franklin drew his attention away from another lady who smiled at the older man invitingly. "Ah yes, Merry does like to dance. She didn't know how, you know?"

Merry? "Nay, I didn't know that." She had Franklin calling her Merry. And believing she didn't know how to dance. She was the daughter of a British peer, for God's sake.

"There are most likely many things you are unaware of," Franklin said, softening the sting of his words with a smile.

"No doubt, however—" Jared's sentence was cut off by another woman who moved up beside Ben. Unlike

197

the other, however, her lascivious gaze was fixed on Jared.

"Ben, my *ami*," she began in halting English. "Introduce me to your friend, *s'il vous plaît*." She leaned forward enough so that Jared could see the dusky crescent of nipple above her gown.

His mind was momentarily distracted from Merideth Banistar. After the introductions were exchanged, Madame de Beaumarchais appeared faint from the wonder of meeting an actual privateer, and a heroic one at that. Jared thought Franklin had embellished his accomplishments a bit, but he didn't object when Madame said she needed a breath of air.

The curved balconies looked out over gardens and fountains lit by hundreds of lanterns. The heady scent of flowers drifted up as Madame de Beaumarchais leaned into his arm. Invitation was written clearly in her brown eyes. Jared dipped his head and her rouged lips parted.

It had been some time since he'd kissed a woman. Not since Lady Merideth. He found himself thinking of the last time he'd touched the Englishwoman as his lips met those of Madame de Beaumarchais. She was an accomplished kisser, using her tongue and teeth to advantage, pressing her breasts to Jared's chest.

He should have been aroused, powerfully so, but the experience left him feeling empty. He didn't want to be out here. The dance was over; Jared could hear the fading strains of violins through the closed door behind him.

With an effort, for one of her arms was now tightly clamped around his neck while the other roamed down the front of his body, Jared set her aside. Her expression of shock matched his own disbelief. Was he losing his mind? Turning aside a beautiful willing woman was not something he usually did. And Madame de Beaumarchais *was* beautiful, though not as much to his liking as others . . . one other.

When he suggested they return to the ballroom, Madame's smile grew chilly. She turned on her heels and preceded him through the door, never looking back as she swept into the crowd.

Across the room, Franklin pointed and said, "Ah, there he is now."

"Who?" Merideth followed the arc of Dr. Franklin's hand in time to see two people enter the ballroom. Her breathing stopped. "Captain Blackstone," she whispered.

Dr. Franklin chatted on to her about how the American privateer had arrived while she was dancing, but Merideth paid little heed. She watched the two across the dance floor.

By the Frenchwoman's demeanor it wasn't difficult to deduce what had happened. Merideth had been forced to turn down several amorous men since she'd been in France. The surprising thing was that Madame *had* refused the captain's advances. She was known for her amours, and she certainly must find the American captain attractive . . . anyone would. But at least Madame de Beaumarchais had the good sense to rebuke him—something Merideth hadn't been able to do. In the past. But from now on it would be different.

Merideth forced herself to remember that as he strode toward them, dark and powerful amid the brilliantly clad revelers. He was compellingly handsome. The shifting of flirting eyes following in his wake told Merideth she wasn't the only one to think so. Even if Madame de Beaumarchais had refused his advances, there seemed to be several ladies willing—nay, eager, judging by the manner of their preening as he walked past them—to take her place.

But his attention was riveted on her. Even when the captain reached them, he barely glanced toward Dr. Franklin.

"What are you doing here?" She hadn't meant to blurt out the question, but it was what she wanted to know. Merideth wasn't sure why his presence was so unsettling. She had thought herself rid of him. Had worked on forgetting him, only to look up and see him standing across the room.

Gone was the coy flirt. Blue eyes, which had previously danced with laughter, now shone cold. Her mouth was a tight line. No quick smiles for him. His own expression was derisive. "One might ask the same of you, Merry," he said, watching her chin rise at his use of her pet name. If Franklin and half of France could use it, then dammit, so could he.

"I'm a guest of Madame d'Abbeville."

"As it happens, so am I."

"I gathered as much. My question is, why have you returned to Passy?" It was disconcerting.

"*I* summoned Captain Blackstone, dear."

"Why?" Merideth turned on Dr. Franklin. "No, please." Merideth held up her hand. "I apologize for

200

questioning you. It is none of my concern."

"But it is mine. Why did you have me come here?" Jared had certainly assumed there was some emergency when he received the letter. But Franklin seemed unconcerned about anything but enjoying himself with his friends. His next words confirmed Jared's conclusion. Instead of answering Jared's inquiry, the older man suggested Jared partner Lady Merideth in the next round.

"I'm afraid my old foe, Sir Gout, forces me to sit and watch or I would do it myself," Franklin said.

"I really am too fatigued to dance." Opening her fan with a flourish, Merideth swiped it through the perfume-laden air.

"I'm quite sure Lady Merideth has her pick of partners should she change her mind," Jared said, causing Ben to chuckle.

"She does, doesn't she?" Franklin agreed. "But come now, children." He took them each by the arm, leading them through the throng of people, toward the dancers. "Certainly you won't deny an old man's wish."

When he paused there didn't seem to be anything for Jared to do but offer his arm. She took it, albeit reluctantly, and they joined the procession for *L'Escapade*.

They circled to the left four counts, then back again, the tall, dark man and his golden partner. When they met in the middle, Jared arched his brow.

"For a novice you dance very well."

Merideth ignored the sarcasm-drenched comment, twisting away from him as soon as the music allowed. When they came together again it was Merideth who broke the silence. "Why did Dr. Franklin summon you here?"

"I haven't a clue." He watched her brow wrinkle in concentration. "Perhaps it has something to do with you."

"That hardly seems likely."

They moved on, bowing to the next couple in line, allemanding right. It was several minutes until they sidestepped back to face each other.

"Why would you think Dr. Franklin brought you here on my account?"

Jared shrugged. His gaze traveled down over her gown. "The expense of keeping you?"

"The gown is borrowed."

The dance brought them closer. "Perhaps he resents your using his hospitality as a means of gathering state secrets."

His words were low, spoken in an intimate, sensual tone, and for a moment Merideth didn't comprehend his meaning. The instant she did, she stopped, causing the lady to her right to bump into her. Without a word Merideth turned and walked from the dance floor.

"Insufferably rude man," Merideth mumbled to herself as she made her way through the crowd. When she spotted Dr. Franklin, she tried to replace her scowl with a smile. His first words to her showed she hadn't succeeded.

"Are you well, my dear?"

"No, actually, I've a terrible headache. Would you mind terribly if I returned to my room at the estate? I'd send the carriage back for you."

"I'll go with you."

"You'll do no such thing. I can see how much you're enjoying yourself, *and* I also know that you've planned a meeting with Monsieur Gerald later to discuss politics."

"I don't feel right letting you go alone."

"Because of what happened in Paris?"

"'Twas an accident. You said you were sure."

"Yes. Yes, I was sure," Merideth said. "I *am* sure." What else could it have been? It had simply been so frightening to look up and see a team of horses bearing down on her. To see the face of the woman driving the coach. She'd obviously lost control, and Merideth had panicked, nearly freezing in their path. If not for Dr. Franklin's frantic yelling, she would have been killed. As it was, she'd barely made it out of the horses' path before they bore down on the spot where she had stood. The coach sped by. No one recognized the woman or the livery.

It had been a freak accident. But ever since that day, Dr. Franklin had kept a close eye on her.

"The accident is not why you . . . ?"

"What?" Franklin lifted his brow.

"Never mind. 'Tis silly." She had almost asked if Captain Blackstone had returned to watch out for her. But that was ridiculous. He was the man accused of killing her father. She sighed. "At any rate, I really do wish to return to the house. And please." She clasped his hand in hers. "Don't trouble yourself. I shall be fine."

Allowing him no time to protest, Merideth turned and swept through the crowd of people.

Jared watched her go and hesitated only a moment

before approaching Franklin. He'd been riding for hours, was tired and in no mood to remain at this soiree. In no mood to remain in Passy, for that matter. Franklin's message had implied the need for haste. Jared had complied, only to be repeatedly put off and dragged to a ball.

And shown the error of his ways for having brought Merideth Banistar to Passy. She'd obviously made out quite nicely. Society seemed to adore her. Ben Franklin sang her praises. And no one even suspected that she committed treason in exchange for coin.

"Ah, there you are, my boy." Ben hailed Jared closer when he noticed him approach.

"Dr. Franklin," Jared began. "I shall wait on you in the morning, but, for now, I must take my leave."

"Of course you must." Franklin's voice had the edge of panic. "She's off by herself."

"Who?"

"Merry."

The tone of that one word seemed to imply that Jared should know what Dr. Franklin was talking about—which he assuredly did not. "I'm sure Lady Merideth is fine."

"No, no, you don't understand. It's not safe for her. I've tried not to alarm her, but she mustn't be alone. Please, go after her. She took the carriage."

Jared still didn't understand, but, for whatever reason, Franklin was concerned. Nay, more than concerned—deeply worried. He gave Jared's arm a push. "Go," was all he said.

Turning on his heel, Jared headed for the ballroom doorway. As he moved, the tension inside him built, so that by the time Jared reached the spiral staircase he was nearly running. He took the stairs quickly, offhandedly excusing himself when he pushed past a group of perfumed dandies taking the stairs at their own leisurely pace.

The night air felt cool and inviting as Jared burst through the door, startling the servant standing off to the side on the giant portico. "Lady Merideth Banistar. Have you seen her?" Jared asked as he scanned the curved drive.

The man merely shook his head, filtering fine powder over his jacket.

"A mademoiselle. Beautiful. Did she—" Jared's eyes snagged on a coach just passing through the stone gates at the foot of the drive. Without another word he took off at a run. His boots kicked up gravel as he sped after the coach. It was perhaps twenty-five rods away, but slowed to turn the corner onto the main road. Jared caught up with the conveyance, just as it picked up speed.

Grabbing onto the window, he swung himself up, pulling open the door and throwing himself inside. He landed with a thud on the leather seat and was immediately pummeled about the face. Lifting his forearms, Jared warded off Merideth's blows. He pushed her back onto the opposite seat, covering her mouth when she tried to scream.

"Be still. It's me."

It was dark in the carriage. She hadn't lit the lamp, but apparently she recognized his voice, because he felt her body relax once he spoke. But the next moment she tensed, clawing at his hand with her fingers. His body covered hers, but he tentatively loosened his grip on her mouth.

"What are you doing?" she sputtered. "Have you . . . have you lost your mind?" Her breath came in ragged gulps. She had been so frightened her voice still quivered. And she wasn't certain she shouldn't be frightened yet.

"Perhaps." Jared too was short of breath from his run, and lying as he was on top of her wasn't helping. He shifted, bringing his mouth on a level with hers. "As to what I want, I imagine it is the same thing most of the male population of Passy wants."

"Get off me, you uncouth barbarian!"

"Ay, the lady prefers seduction by perfumed dandies with powdered wigs and beauty patches. Or is it simply that men such as that have secrets they are willing to share for a taste of your delightful—"

Whack!

The slap was hard and unexpected and it caught Jared square on his cheek, burning his flesh and causing him to grab her hands. He pulled them above her head. His face was close to hers and he could make out her large eyes, luminous in the dim light, and her lips, open and inviting.

His breath fanned her face and she waited, the tension near unbearable. He was angry, angry as she. There was no denying that. But there was something else, something primal and erotic that bound them as tightly as the anger. Merideth could feel the promise of passion racing through her body. She tried to fight it, but the moment his lips touched hers it flared, and she could do naught to stem the feelings that engulfed her.

Hard and aggressive, his mouth ravaged hers. And she met him with equal desire and fervor. When he let loose her hands she used them to clutch at his shoulders, so broad and firm beneath the fine broadcloth. His mouth tore along her jaw, nipping and wetting, then returned to her mouth. She met the thrust of his tongue with her own . . . intimate interplay that made their blood boil.

His whiskers abraded her soft skin, but she cared not. He forged a trail under her chin, down the slender column of her throat, and she writhed beneath him. With a swipe of his hand her cape was gone, and his mouth feasted upon the flesh of her chest. He followed the border of low-cut lace, then nudged lower, biting the tip of her straining nipple through the heated silk.

Merideth arched, grabbing handfuls of his raven hair, pulling him closer. His body was hard, burning into hers through the layers of ruffles and lace. And Merideth moaned. The ache for him was nigh unbearable. Her legs spread in the tangle of petticoats, but that didn't assuage the gnawing hunger. She didn't know what would, until his hand grasped her.

There was no gentle exploration of her thighs or the curve of her hip. His fingers delved straight for the moist heated core of her passion. And oh, the splendor of it!

He prodded, touching, and like a flame to powder she exploded. Her body bucked, shivering and trembling uncontrollably. Her eyes drifted shut and her mouth went slack, till his covered it, consuming her with a kiss full of carnal delights.

She soared, then slowly, sensually floated back to

earth. She was spent, emotionally and physically. Her lashes lifted and in the darkness she saw the flash of white teeth . . . his grin. She couldn't help responding in kind.

"You are full of surprises, Lady Merideth."

"I . . . I don't understand. What happened?"

"Only a prelude," Jared assured, then lowered his mouth again for a probing kiss that proved him right. She longed for more. He longed for the feel of her heat surrounding him.

The sound of the shot caught them both off guard.

"What was that?"

Jared jerked up, then pushed her onto the floor. She landed in a pile of lace and petticoats. The coach slowed, then rolled to a stop. Jared could hear voices outside. The driver, and someone else. A coarse, ill-bred voice that yelled for the driver to get off the box.

Cursing the fact that he had left his pistols at the Hôtel de Valentinois, Jared lifted the flap and peered out. By the light of the lanterns mounted on the side of the carriage, Jared could see that the road was surrounded by forest . . . the perfect place for a highwayman.

"What is it? Who's out there?"

Jared hushed Merideth, pushing her back when she tried to climb up to see for herself.

"Come on out with ye, yer ladyship. I know yer in there."

The burly man who spoke stood close to the coach, his pistol trained at the door. Jared couldn't see any sign of the driver. Or of the highwayman's horse.

208

"Now, let's don't make this harder on ye. Come on out."

Jared could hear her ragged breathing . . . or was it his own? At any rate, he reached down and squeezed her knee. A gesture of hope? Or despair?

The handle jiggled.

"I'm through playin' games, yer Ladyship."

The door opened. The highwayman stuck his gun inside the coach and Merideth screamed. In the same instant, Jared chopped his fist down hard over the assailant's hand. The pistol clattered to the coach floor, and the highwayman looked up at Jared with a shocked expression. Then he turned and fled.

Jared leaped from the coach. It took him little time to overtake the lumbering outlaw. Jared grabbed him from behind as the man headed into the woods. He jerked him around, knocking away the man's hands when he tried to protect himself.

"What in the hell is going on here?" Jared demanded. "What did you want with Lady Merideth?" When he didn't answer immediately, Jared shook the man like a rat terrier would its prey.

"I ain't got nothin' against her meself. It was him that hired me to kill her that does."

"To kill her?" Jared tried to control his anger. "Who? Who hired you? Tell me or I'll tear you limb from limb with my bare hands." Jared jerked the trembling man forward by the front of his jacket, ready to do just that. He saw the slobbery mouth quiver . . . open to speak.

And then a shot rang through the forest.

Chapter Eleven

The highwayman's body jerked, then went limp. All that held him upright were Jared's hands grasping his bloodstained jacket. When Jared let go, the body slumped to the ground. Stunned, Jared crouched down beside him, peering through the darkness for any sign of who had fired the shot. The only light, thrown off by the coach lanterns, was behind, silhouetting him. Before him was darkness and shadows.

He waited, listening intently, the beat of his heart pounding in his ears. Then from the rear he heard the rustle of leaves. Shifting, Jared followed the sound of the footsteps coming ever closer. When they were almost upon him he turned and sprang, flattening the intruder beneath his body.

He heard a squeal and froze.

"What in the hell are you doing sneaking around?" he whispered, lifting his head just enough to recognize Merideth's face.

"I wanted to see what happened. I heard a shot."

"Aye, you heard a shot. And 'tis lucky you didn't take a musket ball yourself."

"I also brought you the highwayman's pistol," Merideth pointed out, not surprised when the captain quickly grabbed for the gun.

"Stay here," was all he said as he rose to a crouch. But before he could move into the shadows, the clip-clop of horses riding off came from the woods. Jared stood, and ran a few paces toward the sound, stopping when the hoofbeats faded.

"I think they're gone."

"Who?" Merideth rolled over to get up. "Who's gone? What hap—" Her breath caught and she let out a shriek. Before Jared could reach her, Merideth was on her feet, backing away from the body sprawled on the ground.

"The highwayman," Jared said, answering her silent inquiry.

"Is he . . . ?"

"Dead?" Bending down, Jared held his hand over the man's chest. "Aye." He paused. "He was shot."

"Shot? But you didn't have a pistol."

"*I* didn't shoot him."

"But how did he . . . ?"

Jared shook his head in the direction of the woods. "It appears one of his fellow highwaymen did the job."

"Why would they do that?"

Jared hesitated only a moment. "I don't know." Now was not the time to tell her what the assailant had said before he'd died—before someone had stopped him from saying more. "Let's get out of here." Jared turned Merideth away from her study of the body. She was trembling when he touched her shoulder.

"Shouldn't we . . . ? We can't just leave him here."

"I'll send someone back to handle it." His arm draped around her. "Let's see if we can find the driver."

"He's on the other side of the coach," Merideth said, but she held back, her attention uncontrollably drawn to the dark heap on the side of the road. Another murdered man. Before she'd met Captain Blackstone, the only dead people she'd ever seen were victims of age and disease.

But since that night Jared Blackstone blew in with the storm, there seemed no end to the violence she witnessed—blank-eyed stares, chests abloom with crimson . . .

"Come on, Merideth." Jared nudged her toward the coach and she started moving. He found the driver propped against a wheel, his knees pulled up and his head cradled in his palms. There was a knot on the side of his head and blood matted on his powdered wig, but he was able to stand. With help from Merideth, Jared settled him inside the coach. "You ride with him," Jared ordered. "I'll drive the coach."

Outside of admitting to a terrible ache above his ear, the driver had little to say as they jostled along the road toward Passy. Once in the village, Jared steered the horses to the Hôtel de Valentinois.

"We've a hurt man," Merideth heard Captain Blackstone announce as servants came toward the carriage. But she didn't stay to hear what else went on. Nearly unnoticed, she slipped from the carriage and through the front door. Once inside she sought out her room, stopping only once to assure Will that nothing was amiss. He'd wandered into the hallway in his nightshirt and stocking feet, rubbing at his eyes. With very little persuasion he returned to his room.

Merideth envied him his innocence as she closed her bedroom door behind her. Her bottom lip quivered as it had threatened to do all evening—at least since her encounter with Captain Blackstone. But she didn't let herself surrender to tears.

How long she stood there, clutching the back of a brocaded chair, Merideth didn't know. She tried to block what had happened from her thoughts, but flashes of memory seared through her mind.

The moment of fear when the highwayman aimed the pistol at her. The blank expression in his lifeless eyes. And always the captain. She could no more forget him, forget the dark passion of his touch, than she could shy away from the other realities.

The bedroom door opened and Merideth turned, not in the least surprised to see Jared Blackstone standing there. He paused for a moment, his form filling the entryway, then entered the room, closing the door behind him.

"I've sent word to the authorities."

Merideth merely nodded, wishing he would speak no more of it. He seemed to understand her reluctance, for his expression grew serious. Striding to the window, he pushed aside the heavy silk drapes before asking, "Why would anyone want you dead?"

"Dead?" Merideth couldn't help being taken aback by his question. "I . . . I . . . That's preposterous. No one wants me dead."

For long moments, during which Merideth forgot to

breathe, he stared at her, his sea-green eyes searching. Then he shrugged, seemingly accepting her contention. Without another word he advanced on her, his pace steady. Merideth retreated one step, then—when she saw the unbridled passion in his expression—another. The chair separated them, but he skirted it easily, grabbing her shoulders when she turned to reach for the door.

"Don't. I don't want you to—" He silenced the remainder of her denial with his lips, pressing them firmly to hers. Her halfhearted attempts to push him away proved futile. His body engulfed her . . . he engulfed her. His smell, his taste, the feel of his work-roughened hands on her skin, proved as tantalizing as before.

This, this is why she'd allowed him to touch her in the coach, the answer to the question that nagged at her. She simply couldn't help herself. Even now, as the feel of his fingers unfastening her gown sent warnings to her mind, she couldn't resist him.

Her hands tangled in the rough silk of his hair, loosening the black ribbon and freeing the raven locks. His head dipped to her throat and he nudged aside her gold locket, wetting the small hollow of skin beneath with his tongue. Merideth's pulse raced, her body arched, and the craving intensified.

When the silvery-blue silk slipped from her shoulders, Merideth felt no remorse. His gaze raked her, sweeping over the distended nipples that pressed against the fine linen of her shift. His fingers spread, covering her upper chest, pushing aside the fabric. When his thumbs scraped over the sensitive nubs,

215

Merideth moaned a siren song of surrender.

"You like that." There was no question in his voice, nothing but a simple declaration of fact, as his thumbs circled, then whisked across, her flesh.

She should protest. Deep in the recesses of her mind, Merideth knew no good could come from this. She stood, clutching his broad shoulders while he caressed her. He, fully dressed in his black waistcoat, the untamed fall of raven hair and dark, heavy-lidded eyes the only break from his civilized attire. While she displayed herself for him, her breasts bared, begging for his touch, her curls a tangle across her naked shoulders.

But objecting was beyond her. All she could do was acquiesce. His mouth replaced the gentle rub of his thumb, the moist heat making her knees tremble and the ache deep inside grow stronger.

With practiced hands the corset ties came undone, freeing even more of her flesh to his touch, his mouth. The gown drifted to the carpeted floor on a whisper of silk, followed by the shift and petticoats.

When she stood before him in nothing but clocked stockings and satin slippers, Jared skimmed his hands down over her hips. "You are so beautiful," he said, his voice thick. Up and down, his fingers roamed over her satin-soft skin, brushing her ribs, then rounding to shape her buttocks.

Merideth watched him, her eyes no more than blue slits, her breathing shallow. Everywhere he touched she burned.

"I want you." His hand filtered down her stomach and Merideth gasped as it tangled in the delta of tight curls. Her body quivered, tight as a bowstring, fraught with anticipation. She knew what he could do to her with just the touch of a finger. She longed for the release he had given her in the coach. But though she arched, inviting him to further exploration, he hesitated.

Merideth tried to control her breathing, but it came in short gulps. She swallowed, poised . . . waiting . . . but still he didn't move.

"Touch me." The words were softly spoken, and Merideth wasn't certain she'd heard him until his hand closed over hers. Then he was guiding, filling her fingers with the rock-hard proof of his passion.

His dark lashes drifted shut, closing off the primal vestige of desire. But Merideth had seen, and she gloried in it all the while her caress measured his length.

The swoop of his mouth caught her by surprise, but she matched his ardor, matched the sensual dance of his tongue, as her fingers stretched to surround him.

She was off her feet before she knew what he was about. The bed was high with a fanciful tester and gold brocaded hangings. He deposited her in the center, then turned to shuck off his waistcoat. His cravat followed, then his shirt.

Merideth watched unabashedly as he yanked off his breeches and boots. He stood before her, splendid in his dark beauty, and she could do naught but reach for him. Taking her hand, Jared brushed his lips across her knuckles, then placed them, palms flat, on his chest while he reached for the ribbons holding her stockings.

The dark pelt of hair enticed, curled around her fingers as Merideth slid them across his chest. She skimmed the hard nub of his breast and he sucked in air. His movements quickened, sweeping the white stockings over her toes and tossing them to the floor.

"I can't wait any longer," he said, and Merideth couldn't agree more. She longed to have him touch her like he had earlier. Her body arched, but instead of the magic of before, he settled atop her.

At first she found his weight an oddity, but then he kissed her and all but the most sensual of thoughts escaped her.

Jared wanted to go slowly, to savor being with her to its fullest. From the first time he'd seen her he'd thought of this, of how her skin would feel, like warmed silk. And how the heat of her would drive him insane. When he'd seen her tonight, radiant in her finery, dancing, smiling, flirting, he'd been incensed. Other men knew what he'd only dreamed of.

She was a traitor; at this moment he didn't care. She had parlayed her body for secrets. But the only secret he knew was told him by the highwayman moments before he died. A secret he would tell her anyway. But not now.

He'd reached the limits of his endurance.

"Lift your legs." Jared whispered his request, not surprised when she complied immediately. She was a passionate lover, free and giving with her favors. He sank into the cradle of her body, pressing against her heat. His first thrust penetrated but slightly, and Jared sucked in his breath at the pleasure that shot through him. Anxious to experience all the satisfaction she could offer, he pushed.

And stopped cold.

Resting his weight on his elbows, Jared tried again,

his passion-drugged mind barely comprehending the barrier he felt. He'd been so certain she was an experienced courtesan, a seductress who traded her delectable body for a traitor's secrets. But the proof that she wasn't couldn't be denied.

"What . . . what is it?" Merideth knew there was something amiss, but she couldn't imagine what she'd done wrong. But he stared at her, a strange expression darkening his handsome features. And his wonderful caresses had stopped. She wanted them to continue. Her body moved, seemingly of its own accord, and she felt the captain stiffen, but not before a sharp pain tore through her.

"Oh." Tears filled her eyes and she tried to blink them away. But one rolled down the side of her face. With the pad of his thumb, Jared brushed it away.

"Don't cry," he whispered. "I didn't mean to hurt you."

"You didn't. I mean, not really. I just didn't expect . . ."

"Nor did I." Jared tried to pull away, but found her hands tighten on his shoulders.

"What . . . what's wrong?"

"There's nothing awry." Jared lowered his head, a brush of lips to convince her of his words, but the contact lengthened, and heightened. Soon the probing of his tongue matched the thrust of his body. There was no more barrier, nothing but the smooth glide of flesh inside moist flesh.

Instinct took over, and Jared basked in the heat they produced. She was so sensual, so willing, that he almost forgot the proof of her inexperience.

Merideth clung to him, drowning in all the sensations he awakened in her. It was overpowering. *He* was overpowering. She rushed toward a precipice, a dark, almost frightening precipice. Something in her shied away, warned her that she shouldn't explore. She should keep herself safe. But she knew, in her heart she knew, it was already too late for that.

The waves of wonder hit her, tossing her toward the dark spiral, dissolving her control. Her breath came in shallow gasps and she cried out, unable to stop herself. It went on and on, this whirl through the darkness, till an explosion of bright lights shattered through her.

The captain's groan echoed in her ear as he collapsed, his body poker hot and searing. Merideth became vaguely aware that he had shifted some of his weight to his elbows, but she was too tired and replete to comment upon it. They seemed to float, surrounded by the feather softness of the down comforter.

His voice was husky, his words tickled the fine hairs curling about her ear. "Are you all right?"

Merideth didn't remember ever being so all right. But she didn't want to talk, she didn't want to think. The captain obviously wasn't going to allow her that luxury. When she didn't answer he shifted again, pulling away his marvelous weight and allowing the night chill to creep over her naked body.

"Did I hurt you?"

Merideth thought she heard genuine concern in his voice, a novelty in itself. She had evoked many emotions in the captain since she'd met him, but concern was not one of them. Without knowing why, she found she liked the idea. "I'm fine. Perhaps a little

220

tired." Her last words were slurred by sleep as her lashes drifted shut.

"That's right. Just rest," Jared whispered. He settled onto the mattress beside her, cradling her head against his shoulder. He was replete. He was comfortable. But he harbored no thoughts of slumber for himself.

For an old man with gout, he could move rather quickly.

Jared watched from the anteroom window as Dr. Franklin bustled from the carriage. His flannel hat sat askew on his head, and he used his walking stick to shoo servants from his path as he climbed the stone stairs leading to the front door.

He was halfway across the marble great hall before Jared's voice stopped him.

"Ah, there you are, my boy." Franklin motioned Jared to his side. "Where is she? Where is Lady Merideth? Did she come to any harm?"

"Nay. She is safe, asleep in her bed." Jared moved, blocking Franklin's path when he started toward the stairs. "She is fine, I tell you. But we need to talk."

Jared watched as the worry left Franklin's eyes, to be replaced by a shrewdness that belied his backwoods appearance.

"I suppose you're right. But not here," Franklin said with a cursory look around the huge hall. "Follow me."

Franklin led them up the curved stairway and down a series of portrait-lined hallways. "Are you certain she wasn't hurt? Word reached Madame d'Abbeville's that your coach had been attacked by highwaymen, and I came rushing home."

"Because you suspected someone might harm her." Jared's statement elicited nothing but a straightforward stare from Franklin, so he reassured the older man again. "As I said, she is safely asleep in her room. A room for which I have the key." Jared produced the brass key from his waistcoat. It shone dully in the candlelight as he held out his palm for Franklin to see.

Jared wondered how Franklin might view his locking Lady Merideth in her room, but one look at the twinkling eyes and Jared knew better.

"Good work, my boy. I knew you were the man for the job." He opened a door and motioned Jared into a small, cluttered room. After lighting a candle from a sconce in the hallway, Franklin shut the door. He placed the candlestick on a drop-leaf table piled with stacks of parchment. Then he settled into a delicately wrought chair that creaked under his weight.

Jared wasted no time getting to the point. "I wish to know what's going on. You send me after Lady Merideth because you fear for her safety." He paused, leaning toward Franklin, his hands planted on the table separating them. "How did you know a highwayman was going to attack the carriage?"

"I didn't." When he noticed Jared's skeptically raised brow, he continued. "Not for certain, anyway. But I feared something might happen." Franklin stood and moved awkwardly toward the window. "There have been a series of . . . *accidents.*"

"Accidents?"

"I call them that for want of a better word. At first I thought them just that. A runaway coach that barely

222

missed hitting her. A footpad who attacked as we walked along the ramparts of the Quarter Bonne Nouvelle. They all seemed coincidental. Even after I spoke with Merideth about it, she assured me that the only person she had to fear was you. And you, of course, were liberating English supplies on the channel."

A pang of guilt shot through Jared. He had indeed been the cause of fear in Merideth more than once. He opened his mouth to explain, but Franklin waved his interruption aside.

"At any rate, she nearly had me convinced that they were just a series of accidents until one of the grooms surprised an intruder in the stables." Franklin settled back into his chair. "The man was doing something to the saddle Merry used for her everyday ride. The groom scared him away, then luckily examined the saddle and found the cinch had been cut almost clear through."

"So she would have taken an 'accidental' spill."

"Exactly." Franklin peered through his spectacles. "Possibly a fatal one."

Jared grew tired of pacing and took the seat across from Franklin. "What did Lady Merideth say when you told her?"

"I didn't."

"But I don't under—"

"I'm nearly convinced someone is trying to kill our Merry," Franklin interrupted. "I'm also confident she doesn't know who or why. I know you find that hard to believe." Ruffles fell away from his wrist as Franklin held up his hand. "But I've come to know her very well, and I think she can be trusted."

Two hours ago Jared would have argued that point vehemently. Now, after making love to her, he wasn't certain enough to offer any response.

"You probably think this the result of an old man's imagination, but—"

"Nay. I also believe someone is trying to kill Lady Merideth." As concisely as he could, Jared related the experience with the highwayman.

"And he gave you neither name nor reason?"

"He was killed before he could say anything more."

"Hmmm." Franklin's head sank into his neck and he rubbed at his chin. "It's obvious you'll have to take her to safety."

"Me?" The words had been uttered so quietly it took Jared a moment to appreciate what the older man was saying. When he did, Jared's surprise was evident. "I can't protect Merideth."

"You did tonight."

"Only by a stroke of dumb luck, I assure you." Jared tried to explain the situation logically. After all, wasn't Dr. Franklin known for his logic? "If there is a threat against her life, perhaps the police—"

Franklin waved that suggestion away with a swish of his hand. "They wouldn't know where to begin. Besides, Lady Merideth is British. You are the one to do it, my boy. Need I remind you that you are the one who brought Merry here, thus exposing her to this danger?"

A rush of guilt shot through Jared, but he still countered Franklin's argument. "She possessed information I was sent to retrieve. Hell, she still possesses it."

224

"Poppycock! Merry doesn't know anything." Franklin's expression sobered. "I want you to take her back to Land's End."

"What of your diplomatic channels?"

"Nothing moves as slowly as diplomats. And we haven't the luxury of time." Franklin pushed himself to his feet. "I should think you'd feel some responsibility toward the girl."

Jared wanted to argue the point, but the truth was, he *did* feel responsible for Merideth Banistar . . . especially after tonight. He let out a gust of air, then leaned back in his chair. "I suppose I can see her safely home."

Franklin's face brightened. The crinkles around his eyes deepened. "That's splendid. I knew I could count on you."

Jared hadn't a clue as to why Dr. Franklin felt that way, but he merely shrugged. He stood, and was almost to the door of the small room when Franklin stopped him. "She isn't likely to go with you voluntarily."

Jared turned. "Why is that?"

"I believe Merry still harbors a dislike for you."

If that were true, her actions earlier would be difficult to explain. "I shall handle it."

"Good. Now I believe I shall seek my bed, knowing Merry is in safekeeping."

Merideth jerked awake.

It only took a moment for her to remember what she'd done in this bed, and to realize she was alone. She sat up, brushing tangled hair from her eyes, her mind

225

riddled with disbelief.

Not about Captain Blackstone abandoning her. She'd expected no less from him.

It was her own behavior that astounded her. It had, almost from the moment she'd first seen him. This inability to think . . . or behave rationally while in his presence.

Burying her face in her hands, Merideth tried to tell herself it was the American's fault. But though he had come to her room, she knew there had been no force. She had wanted him . . . wanted him to make real the dreams she'd had about him.

And now that he had, he was gone.

Telling herself she was pleased, at least about that, Merideth slipped from the bed. The room was dark and still, closed up. The stifling closeness was breeding a panic in the pit of her stomach. Earlier, the captain's appearance had kept her from opening the doors that led onto the terrace. But now she planned to rectify that.

She scooped the silk wrapper from the gilt-front chifforobe and flung it around her body just as the sound of a lock being turned came from her door.

Dual realization hit her. She'd been locked in her room. And someone . . . someone with the key was entering. After all that had happened tonight, she wasn't surprised to see Captain Blackstone standing in the doorway, silhouetted by the light from the hall.

"You're awake. Good," was all he said as he entered, carrying a branch of candles.

The light splashed into the room, filling all but the deepest corners. Merideth's wrapper hung open and she hastily tied the sash, lifting her chin when she noticed the captain's steady appraisal.

"What . . . ?" Merideth's voice quivered and she took a steadying breath. There was something about his hot, green gaze that made her remember the feel of his mouth on her flesh. "What are you doing here?"

The slight lift of his brows and quirk of his lips told her he remembered it too. His words confirmed it. "I'd have thought you would be expecting my return."

He was so arrogant. So certain she would succumb to him. And why not? Merideth chastised herself. She'd done it quickly enough before.

But not this time.

Folding her arms over breasts tight with longing for his touch, Merideth marched to the doors leading to the balcony. She'd barely gripped the brass handle when he grabbed her from behind, pushing her away from the glass-paned doors and pressing her against the watered-silk wall.

"What do you think you're doing?" she sputtered, shoving at his hard chest to no avail.

All manner of responses came to mind. His attempt to keep her from opening the balcony door. His fear that Franklin was right and there might be someone out there right now waiting to kill her. But he didn't think she'd believe him.

And then, Jared wasn't sure that *was* the real reason he was pressed against her. When he'd entered, her expression had been so full of disdain. He hadn't expected a loving welcome . . . but disdain? It would be interesting to see how long her eyes held their frosty edge if he kissed her.

"Don't! I'll scream." Merideth jerked her head to the side to avoid the descent of his lips. But his attack was only deterred, not repelled. His mouth wet a spot on the side of her neck, just below her ear, and Merideth couldn't suppress the moan of desire.

Jared smiled against her flesh. His palm slid between their bodies and found her breast, berry hard and straining against the clinging silk. His lower body arched forward, showing her his desire was as hot as hers.

And she seemed to melt around him.

For a moment Jared found his control sifting away. What had started as an attempt to prove something to her, as well as to himself, was fast taking over his good sense. He'd decided, after leaving Franklin, to spirit her away as quickly as possible. Tonight. Before anyone was the wiser.

If he had to take her back to Land's End . . . and it appeared he did . . . it was best to accomplish it quickly.

But now his resolve was battling his desire. Carrying her to the bed and burying himself deep inside her, or just taking her here, against the wall—such was all he could think about. And she'd let him. Jared didn't have to plunge into her moist heat to know she was ready for him.

He closed his eyes and tasted the sweet honey of her lips. But with the sensual thrill came the flash of a memory—the expression on her face when the highwayman had aimed his pistol at her.

With a final sweep of his tongue, Jared broke the kiss. His forehead rested momentarily against hers as

228

he fought for control. Then, before she could protest, he grabbed her arm and pulled her toward the chifforobe. Still holding onto her, he yanked open the door and pulled out a gown.

"Get dressed," he said, holding it out toward her.

"But I . . ." Merideth sucked in her breath as he snatched open the wrapper and drew it off her shoulders. "Stop that." Before she was certain what "that" was, he was gathering the gown and tossing it over her head, not bothering to hide the regret in his eyes as he covered her nakedness. "What?" Merideth spit hair from her mouth as he pulled the neckline over her head. "What are you doing?"

"Remember what I told you about my great-grandfather?" Jared smoothed the bodice down over her breasts and waist.

"Your . . . You mean the pirate?"

"Aye." Jared glanced up from his search for a pair of slippers.

"What about him?" Merideth was having a hard time following what he was doing. What he was saying.

"I told you what he did with beautiful women."

Merideth hopped on one foot as the captain grabbed her ankle and stuck her foot into a shoe. "You mean that he kidnapped them?"

Jared stood, towering over her. For a moment he only stared. Then he grinned, the dimple dancing to life in his cheek. "Consider yourself kidnapped . . . again."

Chapter Twelve

"Where in the hell have you been?"

Jared stood hands-on-hips on the *Carolina*'s deck, glaring at his cousin. Daniel Wallis appeared nonplussed as he crossed the gangplank and ambled toward the ship's captain.

"Greetings to you too, Cousin Jared."

"Don't give me any of your dubious charm. I asked you a question."

"A question I'm not at liberty to answer, cousin." Daniel shaded his eyes and stared into the rigging. "My, the *Carolina* looks in fine form."

"She is, no thanks to you. She could have been lost off the coast of England along with all on board. All because I was off running some wild-goose chase for you."

The mirth left Daniel's pale-green eyes. "This is not something we should discuss here. As a matter of fact, I've come to ask you to join me in town. I've let a room and we can talk there without being disturbed."

Jared held up his hand. "I don't wish to hear any more. We set sail from Morlaix with the evening tide, and I've work to do."

"Your destination is what I must speak with you about."

"My destination is none of your business."

"You misunderstand, cousin. I already know your destination. I also know taking Lady Merideth back to Land's End is ill advised."

Jared tried to hide his surprise that Daniel knew where he was going and why. He had told no one . . . not even his crew. They might have suspected when he brought Merideth Banistar back on board that they were taking her home, but Jared had tried to make it appear that she was only staying with him for their mutual enjoyment. He had kept her in the cabin—not without protest from her. And he'd stayed close by her side. Even Padriac looked on him with envy, thinking he was enjoying a passionate affair before facing the rigors of sea battle again.

But contrary to the impression Jared had tried to convey, he'd kept his distance from Merideth. And having her near, not touching her, was taking its toll on his patience.

It showed in the narrowing of his eyes, and the set of his jaw. "I won't listen to any more. You refuse to tell me where you've been. Fine. I'll accept this misadventure for what it is. But I am out, repeat, *out,* of the spy business."

"I understand your reluctance—"

"You misunderstand, Daniel." Jared turned his face into the brisk breeze blowing up the river and strove to control his anger. "It isn't a matter of my being reluctant. A man was killed—Lord Alfred was killed over this scrap of information that the Americans don't even desire." Jared clenched his hands behind his back. "*I* was to be hanged for his murder." Jared's brow arched. "You don't appear surprised."

"Because I'm not. Listen, cousin, this is far more complex than you can imagine."

"Not according to Dr. Franklin."

Daniel made a noise with his mouth that bordered on disdain. "I admire Ben," he said, belying his obvious attitude. "But he doesn't always know what's best as far as negotiations with the French are concerned."

"He isn't interested in the name of any traitors."

"Which in itself should have given you a sense of his incompetence. How couldn't he be interested to know the name of a Judas in his midst?"

Jared shrugged, unable to argue the point, unwilling to even try. "It matters naught. I had no name to give him. Lord Alfred died before he could do anything but tell me his daughter was involved. And she refuses to say . . . or mayhap she doesn't know," Jared added. As time went by he was more and more inclined to believe the latter.

"So that's it then?" Daniel followed Jared up the ladder to the quarterdeck.

"As far as I'm concerned, aye." Unrolling a chart, Jared began to examine it, hoping the discussion closed. But in the end he relented and accompanied his cousin into town.

The chance to learn more about his brother's death was something Jared could not resist. Daniel knew it.

Jared knew he did. So when Daniel intimated a link existed between Lord Alfred's death and John's, Jared couldn't resist trying to find out more.

"How long do you plan to keep me a prisoner down here?" It was the question she had asked near every day since she and the captain had arrived in Morlaix. And in truth she asked it now more out of habit than with any thought that she'd discover the answer.

"Until I deposit you safely on British soil," her captor answered offhandedly.

Merideth leaned back against the window seat, where she was reading a book about the growing seasons of Carolina—one of several the captain had on the subject. Cocking her head to the side, she watched Jared Blackstone as he settled into the chair beside his desk. He usually bristled at her inquiries about her captivity. Actually, that was the main reason she continued to ask. But today he barely seemed to notice her or her question.

"It's been so long since I've seen the sun." Merideth closed the book and set it upon the cushion beside her.

"May I suggest you but turn your head," Jared said without looking up.

Merideth glanced out the transom window and scowled. "I meant to say, 'tis been so long since I've been *out* in the sunshine."

"Think of all the sunspots you've avoided getting on your nose."

"I do *not* get sunspots."

He glanced up at her and Merideth felt heat seep up

234

her neck into her cheeks. She hadn't been able to meet his eyes without blushing since the night he'd kidnapped her for the second time . . . the night they'd made love. Merideth raised her chin, daring him to say anything about her high color, but he only looked back down at the chart on his desk.

He basically ignored her.

He'd basically ignored her since they'd stolen away from Passy.

And it was irritating beyond belief.

Not that Merideth wanted a repeat of the night in his arms. After considerable reflection she decided that that had been caused by a temporary—hopefully— lapse in her ability to reason.

But she didn't like being ignored.

"Is that a map of the waters around Land's End?" Merideth kept her gaze carefully fixed on the desk top so she wouldn't meet his green eyes when he looked up.

"Nay. 'Tis of the route to the Carolinas."

"In the New World?" Merideth forgot to keep her lashes lowered.

"Aye." Jared forgot to ignore his captive.

For long moments their gazes locked.

Merideth's knees felt weak, and she could hear her heart pounding in her chest. His gaze warmed her. The green eyes, so like the color of the sea on a clear day, drew her with a force she couldn't resist.

Pressing palms to desk top, Jared stood. He was around the side of the chair before he realized he'd moved. Going to her seemed the most natural thing in the world.

The knock on the cabin door jolted them both.

Merideth flopped back onto the window seat, wondering when she'd stood. She grabbed up the book on agriculture. Jared turned, scooping up the chart and rolling it into a cylinder, which he passed from one hand to the other. "Enter," he said, not surprised at the gruffness in his voice.

"Ah, Cousin Jared, there you are."

Jared's eyes widened in surprise, then narrowed as he stared at Daniel. After listening to Daniel this morning, Jared had agreed to take him, and his cargo, to Charles Town. But Jared had also insisted upon one stipulation—and Daniel was breaking it by coming to the cabin.

But Daniel, as he strolled into the captain's cabin, acted as if he'd never promised to avoid any contact with Merideth Banistar. "Oh, do present me to this lovely lady or I shall perish." He moved steadily toward Merideth, and Jared had no alternative but to make the introductions. He saw a spark of recognition light up Merideth's eyes when he said his cousin's name. She glanced at Jared; then her attention returned to Daniel.

"Daniel Wallis," she repeated the name. "Captain Blackstone's cousin." Her voice was tight. "I see the family resemblance." In actuality, Daniel was almost like a pale, miniature copy of the captain. The features were similar, regular and aristocratic. But what on Jared appeared undeniably strong and handsome, was on the cousin feminine . . . almost pretty.

"You flatter me, your Ladyship." Daniel bowed.

"Do I?" Merideth's chin notched higher. She didn't have a clue why Daniel was here, but she didn't intend to play along with whatever game the captain and he had planned for her. "I understand you are my *contact,* Mr. Wallis. My contact in some bit of international intrigue."

"My dear Lady Merideth—"

"Did you or did you not send Captain Blackstone to Banistar Hall?"

Jared watched his cousin squirm under Merideth's direct gaze. Any thoughts of intervening vanished as Jared waited to hear his cousin's answer.

"I received a communication that somone at Land's End wished to speak with me concerning a spy."

"Someone?" Merideth's brow arched.

"The sender was somewhat vague about his identity. Traitors often are."

"What the hell are you saying? You told me it was Lord Alfred."

Merideth ignored the captain's outburst. "So it wasn't necessarily my father who contacted you."

"I assumed it was Lord Alfred. But . . ." Daniel swished the air with his fingers. "I suppose it could have been someone else."

Merideth shot Jared a triumphant look—one he returned with steely determination. She opened her mouth to question Daniel further. But before she could the captain had his cousin by the arm and was propelling him from the cabin.

"You, stay put," Jared ordered over his shoulder to Merideth as he slammed the door.

Then he dragged Daniel along the passageway until he was sure they were out of earshot of the cabin. "What in the hell was that all about?"

Daniel jerked his arm and Jared let go of the silk sleeve. With infinite care Daniel smoothed out the ruffles at his wrist. "You always did think brute force the answer to everything, didn't you, *dear* cousin?"

Jared's jaw clenched. "I want to know what you thought you were doing back there. You and I both know Lord Alfred was going to traitor himself for money."

"Of course we do. But for some reason Lady Merideth wishes to be coy. So I shall simply have to do my job." Daniel took a small jeweled container from his pocket and pinched snuff between his thumb and finger. He breathed deeply, wiping the end of his nose with a lace-edged handkerchief. "How can you endure the smell down here, cousin?"

Jared resisted the urge to knock the snuffbox from his fingers. "What *job,* exactly, are you speaking of?"

"Charming Lady Merideth, naturally. She *is* in possession of information I want—you said so yourself. Obviously she doesn't respond well to threats and kidnappings or you would know the name by now. It's time a more subtle approach was used with the lovely lady."

"You said you'd stay away from her." Jared was having a difficult time controlling his anger.

"No, dear cousin. You ordered me to keep my distance. There *is* a difference." He slipped the snuffbox into his pocket and straightened his powdered wig. "I'm more experienced in these intrigues. I suggest you allow me to handle this."

"There's nothing to handle. I told you Dr. Franklin doesn't wish to know who the traitor is, and I also promised him I'd return Lady Merideth safely to Land's End."

"And I told you your brother was in Land's End when he died."

"That doesn't mean—"

"What I didn't tell you, dear cousin, is that he was also trying to discover the identity of the spy."

Jared paled beneath his sun-darkened skin. "What are you implying?"

"Not a thing . . . except I intend to do what I can to persuade Merideth Banistar to tell me what she knows."

"I don't want her hurt."

Daniel smirked. "I never imagined you did. She's quite lovely . . . and no doubt very passionate." He held up his hands when Jared reached out to grab him. "No need for violence, cousin. I have no intention of harming Lady Merideth. And as for your dalliance with her, you needn't concern yourself with me. 'Tis information I want. Nothing more."

Jared wished he could argue Daniel's words . . . deny his attraction to Merideth. But he couldn't. Anymore than he could overlook the circumstances of his brother's death. In the end he merely nodded and led Daniel along the companionway to the first mate's cabin. Padraic had volunteered to move his own things in with the boatswain while Daniel was aboard. Jared appreciated his friend's sacrifice; apparently Daniel didn't.

"Good Lord, is this the best you can do?" Daniel's gaze swept the small, windowless cubbyhole.

"Other than my cabin, aye. Which you are not

getting, by the by. You're on a privateer now. We haven't room for luxuries." Jared resisted the temptation to show his cousin to the berth deck, where the crew slept in hammocks. It would do Daniel good to cross the ocean like a common seaman . . . or maybe it would do Jared good to witness it.

"So I see," Daniel said, his expression full of disdain.

"You can always find other transport to America," Jared pointed out.

"Does that go for the guns and powder I've arranged for you to take to Charles Town?" Daniel asked slyly. "You needn't reply. I think I know the answer. Just remember, cousin. We're on the same side. Besides, I certainly didn't intend to insult your schooner."

Jared turned on his heel and walked out of the small cabin, leaving Daniel to flick dust from the narrow cot with his handkerchief.

The wardroom was empty, which suited Jared. He poured himself a tankard of grog and slumped down on a bench.

Was there a link between his brother's accident and Merideth? Daniel, for all his evasive answers and foolish smirks, seemed to imply as much. Jared took a deep swallow, backhanding the moisture from his lips.

Perhaps Daniel was right. Perhaps he was the one to deal with Merideth. His cousin could be all ingratiating smiles and sweet words.

Watching him earlier with Merideth had brought to mind times when Jared and his brother John shook their heads over Daniel's behavior toward the fairer sex back at Royal Oak.

"How could any female be taken in by him?" John had asked as they leaned against the broad, white-washed columns of Royal Oaks's front porch. Daniel was handing Millicent Waters into her coach, gushing over the sunlight sparkling in her hair and the blush of her cheeks.

When Jared simply shook his head, John laughed. "'Tis easy for you not to concern yourself. More often than not, the ladies prefer your handsome face and devil-may-care ways. But for me, 'tis a problem. Why do you think I've decided to go to France with Daniel? I want women to see me as a dashing hero."

Jared laughed and looped his arm around his brother's neck, promising to leave one or two beauties behind when he sailed the following day.

It was the last time he'd seen his brother.

The *Carolina* sailed with the evening tide and by nightfall was skimming along off the coast of France, searching for a westward wind. Jared stood on the quarterdeck long after the bo'sun piped the end of his watch. He told himself it was the beauty of the moon-drenched sails or the feel of salt-laced breeze stinging his cheeks that kept him above.

But he knew better.

Tonight he had nowhere to sleep except his own cabin. Tonight he could not slip ashore and rent a room at a dockside tavern as he had since bringing Merideth to Morlaix.

His crew thought the two had cohabited the cabin—and that's what he wanted them to think. And tonight the crew would be correct.

The prospect had caused him only minor concern . . . until today. Today he'd broken his own rule and talked to her . . . looked at her . . . and all the desire she'd evoked in him had come racing back. Racing back completely out of control.

He hated to think what would have happened today had Daniel not come below. But Daniel had knocked on the cabin door and nothing had happened, Jared reminded himself as he stared out over the trail of reflected moonlight leading to the horizon. His vow to himself was still intact. He would not touch Lady Merideth again.

His lungs full of tangy sea air, Jared headed for the hatch, assuring himself that his willpower was up to anything that came his way. He knew exactly where the hammock was stashed in the cabin, and could easily hang it from the hooks in the dark. The hour was late enough that Merideth was certainly asleep. And he would be up and gone before she woke. All in all, she'd probably never realize he'd slept in his cabin.

Feeling a bit smug with his planning, Jared made his way aft along the companionway. Tallow candles, their iron holders stuck in the bulwarks, lit the way. He was nearly upon his cabin before he noticed something amiss.

The door was ajar.

Though he doubted anyone on board meant Lady Merideth any harm, he'd instructed her to lock the door. He had the only other key in his pocket.

Fear raced through him as he rushed toward the open door. Fear that someone had managed to enter the cabin and hurt her. Jared reached for his sword and was quickly reminded it wasn't strapped to his side.

He rushed through the doorway slightly disoriented, to find nothing amiss. As his eyes accustomed to the darkness he saw Merideth, asleep on his bunk. No armed men lurked in the shadows.

As he watched, her eyes opened, and she sat up with a start.

"What . . . ? What are you doing in here?" Merideth grasped the blanket and pulled it under her chin.

"What am I doing?" Jared tossed up his hands in disgust. "I'm simply entering a cabin that anyone on this ship could walk into. Did I or did I not tell you to lock the door?"

Merideth angled her chin. "You did."

"Then why, pray tell, is it not only unlocked but wide open?"

Merideth took a deep breath, ready to explain, then stopped. He wouldn't understand. She didn't completely understand herself. She only knew that closed-up places made her skin prickle, and she didn't feel comfortable until she opened something . . . a door, a window . . . something.

He stood watching her for a long time, the light from the passageway spilling in around him. Then he turned and slowly, deliberately, shut the door.

"Don't—" Merideth started to protest, but caught herself. The room was dark now, so dark she couldn't make out the captain's form. But she could hear him moving about in the cabin. Merideth inched herself back against the bulwark, pressing her back into the rough wood.

The blossom of light as he struck flint surprised her. Carefully he lit the lantern suspended above his desk and moved to sit on the edge of the bunk.

Some of her panic disappeared when the cabin was bathed in light, but Merideth still had to struggle for control. The fingers that grasped the blanket were white-knuckled. He covered her cold hands with his own.

"This is what happened to you when I mentioned the cave, isn't it?"

Merideth didn't answer. She simply stared at him, her blue eyes large in her pale face.

"What is it? What scares you so?"

"I don't know." Merideth's words were barely a whisper.

"You're much safer with the door shut and locked." He was using reason, and Merideth admired him for it. Unfortunately she'd long ago learned that when it came to her fear, reason didn't work.

She shook her head, her gaze dropping to the bunched-up blanket in her lap, her hair forming a cascading golden veil.

"Merideth?" His hand on her chin forced her to look up at him.

"I don't know," she repeated. "I don't know what caused it . . . or how to fight it. I try. Don't you think I try?" Her teeth caught the soft, fleshy underside of her bottom lip and kept it from trembling. "I can't help myself from being afraid."

Jared reached out, pulling her into his arms . . . surprising them both. Her initial reaction was to protest. She raised her hands to his chest to do so, but the feel of him, so solid and strong, made her change her mind. He shifted, leaning back against the wall and pulling her across his lap. And she went readily.

"Are you frightened now?" Jared could feel the tension in her muscles and he ran a hand down her upper arm.

Merideth shook her head, then decided upon honesty. "A little. It's much worse when it's dark . . . and when I'm alone."

Jared made a noise as if he were pondering what she had said. He continued his caress until the tenseness seeped from her. "Is that better?"

"Yes." Merideth snuggled deeper into the folds of his loose shirt, reveling in his male scent and the strength of his hard body. In the security he offered.

"How long have you been this way?" he asked. "Frightened of a closed room?"

"I can't remember when it started. But the more she locked me up, the worse it got."

"Who? Who locked you up?"

"Miss Alice, my nanny. She didn't want me to disturb anything, so she locked the door. But I found the key and would wander about the hall while she slept. Except one day I found the caves."

"What happened in the caves?" She clutched his forearm, holding on tight. Jared didn't think she even noticed.

"Shouldn't have gone down to the sea. I was bad. Miss Alice told me it was bad, but I wanted to know." Merideth lifted her head, staring into Jared's eyes.

"You understand, though. I wanted to find out what it was like . . . the sand and the sea." Her voice thickened. "But the caves were dark and cold. And I couldn't find my way out."

She shivered and Jared wrapped his arms around her tightly. "What happened then?"

"They found me. It was the next day."

"At least you were safe."

"Yes." Merideth swallowed. "Mistress Alice was very angry. She locked me in my room, and this time I couldn't find the key."

The bitch. Jared found himself disliking the governess and berating the father that would allow such a punishment. "How old were you when this happened?"

"Eight. 'Twas my birthday." Merideth sighed and her lashes drifted shut. She was so very tired. She'd never told anyone of her fear . . . except her father. And he only laughed and made light of it. To be honest, she couldn't imagine why the captain didn't chide her for her foolishness. But he didn't.

And because of that she completely relaxed against him.

She was asleep. Jared tucked his chin and stared at the golden head resting against his shoulder. His arms tightened and she made a noise of contentment. He discarded his plan to shift her down onto the mattress and hang the hammock for himself.

At least for now. He'd hold her a while longer. As he did he thought of her childhood, of the punishments she'd endured. It was hard for him to imagine; he who'd grown to manhood surrounded by loving parents and siblings.

But though he found her descriptions incredible, he didn't doubt her. That in itself surprised him, and he fell asleep wondering when he'd started believing her.

Wakefulnes came in small, pleasant degrees.

Merideth was first only aware of a general feeling of contentment. It seemed strange. Then as her senses greeted the dawn she recognized a scent that she associated with desire. She also realized she wasn't that comfortable. Her neck was bent at an odd angle, and her head was resting against something hard. And her hip . . .

Merideth's eyes opened and she found herself staring at Captain Blackstone's profile. He was asleep, his black-as-coal lashes forming a crescent across his chiseled cheekbones. Even with the sea-green eyes hidden from view, he was so handsome. His nose was straight, and his sensual mouth with the full bottom lip was slightly open. Merideth lifted her fingers and very gently traced the curve of his black-whiskered jaw, barely touching him.

When she came to his chin with its cleft, she paused. What was she doing? Falling asleep on his shoulder was one thing. Apparently he'd taken it as an invitation to spend the night in the bunk with her—though by the looks of him, with his back pressed against the bulwark, he hadn't had a very comfortable time of it.

Touching him, if he knew about it, would make him think she wanted a lot more than a pillow for her head.

Yet she could scarcely resist. She looked again at his mouth and remembered what it could do to her. She lifted her hand, then hesitated, afraid to touch . . . afraid she wouldn't be able to stop.

"Please." The word was barely more than a breath whispered in the early-morning air, but it startled her. Merideth lifted her eyes to his, drawn by the desire she saw there.

"I didn't think you were awake." He caught her hand before she could pull it away. Then her fingers were pressed against his lips and Merideth felt herself melt.

Last night he'd felt a kinship with her, a deep caring. It had prompted holding her in his arms as she slept. And it had even overshadowed the desire that unfailingly ruled his emotions when around her.

But this morning he had awakened to her lying across him, her hair a tangle of gold, her caress feather-soft on his face, and he'd thought himself in heaven. He was almost afraid to move, lest he scare her off, this angel of the dawn.

He shifted, settling her more fully on the mattress, and lay on top of her. Her hand still cupped his face, but when she looked up at him her fingers stilled. Her breath caught and she swallowed. "I don't think we should—"

Merideth never finished her sentence. The hot hunger of his lips cut her off, made her forget what she'd planned to say. Her arms crept around his neck, pulling him closer, luxuriating in the feel of him, hard and heavy upon her.

What had started as a slow flame now exploded upon Jared with startling force. He couldn't seem to get enough of her. And she matched his passion, kiss for kiss.

He barely knew what he was doing as he yanked the tie of her shift and pulled it down, exposing her rounded breasts to his hands and mouth. She writhed beneath him and his hand delved lower, lifting the shift's skirt and burying his fingers in the moist heat between her thighs.

She climaxed instantly, her erotic moans flaming the blaze of his body even hotter. He kissed her—her lips, her cheek, the berry-hard tips of her breasts—and all the while their bodies moved in unison, aching to draw together.

Jared pulled away to shed his breeches, then unable to bear the separation settled his mouth on her smooth stomach. In his haste the fastenings proved difficult, but her hands were there too, urging him on, helping to free him.

They sighed in unison when his first thrust brought them together. His probes were deep, and grew more frenzied with each passing second. Jared felt his control slipping away, and then she arched, her body flexing around his, and he exploded within her.

How long they rode the stormy splendor, Jared didn't know, but when he finally collapsed by her side he was replete and exhausted. Drawing her close, smiling when she came readily, he fell asleep.

The call to arms, the loud rattling sound, woke him quickly. Years at sea had conditioned him to the speed with which he donned his breeches and shirt.

For Merideth the sound was frightening, for she'd heard it before and knew what it heralded. The thought of another battle, of the pain and suffering that accompanied it, shoved from her mind any embarrassment about their making love. She jumped up and grabbed her shift, yanking it over her head. By the time she stepped into her gown and was pulling it over her shoulders, she felt the captain's eyes on her. She couldn't help the flush that suffused her cheeks.

"Where do you think you're going?" Jared checked the priming in his pistol, then jammed it into his breeches.

"To the surgery, of course." Merideth barely took the time to glance up.

"Nay!"

"What?" Now she looked at him, moving into his path when he continued to ready himself and refused to meet her stare. "Why not?"

"Because I don't know what is going on. Maybe 'tis nothing." Jared shook his head when she began to argue, his unbound hair skimming the breadth of his shoulders. "I'll send Tim down to let you know." Grabbing up his cutlass, he headed for the door, pausing before he shut it behind him.

"Are you going to be all right?" He cocked his head toward the portal. "Can I close it?"

"Yes." Merideth gave him a shy smile. "Yes, I'll be fine."

He nodded, then rushed into the passageway, shutting the door behind him.

Merideth stood, her fingers twisted together, wondering if she spoke the truth. She could handle the door being closed. It was daylight, after all. But what of everything else?

250

She could hear the commotion from overhead; cannons rolled, men scurried to battle stations. But there was something else, something that resisted all efforts to make her "fine," as she'd told the captain.

She feared she was falling in love with him. And she didn't know what to do about it.

Chapter Thirteen

As sea battles went, Merideth decided, the one this morning was unimpressive. Not that she wasn't very relieved. The actual fighting lasted less than a quarter of an hour. Just enough time for the *Carolina* to fire a warning shot and the collier from Wales to strike her colors.

After that, the privateers made quick work of boarding a prize crew that set off for Morlaix with the captured vessel loaded with coal.

There was no fighting, no injuries, and for that Merideth was grateful. But there was no marked delay in their arrival time at Land's End. As strange as it seemed to her, that bothered Merideth.

No more than a sennight ago, her fondest wish was to return to Banistar Hall and put as much of this unpleasantness as she could behind her. But now . . .

Merideth turned her face into the breeze, shading her eyes as she stared toward the setting sun. She took a deep breath of salty air and sighed. Wind whipped through the sails, skimming the schooner ever closer to England. They would arrive off Land's End by nightfall, a mere twenty-four hours after leaving the roadstand at Morlaix. The fifty-or-so leagues that took three days to sail when traveling east passed quickly with the aid of the prevailing westerly winds.

Turning, she caught sight of Jared Blackstone standing on the quarterdeck behind her. Garbed in his usual dark breeches and loose-fitting white shirt, he made an impressive sight. His legs were apart, braced against the sway of the ship; his hands were clasped behind him. As she had earlier, he faced their destination.

But unlike Merideth, he seemed to harbor no regrets about reaching it quickly. Their one encounter since he'd left the cabin this morn, since they'd lain in each other's arms, was when he'd informed her she would be home by dawn.

Merideth looked away quickly when she noticed him shift. She didn't want to be caught staring. But her concern was unwarranted. He simply nodded toward his friend Padriac, who joined him on the quarterdeck.

"Here's the final reckoning on the collier's cargo." Padriac held out a rolled parchment to Jared. "'Tis likely to sell in France for a handsome sum." Padriac paused, the tally still in his outstretched hand. "Or then again we may all sink to the bottom of the channel."

"What? What nonsense are you blathering about?"

"I thought that might get your notice. What are you thinking about with such intensity? Or need I ask?" Padriac turned, giving an exaggerated nod to where Merideth stood by the rail on the deck below. "She's enough to make anyone's attention wander."

"Don't be ridiculous." Jared grabbed the parchment, ignoring his friend's grin as he unrolled it and began studying the figures.

"Are you telling me the lovely Lady Merideth wasn't on your mind?"

"I'm telling you my thoughts are damn well my own, Paddy."

Shrugging, Padriac ignored the rebuke. "What *do* you plan to do with her?"

"Take her ashore tonight and be done with it." It sounded so simple when he said it aloud. Why couldn't he convince himself it was for the best? Jared scanned over the figures, then rerolled the paper. Paddy was right. They'd made a hefty haul this morning.

He was right about something else too. Jared was thinking about Merideth Banistar earlier. He hadn't been able to think of much else all day. Hell, he hadn't been able to get her off his mind since that first night he'd met her. He looked toward Padriac and realized by his friend's expression that Paddy had spoken again; and again Jared had missed it. "What did you say?"

Paddy just shook his head. "You have it bad, my friend."

"I have nothing . . . good or bad. Now, what is it you were saying?"

"I'm only wondering what she's going to do all alone, with her father dead and all."

"She'll get by. Lady Merideth knows how to take care of herself."

"She looks rather forlorn."

Sparing her a glance, Jared admitted to himself that her stance could be interpreted as such, but he thought it unlikely. "More than not, she's thinking of returning to her home."

"All alone," Paddy reminded.

"You forget, I've seen her Ladyship in action. She managed very nicely in Passy. She had a small legion of dandies at her beck and call."

"Which I assume you took exception to."

"Which," Jared said, knowing he lied as he spoke, "didn't bother me at all. And don't give me that look."

Padraic spread his hands wide, an innocent expression on his face. The gesture irritated Jared, partly because it didn't fool him in the least, and partly because he did feel guilty about Merideth. He strode across the deck, stopping before he reached the ladder to the main deck. "See that a long boat is ready for tonight."

"Aye, Captain," Padraic said. But Jared could hear the Celtic humor in his tone.

When he reached the main deck, Lady Merideth was nowhere to be seen. Not that he sought her, Jared told himself. But he had thought to remind her they'd be going ashore about midnight. That way he'd avoid detection . . . hopefully. There was still a British noose waiting for him if he were ever taken on English soil.

But he didn't plan to be caught. He planned to take Merideth ashore, see her safely to Banistar Hall, and be back aboard the *Carolina* before anyone was the wiser.

That's why he was particularly annoyed to find Daniel waiting for him in the wardroom with a request.

"Nay."

"That's it? A simple nay. Am I to hear no explanation?" Daniel asked as he raised a pewter mug to his lips. "We are cousins."

"You're on board my ship, Daniel. A simple nay is all that's required."

"But it's imperative that I come ashore with you."

With an impatient swipe Jared brushed an unruly lock of hair from his forehead. "The only thing that's imperative is that I get Lady Merideth to Banistar Hall and reboard the *Carolina* without getting my neck stretched by a noose."

"Somewhere there's information about the traitor." Daniel shook his head, hurrying on before Jared could interrupt. "Now, I know you think Lady Merideth doesn't know the name . . . and I now tend to think you may be correct. But I can't fathom that Lord Alfred didn't leave something behind, some clue as to who the person is."

"Perhaps he did. But that doesn't change the fact that you're not going ashore. If there's a clue to be found, Merideth will find it."

"And put the wheels in motion again to sell the information like her father did? In the meantime, who knows how many lives may be lost while this traitor continues to sell information to both sides. Lives like John's."

Jared wondered if Daniel knew how effective that one argument was. "You said John's death was an accident."

When Daniel said nothing, Jared's hands tightened into fists. "Was it?"

"I need the name of the spy, cousin."

That was no answer . . . or was it? *Or* was Daniel using Jared's love for his brother to get his own way? "I'll give you half an hour in Banistar Hall, no more."

"I understand."

"If you've found nothing by the end of that time, we leave, and hope Lady Merideth does decide to sell the information if she finds it."

"Agreed."

Jared forced a gust of air from between his teeth, disgusted with himself that he'd given in so easily. But what the hell did it really matter to him? He *hoped* Daniel found the traitor. There were few people that he despised more than someone who would sell out his countrymen for profit.

The image of Lord Alfred moments before he was killed sprang to Jared's mind. *No one would suspect Merry. She has the name.* If that was true, she represented all he hated. Yet he couldn't hate her.

"Be ready by the end of the night watch," was all Jared said before leaving the wardroom. He stood in the passageway, indecision ruling his mind. He glanced aft toward his cabin, then shut his eyes.

There was no reason to seek her out. He sent Tim to tell her of the time they would go ashore. And after what happened the last time he was alone with her, he was better off keeping his distance.

Yet he couldn't.

Even as he clasped his hands and turned to stare toward the ladder leading to the hatch, Jared knew. With a deep breath he turned and strode toward his cabin.

The door was ajar, which didn't surprise him. What

258

did was that she didn't seem to notice him as he stepped inside and quietly shut the door. She was sitting on the cushioned window seat, legs drawn up beneath her skirt, her forehead pressed to the glass of the transom window. She made such a pretty picture against the backdrop of sea and sky, with her golden curls tied in a ribbon, that he was loath to disturb her.

But she must have sensed his presence, for she turned, a tinge of rose staining her cheeks as she stared at him.

"Nay." Jared held up his hand. "Please stay seated," he said as she started to rise. "I just came to . . ." What in the hell had he come for? He hadn't anticipated it would be this difficult to face her after last night. Even after the first time they'd made love it wasn't this trying.

"I came to tell you we'll be anchoring near Land's End soon. At the end of the night watch I'll take you home."

"Tim told me."

"He did." Jared clasped his hands behind his back. "That's good."

The silence spread uncomfortably. Jared staring down at her. Merideth sitting with her hands folded on the brocade silk of her petticoat.

"Well, then," Jared finally said. "I suppose that's it." He turned to leave, but paused, his hand on the latch when she spoke.

"Captain Blackstone."

"Aye."

"Our . . . our relationship has been rather stormy."

"Aye, it has." A grin softened his expression, deepened his dimple.

259

"When I first saw you, I thought . . . well, you know what I thought."

"That I came to do harm to your father."

"Yes." Merideth paused. "I'm still not certain why you did come to Banistar Hall." Merideth stood and shook her head when he would have answered. "Your contention that my father was a traitor is something I cannot . . . will not accept. Your own cousin, the man who sent you, can't even say he was." After pacing the width of the cabin, she turned to face him. "However, I don't believe you killed him."

Arching his brow, Jared leaned back against the door. "What brought you to that conclusion?"

Merideth couldn't help smiling. "I'm not sure." Her expression sobered. "But when I return to Land's End, I intend to discover who did murder him."

"Don't."

"I . . ." Merideth, who was expecting at least a word of appreciation for her admission that she believed in his innocence, was taken aback. "What are you saying?"

"I'm saying"—Jared moved across the cabin, grabbing her shoulders when she would have retreated from him—"I'm telling you to leave it be."

"But I—"

"Let it go, Merideth." His fingers tightened as he looked down into her blue eyes—eyes shadowed slightly by fear. Jared took a deep breath, knowing he should reinforce that fear, yet loathing to do so. He forced his hands to relax their grip. His palms skimmed the flesh-warmed silk of her sleeves as he turned away. "Go home and forget this ever happened."

"Forget this . . ." Merideth stepped in front of him, forcing Jared to meet her gaze. "How can you suggest such a thing? My father was murdered."

"And the same thing could happen to you!"

Her gasp made Jared lower his voice, but the intensity never left his expression. "It isn't safe for you to pursue this."

Merideth took a step back, then another, dread forming a tight knot in the pit of her stomach. Could she have been wrong to think him blameless in her father's death? "Are you threatening me?"

"Nay. Not I. But someone wishes you harm. At least someone in France did. I can't help but think it was related to your father's death."

"But that's ridiculous. No one—"

"The man who climbed in your window in Brittany, near Morlaix."

"A thief, but—"

"The runaway coach in Paris."

Merideth's eyes widened. "Ben told you of that? But it was only—"

"The highwayman outside of Passy."

"As you say, a mere highwayman. Regrettably they are a menace. However—"

"He was after you. Not money. Not jewels. You."

"How could you possibly know that?" Merideth stood still, barely able to breathe as Jared stared down at her. The color drained from her face when he finally answered.

"He told me. Moments before he was shot, he told me."

Held by the trance of his words, Merideth could do

naught at first. Then she swallowed. The soft rustle of silk sounded as she turned away. "You're saying this to frighten me."

"Hell yes." Jared looked down at his hands. "But that doesn't make it any less true." His eyes closed and he took a deep breath. When he opened them again she was staring at him. "If you have any information about a spy—"

"I don't!" Her eyes flashed in anger. "Is that what this is about? Frightening me into telling you the name of the traitor?"

"Nay." Reaching for her only seemed to fuel her anger. She jerked from his grasp and paced to the windows. When she turned to face him her color was high and her breasts heaved beneath the gold locket.

"I have told you repeatedly I know nothing about your traitor. My father knew nothing." She was less sure of this last statement but in her present state was willing to blame everything on Captain Blackstone. "He was killed because of you. Oh, maybe you didn't shoot the pistol, but it was because of you." Merideth took a deep breath. "You came to inform me when we'd be leaving the ship. I shall be ready." Merideth turned away, signaling his dismissal.

After a long pause, she heard him open the door. "And Captain Blackstone," she said before he left the cabin. She whirled about to face him. "After tonight, you needn't concern yourself with my welfare."

"If only it were that simple, Lady Merideth," he said before slamming the door behind him.

*   *   *

Merideth stared through the murky darkness toward Banistar Hall. Earlier, when the *Carolina* had weighed anchor, moonlight had limned the familiar cliffs near the manor. The sight had evoked a strong feeling of longing. But now clouds and fog shrouded all but the dimmest of outlines.

As she stood on the *Carolina*'s deck she could see no sign of the house itself. No lights shone through the tall casement windows. It was dark and dreary . . . uninviting. And Merideth couldn't control the shiver that ran down her spine as she thought of returning there. Alone.

"It won't be long till you're home again."

The sound of a voice so close in the shadows made Merideth jump. Pressing her hand to her racing heart, she tried to calm her panic.

"I *am* sorry. It was not my intention to startle you."

"Please. Do not trouble yourself over it. I'm afraid the mist and the waves against the hull . . . I simply didn't hear you." Merideth smiled over at Daniel Wallis, though she doubted he could make out the gesture in the dim light. She wasn't certain if it was remnants of her talk with Captain Blackstone or the sight of Land's End looking so foreign and dismal, but suddenly she felt frightened. Which was silly beyond belief.

She should be relieved . . . elated that this nightmare was finally over.

"Jared told you, didn't he, that I would be going ashore with you?"

"Yes." Merideth turned back and grasped the rail. It felt slippery beneath her fingers. He had mentioned it when he'd come below for her not twenty minutes earlier. "Captain Blackstone is seeing to the longboat."

"I know." There was a pause, during which Merideth heard him sigh. "Lady Merideth," he began, only to hesitate again.

"What is it?"

"I hope . . . well, I certainly hope this hasn't been too much of an ordeal for you. I mean, to kidnap a lady such as yourself . . . It's simply unforgivable."

"I've managed." Merideth twisted her head to look up at him. "I think it's my father who received the worst of it."

"Ah, poor Lord Alfred. Such a shame . . . a waste." He sighed again. "Sometimes my dear cousin gets carried away with his zeal for the cause."

"The cause? What are you saying?" Turning, Merideth faced him. Since they were anchored in enemy waters there were no lights on deck, so she had to move closer to see him. "Captain Blackstone swore he had nothing to do with my father's death."

"Oh, and I'm quite certain he didn't. I didn't mean to imply . . . Lady Merideth, let me assure you: if Jared told you he didn't kill your father, he didn't. I only meant that . . . well, he can get carried away at times."

"How do you mean?"

"He's told you of his brother, of course."

"He mentioned his brother to Dr. Franklin. They were acquainted, I believe. But what does that have to do with me . . . or my father?"

"Did you know his brother is dead?"

"Yes, but—"

"I can see you don't know the truth. I assumed . .

Well, you appeared so intimate." He moved his hand along the rail till it touched hers. "Please forgive me."

Merideth pulled her hand away. "What about Captain Blackstone's brother?"

"If Jared didn't tell you, then perhaps I shouldn't." He made a *tsk*ing sound with his mouth. "What harm could it do? It's hardly a secret that Jared had a twin, a brother older by mere minutes. John was his brother's name. They were devoted to each other, nearly inseparable, though they were nothing alike.

"John was born in frail health. Perhaps because of that, he loved books. Very learned. A member of the Royal Society." Daniel shook his head, the tiny droplets of mist from his wig spraying down onto Merideth. "No, John was nothing like Jared."

"I still don't understand what this has to do with me." Though the night was warm, a chill permeated through Merideth and she hugged herself. She swallowed. "What . . . what happened to him?"

"He was betrayed by a woman . . . an English woman."

"Betrayed and . . . ?"

"And killed."

Even though she'd anticipated the answer to her question, Merideth couldn't help her gasp.

"It was sad indeed to see Jared after we got the word. He blamed himself, of course."

"Why?"

"No one was sure. His sister couldn't reason with him. No one could. But it's the reason for his hatred of anything English. He vowed at the time to let no traitor—" Daniel stopped abruptly, giving Merideth

265

an embarrassed smile. "I've said too much. Please forgive me."

"No, really, there's nothing to apologize for. You've been very enlightening."

"Perhaps it's my cousin I should be apologizing for, then. He—"

"I don't think that's necessary, *cousin.*" Jared slipped up behind the two. "I believe I'm quite capable of apologizing for myself . . . if there is the need."

Merideth felt thoroughly flustered. She hadn't heard the captain at all. In truth, she was so caught up in Daniel Wallis's words that she probably wouldn't have heard him if he'd stomped up. But Daniel seemed nonplussed. He simply laughed—a sound Merideth found annoying—and clasped the captain on the shoulder.

Merideth noticed Captain Blackstone didn't respond in kind.

But the tense moment passed when Tim came up to say that the longboat was ready. Merideth, caught up in the moment, gave the boy a hug, which he didn't return at first. But just as she was pulling away, his arms tightened around her waist, and Merideth felt the sting of tears in her eyes.

There were things about the *Carolina* she would miss.

"Take care, Tim."

"Ye too, yer Ladyship." With those words he turned and scurried off, and Merideth sighed.

The trip from the *Carolina* to the beach at Land's End was wet and miserable. Down closer to the white-tipped channel waves, the fog seemed heavier, and

Merideth couldn't imagine how Captain Blackstone kept his bearings. The light from the lantern they carried hardly penetrated the mist. For a while the small boat with the three of them aboard seemed the only thing on the damp, murky earth.

Conversation was limited to the captain's rowing instructions to Daniel. It was obvious the latter was no sailor. But he did try.

Clutching the splintery seat, Merideth wondered if they'd ever reach land. Then, just as she was beginning to give up on the captain, the waves surged them toward a shore that Merideth could barely see. The captain leaped from the boat and dragged it further onto the pebbly sand.

Merideth was home.

She sat in the boat a moment longer waiting for the sense of relief to wash over her. It never came.

Daniel Wallis offered his hand, and with an undeniable feeling of unease, she took it.

Captain Blackstone obviously didn't plan on remaining on English soil long. "This way," he said, and headed off toward the steps carved into the cliff.

"It's dark as pitch. We'll never be able to climb these," Daniel complained, but Jared didn't slow his pace. "Well, at least let me position myself behind Lady Merideth. A fall down the side of this cliff could be deadly."

"All right." Jared stopped at the base of the steps and held the lantern aloft. "We'll take it slow."

Slow for the captain wasn't necessarily what Merideth considered slow. Her skirts got tangled about her legs and she yanked at them, trying to clear her feet and keep one hand free to clutch the bracken rooted in the crevices. It was hard work, but Merideth knew they were nearing the top. From there it would be an easy walk through the gardens to the house.

The light from the lantern bobbed above her. With a sigh she followed the captain's shadowy form up yet another stone step. It happened so quickly she barely had time to scream. Something tangled with her foot, pulling her backwards. Her hands flew up and in her mind's eye she pictured herself tumbling down the black, wind-ravished cliff to the beach below.

Then just as suddenly someone grabbed her arm, the force hurting her shoulder. Her knee knocked against an outcrop of rock, sending sharp pain through her body. The lantern flew past her, plummeting down the wall of granite.

"God, is she all right?" Merideth heard the frantic voice of Daniel Wallis below her.

"Aye." Jared clasped his other hand around Merideth's waist and pulled her up beside him. He had reached the top of the cliff just as he'd heard her scream. It was only luck that he'd managed to grab her before she fell.

Now she collapsed against him, her body trembling, and Jared pulled them both away from the edge of the precipice.

"What happened?" Daniel scurried over the top.

"I don't know." Merideth tried to calm her quivering voice. She was still bundled in the captain's arms, and wanted nothing more than to stay there. "Something tangled with my foot," she began. "I don't know. A branch, perhaps."

"Let's get to the house. Are you able to walk?" the captain asked, and though Merideth assured him she could, he kept his arm around her shoulder as they made their way through the garden.

It was obvious no one lived at Banistar Hall anymore. The place was overgrown and deserted. The front door wasn't even shut. Walking into the great hall was like walking into a tomb. Jared struck a flint and lit a burned-down taper left on the table near the door. When he held up the light, it spread grotesque shadows over the cobweb-laced ceiling and few remaining pieces of furniture.

Merideth could barely keep the tears at bay. She took a deep breath and headed for the stairs. In her room she'd be safe . . . at least for this night. Tomorrow she would see about hiring someone to help her. Of course, with no money that would be difficult. But she simply couldn't think about that now.

Before she had climbed three steps the captain was by her side, bringing the candle. "It isn't so bad," she said, more to convince herself than him. "I shall . . ." But there she paused, not knowing exactly what to say.

Her bedroom door was open, and when Merideth stepped inside she was greeted by scurrying sounds. Her composure cracked. Without another thought she turned and walked into Jared's arms.

Jared placed the candle on the stand by the door and held her. He wasn't sure if she was crying or not, but he felt she had every right to. His thumb angled her chin up, and in the flickering light he saw that her blue eyes were prismed with moisture. Her lips were parted, inviting, and Jared lowered his head.

He hovered for a moment, a heartbeat away, as their breath mingled. Then he was tasting her as he'd wanted to . . . as he always wanted to. His fingers delved into the thick golden hair and she moaned as his mouth forced hers open.

The kiss was deep, and passion exploded between them. Merideth melted against him, giving all the more because she knew this was the last time. Her hands burrowed beneath his shirt to touch the smooth, warm skin of his back.

When he pulled away they were both breathing hard. Jared stood for long minutes looking down into her eyes, and she tried to memorize every feature of his handsome face. For in minutes he would be gone.

Her mind was so disoriented from the night, the kiss, that at first she couldn't comprehend what he was doing when he grabbed her hand, pulling her from the room. "What . . . ? What are you doing?"

He had snatched up the candle, and Merideth could see a devilish grin lit his face as he led her down the hall. "I told you I've pirates in my past."

"Yes, but—"

"The blood must run true, for I find myself unable to control what I'm about to do."

They were at the top of the stairs, and Merideth grabbed hold of the newel, effectively slowing his pace. "What is it you're doing?"

The grin spread. The dimple deepened. "You should know by now. I'm kidnapping you," he said just before he tossed her over his broad shoulder.

Chapter Fourteen

"What in the hell are you doing?" Jared let Merideth slide off his shoulder, down the front of his body, as he stared into the library at Banistar Hall.

She had been too surprised to protest when he'd first hoisted her up. But now settled on the threadbare carpet, Merideth pummeled the captain's broad chest with her fists. "How dare you treat me like that again? I am *not* going anywhere with . . ." As Merideth realized he paid her words no heed, her voice drifted off and her hands stilled. He was looking over her head into her father's library. A gasp of shock escaped her as she turned around.

"I asked what you were doing?" Jared stepped around Merideth, who still stood, her mouth open.

Daniel hesitated only a moment longer, like a hare caught in the lantern light. Then he continued rummaging the desk, yanking papers from the drawers and flinging them onto the already littered floor.

"You said I could conduct a search," he said before

moving behind the desk to the one bookcase whose contents remained intact.

"*He* said! *He* said you could search!" The volume of Merideth's voice rose with every word . . . with every step she took toward the captain's cousin. "Who gave anyone permission to do anything with my things?" The way she felt now she could handle this pale imitation of his cousin, then turn on the captain himself.

"Jared," Daniel said as he took a moment away from leafing through a leather-bound book to glance toward Merideth. "Take care of her, please. I'm very nearly finished."

Crossing his arms, Jared made no move to intercept Merideth. She worked her way across the room toward Daniel, skirting the broken vases and overturned chairs that hindered her progress. "As it happens, Daniel," Jared stated calmly, "I think Lady Merideth has every right to be angry. Look what you've done."

"It was necessary." Daniel tossed another book onto the pile at his feet.

Merideth stooped to pick it up; then, holding the corners with two hands, she swatted at his arm. Strong hands grasped her around the waist, pulling her back.

"There's no need for that," Jared said. "Daniel, stop it."

Looking up from fanning through yet another book, Daniel raised his brow. "There's something you don't seem to understand, cousin." After rubbing his arm through the fine silk of his sleeve, he pulled another book from the shelf.

"I know you're obsessed with finding the identity

of this spy, but I think you're going at it in the wrong—"

"Lady Sinclair is responsible for John's death."

A strained silence settled over the ramshackle room. Merideth glanced at the captain in time to see the color drain from his sun-bronzed face. His jaw tightened, a muscle jumping from the force. His voice was low, obviously restrained. "Who in the hell is Lady Sinclair?"

"That, dear cousin, is what I'm trying to find out. Sinclair isn't her real name, of course."

"The spy is a woman?"

"Yes."

"But what does she have to do with John? His death was an accident." Jared's eyes narrowed. "You told me so yourself."

"I thought it best you believed that. I—"

"You thought it best!" Jared grabbed his cousin by the front of his fancy waistcoat. Seams ripped as he lifted him till they were nose to nose. *"You thought! What in the hell made you think you had the right?"* Jared sucked in his breath. His vision was tinged crimson and he tightened his fists. "You bastard. Tell me what happened to him."

The only response from the captain's cousin was a strangled plea. Merideth placed her hand on Jared's arm. She could feel the heat of his anger, the strength of his straining muscles. "Put him down, Jared." At first he seemed not to notice, but then he jerked his head around toward her. "He can't answer your questions when he's dangling in the air."

It appeared to take a moment for her words to burn

through the fog of his anger. He loosened his fingers and Daniel dropped to the floor, falling back against the shelf-lined wall. He caught himself and straightened, pulling on the front of his waistcoat and smoothing a trembling hand over his cravat. He looked up in shock when he noticed the ripped lace. "Was that show of brute force necessary, cousin?"

"You have thirty seconds to tell me about John's death or that display will seem tame in comparison to what I do to you."

Daniel lifted his chin in a gesture of defiance, but Merideth saw the beads of sweat forming on his upper lip. "Is it any wonder I kept the truth from you?" he said while fluffing the lace at his wrist.

Jared took a step toward him and apparently Daniel thought better of even token resistance, for he began his explanation, speaking quickly. "John was in England, at Penzance near here. He was visiting a fellow member of the Royal Society, someone he met while at Oxford. But the visit was a ruse. John was there to receive information concerning the British peace initiative and to discover, if he could, the identity of a spy known to us only as Lady Sinclair.

"She was selling information to both sides, and by doing so seriously jeopardizing our negotations with the French."

"Keep talking. I'm still listening." Jared crossed his arms, in part to control his urge to shake a quicker explanation from his cousin.

"There isn't too much more." Daniel paused, then quickly continued talking when he saw the thunderous expression on Jared's face. "He received the information about London's peace plan . . . from Lord Alfred, I believe."

"That's a lie." Merideth surged forward only to be stopped by Jared's hand clamping her upper arm.

"Go on," he said after giving Merideth a stern look. "What happened next?"

"I received a post from your brother mentioning he was staying at Land's End longer than planned. At first I believed he had discovered a lead about Lady Sinclair. But after rereading the letter I changed my mind. He'd met a woman and, I think, fallen in love with her."

"What drew you to that conclusion?" Jared couldn't help being surprised. His serious-minded brother was much more at ease with a book or a scientific experiment than with members of the fairer sex.

"The post referred to her often. He spoke of her beauty. Called her his angel."

Jared's gaze cut to Merideth's. She returned his stare with wide blue eyes. Angel eyes. But she said nothing.

"Her name," Jared said. "What was her name?"

"He never mentioned it. I wrote back to him, urging him to leave England. The longer he stayed on enemy soil, the more dangerous it became that someone would realize his real reason for being there." Daniel sighed, pursing his lips in thought, then shaking his head.

"I received only one more correspondence from John . . . and that didn't reach my hands till after word of his death."

"What did it say?"

"I've found Lady Sinclair."

Jared let out the breath he didn't realize he was holding. His eyes blinked shut and he turned to stumble heavily into the chair by the desk. After a few minutes he looked up. "And you think Lady Sinclair killed him?"

"I can't be certain, but yes, I think he discovered her identity and she killed him."

"And Lord Alfred?"

"Somehow he knew also. He contacted me in France." Daniel paused. "He was desperate for money. So desperate he would have sold out almost anyone." His pale eyes rested on Merideth.

She held his gaze, only breaking contact when she felt the captain's eyes upon her too. "This is ridiculous," she said. "My father wasn't a traitor." Her tone was insistent, but in her heart she wasn't sure she spoke the truth. She wasn't even certain if the doubt she read in the captain's green eyes had aught to do with her father.

Unable to tolerate the accusation in his expression, Merideth turned on her heel. She was halfway across the library when the captain's booming voice made her stop.

"Where do you think you're going?"

She refused to turn around. Closing her eyes, Merideth said. "To my room. You gentlemen can find your own way out when you're finished . . . ransacking my home."

Before she knew what he was about, Merideth felt a hand clamp around her elbow. She tried to wrench away, but the captain held her firm as he propelled her into the hallway, closing the door behind them.

"What do you think you're doing?" Merideth managed as she was half dragged, half prodded up the stairs.

"You wanted to go to your room. I'm taking you. But hear me well, Lady Merideth. I'm not leaving here without you."

"Well, I'm not going with you." Merideth broke away from him as they neared her room. Gathering her skirts, she ran, managing to enter ahead of him. Using the weight of her body, she tried to slam the door in his face, but with one hand he thwarted her attempts. "Leave me alone," Merideth cried, finally giving up and retreating toward the window.

"Are you the woman?"

He stalked ever closer, his big body seemingly swallowing up all the space in the room. "Answer me, dammit. Are you the one?"

"What woman? I don't know what you're talking about." Merideth tried not to show how frightened she was, but her sob was self-incriminating.

"My brother's woman. The angel. Did my brother love you?"

"No." Merideth's back met the solid barrier of the wall and she stopped. "I never met your brother. I swear."

He stood towering over her, his eyes searching her face; for what, Merideth wasn't sure. But she didn't look away. She couldn't.

Finally he grabbed her hand, pulling her toward the chifforobe. "Pack some clothes. I'll be back directly."

"I said I'm not going!" Merideth yelled, but she spoke to an empty room. He'd already gone, slamming the door. As Merideth stood, trembling, her balled fist against her mouth, she heard the unmistakable click of the lock.

"Why in the hell didn't you tell me this sooner?" Jared burst into the library in time to see Daniel throw the last book from the shelves onto the floor.

"I thought it better you didn't know." Daniel turned a calm face up to Jared's fulminating gaze.

"*You* thought it better!" Jared took a threatening step forward. "You know who killed my brother and you thought it better I didn't know." His tone was incredulous. "I should tear you limb from limb for this."

"If you think that will do any good, go on." Daniel glanced around for something else to search. Seeing nothing, he sank into the closest chair. "No one has ever doubted your bravery . . . or your love for John. But there are times both border on being foolish."

"What in the hell does that have to do with you keeping the identity of John's killer from me?"

"Besides being brave, you're impetuous and head-strong." Daniel held up his hand when Jared would have interrupted. "And you have a temper that too often burns out of control. Fine-enough attributes for a privateer . . . but not for a spy."

"Damn if I wish to be a spy."

"Exactly." Daniel leaned back in the chair. "However, if I'd told you about Lady Sinclair's connection with your brother, you would have insisted upon storming in and—"

278

"And what? Ruined our chances of finding the bitch's identity? If you recall, that happened anyway. *You* sent me here anyway."

The shoulders of Daniel's ice-blue silk waistcoat lifted with his shrug. "That couldn't be helped. I needed an envoy. And as you just pointed out, I didn't really keep the name of John's killer from you. We don't know who Lady Sinclair is."

Jared's thoughts sprang to Merideth. He couldn't help himself. He'd asked her if she was the woman his brother had loved, and she'd said no. At that moment he believed her. But did her innocent eyes and fiery kisses sway his judgment?

His mind's eye conjured up a picture of her as she was in Passy. Beautiful, refined, on the arm of a French dandy. She looked as if she could be very much at ease with intrigue.

"So you see, I decided not to tell you until we found who killed him. Believe me, it was never my intent for the guilty woman to go unpunished."

His cousin's words brought Jared back to the present. He nodded and blew air out through his mouth. "I still wish you would have told me. I'm not all brass and bluster. There may have been something else I could have done." His brow wrinkled. "The man John was visiting in England . . . the scientist. Perhaps if I—"

"I've already sent an agent to inquire . . . discreetly, of course. He's apolitical. Too interested in his inventions to be bothered with anything else. He apparently didn't even realize John was missing until he wished to discuss an invention with him. Besides"—

Daniel gave the room one more cursory glance before leading the way to the hall—"you can't stay in England. It will do your brother no good for you to hang."

What Daniel said was true. But Jared couldn't simply leave now that he knew about John. "Don't concern yourself. I shall be careful, and when I discover who killed John I'll—"

"No!" Daniel turned on his cousin. "You will do nothing of the kind. I told you I've made inquiries. There's nothing else to be done here. The important thing now is for me to return to America with word of Dr. Franklin's progress in France. And to take the guns and munitions to Charles Town."

"I can't just leave."

"You must." The flickering light from the candle he held cast an eerie glow across Daniel's angry features. "This treaty with France is what John worked for. He'd want you to finish what he began. And . . ." Daniel lifted a finger. As the lace fell away from his delicate wrist, he pointed at Jared. "I assume you're taking Lady Merideth with us."

"Aye." Jared's eyes narrowed. "Why?"

The lift of Daniel's shoulders was nearly indiscernible. "Perhaps if you weren't so . . . blinded by her beauty, you wouldn't need ask."

With that, Daniel settled into a chair and crossed his slender legs. The soft glow of polished silver twinkled from the toes of his shoes.

Jared turned on his heel and headed for the wide, curved stairway. He wanted to protest that his thinking was perfectly clear when it came to Merideth Banistar, but, Lord help him, he couldn't. The sight of her, the smell, the taste had become an obsession that he seemed unable to shake.

Did it *blind* him to reality? To the fact that she might be a spy? Might be the infamous Lady Sinclair herself? He wanted to believe her innocent. But as Jared took the steps two at a time he knew he would have to find out the truth for himself.

But how? Torture was out of the question. For one thing, he didn't think he could order it done, even suspecting she might have killed his brother.

The method was obvious.

Seduction.

A campaign of gaining her trust. Of making her believe he would do anything for her. That might lead him to the truth. Lead him to his brother's killer.

Seduction. The very thought made him hard as he rounded the newel post at the top of the staircase. It scared him how eager he was to put his plan into effect. Lure the moth to the flame. But which of them was the moth?

He gave the paneled door a cursory knock before fitting the brass key into the hole. She had lit a candle and was standing by the window. The window she'd managed to open. Neither of those things surprised him. Jared had regretted locking her in the moment he did it. But his choices had been few.

She looked up when he entered and shut the door, her expression defiant. "I shan't go anywhere with you. This is my home and I intend to stay here. You allude to some danger, but I don't think . . . What are you—"

Merideth didn't even get a chance to finish her question before his mouth molded to hers. Her gasp allowed his tongue inside and he thrust it deep, filling her completely.

His body pressed her back, till she was pressed between the wall and him. She could feel his hardness against her stomach as he continued to make love to her mouth . . . sipping, biting, sucking her lower lip between his teeth until she could do naught but make small whimpering noises of surrender.

When his lips left hers, Merideth sucked in air, all thoughts of protest driven from her mind.

"I want you with me," Jared said as his fingers skimmed the lace edging of her bodice. A flick of his wrist and one breast was free, its extended nipple rucked and begging for his touch. And touch it he did, first with the pad of his thumb, then the tip of his wet tongue.

Merideth's knees gave way, and if not for the strength of his body pressing her into the solid wall, she would have melted into a puddle on the threadbare rug.

Moist heat surrounded her breast and Merideth arched forward, silently begging for more. He heard. He answered. As Merideth fingered the rough silk of his hair, cradling his head to her chest, he fought his way through layers of petticoats.

Without preamble he cupped her mound, stroking between the folds with his finger. Like a spark to dry tinder her body convulsed. Her eyes glazed and the only sound coming from her slack lips was the litany of his name.

"My God, you're so hot and wet." Jared tore at the

front of his breeches. He buried his face in the curve of her shoulder, deep in the softness of her sweet-smelling hair as his first thrust joined them.

Their united sigh of contentment soon gave way to heavy rasps of breathing. Breathing that came as fast and hard as the push of their flesh to come together. Jared's hands skimmed down her body, down the skin-warmed silk covering her ribs. Sorting through her skirts to find the soft fullness of her buttocks was impossible, so Jared grasped handfuls of silk and lace, lifting her up and around him. She clung to his shoulders, and their lips met in an erotic kiss.

And all the while he filled her, each soul-consuming plunge deeper than the last. When she began to quiver, Jared's own release exploded. It rocked through him and seemed to last forever.

When he could think again, Jared lowered her slippered feet to the floor. Her eyes were closed, but she opened them slowly when her skirts slipped down around her legs. Her expression was one of disbelief. Jared was certain it matched his own.

Dropping his head, he rested his forehead against hers, his hands flat against the watered-silk wall. "I'm not leaving without you," he said, his voice low and husky. He thought he heard her sigh . . . or sob, he wasn't sure which, but she said nothing to his pronouncement.

Jared left her against the wall, and after rearranging his breeches he moved to her chifforobe. She'd packed nothing, and so for the second time in his life Jared found himself assembling an array of women's clothing. The glance he spared her showed that she'd settled onto the window seat and was leaning against the deep casement. She looked as drained and debauched as he felt.

He found a small trunk that looked as if it had seldom been used, and stuffed several gowns and petticoats inside before closing the lid and hefting it onto his shoulder. When he crossed the room and reached for her hand, Merideth seemed to pull herself from her lethargy.

"I can't just go with you," she said in a tone that Jared knew she thought was sensible. But he ignored both the tone and the sense behind it.

"You can and you are. Now, I still have a shoulder free if you'd like me to toss you over it."

In the end she didn't require such drastic measures. But even though she followed behind him, carrying the candle to light their way, Merideth continued to expound on the reasons she must stay. All for naught. For like his pirate ancestor, he gave her no choice.

The moon, momentarily freed from the blanket of clouds, cast silvery shadows across Banistar Hall as Merideth glanced back. The walls looked tall and imposing . . . imprisoning. Daniel, the captain, and Merideth were making their way across the garden, walking single file along the overgrown paths, when she stopped. Expecting a terse order to hurry along from the captain, who was behind her, Merideth was surprised when he too paused.

"You'll return," Jared said, though he wasn't sure he wasn't promising something he couldn't deliver.

Merideth stood perfectly still a moment longer, the wind swirling ribbons of hair in her face. She was staring . . . remembering. With a sigh she tilted her head toward Jared. "I'm not certain I wish to," she said before resuming the trek toward the cliff.

They climbed down in the same order as their assent. Jared went first, followed by Merideth, then Daniel. There were no near-accidents. Once, close to the bottom, Merideth's leg brushed against a root. She sucked in her breath, expecting the same feeling of tree limbs snarling about to entangle her legs. But it didn't happen. And the more she thought about the snaring from before, the more it bewildered her.

By the time Daniel reached the rocky beach, Jared had settled Merideth in the longboat. The inky sea was choppy, with crowns of frothy white skimming the swells. 'Twas a foreshadowing of a storm brewing to the east . . . a storm that sent the wind whipping through Merideth's hair and fluttering her skirts.

A fast-moving squall . . . on them before they knew what was happening. What had begun as a simple trip from Land's End to the *Carolina*, became a race against time.

"Keep it straight," Merideth heard the captain yell above the thud of waves splashing against the sides. Lightning raged across the sky, etching the captain in bold relief, his muscles straining against the wind-plastered shirt.

Then the rain began, a deluge of skin-prickling pellets that immediately soaked the three occupants of the longboat. They were almost to the *Carolina*. Merideth could make out the skeletal stand of its mast through the sheets of falling water.

She clutched the seat, digging her fingers into the

splintery wood, holding on as the small boat rocked and heaved into the next trough of sea. Salt water sloshed in the bottom of the boat and Merideth no longer tried to raise her slippers above the wet. It was simply too deep.

"Get the bucket!" At first Merideth didn't realize this growled order was meant for her. But with the next flash of lightning she could see the captain shouting her way.

"I don't know . . ." The wind carried the remainder of her words toward land, but Jared apparently knew what she meant, for he yelled for her to search the bottom of the boat.

Slipping down on hands and knees, Merideth braced herself against the ribs and felt about till her hand closed around a rope handle. "I found it!"

"Bail!" came his snapped command as he bent his back into the next swollen wave.

She made little progress against the steady stream of water that splashed over the hull, but at least her efforts kept her too busy to think. Merideth supposed she should be thankful for that. She was so frightened. Surrounded by open air and still she was frightened.

Were they moving toward the *Carolina*? Merideth couldn't tell. Over the angry rumble of the sea she could hear the captain yelling at Daniel. It wasn't until a web of lightning seared the sky that she saw the hull of the schooner looming beside them.

Then there were more shouts, this time from above. Merideth glanced up, protecting her eyes from the rain with the curve of her hand. Lights bobbed overhead, spilling murky circles of yellow on the ochre-sided ship.

"A rope. They've thrown over a rope." His voice faded as he maneuvered the longboat around toward the *Carolina*'s hull. "Grab hold, Merideth."

But the words were barely out of his mouth before the boat tilted and Daniel lunged toward the dangling hemp. Balancing himself, he twisted the rope around his waist, knotting it frantically, then giving a yank. The crew above lifted, and he used his shoes to keep him from banging against the hull.

By sheer luck, the next rope fell nearly in Merideth's lap. She clutched at it just as a wave smashed the longboat against the hull.

"Hell and damnation," she heard the captain yell above the splintering sound. "Wrap it around your waist," he ordered, "while I try to keep this thing still."

"Still" was obviously a relative word, for they were bobbing all over the place, one minute cracking against the *Carolina*, the next pulling away.

"Not without you." Merideth clutched the slick hemp and crawled toward the bow of the longboat.

". . . hurry . . . up. Tie it!"

"I said . . . not going without you." Merideth fell to her knees as a swell swamped over them.

He barely hesitated before pulling in the oars and grabbing the rope. The longboat seemed caught in a vortex, spinning uncontrollably. For one hideous moment as he lashed the rope around his waist, Merideth saw herself being left on the sea to drown when the longboat sank.

Before she could voice her fear, he stood, lurching to the side, and circled her body with his arms. "Hold on tight, your Ladyship," he yelled as he gave the rope a yank.

Merideth wrapped her arms around his neck as they were lifted, swaying with the yaw of the ship and the fickle wind. She tried to strengthen her grip, linking her legs with his, and her wet skirts tangled with his feet. They were suspended in air, surrounded by water. It poured from the heavens and surged beneath them, ready to swallow them up.

Her sob was born of fear and involuntary . . . a mere extension of her rasping breath.

"Hang on, Merry—" His last word was punctuated by a grunt of pain as they banged into the side of the ship.

The impact jarred her arms loose from their grip around Jared's neck. If not for his bruising hold on her waist, she might have fallen. But she didn't, and within moments she felt herself being lifted. Members of the crew had hauled them close enough to grab them.

It didn't matter that strong hands were pulling her over the rail to the safety of the deck; Merideth found it difficult to give up her regained hold on the captain. When they were both standing on the wave-swept deck and being bundled in blankets, she wanted to sink into his arms.

But there was much to do. Merideth was hustled below deck by Tim, who took her straight to the captain's cabin. Where Jared Blackstone went, she didn't know. The storm raged the rest of the night, finally blowing itself out as the first tinges of pewter softened the line between sea and sky.

She'd spent a fitful night, tossing and turning near as

much as the ship. But with the onset of calm, Merideth fell into a deep sleep. Something, a sound or presence, awoke her and she blinked open her eyes to see the captain silhouetted in the open doorway. The light from the passageway outlined his body as surely as the wet clothes he still wore.

He looked tired and bedraggled, a soldier who'd fought the storm and won. But a victor not without wounds. He stepped into the cabin, his feet bare on the wooden deck, his broad shoulders slumped. And Merideth pushed to sitting. She held the blanket to her chin with one hand as she propped herself up with the other.

"Do you mind if I shut the door?" he asked, his voice low and scratchy.

Merideth shook her head. Strands of golden curls, tangled from drying without benefit of brushing, fell across her cheek. She'd kept the door open last night, for she couldn't stand the thought of being closed in with the tempest raging. But now, with the captain in the room with her, the fear was as fleeting as a wisp of smoke fading in the breeze.

His eyelids drooped, the thick tangle of lashes forming a crescent that partially hid the dark shadows of fatigue staining the skin beneath his eyes. "Do you mind if I . . . ?" His words trailed off, but it was obvious by the tilt of his head that the bed was what he desired. His hair was loose from its ribbon, still damp, and dark and sleek as a raven's wing in the sun.

"Oh, of course." Merideth scooted to the bottom of the bunk, pulling the wool blanket with her. She planned to slide off the end, but he sat down on the bed, catching the blanket beneath his body.

"You needn't leave. There's room for us both."

Perhaps so, for the bunk was large, obviously made to suit his size, but . . .

"If it's your virtue you fear for, you needn't. I'm too tired to take advantage of even you."

Not sure if she'd heard a tinge of sarcasm in his words or not, Merideth sat still a moment longer. After all, her "virtue," what there'd been of it, had been welted a deathblow against the wall in her bedroom.

But she still had her pride.

He may have demonstrated more than once that he could make her forget all else with just the touch of his lips, the subtle caress of his fingertips. A small voice inside her warned that sharing a bed with him voluntarily was something else again.

Yet she couldn't make herself rise. He pulled the damp cotton shirt over his head and she just sat and stared at the strong muscles crossing his back. He shifted, slipping the breeches over his narrow hips, and her mouth went dry. When he lifted his hand to reach for her, Merideth lay down beside him, cuddling close beneath the blanket and closing her eyes.

Chapter Fifteen

The uncomfortable sensation of something tightening around her neck woke Merideth. She swallowed and her eyes flew open.

"It's pretty." Jared brushed the pad of his thumb across the intricate design etched onto the locket. Sunlight slanted through the transom window, reflecting off the gold nestled in his hand. "You wear it all the time?"

"Yes." Merideth tried to ignore the effect of his warm fingers against the sensitive skin of her chest. "It was my mother's." All she had left of her mother.

He leaned further over her, supported on one elbow, and the ribbon that held the locket tightened at the back of her neck. "Pretty," he said again, but this time she didn't think he referred to the necklace. He turned his hand and spread his fingers, then slowly lowered his hand from under the locket. The oval slid onto her skin, the gold hot from his touch, and Merideth let out a breath she didn't realize she was holding.

His hand drifted lower, beneath the blanket, the middle finger following the valley between her breasts. His thumb and little finger rode the crests till they spanned her pouting tip to pouting tip.

Merideth's breathing deepened, and she wet her suddenly dry lips. His gaze was on her, holding her in its sea-green depths.

"You, Lady Merideth, are trembling. And naked."

"My . . . my clothes were wet."

"Mmmm." He nuzzled the blanket away with his chin, and Merideth's eyes drifted shut. His whiskers, shadowy dark, abraded sensually. "I'm glad," Jared informed her as his hand trailed lower, taking the blanket with it. "I've never really seen you . . . Not in the daylight."

Merideth's eyes popped open and she reached down to cover herself—he'd managed to expose her to just past her navel—but he was quicker. Clasping her hands in one of his, he transferred them high above her head. "I haven't had a good . . . look yet." He inched the blanket lower. Cool air licked at her body, but the intense heat of his eyes kept her from feeling the chill.

His head lowered, the untamed hair feathering over her breasts, and he kissed the soft skin of her stomach. Merideth sucked in her breath, and her head lolled to the side. That's when she noticed his maneuverings had left him as exposed as she.

He must have realized it too, for when he raised his head, a devilish grin creased the dimple in his cheek. "It would appear we can both see what we're about this time."

She wanted to push him away, to tell him she had no

intention of lying here with him, of seeing anything. But the truth was, she couldn't. He was beautiful to her, all dark hair and steely muscles. Strong and powerful. As much as she wished it weren't so, she was addicted to him, to his touch.

He slid down her body, pausing briefly to whisper his lips along the curve of her hips. Merideth could barely breathe in anticipation of what was to come. Her stomach grew taut. He slid his hands beneath her bottom, which raised up to meet him. Closer, ever closer. His breath fanned the tight, golden curls. And when he touched her, when his open mouth touched her heated flesh, Merideth thought she would die from the exquisite pleasure.

His tongue danced over her, slowly, sensually, and then, as she began to writhe, more aggressively. She quivered, her body tight, her skin flushed. Then over the edge she fell. As the storm caught her, shattering all but a modicum of reality, Merideth called out his name. Over and over again.

He bent over her, his eyes glazing a path down her body. "You're beautiful," he said, his voice low and husky. And Merideth felt beautiful, and more exposed than ever in her life.

She touched him then, her fingers curling in the hair covering his chest, inching ever lower. Sweat broke out on his forehead and he squeezed his eyes shut when her hand wrapped around his thick staff. She stroked. She caressed. And all the while he swelled, pulsating with need and desire.

"Merry." The word gritted between clenched teeth. His hand covered hers, held for a moment, tightening her grip. Then he pulled them both away.

He poised above her, the only contact that of their locked gazes. Then he plunged, deep and strong. Merideth cried out and wrapped her legs around his body, holding him closer. He filled her completely, then withdrew slowly. Again and again.

Merideth arched to meet him and his pace quickened. Powerful thrusts that stroked and sent her spiraling toward the heavens. His mouth found hers, hot and open, and he clung to her as his climax swept him away.

Then he could do naught but collapse on her, his face nestled in her hair, his mind registering only the sweet scent of her surrender.

He'd tried to bring her to a fever pitch, to make her want him more than reason itself, and he had. He had back at Land's End. And he had again this morning. But there was a price to pay for such total and consuming passion.

And the price had been him.

His desire. His need for her was as overwhelming as hers for him.

Jared lay in the cradle of her body while threads of reality filtered into his brain. To seduce her, to make her so susceptible to him that she'd tell him all she knew, required some finesse on his part. Finesse that eluded him whenever he was around her.

Pushing to his elbows, Jared pulled away. He was still firm, with very little effort could make love to her again. But that would be for him. Not for any other reason. She appeared fully debauched and satiated.

She didn't speak as he yanked the blanket over her

and turned to wash himself with the bucket of seawater near the door. He wondered if she watched him, but hadn't the nerve to turn and see for himself. Instead he rubbed his skin dry with a piece of linen and dressed quickly in clean breeches and shirt.

It wasn't until he reached for the latch that she spoke. And then her voice was so soft he barely heard her. "What's to become of me?" she asked, and Jared swallowed before turning to face her.

"When you've dressed you can come on deck. Unless I say otherwise, you've the run of the ship."

Merideth held his stare, never flinching till he turned and left the cabin. Then very slowly she turned her head toward the bulwark and let the tears flow.

Jared sat at the rough-hewn table of the wardroom, elbows bracketing a pewter trencher of salt fish and sea biscuits. He leaned forward, his head held in his hands, but it wasn't the platter he saw. It was Merideth Banistar's pale face. The way she'd looked at him when he'd left his cabin.

With a muffled curse he dug his fingers through his unbound hair and slanted back in his chair, his long legs crossed beneath the table. He'd forgotten to tie back his hair, but then maybe it had been a conscious omission. He preferred it loose, with the sea breeze blowing through it. It made him feel wild and invincible.

Perhaps it was the pirate blood that flowed through his veins, he thought with a grimace. He blamed too much on the blood of an ancestor. Jack Blackstone had been a pirate true, but one who had given up the rogue life to become a respected planter.

Still, if he was going to act the pirate, he might as well look the part. And he most certainly was acting the pirate.

Kidnapping.

Ravishing a woman.

Shaking his head, Jared conceded that he hadn't forced Merideth to make love to him. But what he'd done was almost as bad. He knew the effect he had on her—the same she had on him. And he'd used that knowledge.

Jared sucked in air and shut his eyes. Could she be the woman who had betrayed his brother? The "angel" of a woman?

"There you are. I've been looking for you everywhere."

Planting his chair on all four legs, Jared stared across the table at his cousin. His jaw tightened. "Aye. Here I am."

"I was just on deck." Daniel paused to pour himself a mug of grog. "It appears we weathered the storm all right."

"Aye, we did."

Daniel hesitated momentarily while sliding onto the bench facing the table. A single candle shone through the glass panels of the lantern gently swinging overhead. "Do I detect a note of disapproval in your tone, dear cousin?"

"I don't recall seeing you after we came aboard the *Carolina* last night. We could have used every man during the squall."

296

"I was below . . . trying to stay dry. I'm not much of a sailor, I'm afraid."

"Not much of a gentleman either." Jared leaned back in his chair, never taking his attention from the man across the table. Daniel drew himself up, obviously taking exception to Jared's assessment.

"Pray tell on what you base that judgment." Daniel lifted the mug and sipped at the brew. When he finished he dabbed at his lip with the corner of a lace-trimmed handkerchief.

"That first rope sent over the side last night was meant for Merideth. You took it without a second thought."

A smile spread across Daniel's face. "Is that all? You think I didn't treat your paramour with enough respect?"

Jared was out of the chair so quickly it flipped back, crashing onto the wooden deck. Palms flattened on the table, he leaned toward his cousin. He spoke each word calmly, in sharp contrast to the agitated rise and fall of his powerful chest. "What she may or not be to me is not the question here. Merideth Banistar is a lady and thus deserves our respect and protection. A Blackstone never—"

"Ah, but there's the rub, dear cousin. We both know I'm not a true Blackstone. You pointed out as much yesterday, did you not?"

Jared hesitated only a second before pushing away from the table. "It was a mere slip of the tongue. I was angry at the time."

"Of course, your temper. Something we've all learned to tread softly around. But I think yesterday was more a matter of declaring a spade a spade. A bastard is not something you call someone who lays valid claim to the title . . . unless reminding him of the fact is your goal."

"Damn you, 'tis not true and you know it." Jared's fist came down on the tabletop. "We all decided— John, you, and me—that your parentage was better left a secret."

"Yes." Daniel played with the lace on his sleeve. "We can't have anything mar the good Blackstone name."

"That wasn't the reason."

"Don't try to tell me it was to spare me the humiliation." Daniel's face grew crimson with rage. "I know better."

"You and Aunt Rose. Aye, 'tis true."

"Ah, dear mother and her deathbed confession. She could no longer live with the horrid secret of my conception. Of course, she no longer had to live period. She could just tell her dirty little story and die." Daniel stopped fiddling with the ruffle and looked up at Jared. "While I . . . *I* had to live with the knowledge that I was a bastard. And I couldn't even conceal this bit of bad business and keep it to myself. She chose to bear her guilty soul in front of the two people I most wished didn't know."

"We never threw our knowledge up to you."

Daniel shrugged. "Perhaps not. But I knew what you thought of me."

Turning away, Jared paced the small room. "You're wrong about several things." But right about a few too, Jared thought, though he wouldn't admit it. "First of all, Aunt Rose did not have a guilty soul . . . a tormented one, perhaps. And John and I never held what she told us against you."

They'd all three been thirteen when Aunt Rose died. Jared and John's parents were in Charles Town. Aunt Rose never went to town. She claimed not to like the people. And she was still in mourning. She'd been in mourning for near fourteen years, ever since her husband had died.

She must have loved him very much. Jared remembered once hearing his mother and father talk about it. They didn't know he was in the library as they stood beneath the open window. The story was bittersweet. Rose had gone to Newport for the summer season, as was the custom among wealthy Carolina planters. While there she met Alexander Wallis. Met and married him before the family knew a thing about it. She was afraid they wouldn't approve, Rose said when she returned to Royal Oak, pregnant, her husband dead. Alexander was only a tradesman. But she had loved him and she mourned. His mother had shaken her head sadly. "'Tis such a shame that it affected her mind so."

They all grew up—John, Jared, and her son, Daniel—knowing Rose wasn't quite right. But no one ever doubted the truth of Rose's story until the day she didn't come back from her ride across the lowlands. Riding was the one thing Rose enjoyed, so there was never a thought of confining her. But John especially was concerned when twilight darkened the sky and she wasn't safely ensconced in her room.

The cousins saddled horses and went to look, following her path through the frost-covered grass. They found her horse first, calmly munching grass.

Then they saw Rose, looking like a spilled ink blotch on the ground. Her black veil fluttered as they bent to lift her up.

"He's after me. He came back to get me." A crimson stream trailed from the side of her mouth.

The boys tried to tell her she was safe. There was no one else about, but she wouldn't believe them. In agitation she clutched her son's hand. And that's when she bared her soul. When she told of the rape those many years ago and the lie she'd lived since. The rape that had been Daniel's conception.

"Be that as it may . . ." Daniel's words brought Jared back to the present. "I realized yesterday when you called me a bastard that you—"

"I called you a bastard as I would call anyone who'd lied to me as you did."

"I explained my reasons."

"Dammit, John was my brother. I had a right to know what happened to him, and why."

"And by whom."

Jared dragged his fingers back through his hair. "What's that supposed to mean?"

"Come now, Jared. We're both thinking the same thing. A woman who looks like an angel. Who else could the mysterious Lady Sinclair be but Merideth Banistar?"

Jared's fists clenched. "I don't think she is."

"You don't want to think she is." Daniel stood. "Is she *that* good in bed?"

Jared's fingers were clutching the front of his cousin's waistcoat before either of them realized what was happening.

"Look at you," Daniel said. "You're as foolish as your brother was, letting a pretty face fog your reason." Jared let go and Daniel straightened his clothing. "Am I the only one who can keep his wits? You curse me for not giving the lady the rope. Why should I? She's English, for God's sake, and most likely a spy to boot. Or have you forgotten?"

"Nay." Jared turned away. "I haven't forgotten." He took a deep breath. "And if she had anything to do with John's death . . . I'll find out about it."

"And you'll tell me?"

"And I'll take care of her myself."

It was midafternoon before Merideth decided to go on deck—and then only at Tim's insistence.

"Come on, yer Ladyship. 'Tis a lovely day it is. Sunny and bright, a pleasure after last night."

"I'm comfortable here . . . really." Merideth settled back further on the cushioned window seat. She had washed and dressed earlier. All her clothes the captain packed at Land's End were lost, presumably sent to a watery grave along with the deserted longboat. But luckily the gowns she'd brought with her from France were still in the cabin. She wore a simple frock of blue with roses embroidered on the underpetticoat. Her hair was brushed, and tied back in a matching blue ribbon.

She was presentable.

She had no excuse to stay below in the stuffy cabin.

Except . . . she was hiding.

From Captain Blackstone.

When the reality of what she was doing hit her she

301

stood, calling out to Tim as he was taking her dinner dishes from the cabin.

"I think I shall take a stroll above deck." She was going to have to face the captain sooner or later. And she might as well get it over with. Besides, though she'd thought to discuss . . . things with him privately, she now decided it better to confront him in public.

After patting her hair and straightening her skirt, she marched over toward the door. "I'm ready," she announced, and followed a bewildered looking Tim into the passageway.

The sun was warm, the wind crisp, as she stuck her head up through the hatch. Merideth had accompanied Tim to the galley with the tray, and now finished climbing the ladder so he could come up too. She tried to glance about casually—the captain wasn't up on the quarterdeck—but apparently Tim noticed her surveillance.

"There he is," he shouted, and pointed toward the rigging.

Shading her eyes with the back of her hand, Merideth looked in the direction Tim indicated. The sails shone blindingly white in the sun. Squinting, Merideth tried to figure out why Tim had pointed her in that direction.

Then she saw him.

High in the rigging, perhaps twenty feet up, bare feet tangled in ropes, one hand holding onto a spar, he stood. His hair, cast blue-black in the light, whipped in the wind. He was shirtless, which explained the sun-darkened skin of his upper torso that Merideth had noticed this morn.

"What . . . what is he doing up there?" Merideth pressed her palm to her chest. He looked so vulnerable with nothing but hard deck and endless sea beneath him.

Tim had grabbed up a long stick and was pushing a brick-shaped stone around the deck, scrubbing the wood. He glanced up and shrugged. "Looks like he's fishin' a spar."

"Fishing?" Merideth knew something of the sport, and it wasn't usually done from such an altitude.

"Fishin', aye. He be fixin' it. Musta cracked last night durin' the storm. He's usin' an old oar as a splint." Tim leaned into the handle and surveyed the rigging. "Look yonder. Chet's doin' the same."

Merideth spared a glance toward the other seaman before her attention returned to the captain. "Isn't that . . . dangerous?"

"Aw, not when your a seafarin' man like Cap'n Blackstone. Could do it in his sleep, if'n he'd a mind to, I reckon."

Merideth didn't care if he could do it in his sleep; watching him move around that high up was frightening. She moved toward the capstan, closer to the captain, and called up to him. "Captain Blackstone." The wind caught her words and carried them aft, away from him. The next time she yelled.

"Aye." Jared hung onto the spar and looked down to the deck. Lady Merideth, her skirts flapping in the breeze, stood staring up at him. Her expression was anxious, which surprised him almost as much as her seeking him out. He thought after this morning she'd be avoiding him like the plague.

"I'd like a word with you, if you don't mind."

"About what?"

Merideth glanced around to see if anyone was listening. All the crew members on deck seemed busy with some chore or another. Many of them seemed to be making repairs to the ship. "It's rather private, if you don't mind."

"Private, huh?" With the heel of his hand Jared shoved a wooden wedge beneath the lashings to tighten them. Then he swung down the shrouds, hand over hand, landing on the deck directly in front of Merideth. "Perhaps we should go below if you've something private to discuss."

Merideth took a step back. He stood before her, big and broad-chested, smelling of sun and sea air and sweat. She swallowed, trying to ignore the tangle of damp curls that spread from armpit to armpit and arrowed down to his breeches. And, Lord help her, she knew how the hair thatched out, forming a nest for his manhood.

"No," she said, then cleared her throat because her voice sounded husky. "I think our discussion can be had here, above deck."

Jared shrugged. "'Tis all the same to me."

"Fine." Merideth crossed her arms. "I wish to go back to Land's End. I can't imagine what came over me last night to leave so readily, but I—"

"Nay."

"What . . . ?" The captain strode to the rail and Merideth followed. "What do you mean, nay? Surely you can't be serious about taking me to the New World."

"I am."

"But why? And don't give me that poppycock about someone trying to kill me. That simply isn't true." At least she hoped it wasn't. Granted, she'd had a run of accidents in France—but they were certainly not the result of someone trying to murder her. Who would want to see her dead? Regardless, those incidents were behind her now. A haunting memory of her foot tangling with the underbrush—the frightening moment when she knew she was falling—came back to her. But she pushed it aside to concentrate on what the captain was saying. He turned to face her and Merideth was struck again by the unexpected clarity of his green eyes, so light compared to the thick fringe of black lashes.

"All right," he said, agreeing quickly with her assertion that there was no killer after her. "What of the fact that your home is deserted. You have no money. Nothing."

"I can manage." Merideth watched as he shifted his stance to look out over the sea. "I can." She had felt less sure the previous night when surrounded by the hauntingly empty manor. But now she recalled that except for the servants she'd been alone at Banistar Hall most of her life. Surely she could handle everything if she could just get him to take her back. But his next words made her grip the polished railing.

"It makes no difference. We've cleared the channel and are on our way across the Atlantic. I couldn't take you back now even if I wanted to." He swept her with a green-eyed gaze that sent heat curling through her stomach and lower, before adding, "And believe me, I don't want to."

Merideth swallowed and took a deep breath to bolster her resistance. "That's it, isn't it?" Her voice lowered, although a quick glance about showed that no one was within hearing distance of them. The crew moved about busily, too occupied to care about their captain and his . . . Merideth couldn't imagine what word they would use to describe her.

Jared's dark brow arched. "What is it?"

"You're keeping me because of . . . because of what we do," she finished in a rush.

"What we do?" Now both brows were raised.

"Don't play stupid with me. You know very well what we've been doing." She moved closer, and though her tone was irritated, her words came out as barely a whisper. "In Passy . . . last night in my bedroom . . ."

"Ah, that." Jared's lips turned up in a sardonic smile. His long, thin finger centered on his chin and he tapped the indentation there several times. "Correct me if I'm wrong, but I believe there were other times we made love. In my cabin this morning. We very nearly did in the coach and—"

"Would you be quiet?" Merideth grabbed hold of his arm, pulling his hand away from his face and causing his smile to deepen. She swept the deck with her gaze. "Do you think I want everyone to know? Besides, we did *not* make love."

"Really?" Again Jared turned to study the vast expanse of glistening white-capped waves. "What would you call it?"

"Madness," Merideth answered without hesitation.

"Madness, and it has to stop." For several long minutes, while Merideth contemplated the harsh lines of his handsome face profiled against the backdrop of sea and sky, Jared said nothing. When she could stand it no more, Merideth continued. "Well, don't you agree?"

"Nay."

That single word, softly spoken, sent Merideth's heart pounding. She dug her nails into the railing. "I refuse to allow you to continue your—"

"My what? Ravishment? Rape?" Each word hung on the air like a raindrop, crystal clear and open for examination. They both knew neither described what he'd done.

"I won't force you, Merideth." His eyes searched hers. "But I won't make any ill-advised promises either."

"What of your contention that I'm a traitor? Surely you find that repugnant enough to cool your ardor."

"I find where my *ardor* is concerned, who you are or what you are makes very little difference."

She couldn't look away. Merideth swallowed and tried to concentrate upon her breathing rather than the desire she saw in the green depths, but it did no good. She wanted to lean into him, to melt into the hardness of his body. Even here. Right on deck, surrounded by his crew of privateers. Why had she thought herself safe from him as long as they weren't alone?

A maverick gust of wind caught hold of Merideth's hair ribbon, tossing it across her lips. She turned her face into the breeze, breaking the hold of his gaze, but the sensual spell he wove still surrounded her. Knowing

307

she was retreating and not caring, Merideth took one step away from him, then another.

Merideth cleared her throat. "All that I ask is that you give me someplace to sleep . . . someplace other than your cabin."

"I'm afraid 'tis impossible."

"But—"

"The *Carolina* is a privateer, Merideth, not a packet. Space is limited. Passenger space is nonexistent."

"I don't care where I have to sleep."

"You would if I put you in the hold, or down with the crew. But the question is moot. I shall sleep elsewhere until . . ."

"Until?"

He shrugged, giving her a knowing smile. "Until we reach Charles Town."

Merideth had the strangest feeling that that wasn't what he really meant, but she ignored it. "When will that be?" There were British troops in the colonies, she knew that. Once she reached land she would find them and somehow make her way back to England. Things were bleak, but there was hope. At least Merideth thought so until the captain answered her question.

"It will take us five weeks at best, more likely six to make the Carolina coast."

Six weeks. How was she ever going to stay away from him on this tiny ship for six weeks?

She would have worried even more had she been able to read Jared Blackstone's mind as he watched her walk away from him on the sun-drenched deck.

He may have had some difficulty keeping his wits about him when he'd looked into her blue angel eyes, but some semblance of logic had returned. And with it came Daniel's description of the woman responsible for his brother's death.

Beautiful.

Angelic.

Was it Merideth Banistar?

She seemed innocent, with her sweet face and guileless expression. But the woman who had betrayed John was wise to the ways of deceit. John may have been naive about women, but he was intelligent, and committed to the cause of liberty. He would have kept his guard up unless he'd trusted someone implicitly.

Unless he had believed in her innocence.

Jared's fingers fisted. He knew Merideth Banistar to be innocent in some ways—at least she had been until she'd encountered Jared. She'd been a virgin when he'd first taken her. Jared was certain of that. But he was just as certain that John would not have pressed the woman he loved to fulfill his physical desires. If it was Lady Merideth that he'd adored—and Jared intended to find out one way or the other—John had done it chastely. John was too much the gentleman, ruled by a creed that Jared never could quite understand . . . or live up to.

For, unlike his brother, Jared had no intention of keeping his distance from Merideth Banistar. Mayhap he'd acquiesce to her request that he sleep elsewhere— for the moment. But he planned to be back in her bed soon.

And he planned to be invited.

Chapter Sixteen

Days on board the *Carolina* weren't as bad as she'd imagined. To be honest, Merideth thought today was exhilarating. She leaned into the rail, watching cottony white clouds form shapes.

Turning her face into the stiff breeze, she took a deep breath of salt air, realizing how much she enjoyed the open feeling on deck. She didn't even mind the cramped cabin anymore. Whether it was the row of windows along the transom or the knowledge that the morn would bring a chance to go above deck, Merideth now slept with the door closed.

Shutting and locking the door had nothing to do with wanting to keep Captain Blackstone out.

"As if a locked door would do any good if he really wanted in," she mumbled to herself, then glanced about to make sure no one had heard her. The men of the forenoon watch were busy with their duties, some high in the rigging, others repairing sail and rope, or scrubbing the deck.

Merideth rested her chin on the heel of her hand, her elbows firmly planted on the polished rail, and sighed. The truth was Captain Blackstone showed no desire to enter his cabin. For which she was extremely grateful, Merideth reminded herself. Still, it was strange the way he ignored her. And had for the sennight since their last conversation. The one when she'd warned him away.

He neither slept in nor visited his cabin. If there was something he needed, a chart or clean shirt, he sent someone, most often Tim, to fetch it for him. If Merideth passed him on deck, he nodded, and spoke, but of nothing personal. And he always kept on his way.

Twisting her head aft, Merideth adjusted the old wide-brimmed hat Tim had lent her when she'd discovered several sun spots across the bridge of her nose. She stared at the captain, who was standing spread-legged on the quarterdeck. If she were to climb the ladder and go up to him right now, he would probably make some polite comment, then stride away.

Not that she intended to go to him, of course. Forcing her attention back to the rolling sea, Merideth decided she'd had quite enough of Captain Blackstone.

But the rest of the crew was fine . . . for American privateers. They'd been so many places, and with the tiniest bit of encouragement they shared tales of foreign ports and exotic lands. Just last night Mr. Keefer, the ship's bo'sun, a wiry fellow with a face as brown and wrinkled as a walnut, told her a story about the time he was attacked by pirates in the Caribbean. He—

"How are you this morn, Lady Merideth? I trust you slept well."

Shutting her eyes for a moment, Merideth forced a smile on her lips and turned to face the one person on board the *Carolina* that she truly didn't like . . . except for the captain, she quickly reminded herself.

"Good day, Mr. Wallis."

"Daniel," he said with an ingratiating smile. "You agreed to call me Daniel."

"So I did." He had been telling her of the vast lands in Carolina at the time. The plantation called Royal Oak, where he lived. Where Captain Blackstone lived as well. Though Daniel hadn't revealed that bit of information, she'd remembered hearing it from the captain earlier.

"We're blessed with uncommonly good weather today," he said, resting his lace-edged sleeve on the rail.

"Yes."

He moved closer. "I wonder if you've given my proposal any more thought."

Merideth couldn't help a glance toward the quarter-deck. The captain was still there, engrossed in talking with Mr. Pochet, the ship's carpenter. But though he couldn't hear them, it surprised her that Daniel Wallis would bring up this subject now. Of course, it had surprised her from the beginning.

He must have sensed her unease, for he waved his fine-boned hand in the air. "You needn't worry about Jared. He takes the running of his ship much too seriously. He hardly knows what else goes on."

"Still, I should think if he heard of your offer to help me . . ." Merideth let her sentence drift off, for she couldn't imagine what the captain might do. Any more than she could fathom why his cousin had made the proposition.

"Poppycock." Daniel shook his perfectly dressed hair, sending a shower of powder onto the padded shoulders of his puce silk waistcoat. "I've a feeling Jared would be secretly pleased. He tends to run off impulsively doing things, then finding himself in a quandary as to how to rectify matters."

"He doesn't strike me as the wavering type."

"Precisely why he gets himself in trouble. For instance, I'm sure he sees the error in his ways concerning kidnapping you, but he's too stubborn to admit it. Believe me, in the end he'll be grateful I've taken care of the problem. He always is."

"I see." Merideth didn't like being referred to as a problem, but she supposed that's what she was, at least in the captain's eyes.

"Now, I obviously can't do anything until we reach port, but once we're in Charles Town I shall be able to see to your safe return to England."

"How are you going to do that?" Merideth had some vague idea of contacting the British army herself once they reached America, but she didn't know exactly how to go about it. Apparently Daniel didn't plan to tell her either.

"I have my ways," he said, his green eyes, so like his cousin's, veiled in secrecy. "You forget that I know

314

many people in the government."

"Do you mean, I forget you're a spy?" The affable expression on his face dissolved, to be replaced by a mask of restrained anger. "Actually, I haven't forgotten," Merideth continued. "Nor have I forgotten that you accused me of being the same."

"'Accused' is hardly the correct word."

"You implied, and please don't deny it," Merideth added when he again shook his head. "You implied that I was this infamous Lady Sinclair. The woman responsible for John Blackstone's death."

He seemed momentarily stunned to silence, but shook it off quickly with a delicate shrug. "Perhaps I did hold some doubts about you."

"Please don't tell me you've seen the error of your ways, for there's been nothing done to change your mind."

"True enough. But I've decided we'll all be better off with you back in England . . . regardless of your political activities."

"We?"

"The Americans, because you can be bought and we can use the information you provide. Myself, because I intend to be the go-between for that information. And you, because once you reach Royal Oak, if Jared even suspects you are the one responsible for his brother's death, he'll kill you."

Air left Merideth's lungs in a rush. "I . . . I don't believe you."

"Don't you?" His winged brow lifted. "Neither of us is certain he didn't murder your father, now are we?"

315

He paused, but Merideth couldn't deny his words. The expression of triumph on his too pretty face made Merideth feel physically ill . . . or was it the fear that he might be right?

"Just be watchful, Lady Merideth. And remember I shall be here if you feel the need to discuss this further." With a bow deep enough for the grandest ballroom, Daniel Wallis backed away, leaving Merideth shaken and clutching the rail.

"You seem to get along famously with my cousin."

Merideth didn't know how long she'd stood staring out to sea, but the sound of the deep, familiar voice startled her. She turned, hand to her chest, to look into the sea-green eyes she knew so well. "What . . . what do you mean?"

Jared shrugged, his powerful shoulders lifting beneath the billowing cotton of his shirt. He glanced away to break the hold of her eyes, but looked back when he spoke. He'd seem them talking, watched them bend close. And all the time he'd thought of the woman who'd betrayed his brother. "It just appeared that you were discussing something of great importance."

"Perhaps Daniel offered to help me escape you."

"Did he?"

Merideth stepped forward, aware of how much she longed to tell Jared exactly what his cousin had said. How anxious she was for him to deny everything once more and assure her that he had taken her from

316

England only for her own protection. Even if that was a ridiculous excuse, she wanted to hear it was his.

But could she believe him? Merideth didn't know. And he didn't seem inclined to convince her.

When she turned away, Merideth realized it was in part because she was beginning not to care. The heat of his body seemed to pull, till she wanted to forget everything but how it felt to be held in his arms. She clutched at her locket as she would a talisman. "I hardly think I need answer to you about anything. If you want so badly to know what Daniel said to me . . ." She leveled her gaze on Jared. "Ask him."

Jared met her defiant stare, then turned on his heel. He didn't look back until he'd climbed down the hatch, and then she was well out of sight.

On deck Merideth sucked in her breath, letting it out slowly. She let go of the brooch, using her free hands to hug herself. She was losing her mind. There was no other explanation. There had been a time when she'd thought herself falling in love with the captain.

Now, knowing what she did, with all the more reason to distrust him, she still couldn't rid herself of those feelings. If anything, they grew stronger.

At least the desire for him did. She couldn't close her eyes at night without him invading her dreams. She thought of him constantly, excessively. Of how it felt when he touched her, when he whispered her name . . . when his body joined hers.

Stepping away from the rail, Merideth shook her head. Her blood ran hot and her heart raced. She had to stop this. To stop thinking of him. But she had five more weeks confined on board the *Carolina*. And then she'd be with him at his plantation.

Unless . . .

Maybe Daniel's offer *was* a good idea. Maybe it was the only thing that made any sense.

"I don't think you're paying much attention."

"I'm sorry, yer Ladyship. Truly I am. I guess I just don't have it in me to study none today."

"Today?" Merideth tilted her head and looked at Tim over the book on the captain's desk . . . the book he attempted to read. "You haven't had your heart in our lessons since we began."

"Aw, now that ain't true, Lady Merideth."

After closing the copy of Payne's *Observations on Gardening,* Merideth crossed her arms. She had been on the *Carolina* only a few days when she'd had the idea of tutoring Tim. Padriac was busy and had let his sessions with Tim slide. And since Merideth had plenty of free time, she'd volunteered to teach the boy.

Nonexistent was a good word for her own formal education. However, before most of the books were sold to pay off his debts, her father's library, begun by earlier Banistars, had been the best in the area.

Merideth, who'd spent much of her time alone, had learned to devour the books . . . the ones she could understand, that is.

Helping Tim seemed the perfect idea. At least it did to her.

But now that she recalled it, Tim's initial reaction

318

hadn't been very enthusiastic. He'd given some excuse about the captain needing him, which had made Merideth annoyed with Captain Blackstone. She'd been ready to go to him herself when Tim had assured her he would.

"I shall be glad to talk to him," she'd said. "I'm sure he will agree to the lessons." Actually, she hadn't been at all certain.

But Tim had insisted he should be the one to broach the subject with the captain. And knowing how tenuous was the trust between her and Captain Blackstone, she'd agreed.

Merideth had been elated when Tim had approached her the following day with word. The lessons were fine with the captain. Fine, but apparently he wasn't enthusiastic about her tutoring, for Tim sure wasn't. Reading ahead and making lessons had been a good way to keep her mind off Captain Blackstone. Now she saw this diversion threatened.

Her mouth flattened.

"I suppose we have Captain Blackstone to thank for this."

"Aye, yer Ladyship. I reckon we do."

Taking a deep breath, Merideth resisted the urge to march out of the cabin and head for the quarterdeck. She'd tell the captain a thing or two. Instead she smiled at Tim. "You can't let Captain Blackstone's reluctance keep you from learning." The boy's expression showed confusion, and Merideth continued. "I realize I shouldn't talk about the captain, but he doesn't know everything and—"

"That's just what he said."

Merideth's brow creased. "What who said?"

"The cap'n. He said there was a lot a things he didn't know. Things ye could learn in books."

"There you are. He admits it. Then he should be the first to want you to read."

Tim screwed up his face. "I reckon he is."

"He . . . But why is he opposed to the lessons?" She had a feeling it was because she was teaching them.

"He ain't. *I'm* the one who don't like 'em none. The cap'n, he said I *had* to do 'em."

"Captain Blackstone said—"

"Captain Blackstone said what?"

Merideth's jaw dropped open as the subject of their conversation strode into the cabin. Learning he had forced Tim to take the lessons was surprising enough, but now to see him back in the room that he'd avoided for a fortnight bewildered her. She tried to answer, but found her words shaky. "We were just . . . well, we . . ."

"I was tellin' her what ye told me about learnin', Cap'n."

"I see."

"Yes." Merideth straightened her shoulders. She refused to allow him to intimidate her. They might be in his cabin, but they certainly weren't alone. "Tim seems to blame both of us for his lessons."

"Hmmm." Jared closed the door behind him and walked into the room. He rubbed his chin as he leaned over the desk and flipped open the book. "Seems to me the word should be 'thanks,' not 'blames.'"

"My thoughts exactly." Merideth retreated behind Tim, laying her hands on his thin shoulders. The cabin seemed suddenly crowded and the air insufficient for breathing.

"Aw, Cap'n." Tim twisted about to glance over his shoulder. "Yer Ladyship. It ain't as if I don't like the learnin'. It's just . . . well . . ."

"You'd rather be scampering about above deck," Jared finished for him, smiling when he saw the relieved expression sweep over Tim's freckled face.

"Aye, Cap'n, I would."

"Then I think that's what you should do."

"Thank ye, Cap'n."

"But what of his reading? Are you simply going to ignore that?" She and Tim both spoke at once, but Merideth kept going after the boy paused. "I can't believe you're just—"

"Wait a minute." Holding up his hand palm out, Jared silenced Merideth. "Neither of you let me finish. First of all, I understand how you feel, Tim. So during the day, you can carry out your duties on deck."

"Oh boy." Tim tried to stand, but Jared's hand restrained him. Merideth pulled her own fingers away when they brushed against his.

"But in the evenings, you report to my cabin for lessons," Jared continued. "That is, if it suits Lady Merideth." His eyes searched hers questioningly.

"Yes. That would be fine."

Jared's gaze lowered to Tim, who had resumed his chair. "And you have to show more enthusiasm for your lessons, or they get moved back to the day." He held out his hand. "Agreed?"

Tim stuck out his hand. It was immediately swallowed up by the captain's. "Ye've got yerself a deal, Cap'n." Tim wriggled out of the seat. "Can I go now?"

"Aye. Tell Mr. Delany I said you're to help with heaving the log."

It was obvious to Merideth as she watched Tim hustle from the room that this was one of his favored activities. It was also obvious that she was now in the cabin, alone with the captain. And he seemed in no hurry to leave.

Settling into the chair Tim had just deserted, he flipped through a few pages of the book, reading a line here and there. "This was my brother's," he said when he finally closed the pages. The heel of his hand rested on the leather cover while he traced the gold-embossed title with a fingertip. "He did love his books."

Merideth, standing safely behind the chair, watched the almost caressing movement of the captain's hand. He leaned forward, his broad back bent. Though he'd tied his hair with a leather thong, the sea wind had loosened some ebony strands. They waved down the column of his sun-browned neck, making him appear vulnerable. Merideth resisted the urge to lay her hand on his bent head and pull him to her breast.

"I never met your brother," she said, swallowing when he twisted to look at her. Merideth caught her lower lip between her teeth and forced herself not to shift her gaze away.

He was the first to break the hold of their stare. When he did, it was to reopen the book, and Merideth let out a breath. "He was brilliant," Jared said. "There was a sort of laboratory in one corner of his room. My mother used to say he would most likely end up burning down Royal Oak." He paused to chuckle. "One time he nearly did. We had to pour water from the pitcher and the slop jar on the fire to put it out."

"The slop jar?" Merideth couldn't control the giggle that escaped her.

"Aye. At the time it seemed preferable to fulfilling Mother's prediction."

Pushing away from the wall, Merideth settled on the window seat. It was to the captain's side, and about as far from him as she could get in the small cabin. "Did you . . . did you work with your brother?"

"Nay." Jared shook his head. "He'd oft try to capture my interest with his experiments. But I never could sit still long enough to understand what he found so interesting about plants." He seemed to prove his restlessness now by standing and walking around the desk. He leaned his hip into the scarred wooden corner. "There was many a time I feigned interest, though," he said with a grin that made Merideth's stomach flutter.

"You must have loved him very much."

The smile faded, leaving but a ghost of his dimple. "Yes, I did."

"I don't know anything about his death," Merideth said, the words rushing out before she could stifle them. His expression changed, from sad to something she couldn't define. He pushed away from the desk and came toward her, his pace reminding her of a stalking animal. It was all she could do not to bolt to the side and run from the cabin.

When he loomed over her, Jared smiled again. "I came below to see if you'd care for a walk above deck. The day is exceptionally clear."

"A walk?" She'd strolled on deck every day since they'd left Land's End, and he'd never accompanied her. Why now did he feel the need? Before Merideth could begin to find an answer, he took her hand and drew her up till she stood nearly plastered to his body. His scent of fresh sea air and musky male drifted about her.

Her breath caught. Of its own accord her head tilted up; her lips parted. She could only stare into the depths of his black-fringed green eyes. His kiss was not unexpected. His slow descent gave her plenty of time to pull away. His tongue filled her mouth, swept the deepest recesses till a moan escaped her.

As always, the fire of desire started not as a slow burn but an explosion of emotion. An explosion that had her ears buzzing. Her limbs felt weighty and weak, and it was with great effort that she dragged her arms up and around the strong pillar of his neck.

When she did he jerked her closer, pressing his hard strength into her softness.

"Oh God, Merideth," The words seemed dragged from his soul as Jared tore his lips from hers. His hand cupped the back of her head, tangling in the thick fall of golden curls, and he pressed her to his heart.

Closing his eyes, he swallowed, trying to steady his breathing. It wasn't supposed to be like this. He was supposed to be in control. His plan . . . his damn plan depended upon gaining what information she had. Seduction was the only way open to him.

It should be fairly easy. He was no fool. His effect on her would be obvious to any but a green boy . . . which he definitely was not. He had to no more than touch her to spark her reaction. But what he hadn't counted on was the way she drew him into the web of passion.

The visit to his cabin was calculated. A moment of togetherness after two weeks of holding himself at bay—a fortnight of watching her and wanting her. The kiss was an afterthought.

Or perhaps it was the moment he first lost control.

Regardless, the impact of his desire hit him instantly, like a squall on a calm afternoon. Within seconds of touching her, all thoughts except having her fled his mind.

It was not his usual way of dealing with women. But he found nothing about Merideth Banistar was usual.

Leaning back, he separated her from the front of his shirt. Her reluctance to leave caused a tightening in his chest. When he gazed into her guileless blue eyes, he found them shiny as crystals with unshed tears.

"I don't want this," she whispered, her words a soft feathering of air on his chin.

"Don't you?" His fingers bracketed her face, his thumb catching the tear that finally slipped through the gold-tipped lashes to start a path down her soft cheek. "I think this is the one thing you do want. The one thing we both want."

"Nooo . . ." Merideth shook her head. His hands loosened, allowing her freedom, but he bent his head, catching her lips with his. 'Twas but a slight brushing, but the contact sparked an eruption of emotion.

"Aye, Merideth," was all he said before scooping her up. Her hair, now loose from its ribbon, fell over one arm, her silk skirts over the other. He shifted, bringing her face closer to his. They shared a breath, a soul-shattering moment of anticipation; then she lifted her mouth to his. The kiss was deep and long, and went unbroken as he carried her across the cabin to his wooden-sided bunk.

Even as he lowered her onto the mattress, following her until he rested in the cradle of her body, he continued the kiss. Only a need for air, and to taste the rest of her, broke the fusion.

Her throat was soft, sweet smelling and sensitive to his touch. She arched, throwing her head back to give him better access as he trailed a line of kisses down the slender column. His tongue wet the flutter of pulse, sending the rhythm off kilter.

"God, Merideth, you taste so good." With his mouth Jared followed the velvet stream of ribbon that led to the locket nestled between her breasts. Ignoring the silken fabric molded to her flesh, Jared nipped and suckled till she wiggled and writhed beneath him. Till she tore at the shirt covering his back, yanking the linen from his breeches and digging her fingers into the crisscrossing cords of muscle.

"How?" he breathed, fumbling with the fasteners on her stomacher. God, he should have undressed her before he tumbled them both onto the bunk. Now all their efforts were frustrated by their reluctant inability to let go of each other.

Jared's teeth and whiskered chin grazed her shoulder as he managed to rid her of the gown's bodice. Now only the fine gauze of her chemise covered her breasts. The thin silk couldn't disguise her rosy nipples, puckered berry hard, nor the distended centers that beckoned to his mouth.

Merideth lifted her buttocks off the bed as he dragged the tangle of skirts and petticoats from her body. He shifted to the side enough to peel clocked hose down the slender calves, lingering a moment to follow the graceful curve of her instep before tossing the silk to the cabin's wooden deck. Then with a flick of the drawstring, the shift's neck widened, enabling him to skim it down her ribs, over her hips, and further.

She lay before him, her body covered by nothing but the flush of sexual arousal. He touched her, his long, slender fingers splaying across her stomach from hipbone to hipbone, and Merideth closed her eyes and moaned. When the heel of his palm inched lower she shamelessly spread her legs, allowing him entrance to her heated core.

But it wasn't his hand that nuzzled between her thighs. A sweep of his midnight hair tightened her muscles, sending them into spasms that flowed and concentrated in the heart of her femininity as his tongue probed, stimulating the sensitive kernel of flesh.

The climax that shook her was so sharp, so carnal, that a scream escaped as wave upon wave of sensual delight spread through her body. Her head twisted to the side and her eyes closed, but the bright celebration of colors continued, each vision brighter than the one before.

Before the swells subsided, he slid up her body. Somehow he'd shed his breeches, for the smooth tip of his manhood, hot as a poker, pressed inside her.

Merideth's body stretched to accept the size and strength of him. She raised her knees, twining her legs around his slim hips, and waited for the rhythmic power of his mating to commence.

But he was still. Her lashes lifted and she gazed into his eyes, smoky and dark with passion. The skin was tight across his straight blade of nose. And his mouth was full and beautiful.

Capturing her hands, he stretched them high above the fan of golden curls till her knuckles skimmed the headboard. Then he twined their fingers, tightening his grip as he began to thrust deep inside her.

He withdrew, then entered with more power than before. His sweat-slick chest skimmed a heartbeat above hers, the tangle of raven hair brushing against her erect nipples.

"Please," she whispered, barely able to recognize her own voice, or to know what she begged for.

A flash of white teeth brightened the dark intensity of his face, then the grin faded. His mouth tightened, the tendons on his neck thickened, stood out in bold relief under his sun-browned skin. When he could stand the anticipation no more, he drove faster, deeper.

When she cried out, his mouth fused with hers. He surged uncontrollably, the frenzied motion cresting into an eruption of pure pleasure that seemed to go on and on.

They collapsed together, his face falling into the tangle of curls above her shoulder, his breath rasping in her ear.

When Jared regained a semblance of composure he lifted himself, resting his weight on his elbows and framing her beautiful face with his hands.

"We may have many differences," he said, his voice still warm and husky. "But we do have this in common."

There was no doubt in Merideth's mind what he meant by "this." Or that he was right. They shared an overpowering passion, and there didn't seem to be anything either of them could do about it.

Then he drew her into his arms, kissing her again, and she felt the swell of his body within hers.

And to her shame, Merideth knew she wouldn't stop this madness even if she could.

Chapter Seventeen

There was no doubt where Captain Blackstone would spend his nights—no doubt, at least, in Merideth's mind.

She readied herself for bed that evening, wondering when he would come to her. She'd seen naught of him since he'd left her late that afternoon.

Swiping the captain's silver brush down through her curls, she glanced toward the bunk. A rose-colored blush darkened her cheeks. She had tried to straighten the linen and blankets, but the mattress still looked rumpled to her. Maybe it was simply her guilty conscience. Tim hadn't seemed to notice anything when he'd come this evening for his lesson. He'd been full of talk of his day, of the measuring of knots, and the direction of the wind. If there was ever a lad born to be a sailor, 'twas Tim, Merideth thought.

But he'd stuck to his word and worked hard at his lessons, reading from the Buffon's *Natural History* in his halting style. He hadn't even acted too relieved when Merideth told him he could go, though she'd known he was.

Not that she hadn't been as well. Truthfully, Merideth had let him go earlier than their normal lessons ended. She didn't want him in the cabin when the captain came.

"'Twas no need to worry about that," she mumbled to herself, starting to work the bristles through her hair with forceful jerks. It was late, nigh on mid-watch, and no sign of him yet.

Merideth tossed the brush onto the desk and folded her arms. Why should she care?

She didn't. "I don't," Merideth whispered to herself.

This afternoon had just . . . happened. Neither of them had wanted it to. After all, nothing was changed. She was still his captive. He still doubted her word. And then there was Daniel's contention that Jared would kill her if he suspected she had betrayed his brother.

And Merideth wasn't convinced Daniel didn't speak the truth. She wasn't even certain her innocence would save her.

So why was she pacing the cabin, anticipating the captain's return?

Merideth tried to deny that that was what she was doing, but saw no reason to lie to herself. She'd been in bed, out of bed, stripped naked, covered by her shift and shawl; she'd finally folded the shawl and tossed it aside. She'd read, paced the cabin, brushed her hair . . . paced the cabin. And he still didn't come.

Finally, exasperated with herself and the weakness that drove her to want him when she shouldn't,

Merideth doused the candle in the lantern and lay down. The pillow smelled of him . . . of his hair and the sea, and she snuggled her face into it and breathed deeply. Then turned her head, disgusted that just the smell of him would evoke such need.

Overhead the timbers groaned and she could hear the faint tingling of bells. One two, three . . . Eight bells. Midnight. She'd learned to tell time by the ringing of the brass bell that hung in the bracket near the edge of the forecastle. Each half hour they rang as the sandglass was turned.

The night watch was over. Tired sailors would be making their way to their hammocks. The thought made Merideth drowsy. Closing her eyes, she sighed, telling herself she was just as glad the captain had decided to keep to himself.

It was the exact moment the cabin door opened.

Startled, Merideth sat up, the blanket clutched to her breast. She recognized the captain silhouetted against the lighted passageway and smiled. She couldn't help herself.

"I took the night watch," he said, stepping into the cabin and shutting the door behind him. "Seemed the least I could do for missing my own this afternoon."

Merideth waited for her eyes to adjust to the dark. The moon was waning, offering no more than a shimmer of light to the cabin. She sensed rather than saw him move toward her. "I suppose that's fair," Merideth said. She could hear his boot treads on the wooden floor. He was almost to her.

When his shadowy form settled onto the side of the bunk, Merideth wriggled over to make room for him.

He hesitated, bending forward, his hands between his knees, his broad back a spanse of white.

"I'm not sure why I came here," he began, then seemed to find his own words amusing, because he laughed. "Actually, I do know why I came. I'm just not certain it's the best thing."

"I'm not sure either."

He turned to face her when she spoke. Merideth caught a glimpse of his shining eyes. "But I don't want to leave."

Merideth bit her bottom lip. Her breathing had slowed and she forced herself to take a big gulp of air. "I don't want you to go either."

He came to her then in the darkness, his fingers braiding through her hair, his lips warm and firm. Heat speared through her as he lowered her down on the mattress. Her arms wrapped around his lean waist, kneading the slabs of taut muscles across his back.

She loved the weight of him, the solid feel of him as his body settled onto her. His kisses were tender at first, less hungry, but no less intense than this afternoon, and Merideth luxuriated in them. When he paused to rid her of the shift, himself of his shirt, breeches, and boots, Merideth found she missed him.

But soon he was back, slipping inside her as smoothly as water over glass. She drew him in, cupping his buttocks and meeting each long, slow plunge.

His mouth slid off hers, following the curve of her jaw till it found the underside of her chin, the slender line of her neck. "Merry, oh God, Merry," he murmured, his breath a hot brand on her flesh. Then she could hear nothing but the soft sensual moans that came from both of them.

She tingled, the thrusts quickened, and her mind hazed with anticipation. When her release came in long undulating crests of pleasure, Jared linked their hands, bracketing her head. Their fingers twined, staying that way long after they'd coaxed the last shivers free.

Merideth lifted her lashes, and though the cabin was dark she could tell he stared at her. But she could not read his expression, and though she thought to ask what he was thinking, the words wouldn't come.

After a moment he settled down on the bunk, pulled her to his side, and covered them with the woolen blanket. Merideth rested her head on his shoulder and fell asleep to the lullaby of his soft snores.

In the morning he was gone.

Waking up with the first blush of dawn shining through the stern windows, Merideth smiled, then stretched, her arms stopping in mid spread when she realized she was alone in the bunk.

Sitting up, she looked around the cabin. In the gritty light she could see he'd taken his clothes. Not a sign of him remained from last night.

"Which is as I expected," Merideth said as she clambered from the bed. Nothing had really changed between them.

Except now they were lovers.

Not in love, though Merideth wasn't certain she didn't suffer from that ailment. But it was obvious the captain didn't. He wanted one thing from her. Two, if you counted the name of the traitor. But she couldn't give him that.

Biting her lip to keep the tears at bay, Merideth

splashed water from the pitcher into the bowl, then onto her face. She dressed quickly, tied back her hair, and stuffed the old felt hat onto her head. With a smile forced on her lips she went on deck.

The day was sharp and clear, a fresh wind sang through the sails, and before she knew it, the smile was genuine. She spoke briefly with Mr. Pochet, the ship's carpenter, then was hailed to the rail by Tim.

"Lady Merideth," he said, his hazel eyes full of excitement. "We spotted sail near dawn."

"You did." Merideth shaded her eyes. "Where?"

Following the line of his finger, Merideth could make out a tiny speck on the horizon. "Cap'n says it's a merchantman probably bound for Kingston from Canada."

"It's English, then?"

"Cap'n says more'n likely."

For hours Merideth watched silently as the spot of white grew larger, till she could finally make out the shape of sails. Tim had left her, to carry on with his duties, so she no longer had his running commentary. Even without it she could tell the *Carolina* was in pursuit.

Visions of another bloody battle came to her, and with it the memory of the men she had nursed . . . the men who had died. She glanced about the deck, at Mr. Pochet, and at Tim. At Padriac, and at the bo'sun who told her such wonderful tales of pirates. She imagined them burned and bleeding. She drew in a shattered breath and her gaze searched the quarterdeck.

"He can't seem to let well enough alone."

"What?" Merideth hadn't noticed Daniel approach

336

her until he was by her side.

He nodded his wigged head in the direction Merideth looked. "My dear cousin is determined to take yet another prize. It doesn't seem to matter to him that our hold is already full."

Glancing around, Merideth stared at him, not knowing what she was to say. But apparently Daniel expected no response. His eyes were still fixed on the captain and he continued. "But that's like Jared. He wants it all. He always has."

"You sound as if you don't like him very much."

His attention shifted to her quickly. His winged brows lifted. "Not like Jared, my own flesh and blood? Why, that's unheard of." His smile sent a chill down Merideth's spine. "We Blackstones stick together. It's a rule. Almost a sacrament. We never speak ill of another Blackstone."

"You seem want to adhere to your own maxim."

"What?" Daniel lifted his hand, slender fingers spread. "Because I point out a few of my relative's deficiencies?" His smile turned ingratiating. "But that's just to you, dear girl, and only because you've become important to me."

He reached out, catching a lock of Merideth's hair, twirling it around his finger before she could step away. He seemed to sense her discomfort, but Merideth was certain that wasn't the reason he let go before she raised her hand to slap at his. His laugh was chilling.

"But then here comes our revered captain now." Merideth glanced up to see Jared approaching, a sober expression on his sun-darkened face. "I'm sure he'll tell you the same. Won't you, dear cousin?" he added, raising his voice for Jared to hear.

"Won't I what?" Jared stopped before them, wondering why it annoyed him so much to see the two of them together.

"I was just giving our lovely Lady Merideth an explanation of why blood is thicker than water."

Jared's eyes narrowed and Daniel brushed the explanation aside with a flick of his wrist. "'Tis nothing. Certainly nothing so important as what you've come to say."

Merideth was sure the captain would find the tone of sarcasm in his cousin's voice offensive—she certainly did—but he merely stared at Daniel a moment before turning his sea-green eyes on her.

"I think it best you go below deck, Lady Merideth."

He spoke with a detachment that belied the intimacy of the previous night. A detachment that offended Merideth. She raised her chin. She could be as haughty and distant as he. "Is that because you plan to attack that innocent ship?" Merideth pointed to where the merchantman was now clearly visible.

Jared didn't bother to turn his head. "Aye," he said, his eyes never leaving hers. "That would be the reason."

The words were spoken without inflection, but Merideth could tell she'd sparked his ire. Though his chiseled face was covered with a day's growth of black whiskers—apparently he'd been so anxious to leave her this morning, he'd neglected to shave—she could see the telltale tightening of his jaw.

She held her ground.

Daniel, however, did not. "I suppose I shall retire below deck. Are you coming, Lady Merideth?" When he received no answer, not even a shift of attention his way, Daniel bowed. "Well then, till later."

Neither Merideth nor Jared noticed him leave. Towering over her, his expression as dark as the tangle of hair that whipped back and forth across his face, he said nothing.

Trying not to feel intimidated, Merideth cleared her throat. "Look at the poor vessel." Though her words demanded an action, neither head turned. "It doesn't even seem to be running from us."

"'Tis no matter. We could catch her anyway." When the sails were spotted by the morning watch just as dawn paled the stars, he'd set the *Carolina* on the same tack and course. He'd ordered canvas unfurled to match the merchantman, and set her position in his compass. He was pleased when her sails drew a point aft. But even if they could outsail the low-riding merchantman, there was no call to cause the enemy ship's captain alarm. Jared didn't want any of her cargo jettisoned in an attempt to outrun a privateer. So he depended on a bluff.

"The ship isn't sailing from us," he told Merideth. "Their captain thinks us to be another merchantman."

"But how—"

"Our gunports are covered with painted canvas, for one thing."

"Why, that's—"

"And we're flying an English ensign, for another."

Her gaze did leave his then—briefly—to search out the flag snapping sharply from the mainmast. It was a brilliant white, sporting a red cross. ". . . not fair," she finished.

"Ruse de guerre," Jared said with a shrug. "I thought you knew war isn't fair."

She did. Hadn't she learned that the hard way? Merideth closed her eyes. When her lashes lifted, the captain had stepped closer. "Now, will you kindly go below?" His voice was low, familiar, reminding her of his long, hard body pressed to hers.

Merideth swallowed. "And if I don't?"

"I shall have to toss you over my shoulder and take you myself."

"You wouldn't." But even as she voiced the words, Merideth knew he most certainly would. He'd done it before, and the gleam in his eyes told her he would do it again. She took a step back, then another. He made no move to follow her, but Merideth decided not to tarry.

Casting a nervous glance over her shoulder as she made her way to the main hatch—the captain no longer stood by the larboard rail—Merideth bumped into a tar she knew as Fleets. He carried two buckets of sand linked by a wooden yoke that rode the curve of his burly tattoo-covered shoulders.

He grabbed her arm. "Beggin' yer pardon, yer Ladyship."

"No, no. It was my fault." Merideth gave him a wan smile and skirted his wide body. Now that she looked about, the deck was full of activity. Sailors were moving here and there, bringing barrels of powder from the hold and stacking handspikes, rammers, and powder horns by the cannons. More tars climbed into the rigging. But to a man they worked in a quiet, casual way that Merideth assumed was meant to throw off the

English captain if he happened to be observing through his spyglass.

Shaking her head, Merideth made her way down the ladder. She made her way aft along the passageway, past the officer's quarters and the wardroom on the starboard side. When she reached the captain's cabin she paused hand-on-latch. The smell of bilge water and tar stung her nostrils and she wished for a deep breath of sea air. Above her she could hear the men moving about, rolling cannon, readying for the battle. She had the strongest urge to run into the cabin, hide her head beneath the blanket, and pretend none of this was happening.

But she couldn't.

Turning on her heel, Merideth retraced her steps along the companionway. She opened a lantern, removing the candle and protecting the flame with her cupped hand as she headed toward the afterhold. The deeper she went, the more the timbers groaned and the darker and danker it became. It reminded her vividly of the caves, but she took a deep breath and continued.

Abner Pochet turned when she climbed down the ladder into the after hold. He stared at her a moment, then continued laying out the tourniquets. "Figured ye might show up," was all he said.

Merideth nodded to him and several other sailors who were readying the hold for surgery, and she set the candle in a holder. They'd already made a floor of wide boards over kegs. There were tables set up for equipment, others for patients needing surgery, and pallets on the floor to accommodate the wounded.

After tying a towel around her waist, she asked, "What should I do?"

"Get out the bandages." He motioned with his pointy chin toward a large wooden box.

Merideth opened the medicine chest, revealing rows of tiny drawers and glass vials. She set out the scraped lint, bunting, and rolls of bandages. As she was preparing the splints, Tim came down the ladder with word from the captain that they were nearly abreast of the enemy ship.

"We're ready down here," Abner said as he carried a bucket of water to one of the tables.

With all prepared, there was naught to do but wait. Merideth paced between the tables and pallets, sometimes straightening a blanket, most of the time simply wringing her hands. Even though she knew it would happen, the thunder of the first salvo caught her unawares. The after hold seemed to tremble, and Merideth caught hold of the ladder as the *Carolina* creaked and swayed.

"That would be the warnin' shot," Abner said, looking as relaxed as if he were strolling along deck. "Doubt this will amount ta much. Cap'n's got the Quakers lined up on deck."

"The what?" Merideth tried to match the ship doctor's nonchalance, but found she couldn't.

"Quakers," Abner repeated. "The fake guns. Made a wood they be, but lookin' for all the world like the real thing. Lookin' down the throat a them plus our real guns is enough to put the fear a God in any respectable merchantman."

"You mean a trick? *Another* trick?" Nervous

laughter escaped her. Jared Blackstone seemed to have a treasure trove of bluffs and ploys. With a sigh Merideth felt some of the tension flow from her shoulders just as another monstrous roar shattered the quiet.

"That wasn't our guns," she said, her eyes large and round. "Was it?"

"God's crutch, nay." Abner sucked in his breath as the *Carolina* strained against the blow. "The bastards mean ta make a fight a it."

And make a fight of it they did—for the next two hours, as Abner and Merideth stopped bleeding with lint and smeared grease on burns.

The wounded that made their way to the after hold told tales of the battle, of the exchange of volleys and tacking for position.

"We'll be boardin' her soon," Tim said as he scrambled down the steps.

Glancing up from giving a sailor a drink, Merideth saw him. After carefully lowering the man's head, she rushed to Tim.

"Are you hurt anyplace?" She grabbed hold of his shoulders and spun the boy around to face her.

"Nay, I'm fine." Tim shrugged out of her hands. "I'm not a baby to be coddled."

"You're right. I'm sorry. I only thought . . ." There was no sense telling him of her worries. "What of the boarding? Are they giving up?"

"Soon." Tim's countenance brightened. "Cap'n sent me down here to help. We're rakin' her stern now," Tim said, raising his voice over the sound of the great guns. "Wouldn't be surprised if she strikes her colors

343

before we come aboard."

But the stubborn merchantman didn't give up. It took a fierce hand-to-hand battle on her decks before her captain handed over his sword.

"Must be carryin' something dear," Tim said when word finally came down that the fighting was over. "Else they wouldn't a put up such a tussle."

"Well, I hope it was dear enough for the suffering it caused." Merideth tied off a bandage around a young tar's leg. His smoke-blackened face sweated profusely.

"Now yer Ladyship, ye shouldn't take on so. 'Tis war, ye know."

"So I've been told."

The crew of the *Carolina* won the day. Which didn't surprise Merideth. And in truth she was hoping they would. Later that evening, in the captain's cabin, she shook her head as she thought of her reaction to the battle.

She was British, daughter of a peer of the realm. Certainly she should be loyal to her homeland. Hadn't the captain's implications to the contrary been enough to send her into a fit of denials?

Yet here she was, content with—nay, actually wishing for—an American victory over her countrymen. Settling back on the window seat, Merideth pulled her knees up under her chemise and propped her chin. Earlier she'd shed her gown, which, despite her efforts to apron the skirt with a towel, bore bloodstains.

At least none of the injuries sustained by the *Carolina*'s crew were serious. Most of the tars who'd made their way down to the after hold required no more than bandaging. Abner hadn't had to use his amputation blade once, thank God.

Her head lolled back against the chilled window-panes. She was tired, too weary to ponder such weighty questions as loyalty, let alone rebellions and liberty. Such words were often bantered around by the *Carolina*'s sailors. The men obviously believed in what they fought for. But Merideth didn't know anymore. She just didn't know.

As she clasped her locket, Merideth's lashes drifted down. She didn't even realize she'd fallen asleep until the opening of the door woke her. She smiled dreamily up at the captain. It was hours since she'd last seen him on deck before the battle. But she'd worried about him all day.

She'd almost begun to think of him as invincible, till her gaze focused. "My God, what happened to you?" Merideth's eyes widened, and she leaped from the padded bench.

"'Tis nothing. I'm fine."

"Fine! Fine?" The captain stood, his muscular legs spread against the sway of the ship, his jacket gone, his once white shirt in shreds. The left sleeve was stained a rusty red, and the arm inside it hung limply at his side.

When Merideth grabbed for his hand, the lines etched about his sensual mouth deepened. "Ouch, dammit! Is this how you minister to the wounded down in the surgery?"

"No, but then they have the sense to come below rather than bleed to death."

"I was never in danger of bleeding to death, Merry." His use of her pet name was surprising, but she made

345

no comment, for the captain didn't seem to realize what he'd said. But the endearment, for that's how she viewed it, softened Merideth's tone. "Come sit on the bunk and let me see."

He looked at her, his green eyes shaded with suspicion and something else Merideth couldn't read. But he followed as she took his right hand and guided him toward the bed. Once the captain, grunting with relief, was settled on the mattress, Merideth carefully peeled the tattered linen from his shoulders. It smelled of gunpowder and sweat, and it bore the coppery scent of blood.

The cords of muscles across his shoulders and down the length of his arms tightened when she tried to unstick the cloth from his wound. And bright crimson mingled with the dark rust stain.

"Christ, Merideth," he hissed, yanking his arm from her hands.

"Be still." Straddling his bent leg, Merideth clutched his elbow. She narrowed her eyes, examining the blood, crusted and fresh, that covered his upper arm.

"But the damn thing hurts," Jared insisted.

"I know that."

"Well, you don't act like you know it."

Merideth just stared at him. It was all she could do to keep from crying and throwing herself at his feet. Her hands trembled from the effort of being brave and trying to help him when she thought of what might have happened.

The wound wasn't mortal, that was apparent, but it could have been. And she wanted to plead with him to never put himself in such danger again.

But that was ridiculous. That was his life.

"Come over to the bucket," she finally said, and knelt on the deck when he did. Using the torn shred of his shirt, she sponged water down his shoulder, biting her bottom lip when his teeth clenched.

"How did this happen?" she asked when the wound was free of material. She could now see the angry, swollen slash starting near his shoulder and slanting down toward his elbow.

"Saber fight. The damn British captain was reluctant to surrender."

"And I suppose you wouldn't have been."

"I didn't lose, Merry," he said, grinning, his teeth shining white in his dirt-streaked face.

Oh, but you could have, Merideth thought, though she didn't say it. She patted his arm dry and motioned for him to resume his seat on the bunk. "Did you kill him?"

"Nay. A saber point to his throat convinced him the battle was over. He's locked in his own brig, and a prize crew is aboard . . . What the hell are you doing?"

"Threading a needle." Merideth held her fingers to the lantern and squinted.

"What the hell for?"

"If I don't sew your arm, there'll be a scar."

"I've my share of scars anyway. Now wait a minute, Merideth, I've no desire for you to go at me with that needle."

"Yet you allow someone to go at you with a saber."

"That's different. 'Tis war."

"Then consider this the price you pay. Now give me your arm and don't make a fuss."

He didn't fuss, though beads of sweat broke out on his forehead and upper lip, where the whiskers were black and coarse. When she finished, Merideth brushed back the raven hair that had come loose from its queue during the battle.

"Would you like some dinner? The galley fires must be relit by now." Her own evening meal had consisted of sea biscuits and cold pork because the cook had not yet relit the flames he'd doused when the battle began.

"Nay." Jared stretched his long legs out on the bunk. "I could use a bit of whiskey." He motioned with his free hand. "In the chest over there."

After finding the bottle among stacks of books, Merideth poured enough to cover the bottom of a pewter cup. His brow arched questioningly when she handed him the paltry amount. "Are you rationing me my own whiskey?"

"What? Oh, no." Merideth shook her head, trying to rid her mind of the memories the smell conjured up. "It's just that my father drank whiskey. Quite a lot of whiskey, actually. He was . . . not pleasant to be around . . ."

"I'm not your father, Merideth. I don't abuse drink."

She knew that. Apparently the bottle, near three-quarters full, had been in his sea chest all the while she'd been on board the *Carolina*, and she hadn't seen him drink from it. Carrying the amber bottle, Merideth moved toward the bunk. She hesitated, then held it out to him.

"'Tis all right." Jared swallowed the fiery liquid. "I think I need rest more than liquor anyway."

348

Merideth removed his boot, then helped him wipe his face clean and shrug out of his breeches. When he was beneath the covers she blew out the lantern.

"Aren't you coming to bed?" he asked, his voice soft in the darkness.

Without another thought Merideth pulled the shift over her head and carefully climbed into the bunk. She snuggled into his good arm and pressed her body to his.

The following weeks were the best Merideth could ever remember. In spite of being on an enemy ship. In spite of the fact that she didn't know what the future would bring. Or maybe it was more that she did know. At least she knew it would bring her unhappiness. So she tried to enjoy every minute.

The weather was perfect, clear skies and freshening winds. The war seemed far away. Not an enemy vessel crossed the *Carolina*'s bow. And the captain himself was agreeable.

At first she thought he spent more time with her in the cabin because of his wound. But only a few days after the battle, he proved to her that he could do, and do well, most everything he'd done before.

She woke early and, being full of energy, decided to take a stroll on deck so as not to disturb him. She had just pulled a saffron-colored gown over her head when she heard his voice.

"What are you about so early?"

"Oh." Merideth's head popped through the neck of the dress and she smoothed the bodice over her ribs. "I didn't mean to wake you. I'm getting dressed."

He slowly shook his head and the sight of his heavily lidded, sleepy eyes and tousled hair fired her blood.

"But I thought I'd go on deck—"

"Take it off, Merry."

Swallowing her breath coming in shallow gasps, Merideth met his eyes. "The gown?"

"Aye, the gown. Take it off."

She did, slowly slipping it down over one shoulder, then the other. If the cabin was chilled, she no longer noticed, for the heat of his stare left her burning. The silk fell about her ankles in a soft whisper.

"Now the shift," he said, propping his shaggy black head on the bend of his elbow.

Releasing the drawstring between her breasts, Merideth let the thin fabric glide down her body. When she stood before him, naked and drunk with desire, she watched as his eyes wandered over her.

Her breasts, their nipples rucked and ripe, swelled beneath his gaze. Her pulse quickened when his eyes strayed lower.

"Come here, Merry." His voice was low and as rich as black velvet.

"What of your wound?" Merideth moved forward.

"'Tis another part of me that aches far worse than any arm." He glanced down to where the blanket tented below his waist.

With a flick of her wrist, Merideth flipped the wool aside. He lay gloriously naked, swirls of midnight-black hair cradling his large, swollen manhood. He let her look her fill before reaching up and grabbing her hand.

"Come, Merry," was all he said as he pulled her down to mount him.

"He was fascinated by plants."

"Who?" They were sitting in the window seat one evening as dusk turned the sea and sky dark. Merideth's feet were in the captain's lap, and he idly traced the curve of her instep.

"My brother. He was a fellow of the Royal Society, and he studied how flowers reproduce."

"Really." This was the first he'd mentioned his twin since the truce between them began, and Merideth feared it might be the end of it. She didn't know what she'd do if he began accusing her of betraying John Blackstone.

"He was a genius. But then so were my parents. Both of them studied nature and kept journals full of observations. My father was in the Royal Society too."

"You're very smart," Merideth said in defense of the man she was growing to love more each day.

He simply snorted as his eyes met hers. "Clever maybe, but not smart like they were. They were the kind of people who leave their mark on the world. Like Dr. Franklin."

"I still think—"

He leaned forward then, brushing his lips across hers to silence her protest.

"I'm a sea captain, Merry. Nothing more."

"Tim thinks you can do no wrong."

Merideth stood beside Jared on the leeward deck. She smiled up at him when he glanced down in surprise.

"He's a fine lad."

"Mmmm," Merideth agreed. "He told me how you found him on the docks after he ran away from the poorhouse at St. Philip's. How you took him in."

"I needed a cabin boy."

"Tim said Skeeter was your cabin boy and you promoted him to sailor."

His eyes narrowed. "What are you implying?"

Merideth shrugged. "Not a thing." She ran her finger along the polished rail. "He also says you teach him all about navigation. That you're an expert."

"There are experts and there are experts," Jared said, draping his arm around Merideth. After a fortnight it was almost as good as new. "Seeing that Tim knew nothing about the subject, I would think anyone would seem knowledgeable."

"He says the entire crew thinks you're the greatest captain ever."

Jared turned to face her, his countenance sober. "Don't make me out to be a saint, Merry. For believe me, 'tis far from the truth. What?" He jerked around to look in the direction she pointed. "What is it?"

"A gull," Merideth said, her heart heavy. "We must be close to land."

"We are. Have been for days. I've been waiting for the moon to wane so we can slip past any British ships that might be blockading the port."

"So we're here? We're off Charles Town?"

"Aye. And the night promises to be a dark one. We'll

352

slip into the harbor tonight."

He was pleased, she could tell that. But as he left their bed during the night watch to steer the *Carolina* through the shoals, all Merideth could think of was that the sojourn was over. Now she had to decide what to do.

About Daniel Wallis.

About Jared Blackstone.

Chapter Eighteen

By first light the *Carolina* sailed past the American guns at Fort Johnson. If there was a blockade of the port, Jared had seen no evidence of it through the night. Even as they entered Rebellion Roads and could see the tall masts lining the wharves like a forest of leafless trees, Jared doubted the British were effectively slowing shipping to *this* city, at least.

At the helm, Jared guided his schooner through the inner channel between James Island and the middle ground, the shoal that had helped protect Charles Town when the British attacked the port in '76. Three of Admiral Parker's ships ran ashore on the shoal in the harbor. Two managed to wrest free, badly damaged, but the third was abandoned and burned.

Jared was in France when the attack took place. When his fellow Carolinians, in a half-finished fort made of palmetto logs, outmanned and outgunned, rebuffed the British fleet. He heard of it weeks later and experienced a swell of pride for his homeland.

Rumor was, the British were now planning another assault. Hopefully the weapons in the *Carolina*'s hold would help the small city repel it. And this time, Jared planned to be here to defend what was his.

"That there's St. Michael's," Tim said, his thin finger pointing toward a steeple, its roof reflecting the morning sun. "And there's St. Philip's." He shifted slightly, drawing Merideth's attention to another equally lovely spire. "That's where Cap'n Blackstone got me."

Merideth turned to look at the boy from under the brim of her hat. They stood on the deck as the *Carolina* skimmed into Charles Town harbor. "I thought he found you in an alley near the docks."

"Aye, he done that. But then he took me back to St. Philip's on account a they take care a the poor and the orphaned.

"'Tweren't too bad there," he continued. "Had me pretty near 'nough ta eat, but I still didn't like it."

"Why not?"

"I wanted ta go ta sea," he replied, obviously surprised she couldn't figure that out for herself.

"I imagine you relayed your wish to Captain Blackstone?"

"Aye." A grin spread across his freckled face. "And he came back for me, he did. Just like that." Tim snapped his fingers.

Laughing, Merideth shook her head. "You're a rogue, Timothy. You and the captain deserve each other."

"What a ye, yer Ladyship? Will ye be stayin' with him?"

The question was asked innocently enough. Merideth was sure Tim didn't realize all the implications of his query. Captain Blackstone had taken him in, and he was fiercely loyal. The boy expected Merideth to be the same.

But the captain hadn't taken her in. He'd kidnapped her. And though she was surely in love with him, she couldn't stay when it wasn't reciprocated. She was not Jared's cabin boy. She was his mistress. And her future was as vague as the mist rising over the twin church steeples.

After giving Tim a noncommittal answer, Merideth went below to ponder her immediate future. She packed her few belongings in the small trunk Jared had given her, then sat on the window seat.

She thought about seeking Daniel Wallis. Though she'd spoken to him rarely since the day he offered to get her back to England, Merideth assumed it was still a possibility. Several times over the last few days, she caught him staring at her, his eyes questioning. When she looked up he raised his brow as if to remind her that she'd given him no answer. But the captain was always there, offering her no time to discuss the matter further with his cousin.

Merideth pressed her forehead to the stern windows. Her breath fogged the glass as she watched small boats skim over the waves in the harbor. With her finger she traced through the moisture. How could she give Daniel an answer when she didn't know what it should be?

By midmorning the captain returned to his cabin. The *Carolina* was docked, and her crew was busy unloading the munitions from her hold.

"I thought you might like a chance to walk on solid ground," he said as he entered the cabin. "We keep a house in Charles Town that is a mite more comfortable than this." Jared's hand swept the cramped quarters. He was dressed in a dark-blue waistcoat. The stock of his pristine white shirt was tied neatly about his neck. His black hair was brushed and clubbed with a dark ribbon.

After weeks of seeing him as wild and free, with his hair blowing in the wind, and his shirt sleeves rolled to reveal muscled forearms, it seemed strange to be reminded that he could appear civilized. However, Merideth doubted any amount of polishing could completely mask the untamed spirit that lay just beneath the surface.

He held out his hand, and tentatively Merideth took it. Remaining on the ship would do her no good. Perhaps at his house she could speak to Daniel in private.

She was slightly surprised when they crossed the gangplank onto the noisy wharf without Daniel. "Isn't your cousin accompanying us?" she asked as her legs adjusted to the lack of sway the solid ground offered.

"He'll be along directly, I imagine."

"But don't you think we should wait for him?"

Her question seemed to surprise the captain, for he stopped. Merideth's hand rested on his sleeve, and she realized she had tightened her fingers. He looked first at her hand, small and pale against the dark-blue fabric, then into her eyes.

Suspicion, an expression of the captain's she knew too well, veiled his handsome features. "Why the sudden interest in my cousin?"

They stood on the crowded dock, a small oasis surrounded by swarms of people. But though she stood still, Merideth's emotions were as jumbled as the activity around her. Her fingers instinctively reached for her locket. She caught herself before she touched the smooth gold, and hoped he didn't notice the nervous movement of her hand. He'd told her once that she touched the locket whenever she was upset . . . or lying. "I have no interest in Daniel," she lied, and turned away from him.

The raucous cries of seagulls served as a backdrop to the noise and bustle on the docks. For a moment it all seemed to close in around her. Then she felt Jared's strong hand grasp her elbow and he forged a path for them.

Men with sleek skin, black as ebony, rolled giant barrels or hefted smaller ones on their broad shoulders. Merideth had seen blackamoors before. There were two among the *Carolina*'s crew. But she'd never imagined to see so many in one place.

"'Tis not far to Tradd Street," he said when they'd cleared the busiest part of the dock. Merideth glanced over her shoulder, catching a glimpse of the *Carolina*'s mast towering above the Cooper River. The sight filled her with a longing to be back on the high seas again. To be free, at least temporarily, from the decision she had to make.

But soon Merideth's natural curiosity overcame even her worry of the future. The captain's walk was brisk, but it didn't stop Merideth from gaping wide-eyed at her surroundings. Everything was new and different, from the trees—Jared called them palmettos—with their top plumage of broad serrated leaves, to the odd-smelling mud that choked the streets.

They crossed East Bay, where there were still signs of earthworks thrown up during the battle two years earlier. On Tradd Street there were pavements, six feet wide and made of brick and mortar, that made the walking easier. The mansions along the tree-lined street were impressive, large with gardens full of strange, sweet-smelling flowers. In Land's End a chill would be in the air, but not here. It was as warm as midsummer.

The house they stopped before didn't appear as large as some, but as they went through the ironwork gate Merideth realized it was really the side of the house that fronted the street. Three stories high, with tall casement windows, shuttered now against the sun, and a pediment-surrounded front door, the house was covered with cream-colored stucco.

An elderly man with frizzled white hair opened the set in front door, his face breaking instantly into a nearly toothless smile. "Master Jared, 'tis really you? Welcome home, sir."

"How are you, Seth?" Jared stepped back to allow Merideth to enter. The hallway was wide and cool, compared to the outside, and smelled faintly of beeswax.

"I'm good, sir. Theo done told us he saw the *Carolina*

360

in the harbor early this mornin' when he went to market, but I had a hard time givin' it credit."

"It has been a long time." Jared squeezed the old man's shoulder. The livery he wore was faded several shades lighter than its original scarlet, but spotless. "I've brought a guest, Seth. This is Lady Banistar."

The old man bowed and Merideth thought she could hear his joints cracking. After that he led them off the hall into a large room with raised paneled walls painted a soft cream like the exterior. Aubusson rugs covered the dark floors that shone in the filtered sunlight coming through the shutters. The room was open and bright, and though not so large as the parlor at Banistar Hall, there were no dark corners to make one feel unwelcome.

While Seth went for refreshments the captain absently wandered about the room, picking up a crystal bowl, following the curve of a winged chair. It was almost as if he were reacquainting himself with the house. Merideth leaned back and then looked around.

Nothing was as she'd expected. Not Charles Town. Certainly not this house. Silk framed the windows and covered the delicate settee where she sat. Silver sconces bracketed a gilded mirror above the carved wooden mantle.

"The main drawing room is on the second floor," Jared said, startling her. "My parents used to hold balls up there. The smaller west parlor's doors open to make one huge room."

"What . . .? Oh." Merideth glanced around to see Jared watching her, an amused smile on his face. Did he know what she was thinking? Merideth felt a blush creep up her neck. He'd obviously caught her examining the room. "Your house . . . It's lovely."

"But not what you expected."

"Well, I didn't—" Merideth cut short her statement, then slowly shook her head. "Not really. I thought it might be a bit more . . ." At a loss for the correct word, Merideth paused.

"Primitive?" Jared supplied, his dark brow arched.

"Yes, I suppose so."

"We 'colonials' are as fond of the creature comforts as the British. Actually, the house doesn't look near as grand as when I left. But then I suppose the war has something to do with that."

Merideth glanced down at her hands, then back at him. He was now leaning against the fireplace, his elbow on the mantel, his ankles crossed. "You sound as if you have wonderful memories of here."

"I do." Jared took a deep breath. "This house stands on the original property where my great-grandmother lived."

"The one who married the pirate?"

"Aye, the very same," he said, nodding. "The house was destroyed when a fire swept through the city in 1740. Some years later my grandparents built this over the ashes." He ran his finger along the carved scrolls. "Before my parents died we all moved to town every winter, for the season. At first I remember hating it, because that meant we had to leave Royal Oak." He shrugged, his smile revealing the dimple. "But as we grew older, John and I decided there were far more beautiful ladies in Charles Town than on the plantation."

Merideth laughed. "Always the rogue."

Jared shook his head, the devilish grin deepening the radiating lines at the corners of his eyes. "Actually, the balls and races were pleasant diversions, but I've always felt more at home at Royal Oak."

"Or on the bow of a ship."

"That too. Ah, here's Seth." Jared pushed away from the mantel and met the older man as he entered the room. He took the large silver tray and set it on the tea table in front of the settee. Then he settled beside Merideth, his thighs brushing against her skirt, and indicated the chair across from them for Seth.

"Tell me how things are," Jared asked while Merideth poured tea from the silver pot. "Is Mr. Guthre in?"

"No sir. He done left day 'fore yesterday for Royal Oak."

"Really." Bartrom Guthre was a distant cousin, son of a ne'er-do-well, yet himself possessing a keen mind for business. When John and Jared had left for France and the English Channel, they'd put Bart in charge of the Blackstone family's business. He supervised the indigo plantation and saw to the warehouses in town.

"I don't rightly know when he's comin' back to Charles Town, sir."

"No matter. Lady Merideth and I are leaving for Port Royal within the hour anyway."

"Within the—" The hand bringing the delicate china cup to her lips stilled as Merideth twisted toward him. "But we can't do that."

"And why is that?"

Why indeed. Merideth could hardly say that she

363

needed time to speak to Daniel Wallis. That he'd promised to see her safely back to England. That though she didn't want to go . . . to leave Jared . . . she couldn't stay. Not the way things were.

"I'm just surprised you wish to leave so soon." Merideth took a sip of tea to wet her suddenly dry mouth. "We . . . we just arrived."

His expression was unreadable as he leveled his green eyes on her . . . waiting. Merideth swallowed. "What of Daniel? Is he to come with us?"

"He'll come to Royal Oak in his own good time, I suppose."

"Surely before he leaves for Philadelphia." She was revealing too much. Merideth knew that, but she didn't seem able to help herself.

The captain's eyes narrowed. "Perhaps you should rest before we go." He rang a small silver bell, and when a round-cheeked black woman appeared at the door he introduced her as Evy and asked her to show Merideth upstairs. With that the captain turned back to Seth. As Merideth retreated from the room she could hear the men discussing the British attack on Charles Town.

"Ya be wantin' anythin' else, ma'am?" the young woman inquired after she'd poured water from the pitcher into the china bowl and set out linen towels.

"No. No, thank you." Merideth bit her lip. "Except . . . When Daniel Wallis is in Charles Town he does live here, doesn't he?" Perhaps he would show up before they departed.

The woman's friendly smile dissolved. She bustled toward the door, turning the knob before answering. "That one lives here most a the time," was all she said before leaving and shutting the door behind her.

Alone in the room, Merideth cupped water in her hands and splashed it onto her hot cheeks. With her eyes closed she leaned forward, wondering how she would ever get away from the man she loved . . . the man who didn't return that love. And worse, who believed her a traitor.

Her one hope, that Daniel would come to the house on Tradd Street before they left, faded as she and the captain mounted horses at the stables to the rear of the property.

They rode south along a sandy dirt road lined with towering pines till they reached the Ashley River. After being ferried across, they continued until it was nearly dark. They stopped at a plantation house owned by the Weller family. Mrs. Weller and her widowed daughter were the only ones at home, and they seemed delighted to see Jared.

He quickly supplied them with news from Charles Town, for which they seemed very eager. Merideth got the impression that news traveled slowly in the Low Country, as the captain referred to this area of Charles Town.

The ladies' reception of Merideth was polite but stilted. At first she thought this the result of her introduction as *Lady* Merideth Banistar. The younger woman's husband was dead as a result of the fighting at Charles Town. Lucy Weller, her mother, spoke often of her son-in-law's bravery when the English attacked the town. He had been one of Colonel Moultrie's officers.

But as they sat in the huge dining room beneath the prismed luster, Merideth suspected the thinly veiled animosity was rooted in more than hatred of the English.

Lucinda Weller King couldn't keep her eyes off of Jared Blackstone.

She smiled at him constantly. She laughed, her lower face hidden beneath the flair of her fan, whenever he said something even remotely humorous, and she touched him at every opportunity.

Merideth found the display disgusting.

As the evening wore on, Merideth grew more withdrawn—not that anyone had been interested in what she'd had to say earlier anyway. It was obvious from the conversation that the Wellers and Blackstones had been friends forever. It was also obvious that Lucinda had had her cap set for Jared before her marriage.

"Oh, do you remember that New Year's ball at Mrs. Gordon's Long Room? I declare, you were *so* upset when Alexander King escorted me to dinner.

"And the Newmarket Race Track at Goose Creek. Do you remember?" she asked as she wove her arm through his and led the way from the dining room into the parlor. "You were so besotted you begged for one of my ribbons to wear as your colors. Just like a knight of old, you said. And you won. Do you remember that, Jared?"

Merideth wasn't close enough to hear the captain's reply, nor to see the way Lucinda looked up at him, but she could imagine the lashes above the woman's limpid brown eyes were fluttering furiously.

It wasn't until the ladies learned of Merideth's recent visit to the French capital that they showed any interest in her. Then they couldn't seem to hear enough. While Lucinda sat by the captain's side, Merideth answered questions, giving detailed description of the gowns she saw and wore.

When she finally pleaded fatigue and was shown to a large well-appointed room by a black servant, she had a throbbing headache.

It was still upon her the following morning.

They spent the night in separate rooms, and rose early to breakfast on ham and eggs, potatoes and biscuits and fish. Lucinda, dressed in a powder-blue gown with rows of lace frothing from the elbow-length sleeve, suggested Jared stay another day.

"Oh, and you too, Lady Merideth," she added sweetly.

But Jared declined, promising to come back for a long visit as soon as he could. He assured them he needed to get to Royal Oak without delay to assure himself it suffered no ill from the war.

They were both silent as they rode side by side along the path. The land was low and swampy in places, the soil dark. As the day progressed, the weather grew hotter, the air thick with moisture and droning insects.

"I imagine we'll have a storm before long. Hopefully we'll make it to Royal Oak before it breaks."

Merideth made a noncommittal noise that made Jared twist in his saddle to look at her.

"What's wrong?"

"Not a thing." Merideth kept her eyes fixed on the path ahead. For several moments they trotted along in silence. Then the captain reached out and grabbed her horse's reins, bringing them both to a halt.

"I asked you a question."

Merideth lifted her chin. "And I answered it." She followed the drift of his eyes till they rested on the locket. As if it were on fire, she jerked her fingers away. "This contention of yours that I touch my necklace when I'm lying is nonsense. It happens to be very dear to me."

Saying nothing, the captain continued to watch her. Around her Merideth could hear the singing of birds and the stirring of the wind through the grasses and trees. "Shouldn't we be on our way if we plan to be at your plantation before it rains?" she said as her horse impatiently stomped his hooves.

"First tell me why you've been so quiet."

"Why I've . . ." She stared at him, momentarily at a loss for words. "What? Am I not pleasant-enough company for you? If that's the case, I suggest you look for someone who wasn't kidnapped and brought to a strange country against her wishes. She might be more accommodating. Besides, I should think you would like a respite from talking after last night. It must have been taxing on you being so charming to Lucinda King."

A grin played around the corners of Jared's mouth. "So you thought I was charming?"

Merideth's lips thinned. "No, actually, I thought you acted silly, but I'm sure the simpering Mrs. King was impressed."

"She always has been."

"Has been what?"

"Easily impressed. I tried to warn Alex about her, but he wouldn't listen."

"Was this before or after he escorted her to dinner?"

Jared's brow arched. "Don't believe everything you hear, Merry."

"I could say the same to you."

Jared shifted in the saddle. The leather creaked, but his attention remained on Merideth. "Besides," Merideth said, folding her hands over the reins to keep herself from touching her locket, "I don't care in the least what Mrs. King had to say."

With that she gave the reins a tug. The captain let them slip through his fingers and they continued on their way.

By afternoon, mountainous clouds billowed up to the east, darkening the sky. The wind picked up and Merideth snatched at her hat—the same flannel one she'd worn on the *Carolina*—and tried to keep up with the captain's hurried pace.

They made it to Royal Oak just as the storm sent its first streaks of lightning shooting across the sky. They raced the raindrops up the crushed-shell drive lined by two rows of moss-draped oaks. Merideth was too concerned with controlling the frightened horse and keeping her seat to notice the house until she was nearly upon it.

Then it loomed up on her, large, with a sweeping veranda across the front. As soon as they reached the brick stairs, Jared jumped from his horse and grabbed Merideth from hers.

They pushed through the front door, shaking raindrops off them like puppies.

"What the . . ." A rotund woman with a bright kerchief around her head came barreling down the curved staircase. She paused near the bottom as Jared glanced toward her. "Why, Mastah Jared, is that you?"

"In the flesh," Jared said, and rushed toward his old nanny. She squealed when he lifted her up.

"Now you stop that," she protested, but her laughter kept the words from being an admonishment. "Where've ya been for so long?"

"England, France. Just about all over the world. But I missed you all the while."

"Oh, you shush that silly talk." The woman straightened her kerchief. "Who's this child you brought me?"

After the introductions, the black woman, whose name was Belle—because Mastah Jared couldn't say Isabel when he was little—took Merideth upstairs.

"Ain't had no chance to air out this room," she said, bustling around, flitting dust around the bureau with her bunched-up apron.

"This is fine, really." The room was lovely, with pale-yellow curtains and a high tester bed draped in silk of the same color. "I'm just glad to be out of the wet."

While the storm raged outside, Merideth munched on cold chicken and rice from the tray brought to the room by another servant. Belle shook out the gown Merideth had managed to pack in the saddlebag. Her trunk had arrived at the Tradd Street house just as they were planning to leave, and she'd hurriedly scrambled through it, packing some clean shifts and the gown. It seemed she was always being forced to go here and there with the captain without a change of clothes.

Merideth napped through the afternoon and awoke refreshed, without any sign of the pesky headache. The storm was over, the air fresher after the drenching. When a young woman named Lily came in to light the candles, she told Merideth the captain had ridden off to look over the fields after the rain had stopped.

"He said ta go on and eat without 'im, 'cause he won't be back ta late."

The evening darkened into night, and despite her nap, Merideth was tired. She hadn't seen the captain, though she did meet the distant cousin of his, Bartrom Guthre. He was a pleasant dinner companion, talking mostly of his wife and young son, who were presently back in Charles Town. Merideth was sorry she hadn't seen them at Jared's house so she could bring Bartrom some word from his family.

He showed her around the house, which was indeed large and lovely, with intricate carvings in the ceiling and walls. Merideth liked it immediately, and wished . . . She couldn't decide what she wished. That she could stay. That the captain wanted her for more than a name she couldn't give him.

That he loved her.

But for now, at least, there was nothing she could do. Being at Royal Oak was almost like being on board the *Carolina*. There was no way she could escape. She fell asleep in a bed draped with mosquito netting, wondering if she didn't prefer it that way.

It was late when he came to her, softly, like a whisper in the night. Before, she had dreaded the shadows, the darkness. But this, the dip of the mattress as he slipped in beside her, the strength of his arms as they enfolded her, was an extension of her sensual dream.

His lips brushed hers, tasting of brandy and him.

Still groggy from sleep, Merideth lifted her hands to his hair, catching the ribbon that held it back and freeing the rough silk strands. Droplets of water showered onto her neck.

"'Tis raining again," Jared whispered as he bent to sip the moisture from her flesh.

Instinctively Merideth arched, braiding her fingers through his damp curls and holding him close.

"I came because I couldn't help myself. But the decision is yours. I'll leave if you want me to." His breath singed her skin.

"No." Her fingers tightened. "Don't go." She guided his mouth back to hers, kissing him with all the intensity, all the expertise, he'd taught her. Her tongue met his, parried, ignited the fires of their passion.

She lay naked under the coverlet and his large hands skimmed down, caressing her. He cupped her breast while he made love to her mouth. The pad of his thumb slid over her nipple and she moaned, lifting her back from the linen sheet and filling his hand more completely.

Nudging the gold locket aside with his chin, Jared kissed a path down the valley of her chest. His whiskers abraded the tender skin, sending shivers of pleasure shooting through her body. Then the moist heat settled over her nipple and he sucked it into his mouth.

Merideth's legs spread, wrapping around his body. The doeskin of his breeches felt damp and rough between her thighs, erotic. But she wanted him, the hair-roughened texture of his skin, the steel-hard manhood that pressed against her stomach.

With eager hands she pulled at his clothing. He

jerked his arms behind him, managing to rid himself of the shirt. It went sailing to the floor, and with a shuddered sigh Merideth ran her hands down the bulging muscles of his arms.

The breeches were more difficult. Jared slid down the bed between her legs, his mouth wetting a path as he went. His hands fumbled with the flap of his breeches; his tongue probed the honeyed folds of her body. She was wet and ready, the tremors setting her aquiver with the first heated contact.

She cried out, a siren song that drove Jared to the brink. He tore at his pants, freeing himself and driving into her with one powerful plunge. She called out his name, clasping him to her with arms and legs while her body writhed, milking him with wave upon shattering wave of pleasure.

When some semblance of reason returned, Jared rolled to his back, his arm thrown over his head, his face toward her. Lightning flashed, searing the room with a split second of white light. Enough time for him to see her clearly. To set an imprint of her perfection on his mind.

He leaned up on an elbow, his fingers tangling in the riot of golden curls spread across the pillow. "You are so beautiful. Like an angel," he whispered, and bent to kiss her lips.

She turned away.

"What is it?" With his fingers he cupped her chin, pulling her back toward him. He could only see the pale image of her face, the sparkle of her eyes.

"I'm not an angel," Merideth breathed, embarrassed that she was close to tears. "I'm but a woman." "A woman who loves you," she almost said, but pride kept her from it. The pride that made her know she could not stay here any longer, when his every touch shattered her soul.

"I know what you are," he murmured, his fingers drifting down the curve of her jaw to her neck. "The locket," he said, lifting the gold oval, feeling the heat from her body stored in the precious metal. "You always wear it. What's inside?"

"'Tis a miniature. A painting of my mother . . . and me. I was three when she died, but I remember her. Her sunshine and light . . . her happy laugh when she was with me."

"What happened to her?"

"I don't know, really." Merideth swallowed. "She became ill. Miss Alice took me to her room. She said I must be very good and very quiet or my mother would leave. Her bedchamber was dark . . . all the curtains were drawn tight, and the only candle was guttered. I could barely see her." She was quiet a moment and Jared thought perhaps she'd fallen asleep. But when she spoke again her voice was strong and clear.

"I asked why it was so dark . . . complained my mother couldn't see. Miss Alice yanked on my ear." Her hair rustled on the pillowcase as she turned her head to face him. "My mother died that night."

His arm slid beneath her, drawing her close. "Was your father there?"

"No. He was . . . I don't know where he was. But he rarely stayed at home. Not until debt limited his traveling."

"I'd like to see it . . . the painting of you and your

mother," Jared whispered into her hair.

"You shall," came her breathy reply.

In the morning he was gone. Merideth awoke to bright sunshine and dressed quickly. When she wandered downstairs Belle told her the master had gone off to the fields again and would be home late.

Disappointed, Merideth ate a quick breakfast. She'd planned to talk with him today. To ask him straight out why he'd brought her here and what he planned to do with her. She wanted the answers, though she dreaded them. Dreaded them because she feared she already knew the answers.

She was a trophy of war to him. Like his ancestor the pirate, he'd captured her. But unlike the long-ago rogue, Jared Blackstone had no intention of marrying his captive.

Feeling more and more dejected as she faced the realities of her situation, Merideth wandered about the house. Mr. Guthre had shown her most, but not all, of the rooms last evening. Today she entered one he hadn't included on his tour.

It was a library, book-lined and smelling of leather and wood. The shutters were closed, but dust motes still danced in the slanted rays of light that filtered through the wooden slats.

The portrait above the mantel caught her eye, and Merideth moved toward it, mesmerized. It was the pirate and his lady, of that she had no doubt. The man was large and blond, with a wildness about him so like his great-grandson. The woman was dark and pretty, and they looked at each other with such love that Merideth was momentarily jealous of the long-dead couple. Surely such devotion as theirs transcended time.

"Ah, I see you've found the skeleton in our closet."

Merideth whirled around, hand at her throat, to see Daniel Wallis blocking the doorway. "The pirate," he said, pointing to the painting. "Though I prefer to think of him as a pariah."

"Jared doesn't seem to think so."

"He wouldn't." Daniel shut the door. "Are you ready?"

"Ready?"

He shrugged delicately. "To begin your return trip to England. You do still want to go, don't you?"

Merideth glanced over her shoulder at the portrait, then back at the captain's cousin. "Yes," she said, her voice low. "I think it time I go home."

Chapter Nineteen

Jared took the winding central stairs three at a time. Small clumps of rich black Carolina mud dirtied the polished treads and he knew he'd get a scolding from Belle, but he didn't care. He was anxious to see Merideth. Too anxious to take the time to remove the boots he'd worn in the fields.

After a sharp rap on the door, which brought no answer, he turned the brass knob. Filtered light drenched the room like melted butter on a biscuit. He glanced at the high bed draped in gossamer netting and couldn't help a smile.

He'd left her in that bed early this morning, rising before dawn so he could finish his tour of the fields and be back by the evening meal. He and Bartrom had spent all day on horseback discussing the plantation, and he was tired.

And he wanted to see Merideth.

Retracing his dash up the stairs, he checked the parlor. She wasn't there either.

Today Jared had reached several decisions. One was to reflood all the fields. His grandmother had converted much of Royal Oak's acreage to the growing of indigo. It had been a smart move in 1743. Indigo was a good cash crop that grew well in the Low Country. It had helped make the Blackstones one of the wealthiest families in the Carolinas.

But indigo couldn't be eaten. And Jared feared a British blockade. Despite the attempt to thwart the British navy by privateers such as himself, England still ruled the seas. It wouldn't be long until Charles Town followed northern cities like New York and Philadelphia in having its ports closed.

Then the people of South Carolina would have to depend upon themselves for food. They would need rice.

Jared never doubted the eventual outcome of the war . . . especially after meeting and conversing with Benjamin Franklin. Eventually the French would enter the conflict. Eventually the Americans would prevail. But in the meantime Jared meant to do all he could to see his homeland provided for.

He had made another decision today while riding beneath wispy beards of Spanish moss. This one concerned Merideth. Jared stuck his head in the dining room, his gaze sweeping over the large room.

"She ain't in there."

Turning, Jared gave Belle a smile, which grew wider when he saw her scowl. "I can see that. Where—"

"What you doin' trackin' mud all over my clean floors? Why, your mama would roll over in her grave if'n she saw it."

"Sorry." Jared bent down and gave the old black woman a quick hug. He was secretly pleased he could no longer receive the punishment of no dessert. "Where is Lady Merideth?"

"She's gone."

"Gone? Is she in the gardens?" His shoulders lifted. "Did she go for a ride?"

"Gone, I said she was gone. Left first thing this mornin'."

Comprehension was slow to come, basically because he'd stopped thinking of Merideth in terms of his captive. But when it hit, Jared was filled with impotent rage. "Where in the hell did she go? How?"

"Don't you go cursin' like that. She went off with Mistah Daniel. He said you knowed about it."

Jared was to the front door before Belle's voice stopped him. He gripped the handle, his knuckles white as he turned. "What did you say?" God, when he got his hands on Daniel, he'd have some explaining to do. What did he think he was doing, spiriting Merideth off like this?

"I said, she done left a letter for ye. In the library. Said to make sure ye got it."

Without another word Jared clomped down the hall toward the library. It was his favorite room at Royal Oak. Even as a child, while John was upstairs observing his plants or collecting rocks, Jared liked to come to the library. He'd look at the portrait of his great-grandfather and imagine himself on the high seas.

But this time when he entered the book-lined room, it wasn't the picture but the letter on the mantel beneath it that drew his gaze.

379

Beside the gold locket.

Picking it up, Jared swallowed as his fingers closed over the oval of gold. He'd never seen it other than around her beautiful neck. Trailing the ribbon from his hand, he grabbed up the folded parchment and tore open the wax seal. Feeling very tired, he sat in the chair behind his desk.

Her handwriting was neat and even. The letter was short, and reading it made his heart ache unbearably.

> Dearest Jared,
> By the time you read this I will be on my way back to England. Leaving you is painful, and the most difficult thing I've ever done, but I think it best. Though I long ago decided you couldn't have killed my father, I know you neither believe nor trust me. And I find I cannot live with that.
> Please don't worry about me. I shall be fine. I'm leaving the locket to help you remember me. I shall always remember you.
> I love you.
> Merideth

Jared looked from the signature on the parchment to his hand. Slowly he unfurled his fingers till the gold locket lay in his palm. Delicate filigree swirls decorated the outside. With a flick of his thumb, he unhooked the tiny latch. The top opened like the shell of a clam.

Jared recognized Lord Alfred on the left, though the Englishman appeared much younger and in better health. But it was the miniature on the right that held his interest. There, looking very much like Merideth, was a young woman with light hair. Beside her sat a beautiful child. A child with the face of an angel.

Merideth.

Jared took a shattered breath and shut his eyes. Belle found him like that when she came to light the candles in the room.

"I thought you lived with Captain Blackstone." It was dark; they'd ridden hard all day and into the night to arrive at Charles Town. And though she'd only been there once, and though she could barely see now, Merideth was certain this wasn't the same house on Tradd Street.

"I do," Daniel answered. They were leading their horses around back to the stables. "But I keep this place too. For when I want to be off to myself."

Merideth looked toward him but could discern no more than a shadowy form.

"It's better that no one knows you're here," he explained. "'Twill be easier to get you north that way. I'm convinced that's the best plan."

She supposed it made sense, as much sense as anything else that had happened to her since Jared Blackstone had come into her life. Besides, she was too tired to think of it now. Her legs felt limp and quivery. Merideth didn't know how she could still stand.

She was startled from her lethargy when Daniel pounded on the stable door. He yelled a name, and some minutes later a bedraggled old man with a gray, straggly beard and torn, filthy clothing opened the door. He held a lantern high, squinting through the light at Daniel and Merideth.

"What ye be wantin'?" he growled as his body blocked their entrance to the stable.

Merideth's horse, obviously as tired as she and anxious for her feed, pawed the ground.

"Make way for your betters, you insufferable swine. I'll tolerate no disrespect from the likes of you." Daniel shoved at the man's chest. The poor old fellow faltered and fell back, catching himself before tumbling to the straw-littered floor.

Merideth thought he would come after Daniel then . . . the look in the old man's eyes was fierce. But he evidently thought better of it. With a scowl he hung the lantern from a hook and grabbed the reins from Merideth's hand. She let go instantly, jumping out of the way when he led the horse past her. This seemed to amuse the old man, for when he looked back a grotesque parody of a smile creased his whiskered face. "So now you're takin' to bringin' girls here too, are ye?"

Before Merideth's surprised eyes Daniel lurched forward, clutching the ragged garment covering the old man's chest and slapping him hard across the face. Merideth gasped as the sharp sound echoed through the stable.

"Shut your filthy mouth," Daniel said before pushing him to the ground. The horse's hooves pounded the straw nervously and Merideth feared the man would be trampled, but he rolled away. The evil laugh that escaped him made Merideth's flesh crawl.

"Come on," Daniel said as he grabbed the lantern. He rushed from the stable, leaving it blanketed in darkness, and Merideth scrambled after him.

"What in heaven's name happened back there?" Her voice was breathless as she rushed to catch up with him. Merideth could see the gardens now, at least the parts where the small puddle of light spilled. They were overgrown and choked with weeds.

"He was insolent," was all Daniel would say.

The house appeared deserted. They approached from the back up brick stairs. Merideth tried to suppress her feelings of apprehension. It was just because it was night and deathly dark, she thought. In the morning things would appear brighter. But she couldn't put the ugly scene in the stable from her mind.

Once inside, Daniel lit a branch of candles and led the way up a narrow back staircase. At the top he turned left and opened a door. The room was large and ornately furnished, from what Merideth could see as he swept the flickering flames in an arch.

"You can stay in here."

As she stepped through the threshold, Daniel shut the door behind her, leaving her in darkness.

Panic swelled in Merideth's breast. She fumbled with the latch, swinging the door open only to find the hallway deserted. The light gone. Stifling a sob, she shut the door. Feeling her way along the chair rail, she inched around the room, all the while fighting her fear.

Her elbow bumped into something hard and she cried out. A chifforobe, she discovered, as her hands framed the wooden wardrobe. She found her way to the bed at last, then across it to the commode at its side. Her fingers fumbled with the objects on top, trying not to knock them to the floor.

Her eyes were adjusting to the darkness slowly, and now she could make out dark shadows. Merideth's breath quickened when she found the flint. Carefully she struck it, the blooming flash of light allowing her to see the candle stuck in a silver holder. The wick caught and Merideth sighed in relief, collapsing onto the bed.

She lay huddled on her side, staring at the flickering flame, wondering why she'd come. Deep in her being she missed the captain. Instinctively her fingers reached for the locket before remembering that even that small measure of comfort was gone. But she was glad she'd left it for Jared . . . left him something of herself.

What was he doing now? She couldn't help wondering what he had thought when he'd read her note. He'd be angry. She knew that. But his rage would pass. Then he'd realize what she'd done was for the best.

Now, if Merideth could only convince herself of that . . .

Sleep, when it came, was fitful. She tossed and turned, her dreams many and varied. One moment she was riding the waves of ecstasy, her body and soul consumed by Jared Blackstone. The next she was torn from his arms, thrown into a dark pit where her screams echoed off into nothingness.

It was from the latter nightmare that she woke with a start. She lay on the bed, her breast heaving, staring at the circle of light reflected on the ceiling.

She hadn't noticed before, but above the bed were paintings. Angels, she thought at first, and smiled. Though the room was chilled, her face and body were covered with a fine sheen of perspiration, and she raised her arm to blot her forehead with her sleeve. When she lowered it she looked up again at the mural.

The figures weren't exactly angels. She squinted her eyes, wishing there was more light. That's when she noticed something strange about the elflike creatures. They were all boys. Merideth blinked her eyes in shock, but couldn't help opening them again; she stared intently to make certain she'd seen it correctly.

There was no doubt. The small, pretty-faced people cavorting across the ceiling were nude from the waist down, and painted in graphic detail.

Making a noise of shock and outrage, Merideth rolled to her side and sat in one motion. Golden curls spilled over her shoulders as her head hung limply forward. She gulped for breath, fearing she would be sick.

That's when she heard voices.

They were raised in laughter, and Merideth thought they came from somewhere downstairs. Slipping off the bed, she straightened her gown and picked up the candlestick. The taper was burning low, sputtering in the melted wax, and Merideth quickly searched for another, to no avail.

Hurriedly she left the room.

Protecting the flame with her cupped hand, Merideth rushed along the hall. Passing by the servant's steps, she found the top of a wide spiraling staircase. The voices were louder now. She recognized Daniel's. There was another, no, two other men she'd never heard before.

The treads were carpeted in an ornate rug that softened her footsteps. When she reached the landing she lifted the stub of a candle to the face of the tall case clock.

Twenty minutes past two.

An hour that should find her abed. But she couldn't return to that room. The voices and the bright light spilling from the room to the right of the wide entrance hall drew her.

Lifting the skirts of her blue silk gown, she moved across the hall. In the doorway she paused, staring into the parlor.

The room was aglow with a multitude of candles. Overhead a crystal luster sparkled with reflected light. And in every conceivable spot tapers burned, their twinkling flames contributing to the brilliance.

Two young men she'd never seen before sat in the room, sprawling across chairs, their jackets off, their shirts loose. Daniel stood before them, his back to Merideth. He wore a floral-patterned banyan of vivid red, and his head, free from the wig, was covered with wispy brown curls. He held a goblet in one hand, a decanter in the other, and he used them both to gesture as he talked.

When one of the men spotted Merideth, he motioned with his head, and Daniel turned around, his loose robe swirling about him.

Merideth gasped and stepped back. She'd never seen anyone look so grotesque. His lips were rouged scarlet and his eyes lined with kohl. At the apex of each cheek rode a velvet beauty patch. Merideth could only stare.

But Daniel seemed not to notice. He waved her in, splashing red wine over his sleeve in the process. "Ah, Lady Merideth, do come join us."

"I heard voices," Merideth began, and faltered. A smoky haze hung in the air, giving the whole scene a surreal quality. "I don't want to disturb you." Suddenly Merideth had the strongest urge to bolt. From the room. From the house.

But Daniel's hand on her elbow stopped any such thoughts. "Nonsense, my dear Merideth. We wouldn't dream of you escaping us." He was stronger than he looked, and Merideth found herself being pulled to the center of the garishly decorated parlor. The couch he led her to was blood red, with rolled bolsters and gilded legs. The cushions enveloped her when she sat.

Merideth swallowed and tried to stand. The force of his hold kept her from it.

Unease burgeoned into fear.

"I really should leave."

This time his voice lost its coating of civility. "Stay where you are." His brows lifted. "The party is in your honor, after all."

"I don't know what you want from me, but I . . ." She what? Merideth couldn't think what to say. What to do. All the while she stared at Daniel, forcing her eyes not to waver. She didn't want him to see her fear. But she couldn't help herself. She was frightened.

He looked so different with his face painted like a French courtesan. Yet something about him seemed familiar. Almost as if she'd seen him like this before. But that was impossible. Certainly she would remember if he'd ever dressed as a woman before.

"Let me see." Daniel brought his hand to his chin, pointing a finger to his rouged cheek. "Now, what could I want from you?" He chortled, and the other two

387

men must have found this amusing, for they both joined him, tittering away.

"I'm leaving." Merideth pushed his hand aside and scrambled to her feet. She was nearly to the door when her shoulders were grabbed and she was whirled about. It was one of the other men who caught her, held her, as Daniel bore down on her, his face a mask of rage.

And in that instant Merideth knew where she'd seen him before.

The coach.

She . . . *he* was driving the coach that nearly ran her down in Paris. He'd worn a hat and veils at the time, but when Merideth had looked up, the wind caught the netting, blowing it aside and exposing the face. She'd thought at the time that the woman was frightened, that the expression on her painted face was fear. Now she saw it again and recognized it for what it truly was. Hatred.

"What are you going to do with me?" Merideth couldn't keep her voice from trembling. "Why are you doing this?"

"As to why, my dear Merideth, I think you know. Was it not recognition I spotted on your angelic face?"

"You tried to run me down with a coach."

"Ah, you did see me. I feared as much."

"But why?" Merideth's voice was insistent. "What did I ever do to you?"

"Not what you did. What you might do." Daniel paused, motioning to the two men. "Go on upstairs with you. I'll join you soon."

"Are you certain we should go?" one of them asked, and Daniel nodded.

"*This* will insure Lady Merideth's cooperation." He pulled a pistol from the silken folds of his banyan.

Merideth stood, her back against the scarlet-covered wall, the gun pointed at her, as the two men left the room. Her mind worked furiously to come up with a plan to escape this madman, for that was what she assumed he was. But nothing came to her, not even when his attention was once again focused on her.

"You still haven't figured it out, have you? Perhaps you aren't as clever as I thought."

"Figured what out? I . . . I don't know what you mean."

"The identity of the traitor. Of Lady Sinclair."

"I don't know who . . ." The truth came in an epiphany. "You?"

His smile was evil, his shrug delicate. "Perhaps you *didn't* know."

"No, I didn't. How could I?"

"Your father did. He knew it all. Which, of course, was why I had to eliminate him."

"*You* killed my father!" Merideth jerked forward, but the barrel of the pistol halted her advance.

"What would you expect me to do?" Daniel questioned logically. "I thought it was all handled very nicely. With your father dead and Jared to hang for the murder. But then my dear cousin shows up in Morlaix with you. Somehow he's escaped the house *and* he's accompanied by another who knows my little secret."

"You tried to kill me then."

"Oh yes. Several times. In the inn, in Paris. I even hired a highwayman . . . such a waste of time and coin." He shook his head. "But my damn cousin kept spoiling things."

"But surely you realized after we met on the *Carolina* that I didn't know who you were."

"At first I thought you were just being clever and coy. That you planned to blackmail me, or were using me to rid yourself of Jared. Then it occurred to me that he was wrong. That you really didn't know. But you'd seen me in Paris. Sooner or later you might remember that. It's better if we simply eliminate you all together. Don't you agree?"

Merideth felt helpless against his cold logic. "Jared won't let you get away with this."

"My dear cousin won't know. Perhaps John could figure it out, but not Jared."

"What does John have to do with this? If you're Lady Sinclair, then he couldn't have been in love with her. You made that up to make Jared think it was me, didn't you? Didn't—"

"Enough. I tire of this game of a thousand questions. Questions it matters naught if you know the answers to. By tomorrow, nothing on this earthly plane will be of consequence to you."

So now she knew. Merideth fought him when he grabbed her, but before she could do more than scratch his cheek, he twisted her around. Her arm was jerked high. The gun jabbed into her back.

He pushed her out the door then, and it was all Merideth could do to keep her footing as he shoved her along the hallway, through the back door, and into the night. She cried out when he twisted her arm higher, but he only laughed.

"There's no one about who will help you, Lady Merideth. No one at all."

And apparently he was right, for no one came to her rescue.

Merideth could barely see, couldn't imagine where they were headed, but suddenly pain exploded in her shoulder as she was rammed into a brick wall. Tears streamed down her cheeks, and her forehead fell forward against the gritty surface. He let go of her arm them, but Merideth was so disoriented she couldn't take advantage of her freedom. Besides, he still held the cocked gun to her ribs.

She could hear him fumbling with something. A lock? And then came the creaking of rusty door hinges. A dank, musty smell assaulted her nostrils even before he grabbed her again, shoving her into a black hole.

The door slammed shut behind her, blocking even the weakest rays of light.

"No! No!" Merideth's screams reverberated off the walls, echoing back to her own ears, increasing her panic. Her heart raced, and try as she might, she couldn't seem to get enough air into her starving lungs.

"No, no," she sobbed. "Let me out. Oh, please, let me out."

But only silence answered her pleas. Her fists pounded the door, scraping and clawing at the thick panels of wood.

Then slowly, as her strength deserted her, Merideth slid to the packed-earth floor. Clutching her knees, she folded her head between her arms and tried to tame the panic, the feeling that the walls were closing in on her. The demons of the past.

Chapter Twenty

"Where in the hell is she?"

Daniel glanced up from the muffin he'd lathered with butter, his brow raised. The heavy curtains were drawn. A branch of candles on the table flickered, a poor substitute for the morning light. "Good day, dear cousin. I didn't expect to see you here. This is the first you've visited my little home away from home. I didn't even know you knew of its existence."

Jared strode into the dining room, ignoring the cheerful chatter. He was sweaty and covered with dust, certainly in no mood for frivolous conversation. "I want to know what you've done with Merideth."

Daniel shrugged. "Why, nothing. Nothing but send her on her way to New York. She wanted to go back to England. I simply helped—" Daniel yelped as he was hauled up out of his chair.

Using the scarlet banyan to hold him, Jared gave his cousin a shake. "I've been riding all night and most of the morning, and I want to know where she is, Not

393

some vague response like 'She's on her way north.'" He twisted his fingers in the silk. "Who is she with and when did she leave?"

"I'll tell you nothing till you put me down." Daniel's slippered feet landed with a thud on the carpet. He straightened his wig and smoothed the wrinkles from his gown. "You always did think your brawn could take care of any problem," Daniel said, his expression cold. "I would have thought you'd have learned by now it doesn't."

Sinking into a chair, Jared rubbed both hands down over his face. His eyes felt gritty from lack of sleep, and two days' worth of whiskers covered his cheeks and chin. Daniel was right. Jared knew better than to fly into a rage, especially around his cousin. He needed information, and though he was anxious to be on his way, he'd have to play the game Daniel's way. "I'm sorry," he said when his emotions were somewhat under control. "This probably isn't your fault. I know how persuasive Merideth can be, but I need to know where she is."

"Why?"

"Why?" Why. The question he'd been asking himself all night as he rode through the Low Country. Why did he care so much that she was gone? The answer was not easy to accept, but nonetheless Jared knew it was true. Looking up with bloodshot eyes, Jared met his cousin's gaze. "I need to see her, Daniel," he said as calmly as he could. "Now please tell me. How long ago did she leave?"

Settling back in his seat, Daniel took his time spreading a lace napkin in his lap. Then carefully he took a bite of his muffin. Butter oozed between his teeth and he gently dabbed at his lips. "You haven't said how you like my house. It's not so grand as the one on Tradd Street, I know, but then ever since your parents died that's belonged to you and John. And no one expects me to have something quite as good as the Blackstones born on the right side of the sheet."

"What in the hell are you talking about? You were always welcome at both Royal Oak and the house in Charles Town." Jared wished Daniel would just tell him about Merideth and be done with it.

"Welcome, perhaps, but we both knew who owned it . . . everything. Didn't we?" When Jared said nothing, only sat staring, his eyes narrowed, Daniel jumped to his feet. His palms flattened on the table, his sleeve caught the knife handle, sending it clattering to the floor. "Didn't we!" he yelled, his face growing red.

"I own both properties," Jared said without emotion.

Daniel's smile was triumphant. He jerked his head and sank down into his seat, seemingly pleased by the admission. "But you don't have everything you want. Do you, dear cousin? You don't have Merideth Banistar."

Leaning back, Jared stayed in his chair for a moment, studying Daniel. He'd thought Daniel was odd before, but he'd always tried to reconcile his feelings with an understanding that people were different. But Daniel's actions now were something he'd never witnessed before. Taking a deep breath, Jared bent forward. "Where is she?"

"She doesn't want you, you know. She wanted to get away from you."

"Where is she?"

"Actually . . ." Daniel picked up an orange and began peeling it, the tangy scent of citrus filling the air. "After the night we spent together, she said she preferred me to—"

Jared was across the table before Daniel could finish his sentence. Grabbing his cousin by the lace about his neck, he hauled him forward, across his plate. Orange peels and muffin crumbs scattered. "If you hurt her—if you touched her—so help me, I'll kill you." Jared's jaw clenched. "Do you understand me?" He held on till Daniel nodded . . . reluctantly. If Jared believed Daniel's claim about spending the night with Merideth, he wouldn't have let him go so easily. But Jared had long suspected his cousin's tastes didn't run toward women.

With a shove Jared sent him back into his chair. Daniel landed in an undignified heap, his composure badly mauled but not broken.

"You uncivilized brute," Daniel yelled, swiping the lace handkerchief down the front of his soiled banyan. "You've ruined this silk. And all for the sake of that slut."

This time Jared went around the table. His teeth gritted in anger as he yanked Daniel from the chair. "I've put up with as much of this as I intend to. Tell me where she is. And never . . . *never* refer to Lady Merideth that way again."

"Of course you'd choose her over me, one of your own family. Or have you forgotten?"

"I haven't forgotten a thing. The only reason I

haven't beaten the information out of you is the memory of your mother."

"That whore!" Daniel spit out the words, his face the embodiment of hatred.

Slowly Jared lowered him to the floor. He was surprised, nay, shocked, by Daniel's portrayal of his mother. Jared's aunt certainly hadn't had an easy life, but the circumstances of Daniel's birth were beyond her control. Jared reminded his cousin of that. Daniel's only response was a snort.

Taking a deep breath, Jared reached in the pocket of his frock coat. He would have to finish this conversation with Daniel at another time. For now, he needed to continue his pursuit of Merideth. He took out the gold oval and, following Daniel to a small desk in the corner of the room, laid it on the polished surface. If demands and threats didn't work, he would plead.

"What's this?" Daniel hesitated, his hand on the drawer pull.

"Merideth's locket. She left it for me, when she departed Royal Oak. It was with her note." Jared flicked open the clasp to reveal the miniatures inside. "She loves me, Daniel . . . and I love her. I must bring her back."

"Love," Daniel laughed, the sound anything but joyous. "So you love each other." The drawer slid open. "How . . ." He shrugged. "How very sweet." He reached into the drawer. "Unfortunately, this romance is doomed to failure." With that, Daniel picked up the locket with his free hand and threw it onto the floor.

"What the hell are you doing?" Angrily Jared bent over to snatch it up. The miniature of Merideth and her mother had fallen out. Jared picked it up. He started to slide the painting back into the tiny frame when some scrolled writing etched into the gold beneath where the painting had been caught his attention.

He read the words; blinked; then read them again. His expression changed from one of disbelief to one of rage. Clutching the locket, he looked up, ready to attack. But the small pocket pistol pointed at him brought him to a halt.

"You," Jared began. "You're Lady Sinclair."

Daniel kept the gun trained on Jared's chest, but he did glance down at the ribbon streaming from Jared's hand. "So that's where he hid the information. I suspected Lord Alfred might do something like that." Daniel shrugged delicately. "That's why I searched his library so carefully." He sighed. "I'd hoped getting rid of his offspring would be the end of it, but . . ."

Jared took a step forward until he heard the pistol cock. "What did you do with her?"

"Lady Merideth is the least of your concerns, dear cousin." Daniel thrust out the gun when Jared took another step. "Don't think I won't use this dear, dear cousin Jared. I've killed before."

"Lord Alfred?"

"Why, yes," Daniel smiled. "I did do the old man in. He knew I was being paid by both sides in this silly little conflict. Don't look so shocked, cousin. We bastards of the world must earn our coin some way. Anyway, Lord Alfred threatened me with the information. I paid him at first to keep quiet. But that arrangement wasn't to my liking. So I waited for him to contact someone in the American government . . . the old fool didn't even realize the message went through me."

"And stopped there, I presume."

"Not entirely. That's when I pulled you into the intrigue."

"Why? Why involve me if you intended to kill him?"

"Let's just say I enjoy seeing you Blackstones squirm." Daniel giggled. "I'd been at Banistar Hall before, and knew the right places to hide. With their lack of staff, I could have stayed there a fortnight without being detected. But it didn't take that long. You came along with your usual bravado, during the storm, and I just sat back and waited for the right moment."

"To kill him."

"Oh, not just him, dear Jared. You." He laughed again. "You were to die also. Hanged, no less. Such a fitting demise for the descendant of a pirate, don't you think?"

"I think you've lost your mind." Jared slipped the locket into his pocket.

"You'd like to think so, wouldn't you?" Daniel's features contorted in anger. "You'd like to think me crazy. Just like John. That's right, John discovered I was Lady Sinclair. Of course there was no love affair. I made all that up. But he found out about my very profitable undertakings with the British."

"And so you killed him too." The deadly calm of Jared's voice belied the surging emotions inside.

"Oh, yes, I did. You figured it out," Daniel smirked. "I always did think you as clever as the others, even if they did have their noses in a book every moment of the day."

"What did you do with Merideth?" A knot formed in Jared's throat, so large he could barely get the words out. "Did you kill her too?"

"No. But don't worry, I shall. What I can't decide is whether to kill her first and let you watch, or vice versa." Daniel bobbed his head as he spoke. "I think I shall let you see her demise. After all, I really don't have anything personal against her." His face contorted. "Though she did play the role of your whore."

Jared lunged forward, and the pistol fired. Something solid, like a fist, rammed into his side, and Jared faltered. But his anger was stronger than the pain. Jared caught a quick glimpse of the shock and fear on Daniel's face as he knocked the spent gun from his cousin's hand. The weapon went flying to the floor. And under Jared's weight Daniel fell back, sprawling against the desk.

Panic filled Daniel's eyes and his hands flailed out. Feeling the solid strength of the candlestick, Daniel tried to grip the ornate silver. But Jared grabbed hold of the silk robe, pulling him up, then slamming his head back against the smooth wood surface.

"Where is she? Where is she, damn you?"

Daniel's hand knocked the candlestick. Hot wax dripped from the top of the taper, down the side of the thick brocade drapes. The flame followed the arc. It took the fire only a moment to recognize the new supply of rich fuel. Then eagerly it sent tentacles dancing up the silk, consuming all in its path.

"Fire! The room's on fire!" Daniel's voice squeaked as Jared tightened his hold. "We have to get out!"

The wallpaper was next in the path of the voracious

flames, and soon the entire wall was aglow. Choking threads of smoke filled the air. Jared's eyes burned and his lungs cried for a breath of fresh air, but he didn't move. "Nowhere, you bastard. We're going nowhere till you tell me where she is."

"We'll die!" Daniel's face was purple and his eyes bulged. "We'll die," he choked out again. By now the rug was smoldering, sending off the nauseating smell of charred wool.

"Tell me," Jared rasped. "Or so help me God, I'll kill you with my bare hands and leave your body to burn. You think I care about myself? You've taken all from me." Overcome by a bout of coughing, Jared stopped talking, but he tightened his grip. Sweat poured from his forehead and rolled down his chest. But his eyes were deadly serious.

"Smokehouse."

The word was so wracked with coughing, so choked, that at first Jared thought Daniel was complaining about the smoke. It wasn't till Daniel said it again that Jared realized he was referring to an outbuilding.

"She's in the smokehouse? Are you telling me that's where she is?" Jared realized he was shaking Daniel almost uncontrollably and stopped.

"Yes . . . yes. Save me!" Daniel clutched at Jared's sleeve. His wig was gone, his curls plastered to his head with sweat. "Oh, please, save me." His voice quivered piteously between hacking coughs. "Jared, cousin, don't let me die."

The air was thick with smoke, disorienting Jared's best efforts to find the door. He stumbled forward, yanking a nearly limp Daniel in his wake. The fire had a voice of its own, loud and roaring, punctuated by the shattering crash of a rafter by the window. Where Jared had stood moments earlier.

It was too late. He'd stayed in the burning inferno too long and now the fire surrounded him. His side hurt and he glanced down, but the smoke was so thick he couldn't see if he was bleeding. He just knew that Merideth could die if no one released her from the smokehouse. This last thought galvanized him to action. Eyes streaming, lungs raw and burning, he plunged forward, through the thick black smoke.

Why he dragged Daniel along, Jared didn't know. Perhaps if he'd thought, about John . . . even about Merideth's father, the fingers clutching his arm would have slackened. But when he surged forward into the hallway where the smoke only laced the air with wispy streamers, Daniel was still with him, though he was almost a dead weight.

Gasping for breath, Jared burst through the front door into the sunshine. Several servants were in the yard. One had grabbed a bucket, but the others simply stood, staring up at the house. They all jumped back when one side of the roof collapsed into the flaming caldron, sending sparks and burning coals spraying across the yard.

Jared dropped Daniel's body beside the huddled group of servants. It fell in a lifeless heap. Then Jared ran around the side of the house. His arms and legs felt as if they were swimming through molasses, and his hip ached, but he pushed on.

Built of brick, the circular smokehouse was compact and windowless. And Jared couldn't imagine how

Merideth must feel, locked inside. As he raced toward the door he remembered her fear of dark places, of the way she threw open a window or door rather than be enclosed.

"Oh God, please let her be all right."

Jared grabbed the heavy iron padlock and gave it a yank. It bounced back against the heavy wood door with a clunk.

"Merideth!" Jared pounded the splintery wood. "Merideth, honey, answer me!" His hands flattened on the bricks framing the door, Jared leaned his forehead close . . . listening.

But there was no sound, except his own shattered breathing and the heavy thudding of his heart.

Pushing away from the building, Jared loped around the yard, frantically searching for something he could use to pry open the lock. He finally spotted an ax left by the woodpile. Snatching it up, he hurried back to the smokehouse.

Sparks shot out as metal rang against metal. Jared lifted the ax high, then with all his might brought it down across the lock. Again and again. Wood splintered and split. And the metal hasp flew off.

Tossing the ax aside, Jared pushed open the door. Now that the moment was at hand, he was afraid of what he'd find. Daniel had said Merideth was in the smokehouse, and that he hadn't killed her yet. But what if he'd lied or done some other unspeakable thing to her?

Jared took a deep breath and widened the wedge of light spilling into the darkness. His eyes narrowed and he stepped inside. He heard movement behind the door and turned just as Merideth started toward him, a meat hook raised high above her head.

Her hand stopped midway through its downward arc. Blue eyes widened in surprise. "Jared? Oh my God, Jared!" The meat hook thudded to the packed earth and she flew into his outstretched arms.

"Merideth. Merideth." Jared couldn't get enough of holding her, of saying her name. She was crying and clutching at him, and together they sank to their knees. Jared kissed the top of her head, ran his hands down her back. She smelled of woodsmoke and ham and Merideth, and Jared thought there'd never been a better scent.

With his hands he gently cradled her face. His thumbs wiped the tears that streaked through the dirt on her cheeks. "Are you all right, Merry? Did he hurt you?"

"No, I'm fine." Merideth shook her head. It was then she noticed Jared's face, his singed hair. "What happened to you?"

"There was a fire, but it's all right now." Jared paused. He'd almost forgotten about Daniel trying to shoot him. At first Jared thought his cousin had succeeded. But the pain he'd experienced initially was now only a dull ache. Reaching down, Jared found the hole in his jacket where the ball had torn the fabric. But there was no blood and no wound.

"What is it? What's wrong?" Merideth watched as Jared reached into his pocket. "My locket," she said as he slowly pulled the gold oval out by the ribbon. The light from the open doorway shone on the polished surface. "It's dented."

Jared ran his thumb over the metal, then looked up, his expression one of disbelief. "I think the locket saved my life . . . at least saved me from taking the bullet Daniel fired at me."

Merideth stared down at the locket, then back at Jared. "Daniel tried to shoot you?" Her eyes widened when Jared nodded. "Oh, how could I forget, Jared? It was Daniel." She grasped his shoulders. "He killed my father . . . and your brother. He was going to kill me. He locked me in here . . ." Merideth took a deep breath. "I was so terrified." Memories of the fears she'd faced locked in the small, dark building momentarily flooded her. She raised her chin. "But I didn't give up. I crawled around till I found the hook, and then I waited for him to come back."

"My brave, brave girl." Jared touched her cheek, her hair. He couldn't seem to keep his hands off her.

"I wasn't going to let him just murder me, like he did the others. I had to try."

"Shhhh. You don't have to worry about him any more." Jared pressed her close to his heart.

"Are you certain you're all right?"

"Aye, thanks to your locket." Jared took a deep breath. "God, Merry, I was so worried about you. And it was all my fault. I pushed you away with my doubts and suspicions—" His voice cracked, and for the first time since he'd gotten word of his brother's death, tears threatened. "Oh God, Merideth, can you ever forgive me? I love you so."

She looked up, searching the clear green of his eyes with her own. "You do? You love me?"

"With all my heart."

Her own heart was near bursting as she stared at him. "I never knew a thing about any spy."

"I know that, Merry. I was wrong, so wrong to think you did." His fingers tangled in her golden hair. "Can . . . can you ever love me?"

Merideth's smile was beautiful . . . angelic. "Oh, Jared," she said, her voice full of emotion. "I do."

His lips brushed hers lightly. Then he gently tied the dented locket around her neck. Soon he would tell her of the secret message she'd worn. But not now.

Jared took Merideth's hand and together they stood. And walked out into the light.

Epilogue

A storm was coming.

Merideth yanked the straw hat from her head before the wind could claim it. She stood close to the house at the head of the avenue of oaks. Filmy strands of moss whipped about the trees, looking like gossamer veils in the twilight.

"Mama, you best come in before you get wet." The voice came from the second story of the house and Merideth turned, tilting her face till she saw her daughter's head poking from a window.

"Miranda Elizabeth, what are you doing still awake? You were put to bed an hour ago."

"The shutter woke me, Mama. It was banging. It scared me."

Merideth smiled up at her oldest child, her heart filled with love. "'Tis only the wind, sweetheart. Nothing to fear. Climb back in bed and I'll come and tuck you beneath the covers."

The small nightcap-topped head disappeared, and

407

Merideth sighed. She could hear thunder to the north, towards Charles Town. Where the British troops were.

Giving one last look around the grounds, she walked across the crushed-shell drive and climbed the steps to Royal Oak's front portico.

Nothing to fear.

She'd said those words to Miranda. But they weren't true. There was much to fear, and had been since the British occupied Charles Town almost two and half years ago.

That's when Merideth began her double life.

That's when she became a widow.

Merideth turned the large brass knob and entered the wide central hall of her home. Perhaps it was the weather, so reminiscent of the first time she'd seen him, but Merideth couldn't stop thinking of Jared . . . of the life they'd had before the fall of Charles Town.

They'd married soon after the fire at Daniel Wallis's house. Jared's cousin never recovered from the blaze, and died within days of an infection of the lungs.

His death saved Jared from killing him.

Merideth shivered as she climbed the wide spiral staircase. She didn't like to think of Daniel and his treachery. Better to dwell on the good times, the happy times she'd had with Jared.

Merideth carefully opened the nursery door. Tiptoeing across the room, she leaned over her daughter, giving her cheek a kiss. She was fast asleep. At five she was inquisitive, with black hair like her father's and a ready smile. She loved to walk down by the river, collecting insects and plants.

Next Merideth moved to John's bed. Named for

Jared's brother, John was three and never still. Reaching under the mosquito netting, Merideth straightened his tangled blanket and brushed her lips across his forehead. Then she left the children's room for her own.

A single candle on the washstand tried to brighten the shadows in her bedroom and failed. But Merideth was too tired to light more. Today she'd overseen the loading of rice and corn to be sent to Patriot families whose property had been confiscated by General Tarleton. Because she was British and daughter of an earl, the British trusted Merideth. In their condescending manner, the British officers in charge at Charles Town forgave the privateer's widow the peccadillo of her marriage and allowed her to travel freely and to keep her property.

But if they ever found out what she did when she traveled—the ammunition and foodstuffs she managed to get to the American army—her title would mean naught. But so far they didn't seem to suspect. Perhaps out of homesickness, British officers even visited, finding the mistress of Royal Oak charming company. It was hard to maintain the ruse.

Taking the wooden pins from her hair, Merideth let the golden curls fall about her shoulders. She was glad she could help her husband's people—her own people—but the charade was wearing, and she was growing tired.

With a sigh she unhooked her simple gown of sprigged muslin. It fell to the floor and she stepped from the circle of skirts, picking it up and draping the dress across a chair. Dressed in her shift, she splashed water from the pitcher to the bowl and wet a scrap of linen. As the first flash of lightning lit up the sky outside the tall casement windows, Merideth touched the damp cloth to her neck.

"Don't stop there, Lady Merideth. Take off the shift too."

The sound of the voice coming from the shadowy recesses of the room made Merideth stiffen. She dropped the linen. It landed in the water, splashing silver droplets of water across the polished wood.

"Untie the ribbon," came the next command, and Merideth had no choice. Slowly she reached for the pale-blue bow that held the gathered neckline of her shift taut. Her fingers pulled. The ruffed decolletage spread. When it grew wider than her shoulders, the fine gauze hesitated, then whispered to the floor. Merideth shut her eyes as the shift skimmed down her body, leaving her wearing nothing but the dented locket.

"Now turn around."

She did. Her limbs were trembling, but she held her head high.

"And come here."

Lightning flashed again and she saw him sitting on a chair beside the bed, his long legs spread out, crossed at the ankles. He wore no coat, and his shirt, shining white in the grainy light, was open to reveal the thick hair on his chest. Merideth swallowed as she walked toward him. His britches were tight, revealing the large raised ridge of his manhood.

When she approached he opened his legs, and Merideth moved into the V. He leaned forward, touching his open mouth to her stomach, and

Merideth's hands surged through his raven hair, pulling him closer.

"You shouldn't have risked coming," she said, then could say no more. For his lips had moved lower. Her head fell back and her knees grew weak, but by this time he'd cradled her buttocks with his large hands.

"I can't stay away from you." His breath fanned across the tight curls at the apex of her thighs. "Would you really want me not to come?"

She could barely think for wanting him. She'd always wanted him. There were times Merideth thought she might die from the deep desire she felt for him. But there were other things to consider. "I want you safe."

"And I am safe, Merry. Right here in your arms." He nudged. His tongue probed and Merideth cried out.

"I dream of that sound," he said. "You're with me, and I hear you, taste you, and I wake up so hard I ache."

"Oh, Jared." Merideth dropped to her knees, her head against his chest. Her cheek rubbed his skin and she breathed in the manly smell of him. "Take me with you this time. Me and the children."

"Nay, I won't have you on the *Carolina*. 'Tis too dangerous."

She looked up, her blue eyes shining with unshed tears. "But—"

"Listen to me, Merry." Jared's hands bracketed her face. "We devised this scheme of pretending I'm dead to keep you and the children safe. I want no retributions on my family for things I might do. Besides, there's to be a change. There's a convoy of forty British ships in Charles Town harbor."

"More British?" There didn't seem like there could be any more.

"Less."

"Less?"

"They're leaving, Merry. The British are withdrawing from South Carolina." He reached down, pulling his wife onto his lap. His hand splayed her hip, his face was buried in the rich gold of her hair. "It's not over yet. But with the French helping us defeat Cornwallis in Virginia, and Charles Town free, it can't be much longer."

"Oh, Jared, I'm so glad."

"Soon, Merry, I'll be able to stay here with you and our two children."

"Three," she corrected, turning to see the expression on her husband's face when he realized what she was saying.

"You mean . . . ?" His hand curved around to her stomach.

"Yes, and I was going to have a difficult time explaining how a respectable widow managed to get herself with child."

Jared laughed as he stood, gathering Merideth into his arms. In three strides he was beside the tester bed. "Probably because her husband isn't really dead. And he loves his wife so much he can't stay away from her."

Outside, lightning flashed and thunder roared, but in the bedroom—the bedroom once used by the pirate and his wife—Merideth and Jared Blackstone didn't even notice the storm.

To My Readers

I hope you enjoyed the second book in the Charleston Trilogy—tales of the Blackstone men. I loved writing about Merideth and her dark, dangerous privateer, Jared Blackstone.

The Revolutionary War era is one of my favorites. Researching the period with all its different facets is so interesting. I never tire of learning about the brave men and women who forged our country.

The Blackstone family is fictitious—though I certainly hope they seem as real to you as they do to me—but many of the people and events in this book are historically true.

Benjamin Franklin, of course, did much more than experiment with electricity. His diplomatic endeavors in France during the war greatly helped the eventual American victory. He was a fascinating man with many varied interests—including the ladies—and I tried to portray him accurately. And yes, he really didn't worry about spies. If anything, he considered details of his negotiations with France reaching English ears a bonus. And when it was discovered that the English had sent a representative to discuss peace with Franklin—a fact he didn't try to hide—the French decided to speed up negotiations with the Americans.

Privateers like Jared Blackstone also made a great contribution to the cause of liberty. They helped "even the odds" by harassing British shipping and capturing countless prizes. Much of this, as the book indicated, was done in and around England. But privateers also sailed from ports like Charles Town, and it was there, to home, that Jared brought Merideth.

Charleston, like her native sons and daughters, is beautiful and proud . . . a survivor. During the years after the pirate Gentleman Jack Blackstone (from *Sea Fires*) wooed and married Miranda, before Jared and Merideth settled down in Charles Town, the city experienced fires, killer storms, plagues, and enemy occupation. But she endured.

In the final book of the Charleston Trilogy, Jared and Merideth's great-grandson, Devon Blackstone, is a blockade runner during the American Civil War. Like his ancestors, he's a man of the sea and a rogue . . . a hero in the true Blackstone tradition. Fearless and charming, Devon doesn't know what trouble is until he meets abolitionist Felicity Wentworth and the group of children she's come south to rescue.

I truly hope you enjoy the Charleston Trilogy. The Blackstone men and the women who love them are very special to me. Please let me know what you think. For a bookmark and newsletter write me care of:

Zebra Books
475 Park Avenue South
New York, NY 10016

A SASE is appreciated.

To Happy Endings,
Christine Dorsey